THE TIES THAT BIND

IRINA SHAPIRO

This is a work of fiction. Names, characters, business, events and incidents are the products of the author's imagination. Any resemblance to actual persons, living or dead, or actual events is purely coincidental.

Copyright © Irina Shapiro, 2017, 2024

The moral right of the author has been asserted.

Previously published in 2017 as *The Ties that Bind* by Merlin Press LLC.

All rights reserved. No part of this book may be reproduced or used in any manner without the prior written permission of the copyright owner.

To request permissions, contact the publisher at rights@stormpublishing.co

Ebook ISBN: 978-1-80508-657-4
Paperback ISBN: 978-1-80508-658-1

Cover design: Debbie Clement
Cover images: Shutterstock

Published by Storm Publishing.
For further information, visit:
www.stormpublishing.co

ALSO BY IRINA SHAPIRO

A Tate and Bell Mystery

The Highgate Cemetery Murder

Murder at Traitors' Gate

Wonderland Series

The Passage

Wonderland

Sins of Omission

The Queen's Gambit

Comes the Dawn

The Hands of Time Series

The Hands of Time

A Leap of Faith

A World Apart

A Game of Shadows

Shattered Moments

The Winter Solstice

The Summer Solstice

The Christmas Gift

ONE

VIRGINIA AUGUST 1628

It was nearly twilight by the time the party finally broke up and the children were returned to their parents. There weren't that many, but it felt as if the house had been under siege for several hours as kids ranging from three to ten enjoyed their first-ever birthday party, thrown for Robbie, who turned five. Louisa felt that this milestone just couldn't be ignored. People in the seventeenth century did not, as a rule, celebrate their children's birthdays. Partly because they were wary of tempting fate in an age when children routinely died, and partly because birthdays were not the big deal they were in the future where every birthday was celebrated with parties, gifts, mountains of food, and specially ordered cakes. Birthday cakes with the likeness of the child computer-generated onto the cake were something that Valerie found slightly macabre, especially when cut into with a cake knife. Many colonists were illiterate and didn't own a family bible, so never even marked the actual date of the birth, knowing only that their child was born in a particular month of a particular year. They knew the approximate age, and that was good enough.

"You look done in," Louisa said to Valerie as she carried a

stack of dirty plates into the kitchen for washing. "Why don't you get a little air, clear your head? We'll finish clearing up."

Cook nodded in agreement. "Go on. We'll finish up. Perhaps you can escort Fred back to our cabin," Cook added, a note of concern creeping into her otherwise light tone.

Frederick Taylor had often been unwell these past few months, and although he strenuously denied being ill and blamed the symptoms on his advanced years, everyone knew that something had changed. At seventy-seven, Fred was ancient by colonial standards, and even if he were ill, there wasn't much to be done. Fred was suffering from fatigue, lack of appetite, and occasional bouts of nausea—symptoms that could be attributed to a myriad of illnesses, or none at all. Perhaps he was right, and this was simply encroaching old age and not something altogether more sinister.

"Stop fussing," Fred mumbled as he peeked into the kitchen, but he appeared pleased by the prospect of Valerie's company. He gave his wife a peck on the cheek and smiled at Valerie. "I just need a few minutes. Wait for me by the pond?"

"Sure."

It was warm and humid outside, but Valerie longed to be out in the fresh air and away from all the noise. She stepped outside and took a deep breath, enjoying the hint of pine resin and the fragrant smell of hay. The sky was just beginning to turn a deep lavender, a bright pink streak visible on the horizon where the sun had set only a few moments before.

Valerie made her way toward the pond, where she took a seat on the bench Alec had built for her all those years ago. The water was as clear as a looking glass, the surface reflecting the purpling heavens that were just beginning to twinkle with the first stars of the night. The fuzzy heads of reeds swayed in the breeze and appeared almost black in the gathering dusk. Another half-hour and it would be fully dark, but Valerie didn't mind; she had the light from the windows to guide her back home.

Valerie leaned back and closed her eyes, enjoying a moment of perfect silence. It wasn't completely silent, of course. The wind moved stealthily through the trees, the frogs croaked noisily in the pond, and birds twittered endlessly, as if they had to get it all out before night descended and they grew quiet at last. Valerie could hear the cows lowing in the barn and the snorting of the horses coming from the stable. These were the sounds of her life, and she barely noticed them as she stared into the still waters of the pond.

Today was Robbie's birthday, but it was Tom on Valerie's mind, and his mother, who had been Valerie's beloved daughter. Not a day went by that Valerie didn't miss her Louisa or thank God for giving her and Alec little Tom as a consolation prize for losing their only daughter. But Tom was getting older, and Valerie could no longer deny her fears or sweep them under the rug. Tom was a bright little boy who noticed everything and asked endless questions. Unlike many children his age who talked non-stop, Tom was often quiet, watching the world around him with round blue eyes that so reminded Valerie of his hapless father, Thomas Gaines. Already Tom was beginning to ask questions about Finn and his family, and begging to play with his cousins: Diana, Ben, and Nat. He couldn't understand why they were so far away, nor why no one mentioned them when at home. How did one explain to a three-year-old that Finn and his family lived one hundred and fifty years in the future and the only way to see them was to use a time-travel device fashioned by a retired physicist from Princeton, New Jersey in the twenty-first century?

It wasn't only Tom who had questions. Abbie and her parents were too polite to ask outright, but Valerie knew full well that there were comments made about Finn's relations and their odd appearances. Where did they live? Why had no one ever been invited to their home? And why did they never write or respond to letters? All legitimate questions that would have been easy enough to answer had they actually lived in the same time and place.

Alec never really talked about it, but Valerie had seen that faraway look in his eyes more than once, especially in the weeks following a visit to Finn. He had the same worries, and the same longing, only neither one of them had put their feelings into words. Saying it out loud, even to each other, would make it real, would turn it from a thought into a problem that needed to be solved. But this problem had no solution. Valerie's heart lived in two places, as did Alec's. Their family had been torn asunder, and nothing could put it back together. Their only son had chosen to remain in the eighteenth century, to marry the girl he loved, and fight for a cause he passionately believed in. There was no going back, no turning back the clock.

But the clock was ticking, time moving forward, and soon it would become impossible to travel into the future. With every year it would become harder to pull the wool over Tom's eyes and make him believe that he'd slept during the journey and woken up at the Mallory farm. And Valerie would never leave Tom behind—never, not after what happened last time. She would not be parted from this little boy who held her heart in his hands, the only reminder of her Louisa, and their last living child, at least in this century.

Valerie glanced up with a start as a shadowy figure appeared seemingly out of nowhere. Frederick Taylor, the unwitting architect of everything that had happened to Valerie and her sister, sat down on the bench and smiled benignly.

"Tired?" Fred asked.

"A bit."

"You haven't been yourself for quite some time," Fred ventured.

"Neither have you. Fred, are you all right?" Valerie asked, knowing exactly how he would respond.

"I'm splendid. Just a bit tired, is all. I look forward to an hour of peace and quiet before Barbara gets back and starts fussing," he added with an indulgent smile. "Now, what about you?"

"What about me?" Valerie asked, but she was glad of the opening. She needed to talk. Strangely enough, the man who'd been responsible for her journey to the seventeenth century all those years ago was now the closest thing she had to a parent, and the only person who could understand her predicament. Mr. Taylor had followed them to the seventeenth century and chosen to make it his home. Now he was married for the first time in his life and enjoying newfound domestic bliss with their cook. There were things he missed about the future, but he'd left nothing of value behind, no friends or family, no one to miss him or to miss.

"What is it, Valerie? You can tell me," he said kindly. "Or I can just leave you in peace and go home. You must be knackered."

"I don't know what to do, Fred, and I'm reluctant to talk to Alec about it. It's too big to just put out there without knowing what I want to do about it first."

"And what is it that you wish to do, my dear?"

Valerie could tell from Fred's expression that he could hazard a good guess, but he wasn't the type of person to impose his own thoughts and observations on a situation. He did not like to overstep his boundaries, and instead waited to be confided in.

Valerie took a deep breath and plunged in. This was the first time she was voicing her thoughts and feelings out loud, and she was terrified of what this confession would set in motion. "Fred, I miss my son. I long to be where he is and be a part of his family's life. I have grandchildren who barely know me, and Finn's my only living child. I've already buried two children, and I don't want to live apart from the one I have left."

"But you think Alec would be against going to the eighteenth century?" Fred asked.

"No, I don't think he would be, which is why I haven't brought it up to him yet. I don't want to get him all fired up. He hasn't been himself since coming back from the future. Having lived in the eighteenth and twenty-first centuries, Alec can no longer say with any honesty that he feels at home here. He's seen and learned too much of what's going to happen to simply revert to this life without second thoughts or hidden hopes. Alec never expressed any desire to live in the twenty-first century; it's too modern for him, too advanced, but I know that he would embrace life in the eighteenth century, and he misses Finn more than he lets on."

Fred nodded and reached for Valerie's hand. "But you can't leave Louisa."

"How can I?" Valerie exclaimed. "Louisa followed me here, gave up her own life to come and find me. Her life is here, in this time and this place. She cares about Finn, of course, but her husband and children are here, so if I go, I go without her."

"A conundrum, indeed, isn't it?"

"What am I to do, Fred?" Valerie asked miserably.

Fred patted Valerie's hand and stood up. "You already know what you are going to do," he said with a small smile. "People always do. Deep down, your decision was made some time ago, and now you are looking for ways to justify it, not only to others, but to yourself. Valerie, at the end of the day, we must all do what's right for us. You can't please everyone, nor can you bend the laws of the universe to resolve this dilemma. Only you can make this choice, and I think you already have."

Valerie nodded, acknowledging the truth of Fred's words. "Shall I walk you home?"

"No, I'm fine on my own. I only agreed so Barbara would stop worrying. Good night, Valerie."

"Good night."

Valerie looked after the retreating figure until it melted into the shadows, bound for the cabin he shared with his wife. She rose to her feet and walked slowly toward the house. Fred was right, of course. She knew what she wanted to do, but that didn't make it any easier. No matter what she chose, her heart would be torn in half, the only question being which half was bigger and would suffer more. Son or sister? Child of her heart or dearest friend and confidant? Grown man who didn't need her anymore, or the only person who understood where she came from and what she'd sacrificed? Heartache or heartbreak?

TWO

Louisa watched through the window as Valerie walked slowly toward the house. Valerie had gone out of her way to help with the party, and even drew funny cartoons to entertain the children once they'd eaten all the goodies and run out of games, but Valerie's heart was clearly heavy on this day of celebration. Perhaps she was thinking of Finn and all the birthdays she'd missed in the eighteenth century. Louisa had never met Finn's wife or her family, nor had she ever seen Valerie's grandchildren, but they were as real to her as if they lived down the road in Jamestown. Louisa wished she could help Valerie reconcile herself to this dual existence, but there was nothing she could say that would be of any comfort. She was carrying a weight of her own, a weight that was growing heavier by the day. Louisa didn't turn around when Kit entered the kitchen and wrapped his arms about her middle, drawing her against him. She leaned into him, but a part of her remained aloof, detached.

"I'm sorry, Lou," he whispered into her ear. "I really am, but this was inevitable. You knew that all along."

Louisa sighed and walked out of his embrace, still upset. Yes, she'd known it all along, but that didn't make things any easier. He was forcing her to make a choice, but there was no choice to be made. How could she choose Valerie over her husband and children? Louisa headed upstairs to check on the children before Valerie walked through the door. They would have to talk sooner or later, but today wasn't the day. They still had time—but not long.

Kit's eyes followed Louisa as she walked up the stairs, but he did not go after her. She needed time to think and accept the situation; he knew that. Louisa liked to live life on her own terms, which was something he loved and respected about her, so she would need to shape the facts into something that made sense and convince herself that this decision was for the best. Instead, he headed for the study where Alec was hiding with a bottle of brandy. He would speak to Alec. Alec would understand, but that made it harder somehow. Alec was the brother Kit never had, the friend he could rely on in any situation, the man who always had his back, no matter what. This would be hard for all of them, not just for Valerie and Louisa.

Kit closed the door behind him and accepted a cup of brandy from Alec. Alec sat in his favorite chair by the cold hearth, his legs outstretched. He looked tired, and sad. Alec had aged these past few years. A few more gray hairs silvered his temples, and he'd filled out a little around the middle. He wasn't stout by any means, but he was no longer the lean, virile young man Kit had met when he'd first arrived in Virginia. Alec often used a magnifying glass to read correspondence and balance ledgers. He needed spectacles, but there was nowhere to obtain them in Jamestown, and his bout with appendicitis a few years ago left him acutely aware of the lack of proper medical care in the colony, and the acute possibility of one of the family coming down with something equally or more life-threatening. Alec worried about Valerie, and about Tom. He'd lost too many people over the years to comfort himself with the lie that nothing terrible could happen. He knew better, and he was afraid.

Kit sat down and took a sip of brandy. Having a drink with Alec always made him feel more balanced, but he had to be honest with him, and there was no point putting things off. Louisa would tell Valerie, and then Alec would find out anyway.

"Alec, there's something I'd like to talk to you about. I know today probably isn't ideal, but I can't carry this around any longer. I need your support in this."

Alec set down his cup and looked at Kit, a slight smile on his face. "I know what you're going to tell me. I've been expecting it for some time."

"Have you?" Kit asked. He supposed he should have expected Alec to guess. Alec wasn't like Louisa and Valerie; he was a man of the seventeenth century, and he understood the way things were done. He understood duty, unlike his wife, who believed that it was important to follow one's heart and desires. Perhaps she was right and such things were possible in her own time, but in this day and age, people did what was expected of them, and often denied their own wishes to fulfill their obligations and do their duty.

"I've wanted to bring this up time and again, but held off knowing how Louisa would feel, but I can't wait any longer. I've neglected my estate long enough, and now that Master Gibson has passed, a new estate manager needs to be found, and soon. I've charged my nephew Robin with finding a new man, but it's not his responsibility to run my estate. He's got obligations of his own. And, of course, there's Robbie. He's getting older, Alec. It's time he started learning about the running of the estate and attended to his education. He needs qualified tutors and hands-on experience. He will succeed me once I'm gone, and I must see that he is ready."

"And what of Evie?" Alec asked with a smile. Kit doted on

his willful daughter, but he hadn't mentioned her at all when speaking of his plans.

Kit sighed heavily. "Evie will be a fight. Louisa has her own ideas about what a girl should be taught to expect, but I'm afraid those ideas don't quite fall in line with what's expected of girls in this century. I would rather die than see Evie unhappy, but I must be realistic. I am not against offering girls an education but teaching her too much will make her unpopular among the men of her class. Being clever and witty is one thing, but an overly bookish female will put off prospective suitors. Evie is still too young, of course, but it won't be long before the question of marriage comes up. Louisa refuses to discuss it, but girls in this century don't wait until their mid-twenties to contemplate marriage. If Evie wants to make a good match, she'll have to wed in her late teens. Louisa wants to gut me like a fish when I make statements like that, but it's the reality of our life. Am I wrong, Alec? Am I too old-fashioned, in your view?"

Alec refilled Kit's glass and smiled at him. "That's one thing you don't have to worry about. It doesn't matter what you and Louisa decide; Evie will tell you what's what, just as Louisa did with us. We had our arguments about education and marriage, much like you, but Louisa had her own plan all along. As a father, you're blinded to the true nature of your child, but eventually, we begin to see clearly, albeit sometimes too late."

"Yes, you are right there. Evie has a mind of her own and has had since the day she was born. Another mulish female to deal with, and she is still only a child. I can't even begin to imagine what she'll be like as a young woman of marriageable age." Kit shuddered dramatically and made Alec laugh.

"Valerie says that parenting is just a lifelong process of letting go."

"But it's not so easy, is it?"

"No. You have no choice but to let go when you lose a child, but when your child is alive and you can't be near them, it's that much harder," Alec replied.

"Perhaps Valerie will be easier to convince once we leave for England," Kit suggested.

"*Will* you leave for England?" Alec asked with a knowing smile. "I can't see Louisa agreeing to this readily. She will argue that Robbie is still a child and you have plenty of time before any decisions need to be made."

"She's said that already, but I will not be fobbed off this time. I try to make her happy and take her opinion into account, but ultimately, I'm the man of the family and she must obey me in all things."

Both Alec and Kit snorted with laughter at this, knowing only too well that Louisa and Valerie were about as good at obeying as a donkey who'd dug in its heels and was hee-hawing belligerently.

"You can't order her to go, Kit. You must convince her."

"I've tried, Alec, but she won't see sense. She doesn't want to leave Valerie."

"I know."

"What of you and Charles?" Kit asked. "Would you leave Charles behind?"

"Charlie and I haven't had the easiest relationship," Alec reminded Kit.

"Still, he's your only brother. You've already lost a brother and a sister. Speaking of which, have you heard from Jenny?"

"I had a letter from her about a month ago. She always says that all is well, and she couldn't be happier. I'd like to believe that," Alec said, his expression thoughtful.

"Why don't you?"

"Just an impression I get. Jenny is not the type of girl to share her feelings unreservedly. It comes from years of living in a convent and keeping her thoughts to herself. Besides, even if she isn't happy, there isn't much I can do to help from the other side of the world. I believe Cameron is a good man and takes care of her, but I have nothing to go on besides her letters, which tell me she is fine, then go on to ask all about the family in exquisite detail. She avoids saying much about herself or her life in Scotland."

"Alec, if you like, I'll go up there and see her once we return to England."

"That's a lot to ask," Alec balked.

"It would be my pleasure. Besides, Louisa would love to see Jenny. She misses her, as do the children."

"I would appreciate that, Kit. I worry about Jenny as if she were my own daughter. She's been wounded deeply by the revelations about her parents. I just want to know that she's found contentment at last."

"You can count on me, Alec. I'll make sure she's well and do anything I can to help if she isn't."

"Thank you." Alec's eyes grew misty as he smiled ruefully at Kit. "I'd have no trouble leaving Charles, but I will miss you, brother."

"Likewise." They clinked cups in a silent toast to friendship and loyalty. The next few months weren't going to be smooth sailing for either the Whitfields or the Sheridans.

THREE

SCOTLAND AUGUST 1628

Cameron accepted a bowl of parritch from Jenny, added a lump of butter and drizzled a bit of honey to sweeten it. Jenny made the pot two days ago, so the oats were a bit lumpy and thick, but Cameron wasn't a picky eater. Anything she chose to put in front of him was good enough. She was still learning, not having had much experience in running a household of her own. The Whitfields had a cook and a servant, so Jenny never really learned to cook, although she was a deft hand at mending and spinning wool.

Cameron's mother showed Jenny how to make a few basic things such as stew, bannocks, and blood sausage, fearing that her son would starve otherwise. Jenny got the hang of the stew and the bannocks, but the sausage was beyond her, the process of making it too disgusting for a girl who'd never had to get her hands dirty, much less submerge her arm to the elbow in pig's blood. Cameron didn't blame her. He could very happily live without black pudding as long as Jenny was all right, and he wasn't at all sure that she was.

"Aren't ye eating?" Cameron asked, watching his wife as she picked up a basket of dirty clouts and made for the door. It was still barely light outside, and windy by the sound of it. A steady rain had been falling since last night, so the yard would be muddy and slippery.

"No, I'll eat later. Just mind the baby while I wash these clouts, or I won't have enough to last me through the day. Ian's been fed and changed. He fell back asleep," she added as she opened the door and let in a gust of damp air, which inevitably woke the baby. Cameron lifted the baby out of the cot and settled him on his knee while he attended to his breakfast. He needed to eat before he went out since he wouldn't get a chance to grab anything until midday. Cameron laughed as Ian craned his neck to try to get a bit of parritch, opening his mouth like a baby bird who was hoping for a juicy worm.

"Here ye are, my wee laddie. Always hungry, just like yer da."

Ian greedily swallowed a bit of parritch and opened his mouth for more, his expression hopeful. "Mayhap it's time yer mam give ye more solid food," Cameron mused as he shared the rest of his breakfast with the little boy. Ian smiled happily, revealing two teeth on the bottom. He was a bonny little lad with Jenny's chestnut curls and Cameron's wide blue eyes. In Cameron's opinion, there was no sweeter baby in all of Scotland.

Cameron pushed away the empty bowl and settled Ian on the floor, propping him up with his legs. Ian still needed support when sitting, and he leaned against Cameron, full of trust that his father would be there to support him. Cameron handed Ian a wooden spoon. He'd made several toys for the child, but Ian was obsessed with the spoon these past few weeks. Just couldn't get enough of it. Cameron leaned forward and kissed Ian's sweet-smelling head, but the child was no longer interested in him, the wooden spoon had all his attention as he banged it on the floor.

Cameron still thanked God every day that both Jenny and

the baby had survived the birth. So many didn't. His family was a miracle, not only because the good Lord had seen fit to let his wife and son live, but because God, in his wisdom, had also allowed Cameron to escape captivity and make it back home to Scotland, giving him a second chance at life.

Another blast of air announced the return of his wife. Jenny's face was pink, and her hair windblown and damp, but there was an air of grim satisfaction about her. That was one task out of the way, a hundred more still left to tackle.

"I've got to get going, love," Cameron said as he got to his feet and handed Ian to Jenny, who accepted him happily. Ian smiled and grabbed a damp curl in his fist, pulling until Jenny yelped, making him giggle. "He ate some of my parritch. I don't think he's getting enough to eat, Jenny. He always seems hungry."

Jenny nodded. She was still nursing Ian, but perhaps Cameron was right. He needed more solid food now that he was nearly seven months old. Problem was, she had no one to ask. She'd been in Scotland for nearly two years now, but she had no friends, and although the other women were coolly polite, they never included her in their conversations or treated her as one of their own. Jenny had some experience of children, but none of newborn babies, since the only baby she'd been exposed to was Tom, and he had been breastfed until arriving in Virginia with his wet-nurse after his father succumbed to the plague.

"I've packed a couple of oatcakes and a bottle of milk for your break. I'll see you at midday."

Cameron grabbed Jenny about the waist and pulled her close, the baby gurgling between them. "I love ye, and ye," Cameron said as he kissed first Ian then Jenny.

"And we love you. Wave bye-bye to Dada."

Jenny took Ian's hand and waved with it, then stepped away from the door to protect the child from the cool draft. Cameron grabbed the food and set out. A couple of oatcakes wouldn't do much to tide him over until midday, but he was grateful for Jenny's thoughtfulness. He had much to do this morning, starting with the milking. His mother always reminded him that milking was woman's work, but he didn't mind. It didn't take that long, and it was a way to lighten Jenny's load.

In a few weeks, the harvest would need to be brought in and then the haying taken care of, so he wouldn't have as much time to help Jenny, but until then, he'd do everything he could. Cameron went over all the things he had to do while leaning against the warm side of the cow. His hands moved rhythmically, squeezing the udders just the way Mary had taught him when he was a lad.

Then, it had been a game, with him trying to impress Mary with his willingness to help, asking for nothing more than a kiss in return. He still thought of Mary from time to time, especially when he found himself alone in the barn. It wasn't disloyal; Mary had been a part of his life since he was a boy, and they'd been promised to each other and would have wed had Mary not been murdered by that bastard Aloysius Deverell.

Cameron still seethed with anger every time he remembered the day Mary died and the callous way in which her death had been treated by the authorities. He supposed he should feel remorseful for killing the man in cold blood, but he didn't. There was such a thing as justice, and he'd meted it out. And now he had a beautiful, loving wife and a healthy son. He'd moved on.

Cameron patted the cow on the rump affectionately and grabbed hold of the bucket. He'd bring the milk in for Jenny then get on with his own chores. There were fences to mend, wood to chop, a leaky barn roof to fix, and a hundred other things he could think of. Jenny was equally busy all day long. She had to see to the animals, cook, bake, clean, wash, care for the baby, and finish her day by sewing new gowns for Ian and mending Cameron's hose and shirts. Jenny had no help, and even though Cameron had tried to hire a girl from the village to give a hand with the chores, no one was interested in the job.

Cameron felt anger building up in him, the same anger he felt every time he recalled how Jenny was treated. He'd been mad with joy when Jenny finally arrived from Virginia. The voyage had taken her over two months, and she was nervous, having had all that time to wonder what type of reception she was going to get. Cameron spent over a week in Glasgow waiting for the ship to arrive, and when it finally did, he waited with bated breath as the anchor was dropped and the wooden gangplank was lowered to allow passengers and crew to disembark.

Cameron waited patiently as a family with two children came ashore, followed by a prosperous-looking man, who demanded that his trunk be off-loaded immediately. Several seamen dragged heavy chests belonging to the passengers. Cameron peered at the deck. Where was Jenny? And then he finally saw her. She stood still for a moment, looking over the quay, her lovely face full of apprehension. There was a moment of panic until she spotted Cameron, who was waving madly. A huge smile spread across her face and she rushed down the gangplank and straight into his arms, all her worries forgotten as he swung her around and kissed her soundly to the whistling of the sailors and loud disapproval of the other passengers.

"Ye're a sight for sore eyes," he said as he finally set her down. "Oh, I thought I might never see ye again, lass. How bonny ye look."

"You look fairly bonny yourself," Jenny laughed. "Freedom suits you."

"Come now. I've booked us into an inn, Mistress Brody. There'll be a fine supper served in a private parlor followed by bed," he said smiling meaningfully. "To be honest, I might like them in the reverse order."

"Surely there's time before supper," Jenny replied, her face all innocence. "A lady does need to freshen up."

Cameron smiled happily. He'd waited so long for her to come, and now she was really there, with him. He couldn't think of a greater happiness than finally settling down with his bride. By the time they made it down to supper, the food was cold, and the innkeeper's wife gave them evil looks, but they didn't care. They shone like newly minted copper coins, and their joy was there for everyone to see.

"We'll have a proper wedding now that ye're here. I'll arrange everything. We'll invite the whole village, so they all have a chance to meet ye."

The wedding had gone off without a hitch, and Cameron had been too happy and drunk to notice that his bride looked less than joyous. She sat by herself, not quite part of the festivities going on around her. The women flocked to her as soon as she'd arrived, but once their curiosity about Cameron Brody's bride was sated, they kept their distance. Jenny wasn't one of them. She was a well-bred, educated young lady, not an illiterate wife or daughter of a farmer. These women were coarse and work-worn like draft horses, while Jenny was an Arabian stallion, gleaming white and so beautiful that she dazzled the senses, especially the senses of the men who'd never had a lady so fine amongst them. They were intimidated by Genevieve Brody, but they admired her nonetheless, which made her even less popular with the womenfolk, who refused to let any of their daughters work at the Cameron farm for fear of their girls catching Jenny's fancy ways and getting untoward ideas into their heads.

Jenny tried to fit in, but her natural refinement and melodious French accent did little to help. She was modest and unassuming, but she still made the women feel plain and dowdy, and they resented her for it. After a while, Jenny became a recluse. She no longer tried to befriend the women and preferred to stay on the farm, only going into the village to attend church.

Cameron hoped that once Jenny got with child the women would be more welcoming. Nothing bound women more than talk of birthing and bairns, but they closed ranks, and even the midwife, who was a plump older woman with a face like a potato wasn't as kind to Jenny as she might have been. Jenny was an outcast, and it pained Cameron to see her so unhappy. She never complained, but he knew that she felt lonely and isolated, and missed her family. She'd loved Uncle Alec and Aunt Valerie and had grown very fond of Lord and Lady Sheridan.

Jenny hadn't spent as much time with Charles Whitfield and his haughty wife, but she missed them too, and especially their children. For the first time in her life, Jenny had been part of a large, loving family, and now suddenly she was alone again with only Cameron for company.

Cameron never asked if Jenny was sorry she'd followed him to Scotland, because he was afraid to hear the answer. He knew Jenny loved him fiercely, but what if he simply wasn't enough? A woman needed other women in her life. She needed support and comfort, and that special kind of understanding that he couldn't provide. How long would it be before Jenny grew to resent him and wish she'd stayed in Virginia?

His mother could have made all the difference, but she was the worst of the lot. Had she publicly welcomed Jenny and tried to include her, the other women would have followed suit, but Fiona Brody loved Mary like a daughter, and compared Jenny to Mary all the time with Mary coming out the winner every time. How could Jenny compete with a dead woman? There had been an incident early on when Fiona made her feelings known in front of the whole village, and Jenny had never forgotten the slight. Cameron's aunt, Fiona's sister Meg, had passed about a month after Jenny arrived from Virginia. This was Jenny's first Scottish funeral and Cameron spent a bit of time explaining the rituals to her. Jenny was accustomed to a basic Catholic burial with a church mass and prayer at the graveside, but a Scottish funeral was a bit different, and he didn't want her to be shocked. Cameron himself hadn't been to a funeral since Mary was killed, but he'd blocked that memory from his mind, finding it too painful to recall.

Jenny listened carefully as Cameron explained the reason for the keening and warned her that a banshee—a professional keener—would be present at the wake. He thought it would be shocking for someone like Jenny, someone who grew up in the dignified silence of a convent, to be exposed to the kind of raw, unbridled grief, often fueled by strong drink, that came pouring out at a Scottish wake. He couldn't imagine Alec Whitfield tolerating such nonsense, but this is the way things were done here and Jenny had to get used to the local customs.

Cameron wasn't sure if a sin-eater had been invited, since his mother always said that Meg was a saint, having put up with her violent, drunken lout of a husband for nearly forty years, but Jenny might find it a bit disturbing to see a pauper taking on the dead woman's sins for the price of a meal. Jenny didn't believe in that sort of thing, and rightly so, Cameron thought. It was all pure foolishness, designed to make the living feel better. Whatever sins Meg had, they'd died with her, and it was no use trying to shift them to someone else. They all had to answer for their own choices and actions, and he would answer for his when the time came and be proud to do so.

Jenny followed Cameron's instructions and stayed back, only coming forward once to pay her respects to the departed woman. She then reached out to give Fiona a hug, a gesture of affection and condolence, which would have been welcomed by Valerie Whitfield and Lady Sheridan in similar circumstances, but Fiona, unused to such public displays of affection, rudely pushed Jenny away for all to see and turned her back on the shocked girl, sending the message that neither her sympathy nor her love were welcome. His mother knew she'd done wrong, but she was a proud and stubborn woman, and refused to offer a word of apology or anything even remotely resembling an olive branch. The relationship between the two women became strained, and not about to get better, since Jenny was too afraid to be rejected again, and his mother simply too pigheaded to abandon her position of misguided moral superiority.

Cameron hefted the axe and went to work chopping wood. At least his anger was good for something. He had a pile of firewood at his feet in record time, and he did feel marginally better. *Perhaps another bairn, a girl, would set things right*, he suddenly thought. A daughter always knew the path to her mother's heart.

FOUR
VIRGINIA AUGUST 1781

Abbie stepped outdoors and sat down on the bench for a moment to enjoy the golden haze that bathed their little corner of the world in its glow. It had been a hot day, but the heat had abated, replaced by a welcome coolness that was so delicious after months of humid heat. The nights were growing cooler and the days a little shorter. Another couple of weeks and this turbulent summer would finally be over. Abbie normally loved the autumn months, but this year she felt inexplicably apprehensive. There was a charge in the air, a restiveness that was barely noticeable but permeated everything they did.

Abbie didn't fully understand all the political maneuvering that her father discussed in hushed tones with Finn and Sam, but she did know that the end was near. There was no clear victor yet, but there was a sense of imminent resolution. Finn kept assuring her the war would be over soon, as if he knew something she didn't, but no one could predict what would happen. The colonists had given it their all and had made tremendous sacrifices in the name of freedom, but after six years of conflict the armies were still moving around like pieces on a chess board, gaining and losing ground, but mostly losing men—literally and figuratively.

John Mallory still couldn't bear to speak of General Arnold's defection to the British. He'd admired the man and believed him to be one of the true heroes of the Revolutionary War, a man who was noble, proud, and fearless. But Arnold's betrayal cut John Mallory deeply, especially since the motive appeared to be monetary rather than moral. It had shaken his faith in the people he trusted and had risked his life for and made him question the loyalty and wisdom of those who remained in command. Her father still believed in the cause as fervently as ever, but his zeal had cooled in the face of such faithlessness. He never said anything out loud, especially not in front of Sam and Finn, but Abbie knew her father well, and her feminine instinct told her that her father had grown weary and wanted nothing more than to enjoy a spell of peace, surrounded by his children and grandchildren. The great John Mallory was done.

And so was she. Abbie wished with all her heart that the Continental Army would triumph at last, and they could all get on with the business of living without fear of retribution. She'd never forgotten her own brush with British justice, and she still had occasional nightmares about the night she'd spent awaiting her execution for treason back in New York. They never spoke of it now, but it was always there, at the back of everyone's mind. They could have lost Abbie, Finn, and Sam that day, and their family would have been decimated had it not been for Finn's quick thinking and Sam's sway over a certain whore, who now lay buried in the graveyard of their parish church.

Abbie pushed aside her turbulent thoughts, got to her feet, and walked to the well. She needed water to bathe the children. They were grubby from a day of playing outdoors and a warm bath tended to soothe them before bedtime, helping them to sleep better and giving Abbie and Finn some time alone before going to bed. Abbie was just about to draw the water when she saw a lonely silhouette outlined by the crimson glow of the setting sun. She let go of the bucket and walked toward the stile, her heart heavy. Her mother stood in that spot every evening for days, watching the horizon for any sign of her beloved John, who'd gone on one of his clandestine expeditions for the Committee of Correspondence. The fire might have gone out of John Mallory, but he was an honorable man, and he would do his duty until the end, as would his children.

Abbie joined her mother and put her arm around Hannah's shoulders. "Come inside, Ma. It's no use waiting out here."

"He should have been back days ago," Hannah said stubbornly. "He promised me he'd come back in a fortnight."

"And he will. Things don't always go according to plan, do they? Pa is a clever and resourceful man and he always turns up, like a bad penny."

Hannah smiled at her daughter. "You're right, Abbie, I know you are, but I can't help fretting about him. He's not as young as he used to be."

"No, but still just as wily."

Hannah finally allowed Abbie to lead her back to the house. Abbie knew how her mother worried every time her father went on one of his secret missions. She understood only too well, having stood by the stile herself, scanning the horizon as she waited for Finn to return. Espionage was a dangerous game, but a necessary one. Intelligence gathered by John Mallory, Sam, and Finn had saved lives, and to some extent, had influenced the course of the war. They weren't the only ones, of course. There were many like them, men and women who risked capture and death to help the American forces gain whatever advantage they could over the British.

John had joined the Committee of Correspondence early on and had brought in Sam and Finn when he'd thought they were old enough to bear the responsibility. Only Jonah had chosen to enlist in the army and wear the Continental uniform. He believed in fighting openly and honorably, not skulking in the shadows and meeting in taverns to pass on crucial information, but Jonah understood the value of what his father did well enough and hero-worshiped him with the same devotion he'd had when he was a little boy and had wanted nothing more than to win his father's approval.

Jonah had returned to his unit after recovering from his illness, but he still suffered from occasional bouts of malaria, which left him unable to march for days and fight, so he was eventually discharged from active duty and assigned to serve as an aide-de-camp to General William Phillips. Abbie missed Jonah, but the boy who'd left wasn't the man who'd come back to see them before rejoining his unit. Jonah had always been an idealistic dreamer as a boy, but now he was a war-hardened veteran who spoke little and dreamed even less. The only person who saw glimpses of the old Jonah was his wife, Augusta, who'd saved him from certain death and brought him back to the land of the living in more ways than one. Jonah was a devoted husband and father to their three children, two of them from Augusta's previous marriage. He doted on his baby girl Gemma, whom no one had ever met since Augusta had chosen to remain in her native Georgia while Jonah fought.

Abbie put the water on to boil and led her mother to the table. "Let me make you a cup of tea, Ma. It'll revive you."

"The only thing that will revive me is your father's return," Hannah replied. "Stubborn old fool," she added as tears of frustration slid down her cheeks. "Can't sit a single assignment out. Has to go by himself instead of sending one of the younger men."

Hannah got to her feet and tested the water with her finger. "It's warm enough now. I'll help you bathe the children. Being with them is my only pleasure these days," she said dramatically.

"Oh, Ma, surely it's not as bad as all that," Abbie teased her.

"No," Hannah conceded. "I've been very blessed in my life, and I've no reason to complain. Your father will come back, and I will give him a piece of my mind, make no mistake about that, but in the meantime, I will enjoy my grandchildren. Martha said she'll come by tomorrow after church. I'll make some of those apple fritters the children like so much."

"They'll love that," Abbie said as she hefted the heavy cauldron and poured water into the wooden tub. "Make extra. Last time Joe ate at least ten. I don't know where he puts it all. It's like Martha doesn't feed him. Thin as a reed, that boy."

"It's just his constitution. He's just like Gil, all arms and legs. Boys tend to take after their fathers, don't they? Just look at Sam and Jonah."

"Yes, they do take after Pa, but Eddie is all me," Abbie said with a smile. With his golden hair and flecked brown eyes, Abbie's youngest looked just like her. There wasn't a trace of Finn in the child, but Abbie occasionally caught a glimpse of Alec Whitfield in the child's expressions, especially when Eddie was worried about something and furrowed his brow like a little grown-up.

"Bring the children down," Abbie called up to Sarah and Annie, who were minding the little ones in the loft until the bath was ready. She could hear them laughing as they played some silly game.

"Come on then, before the water gets cold." Abbie helped the children undress and lowered them into the steaming tub where they instantly began to splash each other, soaking her instead. She would use the leftover water to have a quick bath. Waste not, want not, her mother always said, and she could use a nice warm bath after a day of doing laundry. She'd sweated buckets in the August heat. Sarah and Annie could put the children to bed. Abbie was just about to start scrubbing the giggling kids when the door flew open to reveal Finn.

"And where have you been?" Abbie demanded, but grew quiet when she noticed Finn's grim expression.

"Mrs. Mallory, come quick. Mr. Mallory is at Sam's."

Hannah jumped to her feet and reached for her shawl. "What's he doing there? Is he all right?" she asked, suddenly realizing that something must be wrong.

"He's been shot. Susanna is attending to him."

"How bad is it? Tell me the truth, Finn."

"Could have been worse," Finn replied, his gaze sliding toward Abbie. "I'll see you later."

Finn and Hannah were out the door before Abbie could ask any questions. She tried to smile for the sake of the children, but they wouldn't be deceived.

"Mama, has Granddad been shot? Is he going to die? Is there blood? Can we go and see him?" Diana demanded. She was old enough to understand and was at an age when she asked a question every second, needing to comprehend the world around her. Eddie was still too young to grasp the significance of what his father had said, but he sensed the tension in Abbie and the anxiety in his sister and began to cry, his earlier good mood forgotten.

"Granddad will be all right, and we will see him soon. Now, let's get you to bed."

"I want a story," Diana demanded.

"Me too," Eddie chimed in through his tears.

"How about I tell you a story?" Sarah asked, seeing Abbie's flustered face. "Annie and I will put them to bed. You go to Sam's."

Abbie nodded. "Thank you. Don't be frightened. Everything will be all right. If anyone can help Pa, it's Sue."

Abbie toweled the children dry before helping them into their nightshirts. "Off you go. Sarah will tell you a story, and I expect to find you sleeping angelically by the time I return."

"Yes, ma'am," Diana answered, cheeky as ever.

FIVE

Abbie ran out the door into the purpling dusk of the August evening. The first stars twinkled above her head, and the chirping of crickets filled the air as she sprinted toward Sam's cabin. It wasn't that far, but it felt as if she were running to Williamsburg, which was miles away. Finn didn't say how badly her father was injured. Shot. Shot where? By whom? Why?

Abbie slowed down and took a deep breath. She suddenly felt like she couldn't go on, all the urgency having gone out of her. She bent down, rested her hands on her thighs, and took a few moments to catch her breath. She was no good to anyone in this state. She knew it was just a belated reaction to panic, but it happened from time to time. Her heart pounded, and she couldn't get enough air into her lungs. Abbie tore off a few leaves, crushed them between her fingers, and inhaled the fresh scent. That helped a bit, so she began to walk again, reasoning with herself all the while. Susanna used to help her father in his surgery since she was a girl, partly because she was forced to take over for her mother when she died, and partly because she was genuinely interested in medicine and eager to learn as much as she could. Sue had more practical knowledge than any of them, even Hannah, and knew how to clean and bandage a wound.

Susanna was the first line of defense when anyone came down with an illness or did themselves an injury. If Sue felt unequal to the task, they sent for the doctor, who lived in Williamsburg and took at least an hour to get to them. Finn hadn't said anything about getting the doctor, so perhaps things weren't as bad as Abbie feared. Or maybe they were so dire that sending for the doctor was pointless.

"Oh, stop being such a downer," Abbie admonished herself. "Facts first, Whitfield."

She'd become something of a worrywart since her experience in New York, but Finn always tried to put things in perspective by telling her that she needed to get all the facts before jumping to conclusions. "It's never too late to panic, Abs. Begin with the assumption that everything is all right and work your way from there."

"Easy for you to say," Abbie muttered as she picked up the pace. Finally, Sam's cabin came into view, and Abbie took a calming breath before knocking. Sam instantly opened the door and stepped aside to let her in.

"Sam, how is he?" Abbie demanded. Sam looked pale but tried to smile for the benefit of the children who sat around the table eating bread with jam. Normally, they would already be in bed at this hour, but Susanna and Sam clearly needed to keep them out of the way, and food was always the best way to distract the Mallory children from asking too many questions or getting underfoot. The boys looked thrilled to be part of this family drama, but Rachel rested her head on the table, her eyelids fluttering as she tried to stay awake. Her face was smeared with jam, and her hair had come loose from the stubby braids tied with pink ribbons.

"Hello, Aunt Abbie," Ben said as he licked jam off his hand. "Granddad's been shot."

"Through the shoulder," Nat elaborated.

The two boys were born four months apart but looked like twins. Nat had been smaller and thinner than Ben when his mother first brought him to Virginia, but he'd grown and filled out over the past two years and was now the same height as Ben. Their coloring was different, with Ben being dark-haired like Sue and Nat's unruly mane glowing with a reddish hue just like his own mother's, but their eyes were almost identical—a clear gray, fringed by thick dark lashes. The Mallory eyes, Hannah called them, since they came down her husband's side of the family.

Nat hardly ever asked about his mother anymore, accepting Sue and Sam as his parents. Sam was Nathaniel's natural father, of course, but Sue made the selfless decision to bring Nat up with her own children after Diana had been found dead at an inn in Williamsburg. Despite his origins, Sue loved Nat as much as she loved Ben and never uttered a negative word about his mother, who had been far from a saint and had set out to destroy Susanna's marriage and claim Sam for her own.

"Pa's been shot in the shoulder and lost a lot of blood. He walked all the way here. He was barely conscious by the time I found him." Sam spoke in a whisper, but of course, the children heard every word.

"You should see the Indian arrow, Aunt Abbie," Nat said, his eyes huge with wonder.

"Indian arrow?" Abbie gasped. "He was shot by Indians?"

Abbie expected to hear that her father had been discovered by the British and pursued by a patrol, but she never imagined that he might have been the victim of an Indian attack. It didn't make any sense. The Indian nations stood firmly with the British since the beginning of the conflict, believing that the

British would protect their interests and offer them better terms once the war was won, but they were also being courted by the Americans, who needed their support to defeat the British.

The British pursued the Indian alliance relentlessly, sending government-nominated agents to offer enticing gifts and negotiate terms of trade, but the Indians also hosted emissaries from the colonies, and, as a rule, did not randomly target Americans. There had been several instances of settlements being sacked but those attacks had been organized, and usually perceived by the Native Americans as having been provoked. To kill a solitary man accomplished nothing, especially if he hadn't done anything to antagonize the Native Americans if he came upon their party. John Mallory had great sympathy for the Indians and their plight and hoped that once the war was won, the Native Americans would live in peace with the colonists and both sides would prosper through trade.

"I'm not quite sure what happened," Sam explained, "but yes, he was shot by an Indian arrow."

"My God," Abbie exclaimed as she stepped into the other room and firmly closed the door behind her so the children, who were craning their necks to get a better view, wouldn't see. Hannah, Finn, and Susanna surrounded John, who lay on the bed, still and silent. Susanna's hands were covered in blood and a pile of crimson-stained rags lay next to a basin. Susanna washed her hands and turned to Abbie. She looked exhausted.

"Sue, will he recover?" Abbie asked.

"I think so. He broke off the arrow, but the shaft was still lodged in his shoulder. I extracted it and cleaned the wound, but it's very deep, Abbie. The arrow went straight through."

"Has he said anything?" Hannah asked.

"No, he was too weak by the time he got here, and delirium had set in. He mumbled a few random words, but they didn't make any sense," Sue replied apologetically. Susanna was close with Hannah and would have liked to give her something to hold on to in the face of her husband's injury, but just then, there was no good news to give.

"Sue, which way did the arrow point? Was he shot while facing the Indians or in the back?" Finn asked.

"He must have been facing them. The point of the arrow was lodged in his back."

"I don't understand," Sam said. "There hasn't been an Indian attack in these parts in ages. Why would they shoot a single man who posed no threat to them?"

"Perhaps they were hunting and shot him by mistake," Sue suggested.

"That doesn't seem very likely," Finn replied. "They are skilled hunters and can tell the difference between a stag and a man, especially when the man in question is wearing a white shirt. Sam, was your father wearing a coat when you found him?" Finn asked, turning to face Sam with a frown on his face.

"No, he wasn't. Just the shirt."

"Why do you want to know?" Sam asked, instantly alert.

"No reason, just curious."

"We won't know anything until John wakes up," Hannah said firmly as she sat on the bed and took John's hand in hers. "I'll stay with him through the night. Susanna, perhaps you should take the children up to the house."

"You go on, Sue. I'll stay with Ma," Sam offered.

"John might need me during the night," Susanna protested. "Sam, take the children and go. Your mother and I will tend to your father. If he makes it through the night, he is sure to improve."

Sam gave Susanna a tender kiss and went to round up the children. "Sleepover at Grandma's," he announced.

"Yay," the children cheered. Rachel, who had been asleep, raised her head and looked around in confusion, but smiled happily once she understood what was happening. She loved spending time with Diana and Eddie.

"Will Grandma make us biscuits and bacon for breakfast?" Ben demanded.

"Grandma will stay here to look after Granddad, but maybe Aunt Abbie can be persuaded to feed the troops."

"Yes Ben, I'll make you bacon," Abbie promised with a smile. Ben could always be counted on to worry about food, especially bacon, which was his absolute favorite thing in the world. Both Ben and Nat sprang to their feet, but Rachel was too tired to walk, so Sam lifted her into his arms and she wrapped her pudgy arms around his neck and put her head on his shoulder, instantly going back to sleep.

"Come," Finn said as he put his arm around Abbie. "I'll come over here first thing in the morning and check on your father. Keep the faith, Abbie. He's as strong as an ox."

"He is," Abbie said through tears, "but he looks so frail."

"He's lost a lot of blood, but I'm sure he'll pull through. Sue will look after him, and he needs his rest. We are not about to get any," Finn said as Sam followed them with his three children in tow. "They'll be jumping like monkeys until they wear themselves out."

None of them had ever seen real monkeys, but Finn had read about them in a book and showed Abbie the drawing that accompanied the article. The boys were indeed bright-eyed and bursting with energy, and the cheer that went up in the loft when the cousins arrived was worthy of the Continental Army.

"You are to go straight to sleep. The first one asleep gets an extra rasher of bacon for breakfast," Abbie promised, trying to hide a smile. Five pairs of eyes stared back at her, their little faces earnest and hopeful.

"Goodnight," Abbie said and climbed down the ladder. "They'll be up till midnight," she said with a sigh as a shriek followed by wild laughter erupted from the loft.

"Let them have their fun, Abs," Finn said. "They are only

young once. Come outside with me. You look like you could use a few minutes of peace."

"Go on. I'll mind the beasts," Sam said as he helped himself to a cup of beer.

Abbie sighed and followed Finn outside. It was a beautiful summer night, and they sat side by side on the bench, gazing up at the stars. Finn could feel the tension coursing through Abbie as she leaned into him.

"He will recover, Abbie. An arrow through the shoulder is painful, but not fatal. No major organs have been damaged. Your father is as tough as an old boot. He'll be up and about in a few days, giving us all hell for not keeping our spirits up."

Abbie nodded into his shoulder. "I know. I just can't bear the thought of losing him, Finn. I can't imagine how you must feel living so far away from your own parents. Just knowing that Ma and Pa are here makes every burden lighter. I don't have to be a grown-up when I turn to them for help and advice. Even though I have my own children, I'm still their child, and it makes me feel safe knowing that I don't have to bear all the responsibility alone. That kind of understanding and support is irreplaceable."

"I do miss my parents, more than I can say, but I've chosen to remain here with you, and your parents have more or less adopted me. I love them too, Abs."

"I know. I'm feeling a bit maudlin, I suppose. We all know we are going to lose the people we love sooner or later, but we sort of put it out of our minds and hope they'll be around for a long time."

"And this has brought it home," Finn said as he kissed Abbie's temple. "You need to get some sleep, sweetheart. Everything will look brighter in the morning."

"I won't be able to get to sleep," Abbie complained as she stood and stretched.

"I'll help you," Finn replied with an impudent smile, his hand cupping her behind.

"There are five children in our loft," Abbie replied with a giggle.

"No one will pay any attention to us. They're too busy entertaining each other."

Finn took Abbie's hand and pulled her into the house. She didn't protest.

SIX

By the time Finn woke the following morning, Abbie was already downstairs. The appetizing smell of buttermilk biscuits and frying bacon drifted up to the loft, and a chorus of piping voices drowned out Abbie's plea for quiet as the children asked for more milk and bacon. Finn opened the shutters and gazed at the cloudless August sky. It had to be close to eight o'clock and he couldn't fathom how he'd managed to sleep through five children waking up and getting dressed right next to him. He must have been sleeping deeply, since it took him several hours to fall asleep the night before, a nagging feeling that he was missing something important eating away at him until he finally succumbed to fatigue. Finn pulled on his clothes and went downstairs.

Abbie greeted him with a nod as she doled out more food to the children, who were seated around the table with Annie and Sarah. The rest of them would have to wait since there wasn't enough room for everyone. Abbie had relaxed somewhat last night, but now she looked tense again, her mouth pressed into a thin line as she sliced more bacon to put in the pan.

"Come, let's get your hands and faces washed," Sarah

ordered the children as they finished their breakfast and reluctantly left the table. "Who wants to help me in the barn?"

Finn tried to hide his amusement when there was no response from the kids. Helping out in the barn wasn't the treat Sarah hoped it would be.

"I want to go fishing," Nat announced when Sam came in from the outside. His hair was wet, and he had a towel slung over his shoulder. Sam must have gone for an early morning swim. "Pa, can we go fishing? You said we could."

"Not today, son. Granddad is ill, so Uncle Finn and I will go check on him. You can stay here and play with your cousins."

"But I want to go fishing," Nat protested, stubborn as ever.

"And you will, but not this morning. I'm sure Aunt Sarah can come up with some fascinating things for you to do in the barn," he replied.

"Pa!" Nat screeched as Ben covered his mouth to hide his laughter.

"I will happily take you all fishing tomorrow, if Granddad is on the mend," Sam promised.

"Even the girls?" Ben demanded.

"Even the girls."

This brought on a new bout of dissent, but Sam was no longer listening. He grabbed a biscuit, broke it in half and stuffed a piece of bacon inside.

"Ready to go, Finn?" Sam asked.

Finn gazed lovingly at the spread before him before copying Sam's maneuver with the biscuit. He wasn't going on an empty belly. "Yes, ready. Abs, I'll bring news as soon as I'm able."

"Please do."

Finn gave Abbie a kiss, ruffled Ben's hair, and pulled playfully on Diana's braid before stepping into the morning sunshine with Sam. The morning was already hot and hazy, the humidity sucking all the freshness out of the air. The yard smelled of cut grass and sunbaked earth.

"I went for a swim," Sam said as they walked through a lush meadow still sparkling with morning dew. "I couldn't sleep a wink last night. Thought the exercise would help me to calm down."

"And did it?"

"No, not really. I'm worried about him, Finn."

"So am I. Sam, something's bothering me," Finn replied, having finally hit on what had been hovering at the edge of his consciousness last night.

"Is it about Pa?"

"Yes. I couldn't fall asleep last night either and I got to thinking about the ways of the Indians."

Finn never told anyone about his life in the seventeenth century, but he did share something of the knowledge that he'd picked up from his hunting buddies, who were members of the Algonquian tribe. He'd learned much from them, and they had learned something from him as well. It had been a mutually beneficial relationship that gave Finn a deeper understanding of their views on life and death.

"Did you happen to notice that the entry wound was much higher than the exit wound?" Finn asked, stopping suddenly to face Sam.

"No, but now that you mention it, yes it was." Sam froze as comprehension dawned. "That would indicate that Pa was shot from above, either from the trees, or while he was sitting down with his attacker standing above him. Why would the Indians shoot a lone man who clearly posed no threat? Perhaps Pa was holding a gun and the Indians felt threatened," Sam suggested.

"Perhaps, but it doesn't seem likely, does it?" Finn asked as he resumed walking. "Your father would not have been anywhere near Indian territory, nor would he suddenly hold someone at gunpoint unless he felt threatened, which would mean that the Indian was already pointing the arrow at him."

Sam shrugged. "We won't know for certain until Pa tells us what happened."

"But if you were an Indian," Finn persisted, "would you shoot someone in the shoulder at such close range? What would be the point?"

"What are you saying?" Sam asked. He stopped walking and stood facing Finn, his brows furrowed with foreboding.

"I'm saying that the Indians are skilled with their bows and arrows. If they shoot, they shoot to kill. Why shoot your father in the shoulder and then allow him to return and tell everyone that he'd been attacked by Indians, possibly provoking some sort of retaliation? If I were to shoot a man, I'd kill him and hide his body. Wouldn't you?"

"You're right," Sam replied. "I hadn't really thought about it, but what you're saying makes perfect sense. So, what's your theory?"

"I don't have one yet. I need to speak to your pa, but I think there's something distinctly odd about this incident. Hopefully, he's awake and alert enough to tell us what really happened. The wound itself is not life-threatening, so he should be on the mend."

"He's lost a lot of blood. Sue says that rest and fluids can help the body regenerate blood. I hope she's right."

"Did she ever receive a reply from her father?" Finn asked. Susanna never spoke of her family, but Sam had mentioned that marrying a rebel had created a rift between Sue and her father and sister, who were fervent supporters of the king. Joseph Freeman had saved Sam's life once, but he probably would not have been as determined to help him if he'd known that Sam would run off with his daughter and convince her to change sides.

"No, Sue wrote to her father and Laura several times but received no reply. It pains her, Finn. She really believed that they would forgive her in time, but she appears to have been mistaken."

"I think I would forgive my children anything," Finn said. "Nothing can be more painful than losing them, especially while they are still alive."

"You mean you'd forgive Diana if she married a scoundrel like me?" Sam joked, smiling for the first time that morning.

"I'd have to, wouldn't I? Who would protect her from a scoundrel like you if not her loving father?"

"Good point. You're just full of them today."

Sam was rattled by Finn's take on the situation, but he put on a brave face and defused the tension with a joke, as was his way. But Finn could see that Sam was struggling to come to terms with the truths he'd chosen to ignore last night. Something about what happened to John Mallory was distinctly odd.

SEVEN

Finn and Sam were surprised to find Susanna sitting outside, her shoulders visibly tense even from a distance, her hands clasped in her lap. She looked tired and melancholy and seemed to be staring off into the distance. She sat up straighter when she spotted them coming toward the house and tried to smile, but the smile never reached her eyes. Whatever news Sue was about to impart wasn't going to be good.

"Sue, what is it?" Sam asked as they came closer. His voice shook and his eyes begged Susanna to tell him that his father wasn't dead. Susanna put a finger to her lips, indicating that whatever she said would be heard inside the house. She stood and walked toward them, drawing them away from the house and into the shade of an old oak. Susanna leaned against the trunk as if she were too tired to stand on her own.

"Sue, please tell me," Sam begged. "How's Pa?"

"He's not well, Sam. Not well at all."

"But you said the wound wasn't fatal. You said the arrow hadn't damaged any major organs. I don't understand."

Sam looked as if he were about to cry. At that moment, he was a little boy who feared losing his father and the look of sympathy on Sue's face implied that she knew that as well. Sam wasn't someone who broke down. He was strong and defused every situation with humor, but this wasn't something that could be turned into a joke to make it more bearable.

"The wound is not fatal on its own, but I discovered something last night. The tip of the arrow and the shaft were coated with something. I believe whatever it was entered the bloodstream. Your father is delirious and fevered this morning."

"What was it slathered with?" Finn demanded, suddenly angry. "Do you still have the arrow?"

Sue nodded. "Yes, I kept it to show you."

"Those bloody Indians," Sam exploded. "I'd like to find the bastard who did this and show him American justice. I'll find him and I'll kill him, and make sure he dies a slow, painful death," Sam hissed. He wasn't using humor this time. He was channeling his fear into anger, which could be a lot more dangerous if he decided to act on it.

"Sam, wait," Finn said, putting a hand on Sam's arm. "Indians rarely use poisoned arrows. They're too good with their bows to need that extra measure, and why would they want to poison their kill? They hunt for food, so they would be compromising their food supply. Besides, if the arrow had been poisoned, chances are Sue would have been dead by now, having touched it with her bare hands. The poisons they use come from snakes and are deadly."

"So, what are you saying, exactly?" Sam demanded, still fuming. His hands were clenched into fists, and if Finn didn't know better, he'd think Sam wanted to punch him.

"I'm saying that maybe this arrow wasn't loosed by an Indian. Sue, I need to see it, please."

"Come back to the house, but please don't say anything to Mrs. Mallory. She doesn't know. The poor woman is exhausted from tending to her husband all night and the last thing she needs is to think that he's been deliberately poisoned."

"I'll be discreet," Finn promised. "Sam, perhaps you should wait for me outside."

"Not a chance," Sam growled as he followed Finn and Susanna into the house.

The house smelled of illness and blood with an underlying odor of vomit. John must have thrown up recently. He looked white, except for the two bright spots of color in his cheeks. His skin glistened with sweat, and his lips were chapped and colorless. Hannah Mallory sat on the bed next to her husband, holding his hand. She looked pale and frightened as she turned to greet them.

"Ma, why don't you come outside for a spell," Sam suggested. "You look like you could use a cool drink and a little fresh air."

"I can't leave him, Sammy. He's very poorly."

Hannah started as John opened his eyes. He was looking at her but didn't seem to recognize her. "Sam, is that you?" John Mallory called out. "Son?"

"I'm here, Pa. What happened?"

John tried to sit up but winced with pain as he moved his injured shoulder. He seemed agitated and confused, his words coming in a rapid stream, as if he needed to get them out while there was still time. "Sam, my pocket. Information. Get it out. Must be delivered. Urgent, you hear? It's urgent."

"Pa, I'll pass on the information. Don't worry. What happened to you?" Sam asked, keeping his voice as calm as possible. "Who shot you? I need to know."

John looked momentarily taken aback by the question. He grew silent, his forehead furrowed in concentration as he tried to remember.

"Pa, was it an Indian?" Sam persisted. "Were you shot by an Indian?"

John shook his head, then looked directly at Sam, his gaze clear and focused.

"It was a white man, Sam. A white man."

"Who was it? Did you recognize him?" Sam asked, but the moment of clarity had passed, and John closed his eyes, too exhausted by his effort to speak.

"Get it out," he whispered before slipping into unconsciousness.

"Sam, what does he mean?" Hannah implored. "I don't understand. "What white man?"

"Sam, can I see you outside?" Finn asked as he peeked into the room.

"I'll be right back, Ma. Sue, please get her a drink," Sam asked as he followed Finn outside.

"What have you found?"

"The arrow is definitely Indian. I've seen many like it, but I don't believe it was loosed by an Indian."

"How could that be?" Sam demanded.

"Poisons have a certain smell that can be detected by someone who's familiar with them. What I'm smelling is cow dung, and it's not just on the tip; it's on the shaft as well."

"Finn, what the hell are you implying?" Sam exploded.

"I'm implying that this arrow was used by someone who intentionally smeared it with dung to ensure that the wound festered. This is a method sometimes used by soldiers on the battlefield to make sure that even if they don't kill their enemy outright, they will still die if wounded. Obviously, they don't use arrows, but some smear bullets with shit to maximize the damage. You see, whoever shot your father wasn't a very skilled archer, nor did he need to finish him off. All he had to do was wound, and I believe that your father was taken unawares, while he was sitting down. I think this was deliberate, Sam."

"Pa said it was a white man."

"I think someone tried to kill him and made it look like an Indian attack. That's why they let him get away, to make sure that it would be known he'd been shot with an arrow."

"They are covering their tracks," Sam said, nodding with understanding. "They had been lying in wait for him."

"And the only reason anyone would wish to kill your father is because they'd discovered his role in the Committee of Correspondence."

EIGHT

VIRGINIA AUGUST 1628

Alec came downstairs, eager for a cup of chicory coffee and almost ready to face the day. The conversation with Kit the night before left him feeling unsettled. He understood Kit's rationale for wishing to return to England. Kit had obligations he could no longer ignore, and he had to do right by his son, but sadness and a terrible sense of foreboding gnawed at Alec. Sometimes not knowing what was to come was a blessing rather than a curse, since the certain knowledge of impending events could be paralyzing.

Kit had time, of course, but in twenty years England would be boiling over like a kettle left over a flame for too long. For the first time in its history a bloody conflict would erupt between the Royalists and the Roundheads, and the people of England would be guilty of regicide, resulting in the type of bloodshed not seen on English soil for generations. Kit might be too old to fight, but not to take sides, but Robbie would be just the right age to get embroiled in the conflict. Given Kit's political views and social position, Robbie would most likely end up on the losing side of history.

But was it fair of Alec to make Kit aware of what was to

come or to try to persuade him to remain in Virginia? Kit was a grown man who had to make up his own mind and follow his own path and Alec had no right to try to influence him one way or the other. Kit had no property of his own in the colony but owned a profitable estate in England that had been managed by proxy for the past several years. Kit had the ready capital to buy a plantation of his own if he chose to do so, but he'd never committed to such an investment, believing it was just a matter of time until he returned home with his family. And now the time had come, as they all knew it would.

Alec took his cup of coffee outside and sat down on the porch, reluctant to converse with anyone just yet, even Valerie. He couldn't talk to her about this, not when her feelings were so deeply involved and her view of the situation far from rational. Valerie was terrified of losing her sister, and for Alec, losing Kit would be as painful as losing a brother. He'd recovered from Finlay's death, or more accurately, he'd learned to live without him, but he still thought of Finn every day and frequently talked to him in his head, telling him what was happening and asking for his advice. They'd rarely agreed on anything while Finn was alive, but they had been as close as any two brothers could be and had understood each other in that instinctive and emotional way siblings often shared.

Kit hadn't replaced Finn, but he'd come closer than any other man to sharing that bond with Alec, and Alec had grown to rely on Kit over the years, seeking Kit's counsel and support a lot more often than that of his remaining brother. Charles had been a sweet boy once, but he'd grown into a self-centered, profit-driven man. Charles was ambitious, and his desire for wealth and influence often led him to make questionable decisions, as well as harsh judgments. Charles had never quite forgiven Alec for inheriting the estate from their uncle and still behaved like the plantation was half his, often interfering with Alec's decisions and undermining his authority. In essence, there were two people running the plantation, and they often clashed.

Alec drained his cup and reluctantly went back inside. Valerie and Louisa were downstairs, enjoying a peaceful breakfast, having fed the children and sent them to play. Alec could hear Minnie reprimanding Evie for something, and Evie's imperious tone as she told Minnie what she could do with her criticism. Evie was strong-willed and opinionated, and Kit would have his hands full a few years from now when Evie began to transition from a child into a woman.

"Alec, come have some breakfast. The buns are still warm, and there's fresh butter and some strawberry jam. We were going to save the jam for the winter months, but Lou and I had a craving for something sweet, so we cracked one jar open."

"Don't mind if I do," Alec replied, glad to see Valerie in better spirits.

Alec buttered a roll and spread it with jam. He normally ate porridge for breakfast, but today the sticky sweetness of the jam and the butter melting into the warm dough gave him immense pleasure. He felt like a child as he licked the jam from his fingers, making Valerie laugh.

"More coffee?" Louisa asked as she got up to fetch some from the kitchen.

"Please."

Alec was just reaching for another roll when he heard the creaking of wheels in the yard. He glanced toward the window to check the position of the sun. It was still early, around eight o'clock.

"Where's Kit?" Alec asked Louisa as she entered the room with a pot of coffee.

"He offered to take breakfast to the workers today. Cook's been complaining of back pain, and the pot is heavy. He should have been back by now," Louisa said as she glanced out the window. "Oh, Good Lord in Heaven. What is he up to now?"

she exclaimed irritably as she motioned for Alec to join her at the window. "That man is as unpredictable as the weather!"

Alec reluctantly left the breakfast table and went to see what had upset Louisa so. She wasn't normally this highly strung, but since Kit had announced his intention of returning to England every little thing set her off, the result being that either someone was reprimanded or Louisa stormed off in tears. Alec had expected to see Kit, but it was Charles who was driving the wagon, with about a dozen dirty children squashed in behind him. They all looked frightened, their young faces tense with foreboding.

Alec swore under his breath and headed outside. "Charles, what's going on? Who are these children?"

Charles jumped off the bench and turned to face Alec, who was surprised to see Charles shining like a new penny. The look of pride on his face was unmistakable. "I've brought the answer to our problem."

"What problem would that be?" Alec demanded, thoroughly annoyed. Charles had been overstepping his authority more and more of late, forcing Alec to clash with him on a regular basis.

"We need more workers, and I got us some at a very reasonable rate," Charles replied, completely ignoring Alec's scowl.

"These are not workers; these are children," Alec exclaimed. "Where did they come from?"

Charles threw an aggrieved look over his shoulder, then beckoned Alec to come back inside the house. "I think we should discuss this privately."

"Discuss what?" Alec spat out as his eyes traveled over the filthy children who looked as if they hadn't eaten in days and were now all staring at him fearfully.

"Valerie, are there enough buns to go round?" he asked as he passed Valerie and Louisa on the way to the study. "These children looked famished."

THE TIES THAT BIND

"I'll get some," Valerie replied. "I'll make sure everyone gets something to eat." She grabbed the plate of buns and went to greet the frightened children, followed by Louisa who was holding a pitcher of milk and several cups.

Charles opened his mouth to say something, but Alec turned his back on him, going into the study and shutting the door. "There's no need for everyone to know our business."

Charles collapsed into a chair and gave Alec a sour look. "Now, don't start in on me until you've heard what I have to say."

"All right. Tell me," Alec replied, striving for patience.

"A large shipment of children came in from England this morning. There was to be an auction in the afternoon, but I happen to be friendly with the captain, so I made him an offer for their indenture contracts, and he accepted. I got an excellent deal on a dozen urchins. They will replace the workers we've lost over the past two years. Children are energetic and nimble, and they have yet to reach their full potential."

"Charles, are you mad?" Alec asked, staring at Charles in disbelief. "What makes you think I wish to own children?"

"Alec, be reasonable. I bought this lot for the price of three adults. We can squeeze a lot of labor out of them before their indenture ends in seven years' time. This was an excellent investment. Admit it."

"I won't have it, Charles. I won't have children working the tobacco fields. It's hard work even for grown men."

Charles winced at Alec's tone. He'd expected high praise, but instead, Alec was treating him like a fool, as usual. Nothing he did was good enough for his older brother. Charles would bet his life that if Kit showed up with a cart full of children, Alec would clap him on the shoulder and say, "Well done." Charles bolted to his feet, eyes blazing with anger.

"Listen Alec, the plantation is suffering. We are barely managing with the laborers we have, and the reason for our failure to turn a better profit is rooted in your inflexible moral principles. You refuse to buy slaves. You refuse to work the men harder to get more done in a day, you refuse to give them cheaper food, and you refuse to punish them to teach them who's in charge. And now you refuse to utilize children? At this rate, we won't survive for much longer."

"My first responsibility is to the people," Alec snapped. "I won't work the men fourteen hours a day seven days a week. They are human beings, not beasts, and even beasts deserve rest and decent food. You've really overstepped your authority this time, Charlie."

Alec glared at Charles, barely holding back what he really wished to say. Charles had no authority at all. The plantation wasn't his to manage. Alec gave Charles a portion of the profits every quarter because he felt guilty that Charles had received nothing from the uncle who raised him. Alec didn't mind helping, but he never actually made Charles his partner. He was a partner in the shipping business, which was doing very well since they began importing rum a few years back. Charles was not only well off, but fairly wealthy. This wasn't about profit; this was about power, and Alec would be damned if he allowed Charles to manipulate him.

"So, what do you suggest? That I take those children back and sell them to other plantation owners? I suppose I can make my money back and turn a profit as well," Charles mused, watching Alec's face with derision. "So, not all is lost."

"Do you not have an ounce of compassion?" Alec fumed.

"Yes, I do, for people of our own class. Those children are thieves and would-be whores. They would surely have starved or died at the end of a rope if they hadn't been taken up by the authorities and shipped to Virginia. If they survive their servitude, they will have a chance at a new life in a growing and prosperous colony. They will be vastly better off than on the streets of London, or wherever they were plucked from. What I have done is merciful, not vicious."

"You just keep telling yourself that," Alec replied, still furiously angry.

"So, shall I take them back then?" Charles demanded. He was goading Alec, and Alec knew it.

"I will decide what to do with them once I've spoken to Kit."

Involving Kit would set Charles off, but he wanted to punish him for his interference. Kit helped run the plantation and earned part of the profit. It was only fair, but Kit never overstepped his boundaries, giving Alec the respect and authority he deserved. Charles, on the other hand, was always one step away from mutiny, which made their relationship less than civil.

"Charles, I think you'd best return home for the time being. I will come and see you when I am ready to discuss this further."

"Damn you, Alec," Charles spat as he strode away. "Damn you."

NINE

"So, what am I to do now?" Alec asked as the four of them sat outside that evening.

It was a pleasant night with countless stars twinkling in a cloudless sky. The haze and humidity of the past few days had given way to a cool breeze and Valerie had insisted that all the windows remain open during the night, despite Cook and Minnie's horror of pestilence infiltrating every inch of the house. Alec and Kit had developed a fondness for going outside on fine evenings ever since Louisa and Valerie assured them that there were no evil humors lurking about and that the night air was not, in fact, dangerous or an instrument of spreading disease. It was a pleasant way to pass time after supper before the cold weather drove them indoors and they spent nearly six months whiling away the frigid evenings reading, playing card games, sewing, or just talking.

"I have to agree with Charles, Alec. These children are orphans and petty criminals who have no one to look out for them. Most of them will not make it to adulthood," Kit replied.

"Same is true here," Valerie chimed in. "Some of the landowners work their laborers to death. They die of exhaustion, malnutrition, and disease. The children won't stand a chance if they wind up on one of those plantations."

"I hadn't realized that they shipped convicts and unwanted children to the colonies before they began ferrying them over to Australia," Louisa said.

"Australia?" Kit asked. "Where's that?"

"It's a continent on the other side of the world, Kit. The British will colonize the eastern part of Australia sometime in the eighteenth century and establish a penal colony called Botany Bay. Thousands will be transported there."

"Really? Is it uninhabited now?" Kit asked. They made it a rule not to talk about the future, so whenever someone slipped up and offered an interesting tidbit, Kit wasn't one to pass it up.

"No, there are indigenous people living there, but they will suffer the same fate as the American Indians," Louisa explained.

"How did the convicts fare in this new land? Will Botany Bay be as prosperous as the American Colonies?" Kit asked.

Alec remained noticeably silent. He'd learned about Australia while in the twenty-first century, so this wasn't new to him, and he was still preoccupied with the fate of the twelve children who were now asleep in one of the barracks.

"It became prosperous in time, but in the beginning, many people perished. You see, Australia's seasons are opposite to those we are used to. Our summer is their winter, and vice versa. It took the colonists a long time to figure out that they needed to plant in the fall rather than in what they believed to be spring. Many starved, and many died either on the way to Australia, or once they got there. I don't envy the poor people who were sent there as punishment for some minor crime, but then, I don't envy anyone who's had a taste of British justice before the twentieth century."

"Come now. You're being too harsh, Lou. The British legal system is the most civilized in the world," Kit protested.

"You think it's civilized to pluck children off the streets without their consent and sell them into slavery? They might be orphans and thieves, but they are still human beings who deserve some consideration. Instead, they are treated as waste, unwanted rubbish shipped off to a place where there's room and work for them. Unpaid, back-breaking work," Louisa added hotly.

"Louisa, we can't change the world as much as we'd like, but we can do something to make it better for those who depend on us," Alec replied. "It's settled. We are keeping the children. You've helped me make up my mind."

"Glad to be of service," Louisa replied sourly.

"Oh, come now," Valerie admonished her. "You can't compare the time we were born into to the seventeenth century. If you do, you'll drive yourself and everyone around you absolutely mad. You knew what you were getting into when you followed me into the past."

"Yes, I did. I apologize," Louisa mumbled, stung by Valerie's words.

"No apologies necessary. You two bear up better than Kit and I would in your situation," Alec said, giving Kit a meaningful look.

"He's right, sweetheart," Kit jumped in hastily, eager to pacify Louisa. "We'll do what we can for the poor mites."

"Good, now I'm going to bed," Louisa announced haughtily, giving Kit a look that clearly indicated he wasn't invited to join her. "Goodnight."

"I'll turn in, too," Valerie said. "Alec, are you coming?"

"I'll be up in a minute. I need to have a word with Kit."

"All right, then. Goodnight, Kit." Valerie covered her mouth as she yawned. It had been a long day, and she was tired.

"Is everything all right between you and Louisa?" Alec asked once Valerie had gone in. "She seems somewhat antagonistic toward you, Kit."

Kit sighed and looked up at the sky, his expression pained. "We had another argument about returning to England. I tried to explain my reasons to her yet again. You can just imagine how well that went over. I always knew she wouldn't be receptive, but she is being downright unreasonable and refuses to even discuss it. Am I wrong in this, Alec?"

"No, you're not, but Louisa is a woman of the twenty-first century. She doesn't care about titles and estates. She cares about family and continuity. Separating Louisa and Valerie will be painful for them both. They were close before traveling through time, but now they're inseparable. They rely on each other emotionally in a way that they will never rely on us. No one can understand them as well as they understand each other."

"Alec, I can't commit to remaining here forever."

"No, you can't, but give her time. Louisa reacts with her heart, but eventually common sense always takes over. Would you like me to talk to Valerie?" Alec offered. Valerie would be devastated, but perhaps she would help Louisa find a way forward.

"Would you? If anyone can sway Louisa, it's Valerie, although I'm not sure which way she'd be swaying her, toward me or away from me."

"That remains to be seen. In the meantime, I'm going to bed. Can't keep the wife waiting."

"At least your wife is waiting. Mine has probably bolted the door," Kit replied with a dramatic sigh.

Alec chuckled at the sight of Kit's miserable expression. "You're probably right, but that doesn't mean you shouldn't try."

"Right," Kit mumbled as he pushed to his feet.

TEN

SCOTLAND AUGUST 1628

How is it possible to be so happy and so miserable at the same time? Jenny wondered as she snuggled next to a comatose Cameron. Cameron had been a light sleeper when she knew him in Virginia, never truly able to let his guard down enough to relax, but since coming home, he learned to sleep deeply again. Jenny liked to watch his face when he wasn't aware of her scrutiny. He looked so peaceful and relaxed in repose, his mouth slightly open and his auburn lashes fanned against the golden hue of his skin. It made her happy to see him rest.

She loved these quiet moments together when they could stay abed just a little longer than usual and not be up before dawn to see to their chores. Most days were a whirlwind of activity with Jenny and Cameron barely seeing each other during the day, but when they were together, Cameron was a considerate and affectionate husband, the type of husband most women could only dream of. And she adored Ian. There was a time when Jenny didn't think she'd ever have a family of her own. She feared she'd spend her days alone, living on the fringes of someone else's family, forever the outsider looking in. Now she had what she'd always dreamed of, but spent every day fighting down the melancholy that threatened to engulf her.

She hadn't been herself since the birth. She'd awaited the arrival of the baby with an anticipation that took her breath away, but once Ian was born, she felt lethargic and sad. She told herself that she was tired from lack of sleep and the constant demands of a nursing baby. Her body needed time to adjust, but Ian was now seven months old and she still felt as if she had to drag herself out of bed every morning if she hoped to get anything done.

There were times when tears came unbidden, and she allowed herself the luxury of crying just to shift the heaviness in her chest. The crying would offer a temporary relief, but within a day or two, the melancholy would start to build up again, dragging her down into its depths like a treacherous swamp. Why couldn't she just be happy with what she had? Cameron and Ian were her life, her reason for being, but something inside her seemed to be broken at a time when she should be most content.

Perhaps if she could bond with other women and seek their advice, she'd feel better, but she had no friends this side of the Atlantic. Jenny missed Valerie and Louisa desperately. They had been so easy to talk to and always ready to offer comfort and support. They were different from any women Jenny had ever met, kind and surprisingly open-minded, where most women of their generation were prone to quick judgments and harsh words. With Valerie and Louisa, Jenny learned to finally open up after years of denying her feelings and suppressing her needs.

In the convent where Jenny grew up, any kind of emotional outburst or desire for physical affection was considered highly inappropriate and shameful. The nuns suppressed all their emotional needs and physical urges and instead turned them into an almost sexual love of God. God was their confidante, their father, and their celibate lover. Jenny had never been able to find comfort in that type of devotion, nor did she wish to. She longed for intimate relationships with others, and actual human contact. Becoming part of the Whitfield family had been a revelation and a dream come true, but she'd been forced to choose between staying with the people who loved her and following Cameron halfway across the world. Was it ever possible to have the best of both worlds?

Jenny tried to forge a bond with Cameron's family, but his mother was a cold and rigid woman, who regarded Jenny with undue suspicion because of her French upbringing. Jenny tried to explain that she'd grown up in a Catholic convent, not the royal court, but to Fiona Brody, the two seemed interchangeable. Deep down, Jenny understood that Fiona felt unworldly and inferior next to a woman who was educated and refined, but all Jenny really wanted was a bit of warmth and sympathy from the woman who claimed to adore her son but couldn't summon a smidgeon of affection for his wife.

They went to Cameron's parents every Sunday after church and Jenny tried to confide in Fiona despite the other woman's resistance to any sort of relationship. Fiona was brusque and impatient, the look of wariness in her eyes unmistakable.

"Ye'll not be the first lassie to feel a wee bit overwhelmed after having her first bairn. Tis normal to feel a bit tearful in the first few months. Don't give in to yer weakness, girl. Yer duty is to care for yer husband and son. Yer tears have no place in the home," Fiona admonished her.

But what Fiona wasn't saying out loud was that she thought Jenny weak and spoiled and well beyond child-bearing years. It was acceptable for a girl of sixteen to feel overwhelmed after giving birth, although they rarely did, since they'd helped their mothers raise a brood of siblings and knew their way around a baby. A woman of Jenny's advanced years should have the situation well in hand.

Jenny had just turned twenty-eight, but she might as well

have turned forty judging by the way the women of the parish viewed her. Most women her age had teenage children and looked decades older than Jenny, having spent their youth birthing numerous babies and doing back-breaking farm work while still caring for their families. These women had not worried about their appearance since they were young maidens of marriageable age, nor had they ever read a book or been more than a few miles from the place of their birth.

To them, Jenny was strange and foreign. She was likely the only woman in the village who could read and write, not only in English, but in French, as well as Latin. They resented her and accused her of putting on airs, when, in reality, Jenny tried hard to dumb herself down to win their acceptance. They laughed at her behind her back, especially when she frowned with concentration in an effort to understand the heavy Scottish brogue and make sense of what was said.

Another source of hilarity in the village was Jenny's desire to maintain hygiene. The nuns at the convent believed cleanliness to be important, and Valerie and Louisa always stressed the importance of washing hands before handling food and after using the chamber pot. Jenny had no idea where their notions came from, but the inhabitants of Rosewood Manor were rarely ill, especially since Valerie and Louisa immediately quarantined anyone who felt unwell and made sure their dishes were washed separately from the others. Uncle Alec and Lord Sheridan periodically checked the workers for any signs of illness and insisted that the men bathe at least once a month. The laborers grumbled but complied. It was well known in Jamestown that Uncle Alec's workers rarely died of sickness or malnutrition. Jenny had lived with Valerie and Louisa long enough to know that their methods worked and had adopted their ways. She didn't care if the women laughed at her. Ian would not grow up dirty and crawling with lice. Jenny bathed him as often as she could and washed every clout rather than letting it dry before using it again.

After a time, Jenny stopped trying to fit in or make herself more acceptable to Cameron's family. The only person who genuinely liked her was Katrina, Cameron's youngest sister. Katrina was only fifteen and somewhat in awe of her cultured and elegant good-sister. Katrina, whose hair was carrot-red and routinely escaped any type of binding, admired Jenny's glossy curls and often asked Jenny to style her hair in the way she imagined ladies wore it at court. Jenny had never been anywhere near the French court but tried to humor the girl by creating elaborate hairstyles that left Katrina well-pleased with the results. She didn't need her hair piled high on her head or decorated with flowers or replicas of ships to be beautiful though. Katrina was genuinely lovely, something no one ever bothered to tell her.

Katrina came by when she could carve out time from her own chores and spent an afternoon with Jenny, cooing over Ian and helping with the cooking. Jenny had no knack for making the Scottish dishes Cameron liked, so Katrina taught her, showing her how to make haggis, bannocks, and sausage in exchange for stories of France and England. Katrina dreamed of seeing the world, but her dreams would never become a reality. She was on the verge of becoming betrothed to a young man she'd known since childhood, and it wouldn't be long before she was wed and expecting her first child. Cameron's parents were in favor of the match but asked that Katrina wait until she turned sixteen to marry.

"Tell me about Paris, Jenny," Katrina pleaded as she rocked Ian in her arms. "I so long to see it. I canna even imagine what a grand palace looks like, on account of never having seen anything bigger than a croft. Tell me about the king's court."

"I've never been to court, Katrina; you know that. I grew up in the town of Loudon, in a convent. I didn't see much of anything, to be honest."

"I ken that well enough, but even a French town must be like something out of a fairy story. And London. Ye've seen London."

"Yes, I have. It's vast; bigger than you can imagine. There are many people from all walks of life. It's noisy and dirty, and it makes one feel small and insignificant."

Jenny could see that Katrina had no idea what insignificant meant, but she didn't ask for fear of appearing stupid.

"But ye did see the king's palace. Did ye no'?"

"I did see it, yes. Whitehall Palace is like a city unto itself. Thousands of people live there, and they all serve the king. I only saw it from a distance, though. Commoners can't just go inside unless they are employed at the palace."

Jenny chose not to tell Katrina that Lord and Lady Sheridan had been frequently invited to Whitehall Palace when they lived in England, and that Lord Sheridan was a member of the Privy Council for a time. If she did, the questions would never stop, and she had no desire to encourage Katrina's daydreaming. Fiona Brody would not thank her for putting ideas into her daughter's head, and Jenny had no wish to annoy her mother-in-law any more than was strictly necessary. She enjoyed Katrina's company and didn't want the girl to be banned from visiting her.

"So, tell me about Jamestown then. The New World," Katrina sighed. "Even the name sounds grand. What's it like, Jenny?"

Jenny was about to say that Jamestown was still a primitive settlement with muddy streets and wooden dwellings, cold in the winter and stifling in the summer, but instead what she saw was Rosewood Manor and the land surrounding it. Her mind flew like an eagle above the house, the pond where she used to meet Cameron on summer nights, and the tobacco fields broiling in the hot Virginia sun. She saw Valerie laughing at something Louisa said and Uncle Alec practicing swordfighting with Lord Sheridan. And she saw the children. She could almost feel Tom's little body as he leaned against her, thumb in his mouth as he listened to a story with rapt attention, or Evie, demanding as ever, asking Jenny to embroider a handkerchief for her. She missed Robbie, Harry, and Millie as well. She missed the feeling of belonging to a family.

"It's wonderful," Jenny said and burst into tears.

"Tis what I thought," Katrina replied in a tone of great satisfaction. "I ken ye miss it, Jenny. Mayhap one day ye'll see yer home again."

"Yes, maybe," Jenny replied, but she wasn't so sure. Why would Cameron ever wish to return to a place where he'd been humiliated and persecuted? This was his home, his land. This was the place he'd dreamed of on those hot summer nights, lying on his pallet surrounded by twenty sleeping men. Jenny sighed and took Ian from Katrina.

"I think he's hungry. Cameron says I should give him real food now," Jenny said, still unsure.

"Oh, aye. Mam says he ought to be eating solid food by now. Give him an oatcake," Katrina suggested, eager to help.

"What if he chokes on it?"

"Nay. He's got teeth, the sweet little lad. He'll be all right."

Katrina took an oatcake and put it into Ian's chubby hand. "Here ye go, laddie. A bit at a time, ye ken?"

Ian went to work, biting, gumming, and drooling, but the oatcake seemed to be growing smaller and Ian grew happier. The front of his gown was covered with a gluey mess, but he was determined to finish his treat.

"See, I told ye he'd like it," Katrina said, smiling at her nephew. "He needs something hard to bite on when the new teeth come in. Helps with the pain."

"I haven't been around babies much," Jenny explained,

feeling foolish. "Tom was a babe when I first knew him, but he had a nurse, and she fed him only breast milk on the crossing since there was nothing appropriate for a baby to eat aboard the ship."

"Don't fash yerself, Jenny. Ye'll learn soon enough, and by the time ye and Cameron have more bairns, ye'll be telling me what to do."

I don't want any more bairns, Jenny suddenly thought. *At least not yet.*

"Well, I best be going. Mam will need me to help with supper. I'll see ye on Sunday then."

"You will. Thank you, Katrina."

"Oh, ye don't need to be thanking me. I like coming here."

Katrina patted Ian affectionately on the head and blew Jenny a kiss before disappearing through the door. Jenny smiled after her. She always felt a little lighter after one of her visits. She only wished that the other women would give her a chance.

ELEVEN
VIRGINIA AUGUST 1781

A shaft of golden sunlight filtered through the window, casting John Mallory in a warm light that disguised his pallor. His eyes were closed and his breathing even, but an angry red welt had formed around the wound and the sickly smell of pus filled the room.

"Susanna, I need you to be straight with me," Hannah Mallory demanded. "I need to know."

Hannah looked terrified, but she squared her shoulders and raised her chin defiantly. She wasn't one to run from the truth, no matter how painful. Susanna met Hannah's gaze straight on, knowing that if she so much as looked away for a moment, Hannah would assume the worst. All she could do was tell her mother-in-law what she knew for certain and keep to herself that which she didn't. And what she didn't know was what type of poison had been used on the arrow. Susanna heard that Native Americans used poisons that were so toxic they killed the victim almost instantly, but this was no true Indian arrow, and no Indian poison. Finn thought it might be dung.

Susanna could recognize the signs of poisoning by arsenic or wolfsbane, having read the literature, but she had no experience treating actual patients while nursing for her father. Joseph Freeman was an army surgeon, a man who extracted bullets, sewed up torn flesh, and amputated limbs when necessary. There were few cases of poisoning in the British Army, if one didn't count the cases of poisoning by tainted food, which happened from time to time and generally required a good purge.

"All I can say with any certainty is that the wound has festered. Mr. Mallory's fever is high, but my father used to say that a fever was a body's way of fighting off the infection," Susanna said, keeping her voice as steady and reassuring as she could manage.

Hannah might have scoffed at this notion had she not been so frightened. "Is there hope, Sue?"

"Hannah, I am doing everything in my power to fight this infection. I've cleaned the wound with vinegar and applied a poultice of minced garlic and honey. If the infection is localized, the treatment will help, but should Mr. Mallory develop blood poisoning, there will be nothing more I can do."

"He will die?" Hannah moaned.

"If the putrefaction enters the blood stream, yes."

Hannah put a hand on Sue's arm and nodded her thanks. She knew it was difficult for Susanna to tell her the truth, and she appreciated her candor. "Thank you. For everything."

Hannah took a moment to compose herself, tucked her hair into her cap, and smoothed down her apron before going into the other room to face Sam, who was shifting from foot to foot, his anxiety palpable. Finn was sitting at the table but sprang to his feet as soon as he saw Hannah. Hannah nodded to Finn, then turned to speak to Sam.

"Son, Susanna is taking good care of your father, so you must carry out his wishes without delay. The information he passed on to you must get to its destination. Without fail."

"But Ma, how can I leave when Pa could be...?" Sam's voice

trailed off. He couldn't say the words out loud, especially to his mother, who seemed to have aged overnight.

"You have a duty, and you must see it carried out. Your father is counting on you. If the worst comes to pass, you will know that you had made your father proud, Sam."

"Yes, Ma. I'll leave this morning. Will you be all right on your own?" Sam asked. Hannah Mallory wasn't known for physical displays of affection, but she walked into Sam's arms and allowed him to hold her for a moment before answering.

"I'm not on my own. I have Abbie and the girls, and Susanna. We will be just fine."

Sam turned to leave but changed his mind and went into the other room to see his father instead. He needed to say goodbye, just in case. Susanna had every intention of giving Sam a moment of privacy but couldn't help watching as he stood at his father's bedside, his head bowed. Sam was always so cocky and confident, but at this moment, he looked like a little boy who was frightened and unsure of what to do next. He grasped his father's hand in his own and bent over the bed to whisper something in John's ear, then straightened up, let go of the hand, and strode from the room.

Finn threw Susanna an apologetic look and followed Sam outside. He could understand Sam's feelings. Finn loved Mr. Mallory as a father, and the thought of losing the man left him gutted. Mr. Mallory had always seemed indestructible, a tower of strength and wisdom. To see him weak and delirious was a shock, as well as a reminder of the frailty of human life and the brevity of one's stay on earth. What if his own father died and he wasn't there to say goodbye? He wouldn't even know unless someone traveled to the future to tell him. Finn felt a pang of despair as he trotted after Sam, who was almost running toward the stables.

"I'm coming with you," Finn called out to Sam.

THE TIES THAT BIND

"You need to stay here and look after the women. We can't leave them without a man about the place."

"Sam, if your father was targeted, then you might be next. I'm coming with you. No arguments. We can stop by Martha's and ask Gil to keep an eye on things. The militia is in the area, so everyone should be safe enough. Now, do you have the message from your father?"

Sam showed Finn a little scroll that he'd extracted from a secret pocket in his father's breeches. Hannah had sewn such pockets into all their clothing to make messages easier to hide. If stopped and searched, the messages were secure enough as most people did not search inside someone's breeches. They rifled through pockets and turned out any purse or satchel, but no one thought to search for hidden compartments inside a man's trousers.

"Have you read it?" Finn asked.

"It's in code, but I got the gist of it. I think we need to make a copy for you in case something happens to me."

"Nothing will happen to you with me there, but you're right; let's make a copy."

Sam nodded and finally turned to face Finn. He looked pale and shaken, something Finn found even more distressing than seeing Mr. Mallory so ill. He wasn't used to seeing Sam's vulnerabilities put on display.

"Finn, what if he dies while we are gone? What if I never see him again?"

Finn laid a steadying hand on Sam's shoulder and fixed him with a steely gaze. "Your father will recover. Do you hear me? He's the strongest person I know, and if you try to fall apart on me, I'll kick you into next Thursday," Finn added for good measure.

Sam gave Finn a watered-down version of his usual smile. "Now you sound like Martha, and that's just plain scary. All right, Finn, I'll hold it together. Now stop wasting time and saddle a horse for yourself."

"We need to stop by the house and tell Abbie that I'm leaving with you. And grab some food for the journey."

"She won't be happy," Sam observed as he lifted a saddle off its hook.

"No, she won't be, but she'll understand."

TWELVE

VIRGINIA AUGUST 1628

"Come on, Tommy, one more spoon for grandma," Valerie cajoled as she tried to get Tom to eat more porridge. He was a finicky eater and preferred anything bready to grains or meat. Valerie always worried that he wasn't getting proper nutrition and added all kinds of things to supplement the porridge. Today's breakfast was dotted with dried blueberries and bits of peanuts, the offering drizzled with a bit of honey to sweeten it for the child.

"No," Tom replied as he crossed his arms and pressed his lips shut. He shook his head to stress his point, a gesture often used by his mother when she was three and refused to do something.

"All right, then. Off you go," Valerie said, capitulating. Tom had eaten half a bowl—good enough.

"Want some oatmeal?" Valerie asked Louisa, who'd just entered the kitchen. Evie and Robbie had already eaten and gone outside. They were currently engaged in a fight-to-the-death duel with sticks in the yard. Valerie could hear Tom pleading to be allowed to join in but was told that he is too young for dueling.

"Girls don't fight," Tom wailed in desperation, only to be rebuffed by Evie, who hated to be told that she couldn't do something just because she wasn't a boy.

"Well, I do. Stop sniveling."

Louisa sank into a chair and glared at Valerie. "No, I don't want anything." Louisa sat with her arms crossed as if she were trying to hold herself together, her puffy eyes a testament to a night spent crying.

"Would you like to talk about it?" Valerie asked as she reluctantly finished off Tom's oatmeal. She would have never done so had she still lived in the twenty-first century, but wasting food was unheard of in colonial Virginia. Any bit of nutrition and sustenance was to be taken advantage of, even by grandmothers who'd already eaten their breakfast.

"Kit fessed up last night. He's already arranged our passage to England. We are leaving at the end of September. Oh Val, I feel wretched. I know I have no right to prevent him from returning home or seeing to his obligations, but the thought of leaving you and Alec is devastating. Who knows when we'll see each other again? And I hated living in England the last time. Here, with you, I am the closest to being my true self. We are far enough removed from Jamestown to be able to live our lives in relative freedom, but in England, I will have to assume the role of Lady Sheridan, and Lady Sheridan is nothing more than an ornament. I must look the part and keep my mouth shut, since voicing my opinion gets me in trouble more often than not."

Louisa grew silent, but the expression on her face remained mutinous as her eyes slid away from Valerie and toward the window where Robbie and Evie had declared a truce and decided to go looking for frogs, this time magnanimously allowing Tom to tag along. Valerie remained quiet, waiting for Louisa to continue. She knew what was on her sister's mind but didn't want to be the one to bring it up. Louisa never mentioned what happened in England, preferring to shut the whole episode in a dusty trunk in the attic of her mind and rebuild her relationship with Kit. They were safe here in Virginia, far away from court and all the political maneuvering and treachery that constituted life at Whitehall Palace. Perhaps they would even be safe at Kit's country estate, but they couldn't hide out there forever, and if Kit were summoned to the palace, he'd have to go, whether he wished to or not.

"I'm scared, Val," Louisa whispered, her frightened eyes once again fixed on Valerie. "I'm scared of Buckingham and the power he wields at court. He could destroy our lives on a whim; he almost did before. Kit swears nothing will happen, but when threatened or blackmailed, people will do anything to protect those they love. Kit is powerless against someone of Buckingham's standing."

Valerie pushed aside the bowl, got up and went over to Louisa. She put her arms around her sister, and they remained that way for a few moments, drawing comfort from each other. Valerie wanted to scream at the thought of losing Louisa, but she had no right to question Kit's decision. He'd gone along with Louisa's wishes from the start, settling in Virginia so that Louisa could be close to her sister, but he couldn't be expected to remain a guest in someone's house forever. The plantation did not belong to him; he had an estate and tenants of his own in England and had decided that it was time to return, despite the Duke of Buckingham, who'd fancied himself in love with Kit and had forced Kit to share his bed for months before setting him free.

Louisa disentangled herself from Valerie's embrace and wiped away the angry tears. "We'd better see what the children are up to. Minnie is doing the morning milking, and they are alone by the pond."

Valerie followed Louisa out the door into the glorious August morning. They could hear Evie and Robbie shrieking as they tried to catch some poor unsuspecting frog. Tom stood off to the side, cradling something in his hands and gazing at it with all the love a three-year-old is capable of.

"Do you think they actually caught a frog for Tom?" Louisa asked as they walked toward the pond.

"Doubtful," Valerie replied with a giggle. "Frogs don't have tails."

"Oh, gross!" Louisa exclaimed as she saw the field mouse in Tom's hands.

"Can I keep it?" Tom pleaded, his face alight with hope. "I'll feed it and keep it safe."

"Of course. Run back to the house and ask Cook for a small box. Make sure to put some grass in there, Tom," Valerie called after Tom, who was already sprinting back to the house.

Louisa sighed and sat down on the bench, her eyes on her children, who were oblivious to the fact that their life was about to change forever. They were hopping about, laughing and shoving each other, their world happy and secure.

"Val, do you remember that summer when we stayed with Aunt Maureen in the Hamptons?" Louisa suddenly asked.

"Yes. She was going through the nautical jewelry phase," Valerie replied, taken aback by Louisa's question. They'd been sent to stay with their father's sister, Maureen, for the whole summer that year since they were too old for camp, but still too young to get proper summer jobs. Maureen had done very well for herself in her divorce from a prominent plastic surgeon and had been granted the house in the Hamptons, as well as a healthy monthly stipend that allowed her to quit her job and devote her time to making jewelry.

"Do you remember the day she took us out to Montauk?" Louisa asked, her expression wistful.

"Yes, I do," Valerie replied. Suddenly, she was right back there, gazing up at the towering lighthouse that to her teenage eyes had looked like an enormous candle. There was no one else around except for the three of them, and suddenly Valerie felt as if she were standing on the tip of the world. She'd been overwhelmed by the wild beauty of the place and intimidated by the feeling of isolation that swept over her as the waves crashed onto the shore, inching closer and closer as the tide came in.

"You didn't want to go up, but I talked you into it," Louisa continued. "I wanted to see the view. It was breathtaking."

"I was scared," Valerie reminded Louisa. Louisa had still been the older sister then, Valerie recalled with a jolt, the sister she'd looked up to. Their fall through the veil of time had reversed their roles, since they'd traveled from nearly the same time and place to different decades in the past. Now Louisa was the youngest, and she was the one who was scared.

"As we stood up there, we made a promise. We swore that we'd always be there for each other, no matter what, and that our bond would be stronger than anything life threw at us," Louisa said, her expression dreamy. "You were scared of being so high up, but I saw that lighthouse as a beacon of hope. I've often wished that there were a shining light to guide me through the treacherous waters of life. I need a light now, Val, because I know what you're contemplating. The next few weeks might be the last we ever spend in the same century. We may never see each other again."

Valerie shook her head stubbornly. "Lou, I refuse to believe that. I thought I'd never see you again after I wound up in the seventeenth century. I thought I would die here, and no one would ever know what happened to me, not you, and not Mom and Dad. But you found your way to me, and I got to see Mom and Dad one last time and say goodbye. Nothing is ever final, at least not while there's still life and hope. Don't lose faith in your light, and don't lose faith in me. And give Kit a break," Valerie added.

Louisa nodded and squeezed Valerie's hand. She wasn't a pessimist by nature. She had allowed herself a few moments of self-pity, but now, in true Louisa fashion, she would find something to focus on that would help her feel in control of her destiny once again. Louisa was a fighter, and a risk-taker, and she would get through this separation in any way she could.

"Where *is* Kit?" Louisa asked, suddenly realizing that she hadn't seen Kit since their argument last night.

"The *Morning Star* docked last night," Valerie replied. "Alec and Kit left early this morning to supervise the unloading. Alec asked that we see to the new indentures. I suppose we should get their names, ages, and find out anything we can about them."

"And check them for lice and signs of scurvy and malnutrition. I'll ask Cook to make an onion soup for lunch. Those poor mites can use all the Vitamin C they can get," Louisa remarked, her mind already on this new problem.

"Tell her to put a few marrow bones into the soup and bake some extra bread. We need to feed them up."

"I can't imagine what it must be like to be all alone in the world at such a young age," Louisa sighed. "No social services, no one to take an interest. Some of those children look as young as seven."

"It's tragic. No matter how long I live in the past, I can't get used to the cruelty and randomness of everyday life," Valerie said.

"Funny how people always complained about things in the twenty-first century. There were food stamps, Medicaid, free education, subsidized rent, and still, nothing was ever enough for some. Can you imagine if they had to live in these conditions and had only themselves to rely on for survival?"

"Many would perish," Valerie replied as she got to her feet. "But those children managed to survive on the streets and made it through a trans-Atlantic voyage. They deserve a second chance at life. Come, let's go meet them."

THIRTEEN

The low wooden building was cool despite the bright summer sunshine. Valerie had advised Alec to leave small openings just beneath the roof to allow for proper airing of the workers' living quarters, and the windows had been thrown open as well to allow for cross-ventilation. Having so many people living in one room created not only a health hazard but left the air stale and reeking of unwashed bodies and flatulence. At this time of the morning, the workers were already out in the fields, but today the large room was still half-full, the new arrivals huddled in the corner, awake and alert.

The children had already had their breakfast of porridge and bread but were told to return to their pallets until further notice. They'd barely been able to keep their eyes open last night, but now that they were better rested were no doubt wondering what this new phase of their lives would bring. The older children glared at Valerie and Louisa belligerently, but the younger children looked at them shyly, their little faces full of hope.

Valerie smiled kindly but couldn't help but be appalled by the state of the poor youngsters. They all looked emaciated, and the rags they wore barely covered their slight bodies. Some were so dirty that Valerie couldn't make out their features beneath the grime. The children looked as if they'd just been liberated from a concentration camp, and she supposed that being cooped up below decks for two months on a ship with no proper food or water for washing was no better. Valerie heard Louisa's intake of breath at the sight of the children. She was horrified and had every reason to be. The fact that Charles had been so gleeful about getting a bargain on the lot made him look even more callous.

"Good morning," Valerie said, trying to sound cheerful. "I hope you slept well. My name is Mistress Whitfield, and this nice lady is my sister, Lady Sheridan. We've brought you a little treat. Would you care to join us in the dining hall?"

The children remained mute, still trying to blend into the wall despite the heavenly aroma coming from Valerie's basket. Valerie removed the linen towel and tilted the basket to display the corn muffins neatly stacked inside. Cook baked them after preparing breakfast for the workers, eager to do something nice for the poor motherless mites. Valerie could see the children salivating, but they didn't surge forward until the two eldest boys budged from their spot by the wall and made for the door, walking with a swagger that belied their situation. The others followed to the mess hall and silently took seats along the trestle table, their eyes on the basket in Valerie's hands. Valerie handed out the muffins while Louisa poured milk into the wooden cups stacked on a side table. They kept a ready supply of clean cups and drinking water, should anyone be thirsty during the day.

The children devoured the muffins, licking their fingers to get every last crumb, but they weren't as enthusiastic about drinking the milk. Few people drank milk in the seventeenth century, and the children likely never had it before arriving at Rosewood Manor. Both adults and children drank beer, ale, and cider, but milk was only used for making dairy products such as cheese and butter. It would be some time yet before the colonists recognized its nutritional value. Most of the children only took a few sips before pushing their cups away and gazing at Valerie's basket with undisguised longing. She'd brought two dozen muffins, but there wasn't a single one left. The children looked around in confusion, unsure what to do next.

Valerie waited until everyone finished eating, then turned to the two boys she'd spotted earlier. They appeared to be the oldest and held a leadership position among the children.

"I would like to learn your names, ages, and anything else you wish to tell me about yourselves. If you have any special skills or enjoy doing something, please feel free to share that as well. How about we begin with you two? What are your names?"

The boys stared back for a moment, clearly wondering how much to tell, but eventually they began to speak.

"I'm Will," one of them said. "I've thirteen summers and I come from London."

"Do you have any special skills, Will?" Valerie asked.

"Ye mean other than liftin' purses?" the second boy asked, making everyone snigger.

"And you are?" Valerie asked, turning to the boy who'd spoken.

"I'm Alfie. I reckon I'm twelve."

"You reckon?"

"I don't rightly know when I were born, mistress. Me mam didn't 'ang about long enough to tell me."

Valerie noticed the children smiling at Alfie's saucy answer. So, Will was the serious one, and Alfie the cheeky one. That could be useful in future dealings with the children. She had been a teacher once, before she'd turned the hands of the clock and found herself in the past. Dealing with children was second nature to her, and she found herself easily slipping into teacher mode, as if no time had passed at all.

Valerie went around the table, taking the time to speak to each child. Will and Alfie were the oldest of the group and seemed to have been sent down for theft. Valerie was fairly sure that all the children had been transported for the same offense. They stole to live, and their fight for survival had landed them on the other side of the world in a place they'd likely never even heard of. There were eight boys and four girls, the girls all under the age of ten. Some of the children were siblings and clung to each other, terrified that they might be torn apart never to see each other again.

"It's a pleasure to meet you all," Valerie said once she got the last child's name. "Now, here's what we're going to do. It's a warm day outside and you all look like you can use a bath after your long journey. We can go down to the pond and you can bathe, and swim for a bit, if you know how. Lady Sheridan and I will have some new clothes for you by the end of the week. In the meantime, you can rest and get used to your new home. Master Whitfield will assign you tasks based on your abilities."

The children looked dubious but didn't protest and followed Valerie and Louisa to the pond. Valerie hoped that splashing around in the cool water would wash away some of their inhibitions as well as dirt. Valerie sat on the bench next to Louisa and looked on as the children shuffled into the pond. They looked as if they were being led to the gallows. Some of the children waded right in, but a few hung back, intimidated by the prospect. Then, they went in only up to their knees and stood there looking uncertain. After a few minutes, their childish natures took over, and the morning became filled with shrieks and laughter as the kids splashed each other and horsed around. The bath also served to wash their filthy clothes, since they could hardly go in naked.

"They're a sad lot, aren't they?" Louisa said. "What are we going to do with them?"

"The boys will work in the fields, I expect, but not a full

day. And the girls can be taught to help with the housework. They are too young and fragile to work in the fields."

Louisa nodded. It went against everything they believed in, putting such young children to work, but there was nothing else they could do with twelve children. The children would require feeding and clothing, so they would have to do something to earn their keep until their period of servitude expired.

Valerie was just about to call the children to come out when she saw Minnie running toward the pond. She was normally an exuberant girl, but she seemed unusually agitated and was waving her arms to get their attention.

"Minnie, what is it?" Valerie called out as she sprang to her feet.

Minnie stopped and took a few moments to catch her breath before finally speaking. "It's Lord Sheridan, ma'am. There's been an accident at the docks."

"What kind of accident?" Louisa cried out, already on her feet.

"I don't rightly know, your ladyship. The boy who delivered the message didn't have any particulars. Just said that Lord Sheridan has been hurt bad, and you were to come quick."

"Go, I'll see to the children," Valerie called out to Louisa, who was already sprinting toward the house. The children gazed after her before returning to their bathing.

"Come on, you lot. Out," Valerie said. "Minnie, please stay with the children while they dry off, and then escort them back to the barracks. I must go with Lady Sheridan."

With that, she took off after Louisa. Whatever happened, Louisa would need her support.

FOURTEEN

By the time Valerie and Louisa made it to Jamestown, a crowd had assembled by the docks. Several children were running around and trying to squeeze between the legs of the onlookers to get a better view of whatever was happening. Louisa saw the tubby form of the Honorable Sir Francis West, new Governor of Virginia, pushing his way through the crowd and parting it long enough for her to glimpse several canvas-wrapped bodies laid out on the dock. Louisa let out a cry of anguish as she grabbed hold of Valerie.

The crowd parted of its own accord to allow the women through. Valerie had expected some degree of chaos, given that something awful must have happened, but the dock was strangely quiet, the wooden boards and canvas-wrapped bodies bathed by the morning sun, and the James River sparkling prettily as it silently flowed by. The *Morning Star* was at anchor, the ramp to the dock empty of sailors who would normally be unloading goods and shouting abuse at each other. The vessel, which would be a beehive of activity for hours after docking, was a ghost ship. Valerie caught a glimpse of the captain standing on the bridge, but he avoided her gaze and pretended not to see her.

Alec was down on the dock, his face shadowed by the ship's hull. He was squatting next to Kit, who was lying on the sun-bleached boards with Doctor Jacobson bending over him. The doctor's hands were slick with blood, and there were streaks of blood on his coat and even his face. He was so intent on what he was doing that he seemed oblivious to the crowd or to Louisa who was running toward him at full speed, shouting like a mad woman.

"Get away from my husband," Louisa screamed.

Doctor Jacobson was known among the residents of the colony as 'The Butcher of Jamestown.' He killed more patients than he healed, but he was the only medical man around, so there wasn't much choice when it came to receiving treatment. Whatever practical knowledge Doctor Jacobson possessed was still greater than that of anyone else, so he was never short of patients. Louisa let out a squeak of shock as she got close enough to see the extent of Kit's injuries.

Alec sprang to his feet and came toward Louisa, carefully avoiding the chunks of splintered wood that littered the dock. A few jagged pieces stuck out over the water like crooked teeth where the dock had been damaged, giving the impression that some huge sea monster had taken a bite out of the wood. There were also deep scratches on the ship's hull, and a coil of frayed rope lay discarded next to the bodies.

"What happened?" Louisa cried as she tried to get past Alec, who grabbed her by the shoulders to keep her from getting any closer to Kit. "I need to go to him," Louisa pleaded, but Alec refused to let go.

"Louisa, you need to come with me," Alec said, his authoritative tone instantly bringing Louisa to her senses. He led her through the crowd toward a shady spot further up the riverbank where they could speak privately. Valerie stole one last glance at Kit before following Alec and her sister.

"Alec, please," Louisa sobbed. "I need to know. Just tell me what happened. I can't bear not knowing." Alec turned to face Louisa and placed his hands squarely on her shoulders, not as a means of restraint, but as a gesture of support. He kept his voice low and steady to keep Louisa from panicking.

"Louisa, there's been a terrible accident. Kit and several sailors were standing on the dock while the ship was being unloaded. A crate containing an armoire for Jane Deverell was being lowered onto the dock when one of the sailors holding the rope slipped on a bit of grease, lost his footing, and let go. The second sailor was unable to hold on and was thrown into the air when the rope slipped through the pulley and the crate came crashing onto the dock. Two people were crushed instantly, but Kit and one other sailor weren't standing directly beneath the crate, so they'd been spared. Louisa, Kit is alive, but he has several broken bones and countless splinters pierced his skin when the crate and armoire shattered. He's in a bad way."

"Let me go to him, Alec. He's in pain," Louisa begged.

"He's not. I gave him enough rum to fell an ox. Doctor Jacobson has set his bones and is in the process of making splints. He will then need to extract the splinters one by one. It will take time and precision. Once he is finished, we will be able to take Kit home."

"And the other man?" Louisa asked.

"The other man was hit on the head. He's unconscious and likely to remain so for some time to come. Now, I need to go back and help the doctor hold Kit still while he applies the splints and binds them. Perhaps you should go to the tavern and get a drink. It will help you to calm down."

"I don't want a drink," Louisa sobbed. "Oh, Alec, I was so awful to him. I accused him of ruining my life and forcing me to leave Valerie. I said that I hoped something would happen to prevent us from sailing back to England."

Alec drew Louisa into a hug and held her close, giving her a moment to cry. He stroked her hair gently while she bawled into his shoulder, mumbling under her breath the whole time, her guilt devouring her from the inside.

"It's not your fault, Louisa," Alec murmured into Louisa's hair. "Kit understands how you feel about leaving and doesn't blame you for being upset. He knows you still love him."

"Does he?" Louisa sobbed. "Does he know that I would follow him to the ends of the earth?"

"I'm sure he does, but if he doesn't, you can tell him yourself once he sobers up."

Alec gave Valerie a loaded look, and she came forward to draw Louisa away. "Come Lou, let's get you a glass of cider. Doctor Jacobson might be a moron, but he can set a bone; I've seen him do it. As long as Kit doesn't need to be operated on, he'll be fine. But he will require a lot of care over the next few months."

"Val, did I bring this on Kit, do you think?" Louisa asked as a tankard of cider was placed in front of her.

"Lou, come on, be reasonable. We all say things in the heat of the moment. If all of them came true, everyone we know would be dead and roasting in Hell by now."

"True," Louisa giggled through tears. "I never wished Kit to go to Hell, but I was angry, and I said things I didn't mean. I called him a tyrant," Louisa confessed, a watery smile tugging at her lips. "I told him I wouldn't go, no matter what he said."

"Well, you got your wish. You won't be going anywhere until the spring. It takes months for bones to knit back together."

"I know. Thank God Alec was with him. I always feel calmer when Alec is in charge," Louisa hiccuped. "Val, I can't just sit here. I know there's nothing I can do to help, but I need to be near Kit, even if he doesn't know I'm there. Please, can we go?"

"Of course."

They paid for the cider and headed back to the docks. Most of the crowd had dispersed, but a few people were still milling around, their curiosity getting the better of them.

"You'd think people had something better to do on a weekday morning than gawk," Louisa grumbled as they walked by. Several people looked shamefaced and hurried away after hearing Louisa's comment, but a few remained, too enthralled with the drama on the dock to walk away. Doctor Jacobson had finished with the splints and was using some sort of metal tweezers to extract splinters from Kit's face.

"Those tweezers aren't sterilized," Louisa whispered, horrified.

"We will clean the wounds with alcohol once we get Kit back home," Valerie promised.

Louisa got as close as she could without disturbing the doctor. Kit's skin appeared ashen beneath the smears of blood, and the right side of his face looked as if he'd been attacked by a tiger. Bloody gashes lined his cheek, and his coat was shredded. Kit's right arm and leg were perfectly straight and still, bound by splints, but his left arm and leg twitched every time the doctor pulled out a piece of wood. Several large splinters were still lodged in Kit's chest and Doctor Jacobson pulled them one by one, having finally finished with the face.

"Oh, dear God," Louisa exclaimed, despite having been asked to remain quiet. Her hand flew to her mouth, but it was too late. Kit's eyes fluttered open at the sound of her voice. His gaze was unfocused, and his pupils dilated from the pain, but he turned his head toward the sound of the voice, searching for his wife.

"Lou, I'm all right," he mumbled, his speech slurred by all the rum Alec had given him. "We won't be sailing to England though," he chuckled, grimacing in his attempt to smile. "See, something good has come out of all this, at least for you."

"You're such an idiot. I'd go anywhere with you, you know that. I couldn't bear it if you were killed." Louisa was valiantly trying not to cry and keep her tone light, but tears were sliding down her face and she was barely keeping it together.

"It takes more than a twenty-stone armoire to kill me," Kit whispered. He was growing tired and his eyes began to close once again, his body doing its best to conserve strength for what lay ahead.

Alec gave Louisa a warning look. Kit was in shock and didn't seem to realize that several people had indeed been killed by the wardrobe which had been made of solid oak. Bits of it still littered the dock. The two bodies had been removed by the sailors and the dead would be given a burial at sea once the *Morning Star* set sail in a few days. The sailor who'd been hit on the head was still unconscious, lying still in the shade of a tree with two of his mates watching over him should he come to.

"If I might be of any assistance," a gentle voice said behind Valerie. She turned around to find Jane Deverell standing off to the side, her hands clasped in front of her. "I'm so very sorry. The armoire was for me. I ordered it from England nearly a year ago," she blathered on in her distress.

"Jane, it was an accident. No one could have foreseen it," Valerie replied.

Jane nodded but didn't look entirely convinced. She still wore black in memory of the husband she'd detested, and mostly kept to herself, but recently she had begun to come out of her shell a little and Valerie found that she quite liked her. Jane was surprisingly warm and outgoing when she felt at ease. She had decided to use the blackmail money she'd inherited from Aloysius Deverell to do some good and purchased the indenture contracts of two young sisters from Southwark who were now in her employ. The girls were ten and twelve, fair-haired and blue-eyed, with a peachy complexion that made them look like a pair of cherubs. Everyone in Jamestown saw the girls as Jane's servants, but to Jane, they were the daughters she never had, and she spoiled the girls and tried to make their life happy and secure. The girls, whose life had not been either until they met Jane, repaid her in kind, and for the first time in her life, Jane had a happy home.

"Jane, if you could spare a blanket," Valerie said, "and perhaps a pillow. I will return them to you tomorrow."

"Of course. You can keep them as long as you like," Jane called over her shoulder as she rushed toward her house. She returned a few moments later with the items, happy to be of some help.

Doctor Jacobson finally finished with Kit, wiped his hands on a handkerchief and came over to speak to Louisa, who was waiting anxiously. He held Lord and Lady Sheridan in particularly high regard since the trial two years ago, which had raised his standing in the community considerably. As far as the doctor knew, he was the first physician to testify in a murder trial, offering his expert opinion on the type of man it would take to strangle a man of Aloysius Deverell's proportions. Doctor Jacobson's testimony swayed the outcome of the trial and saved Kit from being condemned to death.

Louisa and Kit couldn't openly reward the doctor for his help, but he had been invited to dine at Rosewood Manor on several occasions and graciously accepted the gift of a new surgical saw that Kit ordered from England just for him. Valerie always teased Louisa about Doctor Jacobson, saying that the doctor gained a friend in Lord Sheridan but lost his heart to his lady. Louisa laughed at Valerie's teasing, but blushed prettily whenever Doctor Jacobson was mentioned. He might not be a competent doctor, but he was an attractive man and a widower, having lost his wife shortly after arriving in Virginia. Louisa had no romantic interest in Doctor Jacobson whatsoever, but was still flattered by his barely disguised admiration.

"You know, Val," Louisa mused after a visit from Doctor Jacobson, "when men found us attractive in our own time, we enjoyed it and took it for granted. We hardly ever gave it another thought unless we were interested. It was our due and our right to be admired. But when a man admires you in this time, it has a whole new meaning, doesn't it?"

Louisa had been experiencing severe pains in her stomach, and despite her reservations, Doctor Jacobson had been called. Valerie secretly feared that Louisa might be suffering from an ectopic pregnancy and wanted to rule it out. Doctor Jacobson had examined Louisa extensively and prescribed an emetic, believing there to be some minor intestinal blockage. The treatment helped, but Louisa was left emotionally disturbed after the visit.

"It was the way he examined me, Val, the way he touched me. He didn't do anything that another doctor wouldn't have done in his place, but he made me feel violated. I can still feel his fingers inside me. He enjoyed it," Louisa exclaimed, blushing furiously.

Valerie dissolved into giggles at the sight of Louisa's outraged face. "Lou, due to a lack of certain kind of publications and internet access, I'd say this was the closest our good doctor could come to looking at pornography. He finds you attractive, that's obvious enough, and he couldn't help but enjoy examining you so thoroughly. But please keep this from Kit. We don't need another murder trial on our hands."

"You just wait until it's your turn," Louisa retorted, her cheeks stained with embarrassment.

"He did cure your constipation, did he not?" Valerie asked, all innocence.

Louisa had not seen Doctor Jacobson since that visit, but her embarrassment no longer mattered. All her thoughts were for Kit. Louisa reached out a hand and Doctor Jacobson took it gently in his, smiling into her eyes in a reassuring way.

"My lady, it's a blessing that your husband is alive, but he has sustained grave injuries resulting in broken bones in his upper arm, wrist, and thigh bone. He has bruised ribs and several deep cuts which will require stitching, but we must thank God that none of his major organs have been affected, and his collarbone and pelvis are still intact. It will take a long while, and he will be in considerable pain for the next few weeks, but he will recover. I will administer some laudanum before I stitch his face, and it will make the ride back to Rosewood Manor that much more bearable for him. The jolting of the wagon would be agony otherwise."

"Thank you, Doctor," Louisa breathed. "Oh, thank you."

Doctor Jacobson looked as if he wanted to take Louisa in his arms and comfort her, but he quickly got hold of himself and released Louisa's hand. He took a small vial out of his coat pocket and handed it to Louisa.

"Give him a few drops mixed with water whenever you feel he needs it. Sleep is the best medicine in this case. I will come by tomorrow to check on him. Oh, and Lady Sheridan, do try to keep him on a mostly liquid diet for the first few weeks since his lordship will be bedbound for some time."

Louisa nodded and tucked the vial into her pocket, her eyes on Kit. Two men carefully lifted him onto a makeshift stretcher after Alec placed a pillow beneath his head and covered him with a blanket. Kit's clothes were stained and torn, and the bandage covering his leg was already soaked with blood. The men would take Kit to Doctor Jacobson's house to be stitched up before Louisa could finally take him home. She was grateful that Kit was asleep. At least he was spared the pain of being moved, but the next few weeks would be a unique kind of agony for him.

FIFTEEN

Charles watched from a safe distance as Kit was carried into Doctor Jacobson's surgery. He'd heard what happened at the docks and meant to walk over and offer his assistance, but his conscience plagued him. He was meant to be helping unload the vessel with Kit, but had decided to stay abed a little longer, having had something of a hangover. He'd never been much of a drinker, preferring to leave the overindulgence in spirits to Alec, but things had not been at all to his liking lately and he often needed a bit of help just to fall asleep. Besides, both Kit and Alec had been at the dock; he'd only have been in the way, a third wheel as usual.

There was a time when he was happy, married to a woman he loved and running the plantation with his brother. True, he'd still felt resentful about not inheriting the entire estate from their uncle, but he'd made peace with the situation long ago and tried to make the best of things. But everything changed two years ago when Annabel had accused Kit of murder, and no amount of time could make things right again. Annabel had driven a wedge between Charles and Alec and made herself more than a little unpopular with Valerie and Louisa. Charles's family had been banished from Rosewood Manor and from the lives of the people in it. Charles still came by regularly and tried to insert himself into the running of the estate in every way possible, but it was clear to him that his interference wasn't welcome, and neither was he.

Over time, Kit had become the brother Alec needed and trusted, and Charles had taken on the role of pariah, all thanks to Annabel and her thirst for vengeance. She had gambled and lost, but in the process, she forfeited a lot more than she bargained for. She no longer had access to her nephew Tom, nor did she have the friendship of the only two women in Jamestown whose support was worth having, in Charles's opinion. Valerie Whitfield and Lady Sheridan were unique, to say the least, but they were also loyal, intelligent—often more so than was acceptable in women—and warm.

Annabel had taken their friendship for granted, but now that it was no longer freely given, she realized what it was to be without female support. Annabel had no mother, sisters, or even female cousins. She was on good terms with the goodwives of Jamestown, but they tended to view her with suspicion after her obvious attempt at getting Kit hanged. Alec and Kit commanded the kind of respect in the colony that Charles could only dream of, and few would choose Charles and Annabel Whitfield over Alec and Valerie or Lord and Lady Sheridan.

Over the last two years Annabel had grown bitter and angry, constantly reminding Charles that he had been cheated of his birthright and duped by his scheming brother, who'd replaced him at the first opportunity with Kit. She called Valerie and Louisa names that were too crass to be uttered even in the privacy of their bedchamber, and endlessly plotted Alec's downfall. Annabel never actually spoke the words out loud, but Charles knew exactly what she was thinking. If Alec were to die, little Tom would inherit the lot, and Charles and Annabel, being his closest relatives, would be able to move back to Rosewood Manor and assume control of the estate.

Annabel knew better than to wish death on Alec in Charles's presence, but her meaning was clear, and although Charles could see the benefits of such an outcome, he still resented Annabel, for when all was said and done, he loved Alec and craved his approval, and wished more than anything that the events of the past few years could be wiped from memory.

Charles sighed and walked over to the stable to get his horse. He felt a deep sympathy for Kit, but the twinges of resentment planted by Annabel reared their ugly heads when he expected them least, and this was one of those moments. With Kit out of the way, Alec would need Charles again, the way he'd needed him before Kit returned from England and installed himself at Rosewood Manor with his family. Why couldn't he have remained in England, tending to his estate and kissing the posterior of whoever happened to be *courtier du jour*? He'd been close with Buckingham at one time, which had brought him into the personal sphere of the king himself and earned him a seat on the Privy Council.

Hell and damnation, Charles thought as he vaulted into the saddle, *if I had the ear of the king and vast estates in England I would never choose to settle in this cesspool of a colony*. Virginia was the armpit of the world, and a smelly one at that. With all the slaves and indentures being shipped to the colonies, there were hardly any decent folk left. Virginia was becoming a sewage drain for the dregs of British society.

Charles's mood lightened somewhat as he trotted out of Jamestown and headed toward the Abbott homestead. He'd seen Noah Abbott at the docks, fretting about his shipment of something or other. Abbott would be occupied for a few hours at least since all unloading had come to a halt when the crate crashed onto the quay. Abbott was not the kind of man who would simply walk to the nearest tavern and have a drink to calm his nerves. He would harass everyone in sight and make himself a nuisance until he got what was coming to him, in more ways than one. One good thing about his tenacious pursuit of his property was that Bethany would likely be on her own, if spending every hour under the watchful eye of Mistress Abbott counted as being alone.

Charles smiled at the thought of Bethany Warren. She was the only bright light in his otherwise dark existence these days. Bethany gave Charles that which Annabel hadn't given him in many years—a sense of being alive. Part of the fun was the chase itself. Bethany lost her husband just over a year ago and had been as emotionally (and physically) unattainable as any virgin in Virginia. But Charles had plenty of experience with blushing maidens and Bethany eventually agreed to meet him for a walk in the woods.

Naturally, they couldn't be seen together, her being recently widowed and him a married man, but the poor woman was lonely and resentful at having to move in with her brother's family after her husband's death. It would be improper for a woman to live alone and manage her affairs without the benefit of male counsel, so Bethany had been forced to lease her husband's farm and hand over all her assets to her brother. Charles was only too happy to lend her an understanding ear and strong arms of support. It had taken months to even win a kiss from Bethany, but by that time, his desire had reached a boiling point and he was pulsating with emotions and needs that he thought he'd never experience again, at least not with his wife.

Bethany had been shy and frightened, but once she finally submitted to him, all pretense was dropped between them. She was a sensual woman, and her husband had taught her well. She enjoyed carnal pleasures, and once she realized that Charles wouldn't judge her harshly, as many men would, their union became ideal. Charles had no desire to destroy his family or draw the wrath of the community. All he wanted was a bit of pleasure, and he was more than willing to give pleasure and affection in return. He liked Bethany, maybe even loved her, and their trysts became the highlight of his week. He took every precaution to keep her safe, if only for his own sake, and they enjoyed an uncomplicated liaison that could continue until she decided that she wished to marry again.

Charles dug his heels into the flanks of his horse, suddenly desperate to get to Bethany quicker. He hoped she'd be able to meet him at their spot in the woods since his breeches strained uncomfortably against his loins. He throbbed with desire, all thoughts of Kit and Annabel forgotten. All he wanted was to lose himself in Bethany's embrace for a half hour and relieve some of the frustration he was feeling. Charles grinned like a schoolboy when he saw Bethany's slender form in the dooryard. She was hanging laundry, but stopped what she was doing, shaded her eyes with her hand, and watched him canter past, inclining her head in recognition. He tipped his hat in greeting and carried on, glad she'd seen him, and he wouldn't need to find other ways of attracting her attention.

Bethany bent down and lifted the next garment out of the basket. He'd have to wait until she finished and found an excuse to leave the house, but he was in no rush. He didn't wish for her to get into any difficulties with Mistress Abbott or invite suspicion. He'd wait as long as he had to, and in the meantime, there were other ways of getting rid of his bothersome cockstand. If anything, it would make him last longer when she finally came to him, and the prospect of their lovemaking made Charles shiver with anticipation.

Charles bestowed a slow smile on Bethany as she approached. He'd been waiting for a half hour at least, sitting beneath a shady oak and whittling away a stick, but it had been worth it. He felt a familiar stirring, even more urgent this time, but Bethany did not look like a woman eager for a romantic interlude. Her forehead was creased with worry and dark smudges shadowed her eyes, as if she hadn't slept in days. Charles got to his feet and came to greet her.

"Beth, are you all right?" he asked, hoping that she would tell him everything was fine and kiss him instead. He wasn't in the mood for complaints or recriminations; all he wanted was sex, and he meant to have it one way or another.

Bethany walked toward him but stopped before reaching him, leaving a space of about a foot between them that suddenly seemed unbreachable. There was something in her expression that deflated Charles's hopes, and his heart sank. She wanted to talk.

"Beth?" he prompted, now eager to get away from her. He had no desire for conversation, only satiation.

"Charles, I—" Bethany faltered, and Charles patiently waited for her to continue. They'd had several talks like this before. She was a good Christian woman, who believed she was committing a mortal sin by coupling with him without the sanctity of marriage, but her loneliness and her desires were at odds with her beliefs, so a constant battle for supremacy raged within her—understandable, but tiresome, nonetheless.

"Beth, we've been through this," Charles said gently as he finally closed the space between them and cupped her cheek, gazing into her eyes with as much sincerity as he could muster. Perhaps he could seduce her after all. Bethany shook her head but didn't move away. Instead, she rested her forehead on Charles's shoulder as tears began to roll down her cheeks.

"Beth, come now," Charles said as he wiped away the tears. "There's no call for such misery. Do you not enjoy spending time with me?"

Bethany nodded but refused to look up. She wrapped her arms about his waist and he drew her closer, holding her tight. Her breasts heaved against Charles's chest and he moved his hips against hers in silent invitation. She liked to feel his hard length against her belly; it excited her. But Bethany took a step back, rejecting him without a word. She finally looked up at him, her tearstained face full of rancor.

"I'm with child, Charles. Your child. What am I to do?" she asked, watching him with unblinking intensity. Charles's first instinct was to deny that the child could be his. He'd taken every precaution, but he also knew that Bethany wasn't the type of woman to lie with more than one man at a time, and to question the paternity of her baby would wound her to the core.

"Are you certain?" Charles asked, stalling for time.

"Yes."

"How far gone are you?" Charles asked.

"At least six weeks, I reckon," Bethany replied. Her tone was bleak, but her eyes shone with hope. "You must help me, Charles."

"How can I help you?" Charles asked, taking a step toward her, but Bethany stepped back. He was thoroughly annoyed. All he wanted was to stick his cock into someone who wasn't as sullen or disinterested as Annabel, but now that was out of the question, although it's not as if Bethany could get pregnant twice.

"Beth, I can't think straight when I'm aching for you," Charles said, gentling his tone. "Help me, and then I will help you."

Bethany gave him a glare of incredulity, but dutifully lay down on the ground and hiked up her skirt, exposing shapely white legs and a triangle of dark hair. Charles grinned inwardly and tugged at his laces. He was suddenly so aroused that he could barely wait until Bethany was ready, but he took a few moments to prepare her before plunging in. She was dry and tight, not ready for him as she usually was, but Charles didn't care. He ignored her gasp of pain as he thrust into her, desperate for release.

Bethany wasn't enjoying herself, although it would have made her feel better if she gave herself up to the moment. She didn't look at him, nor did she move her hips as she normally did, working toward her own climax. Charles came quickly and withdrew, glad to have gotten what he came for. Bethany grabbed a handful of leaves and wiped all traces of him from her body while Charles tied his laces and shrugged on his coat. Charles helped Bethany to her feet and waited until she adjusted her bodice and smoothed out her skirts.

"Well?" she said. She sounded bitter, which was not something Charles was used to, but it was to be expected under the circumstances.

"Well what? I would marry you in a heartbeat if I weren't married already, but I am not free, Bethany." Charles suddenly remembered the stick he'd been whittling before Bethany came. He picked it up and held it up before Bethany's face. "There are ways to cause a miscarriage," he said. "No one need ever know."

Bethany grabbed the stick from Charles and snapped it in two, bright spots of color appearing on her cheeks. "Are you suggesting I use a sharpened stick to kill our child?"

"There are other ways," Charles replied. Waving the stick about had clearly been a mistake.

"Such as?" Bethany was panting now, her eyes swimming with tears again.

"There are herbs that can bring on your courses. Bethany, you can't have this child. Think of what it would mean," Charles pleaded with her.

To have a child out of wedlock in Jamestown was unheard of. Bethany would be publicly humiliated and punished severely, possibly even banished from the colony. She would have to forfeit all her assets and give up any hope of ever marrying again. And the council would demand to know who fathered her child. Charles would not be exempt, although, as a man, his punishment would not be nearly as severe as Bethany's.

"Oh, I know exactly what it would mean," Bethany retorted and turned her back on Charles. "But don't think that you would escape unscathed. If I am to go down, you will go down with me."

"Beth, I'll come back here in three days' time. Please meet me. We'll talk more once you've calmed down, and I've had time to consider the situation. If you can think of anything I can do short of marrying you, I'll be happy to hear it."

"As you wish," Bethany threw over her shoulder and walked off, leaving Charles feeling angry and depressed.

I wish you'd bleed until your womb was empty, Charles thought bitterly as he jammed his hat onto his head and untied his horse. At least Bethany didn't know that Annabel was expecting as well. That would only add fuel to the fire. Charles mounted his horse and headed back to town. This tryst didn't go quite as planned, but perhaps it hadn't been a total loss. He realized that his desire for Bethany had abated now that he had seen her bitter, angry side. It reminded him too much of Annabel.

SIXTEEN
VIRGINIA AUGUST 1781

Abbie slammed the dough onto the wooden board as if it had personally offended her. She knew her anger was pointless, but she still vibrated with a corrosive energy that needed to be released. She was being unfair and spoiled. She had a good life and had no cause for complaint. She'd been loved by kind, supportive parents and was married to a man who cherished and respected her, but past events had shattered the fragile illusion of well-being and safety and she'd never forgotten them. Things had been fairly quiet for the past two years, Diana's sudden death being the period at the end of a long sentence, but lately, Abbie felt as if she were always waiting for the other shoe to drop, terrified of losing the security she'd come to expect.

The first blow came when her father was wounded by that poisoned arrow, and now Finn and Sam were gone. She'd begged Finn not to go, but nothing she said would have deterred him. He seemed to be burning with a kind of fervor that had not been there before. It's as if something monumental was about to happen and he couldn't bear to miss it. Abbie had no idea what had changed but reasoning with Finn proved pointless. He and Sam left two days ago and were probably well clear of Virginia by now. Abbie punched the dough with all her might and smiled ruefully when she noticed her mother's look of surprise.

"He will recover, Abbie," Hannah said as she took the dough from Abbie and began to knead it carefully, mindful of waking the children, who were napping in the loft. "Sue thinks your father is definitely on the mend. The fever has abated, and he's even asked for a second helping of corn pudding last night. I think I'll be able to take him home in a few days." Hannah smiled at Abbie, who continued to stand there, looking mutinous.

"I'm glad Pa is better, you know I am, but I didn't want Finn to go. I'm scared for him, Ma."

Hannah sighed. The girl who went off to New York five years ago was not the girl who came back. Abbie used to be fearless, but now she saw a threat behind every tree. Hannah could understand, of course. Abbie was a mother now, and being a mother changed everything. Abbie feared not only for herself, but for her children, and she had every right to. Children needed a father, and Finn was as good a father as any child could hope for. He wasn't surly and quick to anger like other men Hannah knew.

Finn was loving and kind and would sooner coddle his children than beat them. He possessed a kind of wisdom that some men never acquired, possibly learned from his own father, who was a decent and even-tempered man. Her own John had had a quick temper when they were first married, and she'd had to teach him to put his love for his children before his own pride. John had mellowed over the years and was a fine example to both Sam and Finn, as was Alec Whitfield.

Hannah greatly admired Alec and liked his wife. They were good people, if a little vague about things. Hannah secretly thought it was bad manners never to invite the Mallory clan to visit them at their home, but Alec and Valerie always appeared furtive when asked about their plantation, so Hannah had given up, telling herself that there was no such thing as perfect in-laws. At least they were well-mannered and generous when they came to visit, and they never interfered.

"Abbie, Finn will be back before you know it. In the meantime, we have much to do to prepare for the winter. Once Sam and Finn are back, the harvest will need to be brought in and the haying done. We should get a start on filling the corn crib and preparing fruit for preserves. And the apples are ripe for picking. Oh, I am looking forward to apple pie."

Abbie normally loved to bake but talk of pies did nothing to distract her. Abbie sat down at the table and propped her flour-smeared cheek with her hand. "I know you're right, Ma, and there's always plenty to do to keep myself occupied, but I just have this feeling," she said.

"What sort of feeling?"

"I don't know—a bad one. A feeling of foreboding. I fear for Finn, Ma. And I'm still worried about Pa. I know he's on the mend, but he could have so easily died. I can't imagine a life without him," Abbie whispered as tears spilled down her cheeks. "Oh, Ma, what if he had died?"

"Now, you stop that sniveling right now, my girl. Your pa did not die. Sue knows what she's doing, and she's taking good care of him. And as for Finn, he's smart, resourceful, and young. He knows what he's about, and he wouldn't appreciate you sitting here doubting him. A woman must stand by her man, Abbie. I know you fear for him, but he's doing important work. If the British win this conflict, it would have all been for naught, so we must bear up and do our bit. You hear me?" Hannah asked sternly, although her heart went out to Abbie. There were more than a few widows made by this never-ending war.

Abbie nodded. "All right, Ma. I will do my bit. But I hope this comes to an end soon. I just can't take the constant threat to our family. We've all been lucky thus far, but even a cat eventually runs out of lives."

"I won't have that kind of defeatist talk in this house, young lady. I suggest you go take a walk to clear your head and bring in the dried laundry when you come back. The children will need clean clothes after their bath tonight. Now go."

Abbie opened her mouth to protest, but the promise of a solitary walk overrode her objections. It wasn't often that she got time to herself, not with everything that needed to be done in the house and with two children under the age of five. She longed for a few quiet moments and promised herself that she would not give in to melancholy. Her mother was right, as she always was. Everything would be all right. Her father was holding his own, and Finn was too smart and resourceful to get caught. He'd learned much from their experiences in New York and his run-in with the British in Savannah. Finn wasn't a fool who beat his chest and screamed his loyalties from an upturned crate in the middle of the square. Finn was stealthy, clever, and most of all, cautious.

Abbie's spirits lifted as she walked toward their little orchard and smiled at the hundreds of red-cheeked apples just waiting to be picked. She loved apple picking and making jellies and preserves. Autumn was almost upon them, and she looked forward to the simple pleasures it brought: a good harvest, chilly evenings and crisp mornings, the smell of wood smoke on the air as the days began to cool, and the first silvery frost. Many people hated the approach of winter, but Abbie always liked the winter months. They were quiet and peaceful, with less to do on the farm and more time to spend indoors, enjoying the fruits of their labor and the things they didn't have time for during the summer.

All would be well. And perhaps the war would be over by Christmas.

SEVENTEEN
SCOTLAND AUGUST 1628

Jenny sank into a chair by the hearth, eternally grateful that Ian had finally fallen asleep. She was exhausted, weepy, and famished. It had been a difficult day, and she hadn't had anything to eat since the night before. Ian had woken up just before dawn, crying as if he were being torn apart. He kept kicking his legs and his arms flailed like a windmill as he screamed for her at the top of his lungs.

"Cameron, what can be wrong with him?" Jenny had cried as she snatched Ian from his cot and held him close. Ian seemed to calm down a little, but continued to cry, hiccupping pitifully between sobs. His huge eyes were fixed on Jenny, seemingly begging her for help, but she had no idea what was troubling him.

"I canna rightly say, lass. I dinna ken much about bairns, but mayhap it's his teeth. Tis about the right age for them to start coming in, is it no'?"

"It is, but I don't think that's what's bothering him. He keeps moving his legs but holding him this way seems to help somewhat."

"Here, let me have him while ye get dressed."

Cameron took the baby from her and walked with him from one end of the room to the other, rocking him gently as he crooned a soft melody. Ian grew quieter, listening to the tune, but his legs continued to jerk. Jenny dressed hastily, built up the fire, and pushed the pot of porridge into the hearth to warm. Cameron had to get going and she couldn't send him off without his breakfast.

"Jenny, make me some bread and cheese for later. If Ian is poorly, ye won't have time to make dinner and bring it to me. Just take care of the bairn and make sure ye eat something, aye?"

"All right," Jenny agreed. She cut some cold pork and slid it between thick slices of bread. Cameron deserved a hot meal for his dinner, and she would bring him one if she were able, but right now she had to make sure that he'd have something to eat if she couldn't settle Ian down long enough to cook. Jenny wrapped the food in a clean cloth and held her arms out for Ian.

"Eat something afore I go, love," Cameron said as he continued to pace with Ian in his arms. Ian was starting to fuss again, the rocking no longer soothing him.

"I'll eat later. Come, have your breakfast. I'll take Ian."

An acrid smell filled the room as Ian noisily filled his clout. He seemed to calm down somewhat after emptying his bowels, even smiling at Jenny as she took him from Cameron. Jenny breathed a sigh of relief. He had a bellyache, that was all, and she'd been imagining all kinds of horrors. Now he'd settle down. Jenny stepped outside into the chilly morning. The day was overcast, and ghostly fingers of fog seemed to beckon to her from behind the barn and wrap themselves around the tree trunks, but at least it wasn't raining yet. Jenny needed to do the laundry, but it would never dry if it pissed down all day.

Ian looked around, his discomfort forgotten. He liked being outside and pointed toward the barn. He liked the animals, especially the donkey, who had kind brown eyes and remained placid while Ian sat on his back supported by Cameron. But now wasn't the time for games. Ian yelped with displeasure as the cold water from the barrel hit his bottom. Jenny murmured words of comfort but continued with her task. Ian needed to be cleaned since the clout was beginning to leak and waiting until the water heated would take some time.

Ian's squawk of protest escalated to a furious roar and he began to squirm in Jenny's arms, trying to escape the cold water. Jenny washed him quickly and wrapped him in his blanket before taking him back inside and putting on a clean clout. Ian remained calm for a little while and Jenny risked putting him back in his cot, but then the screaming began again, even worse this time. Ian filled clout after clout, the diarrhea soaking the fabric and running down his legs. Jenny kept water on the boil all day long to wash him and the pile of filthy clouts that grew by the hour. She kept running outside to hang them up to dry but ran out of clean clouts by midafternoon.

Ian continued to cry and kick his legs, his distress becoming more acute as the day wore on. "You poor baby," Jenny cooed. "Does your belly hurt? I know, it's awful. Here, let me rub it for you."

Rubbing Ian's belly with warm hands seemed to help temporarily, but then he'd begin crying again as soon as she finished. Jenny wasn't sure what else she could do, nor did she know if she ought to feed him while he was in so much pain. He had to be hungry though, especially since everything he'd eaten the day before had already left his body. Jenny put Ian to the breast, and he sucked greedily, but another smelly eruption prevented him from nursing further. Ian began to scream again, his little face crimson and his fists shaking in the air. Only walking with him, his belly pressed to Jenny's side, seemed to help.

Jenny spent the whole day walking, rocking, singing, and washing clouts. She'd had to rip up a sheet to make more clouts since the ones she'd washed were still wet. Thankfully, it was breezy outside, and the laundry dried quickly. By the time it began to grow dark, Jenny was falling off her feet, but Ian was still crying, his belly still bothering him. Jenny tried feeding him again. He had to be famished, and she was right. Ian latched on to her nipple and sucked desperately, finally calming down a little as his belly filled. Jenny sang quietly, and his eyelids began to droop. He had to be exhausted.

"Please, God, let him feel better and go to sleep," Jenny pleaded. "He needs to rest, the poor mite."

Ian finally dropped off, his legs stilling and his little fists relaxing enough for his hands to open. Jenny laid him in his cot and sat down for a moment, utterly drained. There was nothing for Cameron to eat when he got home save the rest of the pork, but it would have to do. She had no time to start a meal just then, not when she had another pile of clouts to wash. She'd just rest for a minute and get to work, but the ache in her lower back left her breathless, and her feet hurt from walking all day.

Jenny suddenly sat up. It had grown dark about an hour ago, but Cameron still hadn't come back. He was usually back by this time. She looked out the window but couldn't see anything at all. The wind howled outside and drops of rain began to fall, hammering against the window and soaking her laundry. She hoped Cameron would be back soon. Jenny stepped outside, filled a basin with water from the barrel and attacked the pile of clouts. She'd hang up the new batch inside. Hopefully, they'd dry overnight.

Jenny looked up with relief when Cameron finally walked in, looking disheveled and dirty. "How is Ian?" he asked as he glanced over at the cot.

"He's better now. Sleeping. Where have you been?"

"Morag is calving, so I have to go back to the barn," Cameron replied.

"Morag?" Jenny asked, surprised. "Isn't it early? I thought

you said she was set for autumn calving." Jenny didn't know much about animal husbandry, but she tried to pay attention and learn. They'd had two foals arrive in the spring, but this was her first bovine delivery.

"Aye, it is early," Cameron replied, his expression grim. "I hope nothing is wrong. Is there ought to eat?"

"I'm sorry. I wasn't able to make anything. But there's still some pork."

"It's all right, lass," Cameron said with a sympathetic smile. "I'll have some oatcakes. I dinna have time to linger anyhow, and ye need to eat. Ye have the pork."

Cameron grabbed a few stale oatcakes, gulped down a cup of milk, gave Jenny a quick kiss, and disappeared out the door. Jenny sank back into a chair, exhausted. She'd just rest for a few moments, then tidy up and have something to eat before going to bed. Cameron might be with Morag for hours yet, and she was simply too tired to wait up for him.

It felt good to sit by the fire, the heat warming her through and making her drowsy. Jenny's eyes began to close, and she allowed herself to drift away, her head drooping like a wilting flower. The chair wasn't very comfortable, but she slipped into a deep sleep immediately, completely oblivious to any discomfort. Jenny dreamed that she was somewhere tropical. She had never seen the tropics herself, but Lady Sheridan told her about Hispaniola and described the sandy beaches, swaying palm trees, and the heady scent of flowers the likes of which she'd never seen. The sun blazed hot during the day, but it was pleasantly cool during the night, fragrant sea air blowing through the window in the captain's cabin and making it easier to sleep.

Jenny saw herself walking along the beach, beads of sweat forming on her forehead from the intense heat of the sun. There was no shade to be found anywhere, and the trees seemed to be moving away from her, as if by magic. Perhaps they were a mirage. Jenny looked around, but there was nothing but sand.

Even the sea seemed to have disappeared, and she was roasting in her woolens, desperate for a cool drink and a bit of shade.

Jenny woke up with a start and looked around. It took her a long moment to comprehend what was happening, but then she leaped to her feet, screaming for Ian. The house was alight, hungry flames licking the walls and devouring everything in sight. Jenny's skirt was aflame, burning her legs. Jenny beat out the flame and grabbed Ian, who was miraculously still asleep after his terrible day. The fire had reached the door, but it was the only way out of the house, so there was no time for hesitation or indecision. Jenny kirtled up her skirt and jumped over the flames, the heat licking her bare calves. She yelped with terror, then threw herself out the door as something inside crashed, producing a shower of sparks. Ian woke, startled by Jenny's scream and gazed up at her, his eyes filled with incomprehension. He stared at the flames erupting from the window, mesmerized by the sight. Jenny looked around wildly. Where was Cameron? What time was it?

The rain had stopped, but it was cold and damp outside, and the wind tore through Jenny's thin dress, making her shiver. She held Ian close and watched her home burn, her mind unable to accept the reality of her situation. How had the fire started? How long had it been burning before she finally woke? What if she hadn't woken up? Ian would have burned to death, and so would she. The clouts must have dried and caught fire somehow, falling to the floor and igniting the hearth rug that Jenny had knitted. She'd been careless because she was tired. She should have made sure that the clouts were securely fastened to the string attached to the mantel before allowing herself to fall asleep. It would take just one square of cloth to catch fire and flutter onto the floor—just one cloth.

Jenny wasn't sure how long she stood there, staring, until she heard Cameron's desperate scream as he erupted out of the darkness. He looked terrified, his eyes searching for them as he took in the conflagration that had been their home.

"We're here," Jenny called out. Her voice barely carried, but Cameron saw them and came running.

"Oh, Jesus, I thought I'd lost ye," he cried as he held them close. "Jenny, what happened? Yer gown," he cried out when he noticed that the bottom of Jenny's dress was gone. Her legs were raw and blistered, but she hardly noticed. She got Ian out in time; that was all that mattered. Ian didn't seem any worse for wear and reached out to his father, eager to be held. Cameron took Ian into his arms and cooed to him, his eyes on Jenny.

I must look a fright, Jenny thought. She felt strangely detached, as if she were still dreaming and would wake up and find everything as it should be. Ian would be asleep in his cot and she would be sitting by the fire: warm, snug, and pleasantly rested. Cameron would come in, undress, climb into bed, and pat the space next to him with a smile of invitation, and she would go to him and snuggle against his strong body.

Jenny suddenly felt overcome and slumped against Cameron, grateful for his strength as her legs went out from under her. Cameron held her against him and talked softly to her, the way he had talked to Ian just a moment ago. He wouldn't let her fall. Jenny felt the world slipping away as she finally gave in to the darkness tugging at her senses. She tried to fight it but couldn't. She was too tired.

EIGHTEEN
VIRGINIA AUGUST 1628

The murky gray light of predawn crept stealthily into the room, reclaiming furnishings from the darkness and settling on the tranquil faces of the occupants of the bed. There was a pleasant chill that made the warmth of the blanket that much more delicious as it cocooned Valerie in its folds. She was having a rather pleasant dream when Louisa's urgent whisper startled her out of a deep sleep.

"Val, wake up," Louisa pleaded. "I need help."

"What is it?" Valerie exclaimed as she sat bolt upright, her dream forgotten. "What's wrong?"

Louisa stood over the bed, her blonde hair cascading around her shoulders, her white nightdress giving her the appearance of a melancholy specter. Alec was still asleep, completely unaware of Louisa's presence in their room. Valerie suspected that he'd overindulged a little last night, given the tragic events of the day. She'd had some brandy as well before retiring, and convinced Louisa to do the same.

"It's Kit. Oh, Val, he's in such pain. I don't know what to do."

"Should we send for Doctor Jacobson?" Valerie asked as she hastily pulled on her dressing gown.

"No, not yet. Maybe there's something you can do. I trust you more than I trust him."

"Lou, I'm no doctor. I have some rudimentary knowledge of healing acquired from years of living without proper medical care, but I can't take it upon myself to play at being a physician."

"I don't expect you to," Louisa retorted. "All I ask is that you take a look and see if there's anything you can do to help."

Valerie closed the door behind her and followed Louisa to her bedroom. Kit was propped up on pillows, his splinted arm and leg stretched out awkwardly beneath the blanket. His face was flushed and swollen where it had been stitched, and his eyes were glazed with pain. Kit's lips were pressed together, as if he were holding back a groan. "Good morning, Valerie," he whispered, polite as ever.

"Kit, may I take a look?" Valerie asked as she sat down on the side of the bed. "Louisa says you're in pain."

"Be my guest."

Valerie moved aside the blanket and gasped at the sight of Kit's leg. It was terribly swollen, the bandage soaked with blood where the bone had perforated the flesh. Kit's skin felt hot to the touch and was mottled with bruises in brilliant shades of blue and purple, clearly visible even by candlelight. Kit's arm was swollen as well, his normally elegant fingers like sausage links.

"I can't feel my hand, and every breath I take is agony," Kit said. Beneath his calm demeanor he was clearly scared.

"Kit, shall I send for the doctor?" Valerie asked, needing to hear from him that it was his decision not to consult Doctor Jacobson.

"No. Not yet. He'll either give me more laudanum or suggest some form of barbaric surgery."

"Are you sure you don't want any laudanum?"

"Not yet," Kit replied stubbornly. Valerie could understand Kit's hesitation. If the wound had begun to fester, the doctor would suggest amputation, which was the only means of healing available to him. The odds of surviving a double amputation were not good, to say the least, and Valerie was certain that Kit would prefer death to life as a double amputee. They had to try to bring down the swelling and lower Kit's temperature by other means.

Valerie motioned for Louisa to follow her as she descended the stairs to fetch her medicine chest. It wasn't large and didn't contain any miraculous cures, but Valerie had learned much from Jenny, who was knowledgeable about plants and herbs.

"Val, I'm scared," Louisa whimpered.

"Lou, we need to remain calm. Look, I don't know much about human physiology, but I know some basic things. Kit has severely bruised ribs, which would account for painful breathing. It's normal for injuries to swell soon after being inflicted. Do you remember how your arm looked after you broke it at camp? Mom and Dad had to come and get you and you cried all the way home. Your fingers were like hot dogs."

"Yes, I remember," Louisa nodded. "I could barely feel my hand, and my fingers tingled from being so swollen. I could feel the skin stretching. So, what do we do? Do we just wait until the swelling subsides?"

"I think maybe we can do something to make Kit more comfortable, but I don't want to loosen the bandages for fear of his bones shifting."

"What can we do? He's suffering, Val."

"Let me think." Valerie looked through her box, searching for something that might help reduce the swelling. She took out a jar of dried dandelion. Jenny often brewed dandelion tea for Cook to help reduce the swelling in her ankles after a day on her feet. If the tea didn't help, at least it wouldn't do any harm.

"Boil some water," Valerie instructed Louisa. "I'll brew dandelion tea and make a catnip compress to apply externally to the wrist and hand, but first, we'll leech him."

Valerie reached up and carefully removed the jar of leeches from a high shelf. She didn't use the leeches often because she couldn't bring herself to handle the slimy creatures, but she acknowledged their efficacy and made sure there were always some on hand should an emergency arise. This case definitely qualified as an emergency.

"Are you sure?" Louisa gasped. She stared at the leeches will disgust. "They're gross."

"Lou, neither leeches nor dandelion tea can do any harm, but they might help. We must give them a try before Doctor Jacobson gets here and proposes something more drastic. Now, get that water on the boil."

Valerie closed the medicine chest, scooped up the jar of leeches, and followed Louisa into the kitchen. She was more scared than she was willing to admit. Although it was true that these remedies wouldn't harm Kit, she couldn't be sure that they would help. Half of Kit's body was broken, and they had no way of knowing how much internal damage he'd suffered. Kit needed X-rays, possible surgery under general anesthesia, and months of rehabilitation. Instead, all she could offer him was tea and leeches. She had to remain calm and think rationally.

It stood to reason that the injuries would get worse before they got better. It would take at least two weeks for the ribs to recover enough to allow for easier breathing, and the swelling and temperature were the body's way of fighting infection. But there could be so many other things going on. Without the benefit of an X-ray, they had no way of knowing if the doctor had set the bones properly, and if he'd found all the fractures. A broken rib could have punctured Kt's lung, causing the pain and shortness of breath he was experiencing. They had to do their best to keep Kit comfortable and hope that the body did the rest and healed itself. In the meantime, he needed to keep up his strength and remain well hydrated.

Valerie was distracted from her thoughts by the arrival of Cook. Mrs. Taylor came in and hung her shawl on a peg in the kitchen. She usually arrived shortly after sunrise to begin her chores for the day. It took hours to heat the oven enough to bake bread and she needed to make porridge for the children's breakfast.

"Good morning, Barbara," Valerie said.

"Were you wanting a cup of coffee?" Cook asked, reaching for a container of ground chicory. "I'll make you some. And there's bread left from yesterday and fresh butter if you don't care to wait for the porridge."

"Not just yet. We are brewing dandelion tea for his lordship. His swelling is very bad," Valerie explained as she measured out the dried flowers.

Cook nodded. "I hope it helps. Is there anything I can do?"

"If you would prepare some beef tea. Don't add any salt," Valerie added.

"No salt? But it will taste terrible," Cook protested.

"Salt forces the body to retain water and we need the swelling to go down. It might not taste good, but it will help."

"Yes, ma'am. I'll put the beef tea on the boil right away. There's a piece of beef I've been saving to make a steak pie for today's luncheon, but I'll boil it for his lordship instead."

"Thank you," Louisa said as she poured the dandelion tea into a cup. "God, it smells dreadful," she said, wrinkling her nose. "I thought it'd be something like chamomile."

"Perhaps we should add a spoonful of honey to sweeten it," Cook suggested.

"Yes," Valerie agreed. "Honey is good," she mused. Kit would benefit from the glucose.

"All right, I'm going up to do the deed," Valerie said as she picked up the jar of leeches. "But first, I need to find a pair of gloves. I can't handle these with my bare hands."

NINETEEN

Valerie recoiled in disgust as she extracted the leeches from the jar and carefully set them in place—two on Kit's hand, and four on his leg. She could never get used to the feel of them in her hands, especially when she removed their engorged bodies after they'd done their work. Valerie gave Kit a smile of encouragement when he cringed with revulsion.

"I've never been leeched before," he said as he watched the creatures latch onto his skin.

"It doesn't hurt."

"I wouldn't feel it even if it did," Kit replied.

Someone who didn't know Kit would take his answer as a sign of self-pity, but that wasn't at all what Kit meant. Even in his condition, he needed to reassure Valerie that she wasn't hurting him or causing him any discomfort. He was worried about her, and that nearly made her cry. Kit's response was so seventeenth century. A modern man would complain and admit to feeling pain. He would lay blame, make threats against those responsible, and probably curse like a sailor, but that wasn't the way of men in this century. Kit and Alec were basically cut from the same cloth, always thinking of others and their responsibility to them and never admitting the extent of their pain or unhappiness.

It never occurred to them to complain or blame someone else. Kit could have been killed, but he didn't hold the sailor who slipped responsible for his injuries, nor did he treat the death of those who weren't as lucky as inconsequential because they weren't of his social standing. Instead, Kit bore his pain quietly and patiently, the only sign of his discomfort the tightening of the jaw and the sharp intake of breath whenever he moved. He closed his eyes as the sun rose higher and illuminated his face, causing him to wince. He probably had a devil of a headache on top of all his other injuries. Valerie went to the window and half-closed the shutters.

Kit looked exhausted despite the laudanum-induced sleep that got him through the night and closed his eyes. Valerie covered the jar and settled in to wait for the leeches to finish and fall off. Focusing on possible treatment was easier than giving way to panic at the sight of his injuries, but now that she was alone with him, there was no need to pretend. Kit was in bad shape, and he knew it. His face was barely recognizable, the skin puckered and angry where Doctor Jacobson had stitched it, his cheek so swollen, he could barely open his eye.

Valerie opened the jar and extracted one more leech. She held it up to Kit's cheekbone until it latched on. Kit grimaced but allowed the creature to remain on his face.

"That bad?" he asked.

"It will help with the swelling around the eye," Valerie replied.

"Thank you."

"I only wish I could do more," Valerie replied, her voice unsteady. She felt helpless in the face of such carnage, so she focused on the leeches instead. They looked like fat commas, punctuating Kit's wounds and glistening in the morning light. After a few minutes, they began to grow fatter and rounder as they feasted on Kit's blood, but the swelling beneath his eye did diminish somewhat, making Valerie feel as if she'd made a difference, no matter how minor.

Kit's eyes remained closed, but Valerie could tell he was awake. His breathing came in short bursts since he couldn't draw in a deep enough breath to fill his lungs.

"Kit, how are you?" Valerie asked as she took his good hand in hers. Kit's eyes fluttered open. They were glazed with pain, but he couldn't bring himself to tell her the truth.

"I've been better," was the best he could manage.

"Doctor Jacobson should be here soon. He'll try to help you."

"That's what I'm afraid of," Kit replied with a weak smile.

"Louisa and I will do everything we can to ease your pain and get you back on your feet."

"I know you will," Kit breathed. Even those few sentences seemed to tire him out, and he shut his eyes again.

Valerie scooped up the leeches and dropped them back in the jar. She'd leech him again tomorrow and every day after that if it helped the swelling go down.

Louisa entered the room carrying a cup of her brew. Her eyes flew to Kit's face, and she exhaled the breath she'd been holding.

"He looks better," she said. "Don't you think so? He'll get through this; I know it."

"Yes," Valerie replied. Louisa needed to hear that Kit would be all right, but Valerie knew no such thing. She suddenly felt sick to her stomach and longed for a breath of fresh air.

"You look green around the gills," Louisa said as she sat down next to Kit to help him drink. "Those leeches will do that to you."

"I just need some air."

Valerie fled the room and ran outside. She took deep breaths of clean, fresh air until she got the stench of blood and fear out of her nostrils. She stood there for a long while until Alec came out of the house and stood behind her, wrapping his arms around her for support. It felt good to lean on him, and Valerie allowed herself to relax into him. They stood quietly for a moment, drawing strength from each other as they so often did.

"How is he, Val?" Alec finally asked.

"He looks so broken, Alec. He needs a hospital, X-rays, and very strong drugs. He's trying to be brave, but he must be in absolute agony. How can an herbal poultice and some leeches ease his pain? It's a joke really, but that's all we have at our disposal."

"Kit is strong. He'll pull through."

"I'd like to believe that, but when I look at him, all I see is someone broken beyond repair." Valerie grew quiet as Louisa stepped from the house. She looked subdued and frightened.

"Was he able to drink the tea?" Valerie asked, for lack of anything else to say.

"Only a little. I feel so helpless," she cried. "I can't stand by and watch him suffer this way."

"Louisa, there's nothing you can do but take care of him and offer your love and support," Alec said.

"That's not enough. My love can't heal his bones."

"But it can heal his spirit, and God will do the rest," Alec replied.

"Oh, spare me your mumbo-jumbo, Alec," Louisa cried. "I know you think everything is God's will and we have to accept it with good grace, but I come from a somewhat different place. I don't even believe in God, if you must know. He's just a fantasy, put forth by desperate, frightened people who needed to find an explanation for the things they couldn't understand. Religion is the best form of PR, putting a positive spin on things when your world is imploding."

With that, Louisa ran toward the woods. Valerie made to go

after her, but Alec held her back. "Let her go, Val. She's angry and scared. She needs a little time alone to calm down and figure out a way to deal with what's happened."

"She didn't mean what she said," Valerie said as she turned to face him.

"I know. But she needed to lash out at someone, and it's easier to lash out at me than at something she can't see or touch. She wants someone to hurt as badly as she's hurting. Louisa is not the first person to question the existence of God when put in a position where nothing makes sense."

"I do envy your faith, Alec. I find it hard to believe in a God who takes everyone you love away from you and still expects you to worship him without bitterness or recrimination."

"It's not God that takes people away, Val—it's life. God can't prevent all bad things from happening, but he is there when you need someone to turn to."

"That doesn't make much sense," Valerie replied. She rarely got involved in theological discussions, but she did find Alec's faith to be both admirable and frustrating. His faith never wavered, and he never lost his way. He suffered, grieved, and occasionally drank too much to dull the pain, but he never lost his belief in a benevolent God, who died for the sins of man and was capable of infinite love and forgiveness.

"There can be no light without darkness, and no joy without pain. The world is all about contrasts, and it's the pain and darkness that bring us to God," Alec explained.

"So, you mean that God allows horrible things to happen to us so that we don't turn away from him?" Valerie asked, failing to grasp the logic of Alec's argument.

"That's not what I meant at all," Alec replied, shaking his head. "It's like when a child falls and scrapes his knee. You, as his mother, can't always stop it from happening, but you can be there to comfort and kiss the hurt away. That's God in a nutshell—a loving parent who is there to ease the pain and soothe away the hurt."

"I like that analogy," Valerie said as she wrapped her arms around Alec's waist. "You have a gift for taking something awful and random and turning it into something logical and manageable."

"I only wish I could do something to help Kit," Alec sighed. "No amount of reasoning will ease Kit's suffering. It will take him months to recover, and that's the best-case scenario," Alec said carefully. Valerie knew what he was alluding to but refused to entertain the idea that Kit wouldn't come out on the other side. He had to, if only for Louisa and the children. The thought of the children jolted Valerie out of her reverie. The children were frightened, and with Louisa off on her emotional rollercoaster there was no one to comfort them aside from Minnie and Cook.

"Alec, why don't you go have breakfast with the children while I go and find Louisa. She needs me, and the children need your calm and presence of mind."

Alec gave Valerie a quick kiss and returned to the house, and Valerie squared her shoulders and went in search of Louisa. They were at the start of this nightmare, and if Louisa hoped to come out of this sane, she needed to get a grip on her emotions and focus all her energies on Kit and the children. Louisa had always been emotional, and at times irrational, and it was Valerie's job to make sure this wasn't going to be one of those times.

TWENTY

Doctor Jacobson arrived just before noon. He tossed the reins of his horse to Alec, as if Alec were a stable boy, and proceeded into the house, his manner bullish and brisk until his gaze alighted on Louisa. Doctor Jacobson's expression softened instantly, becoming one of concern and deference.

"My dear Lady Sheridan. How are you?" he asked as he bowed over Louisa's hand, brushing his lips across her knuckles in a courtly manner.

"As well as can be expected," Louisa replied tersely. She pulled her hand out of the doctor's grasp and crossed her arms over her bosom in what Valerie recognized as a defensive gesture. The man clearly made her uncomfortable.

"Did his lordship have a peaceful night?" Doctor Jacobson inquired.

"Hardly. He's in a great deal of pain, Doctor," Louisa retorted.

"One would hardly expect him not to be after being crushed by a crate," Doctor Jacobson observed. He spoke the truth, but his demeanor was devoid of any sympathy or sensitivity. Perhaps he was repaying Louisa in kind for her obvious rebuke. His gaze, however, was fixed on Louisa's face, his eyes narrowed in speculation. Did he think he would have a chance with her if Kit died? Valerie wondered, unable to control the surge of revulsion she felt toward the man. Vulture! Could he even be trusted to tend to Kit when he so obviously coveted his wife? Louisa must have been having similar thoughts because she looked like she wanted to slap the doctor across his smug face, so Valerie stepped in to defuse the situation. They would deal with Doctor Jacobson's infatuation later, but for now, their priority was Kit.

"Doctor, Lord Sheridan is in extreme pain, and there's some rather bad swelling in his leg and his hand. I've administered a poultice after leeching him."

Doctor Jacobson gaped at her as if she'd just spoken to him in Chinese. Valerie thought it only right to inform him of the steps they'd taken to help Kit, but the doctor saw Valerie's interference as an insult to his professional standing.

"I don't hold with self-doctoring, madam," he snapped. "I did tell you that I was coming this morning. You should have waited."

"Did I do something wrong?" Valerie challenged him.

She'd promised herself that she would remain cool and polite, but something about the man's self-righteous manner provoked her every time. Perhaps it was the fact that he clearly saw all women as nothing more than mentally inferior creatures who were only suited to warming a man's bed and bearing his children. He found Louisa attractive, that was obvious enough, but he had no interest in her mind or her soul; he only wanted her body, and perhaps her submission to his will. He assumed that the only reason behind Louisa's discomfort was the fact that she was married to another man, and it simply never occurred to him that Louisa loathed him and would never welcome his suit, even if she were to become widowed.

"That remains to be seen," Dr. Jacobson replied archly. "Now, may I see the patient, Lady Sheridan?"

Louisa led Doctor Jacobson up the stairs while Valerie remained behind. Provoking him further would do nothing to help Kit, so it was best to let him examine his patient without interference. Valerie had done everything in her power, which was precious little, and now she had to defer to the doctor, although she couldn't begin to imagine what more he could do. The only thing he had at his disposal that Valerie didn't was a rusty saw that he used to amputate limbs, and she would sooner die than let him use it on Kit.

Valerie wandered into the kitchen and helped herself to a bowl of porridge. It was hot and soothing as it went down, the hint of honey and dollop of butter making it more palatable. She thought that the porridge would help Kit keep up his strength and resolved to take him up a bowl after Doctor Jacobson left. She didn't see how a liquid diet would help him heal. If anything, it would weaken him and prevent his body from fighting on its own to recover.

Valerie was just finishing her meal when she heard Doctor Jacobson descending the stairs, followed by Louisa. The door slammed, and the sound of hoofbeats followed shortly after as the doctor trotted away from the house. Louisa sank into a chair next to Valerie. Her head looked like a drooping flower, and she buried her face in her hands as tears slid down her cheeks.

"What did that cretin say?" Valerie demanded. She wasn't sure why she was angry, but as Alec pointed out only an hour ago, they all needed someone to lash out at.

"Nothing. He said nothing."

"What do you mean?" Valerie gaped.

"He said that there's nothing more he can do other than give Kit more laudanum for the pain."

"But what about that terrible swelling and fever? Is that all a part of the healing process? Do we just wait it out?"

"He believes that the leg wound is beginning to fester, and you know what that means. We can either ride it out and hope for the best, or the good doctor will come back with his saw. He gave me twenty-four hours to think that last option over. He would have to take off three-quarters of Kit's leg to save him. God, I can't even envision what that procedure would entail, not to mention the aftermath. Kit would die of shock, or just bleed to death. Can you imagine sawing through a thigh bone with no anesthesia? Whose heart would be strong enough to withstand such torture? And what are the chances that it would actually save his life?"

"So, there are two possible outcomes," Valerie summarized. "Either the infection will clear up on its own and Kit will have a chance at making a full recovery, or he will die with or without the operation."

"Pretty much," Louisa moaned. "And what are the chances of the infection just clearing up? He needs meds, Val. Heavy-duty, twenty-first-century meds."

"Should we take him to a hospital?" Valerie asked, not surprised to see Louisa shake her head in denial.

"Val, Kit would never make the journey. It would take hours by trap over a rutted track to get to where Williamsburg is going to be, and then I'd have to maneuver him on my own to get him to a hospital where he would have to be for weeks. How in the world would I get away with it? I have no money, no ID, no clothes, no place to stay, and no medical insurance."

"There must be something we can do," Valerie persisted. Cold fingers of dread stroked her spine. Louisa was right, Kit would never make it, and even if he did, it would be impossible to pull off a trip to the future without funds. Valerie had virtually no money left in her twenty-first-century bank account, and Louisa couldn't recall her account number or had any ID that could be used to establish her identity. Without money or help from someone on the other side, she could not survive while Kit remained in the hospital. Were they condemning Kit to death by choosing not to transport him to the future? Valerie wondered. There had to be something they could do, but no ideas sprang to mind.

"All we can do is wait. And pray. Oh, I bet Alec would like that," Louisa said, her voice harsh with bitterness.

"Lou, none of this is Alec's fault," Valerie reprimanded Louisa gently.

"I know. I'm just feeling a little irrational at the moment, and I'm desperate for someone to blame."

Valerie got up and walked over to Louisa. She pulled her to her feet, wrapped her arms about her sister, and held her tight, as if her embrace could prevent Louisa from falling apart. Louisa rested her head on Valerie's shoulder as her body quaked with sobs.

"Val, I can't lose him. I just can't. What will I be without him? And there I thought the worst thing that could happen to me was going back to England. How foolish I was. How selfish. I would go to the ends of the earth if it would help him."

"Lou, let's just see what tomorrow brings. Kit is strong and healthy. He might pull through. There are times when a body fights off an infection naturally. People have been known to survive."

Louisa raised her tear-stained face. "Val, you know as well as I do what the mortality rate is in this time and place. What are the chances that Kit will miraculously recover? One in one hundred?"

That sounds about right, Valerie thought.

TWENTY-ONE

Wind moaned outside the nursery window, blowing through the cracks and rattling the shutters. The children were subdued, and for once, eager to go to bed. Valerie helped Tom undress and put on his nightshirt. He clung to her for a moment before allowing himself to be tucked in. Tom normally asked for a story, but tonight he just curled into a ball and was asleep before Valerie even had a chance to kiss him goodnight. Robbie was out too, having spent the day running around with Harry and causing as much mischief as the two boys could manage. Alec had taken the children into Jamestown to visit with Charles's kids in order to allow Louisa and Valerie to look after Kit. Tom had begged to come along, but clearly had a hard time keeping up with the older boys. He had enjoyed the outing though and kept muttering something about playing a 'big boy game' all through supper.

Valerie smoothed back his unruly blond curls and softly kissed him on the forehead, wishing that he would stay three forever. He was so sweet, and still at an age where he welcomed hugs and kisses from his grandparents and needed them to soothe every hurt and fear. Another few years and Tom would start asserting his independence, as Robbie and Harry were doing already. Children didn't remain children for long in seventeenth-century Virginia. Most boys of Robbie's age already helped their parents on their farms and worked from dawn till dusk, especially if the family couldn't afford an indentured servant or a slave.

Valerie turned to leave when she heard Evie call out to her from her bed by the wall. Valerie walked over to Evie's trundle and sat down on the edge. Evie had been quiet all through supper, but that wasn't unusual. Evie had been a real handful when she was younger, but she had changed over the past year, going from a headstrong, attention-grabbing child to a brooding, watchful wraith. Had she been older, everyone would have assumed that she'd reached puberty, but Evie had just turned seven, which made the transformation somewhat surprising.

She still looked like Kit but was beginning to display Louisa's artistic talent and sensitivity. Valerie often found Evie's dark eyes watching her and the other adults, trying to make sense of what was going on in order to determine if she would be affected by it. Valerie suspected that sometimes Evie liked to eavesdrop, perhaps because she feared the truth would be kept from her.

"Mom always did say that little jugs have big handles," Louisa said when Valerie had mentioned this to her. "She's just curious. Actually, she reminds me a lot of Kit's sister, Caro. She had that kind of watchfulness, always listening and assessing the situation and its possible impact on her. Not a bad quality in a woman of this time. Always better to listen more and talk less," Louisa said.

She would never have made that type of observation in her former life, but the role of women was vastly different in this century, and Louisa had finally come to accept that, recognizing that she couldn't rear Evie as she would have in the future. Evie would have to make a life for herself here, and growing up to be an independent, opinionated hoyden would do her no favors when it came to marriage and family, which were her only prospects as a noblewoman of this time.

"I think she's scared," Valerie had replied.

"Why do you say that?" Louisa demanded, shocked that she might have missed something in her own daughter.

Valerie sighed. She'd given this some thought and having at one time been a teacher of young children felt a certain understanding of kids that came from years of experience, as well as her own parenting.

"Evie adored my Louisa, and she had been a bit dazzled by Theo. She might have been little, but her feelings were no less real than those of an adult. And then both Louisa and Theo died, leaving their child behind. Evie might not have grieved their deaths at the time, but their passing left an invisible mark on her. And then Charles and Annabel moved out, taking Millie and Harry to live in Jamestown. They didn't die, but they are no longer a part of Evie's everyday life, which is something she'd come to see as a given," Valerie explained. She was painfully aware that children tended to internalize their feelings rather than deal with them.

"I think the feeling of loss became even more real to her when Jenny left us. Evie had been deeply attached to her, and this was another person she loved who suddenly disappeared from her life. I think she listens and watches because she wants to be prepared should something else happen. I suppose we should have been more honest with her about Jenny and Cameron, but she was too young to understand, and no one told her Jenny was leaving until it was time for her to go. Evie had no time to deal with their separation," Valerie concluded.

Valerie felt a twinge of guilt as she watched Louisa's reaction to her analysis. It was clear that Louisa had never thought of Evie's behavioral changes as anything more than part of the growing process, but now conflicting emotions raced across her features, going from surprise to acknowledgment, to guilt.

"How blind I've been," Louisa stammered as she took in what Valerie had suggested. "It had never occurred to me that Evie might be frightened of losing us. I just thought she'd matured a bit and was more comfortable with having to share attention with Robbie and Tom."

"Lou, don't beat yourself up. Children don't come with instruction manuals, and I could be way off base in my psychoanalysis. I just thought that perhaps she needs a little reassurance."

Louisa shook her head miserably. "What reassurance can I give her when Kit is talking about going back to England? Evie will be torn from people she loves once again, and this time it might be for a much longer stretch. I focused so much on my own feelings that I never stopped to consider how Evie and Robbie might feel. They love you and Alec, and Millie, Harry, and Tom are like siblings to them. They'll be heartbroken to be wrenched away from them. Oh Val, why does everything have to be so complicated? Like it's not difficult enough that we've had to make a life for ourselves in a time that's not our own, but we can't even remain together to shoulder the heavy burden of surviving in these turbulent and backward times."

Valerie hugged her sister and they sat quietly for a few moments, drawing comfort from each other. "Everything will work out, Lou. It has to. Life is like a highway; no matter how often we stop or get lost, we still end up where we're meant to be in the end."

Louisa chuckled through her tears. "Are you saying you now believe in predestination? Our lives have already been mapped out and nothing we do will alter the outcome?"

"I don't know. That's too philosophical for me, but I do believe we each have our own destiny to fulfill, whatever that destiny might be. We are not meant to know how it will all play out, but life often forces us to take a path we'd never considered."

"You mean our celestial GPS recalculates and puts us on a new route to the same destination?" Louisa laughed, her tears forgotten. "All this sounds way too spiritual for me. I am sticking with the idea that we are all a bunch of misfits who make every conceivable effort to screw up our lives and then scramble madly to fix things before it's too late."

"If you truly thought that, you wouldn't have followed me to the past because you wouldn't have believed that we were meant to be reunited. You took a leap of faith, and it had paid off. Perhaps it's time to take another one. Trust that everything will be the way it was always meant to be. I do, otherwise I wouldn't be able to get from day to day without losing my mind."

The conversation with Louisa raced through Valerie's mind as she approached Evie's bed and took in her tense expression. Her eyes were huge in the glow of Valerie's candle, and Valerie realized what Evie was going to ask before she even uttered the words.

"Aunt Valerie, is my father going to die?" Evie whispered. Her breathing was shallow, and she stared at Valerie with unwavering concentration, as if she were afraid to miss some minute facial alteration that might alert her to the truth.

"Evie, we are doing everything we can to help your father recover," Valerie said as she stroked Evie's cheek, but Evie pulled back sharply, tears filling her eyes.

"So you mean he will," she cried.

"I didn't say that."

"You didn't have to. You don't believe he will recover, do you?" Evie was sitting up now, her arms wrapped around her middle in a defensive gesture Valerie recognized only too well. Her own daughter had looked just like that when she'd tried to keep out feelings that might overwhelm her.

"Sweetheart, none of us can predict with any certainty what's going to happen. Your father is very badly hurt, and yes, there's always a chance of things taking a turn for the worse, but he is not dead yet, so there's still hope."

"I don't want hope," Evie protested, shaking her head. "I want you to tell me that he will be all right. I don't want to lose him," Evie wailed, finally dissolving into tears. "I love him," she sobbed.

Valerie drew Evie into a fierce hug and Evie wrapped her arms around her aunt. "Oh, Evie, we all love him."

"Not like I do," Evie moaned.

"No, no one loves him quite like you do," Valerie conceded. She thought her heart had already withstood its share of heartbreak when Louisa and Theo died, but Valerie realized that as long as one lived and breathed, there was always more to come and there was a reason why the heart was the strongest muscle in the body—it had the most to bear.

"We'll save him, Evie," she whispered into Evie's hair. "We'll save him."

It took Evie a long while to calm down, but she finally fell asleep, having worn herself out with crying and grief. Valerie tucked her in and let herself out of the nursery. She always underestimated the sensitivity and perception of little girls, and she'd paid for her ignorance with her own daughter as Louisa might with Evie. They needed to be honest with her, no matter what, and treat her with the respect she deserved. She might be only seven, but she had an old soul that cried out for understanding and comfort. Whatever happened, Evie would handle it better if she knew the truth.

Valerie quickly undressed and blew out the candle so as not to disturb Alec, who was already asleep. She slid into bed and was surprised when Alec's arms came around her as he fitted his body to her back. "What took you so long?" he asked. "Is it Kit?"

"No, I was with Evie. She's terrified, Alec. She is grieving for Kit and wants reassurance that a miracle will happen and save her daddy. I've never seen such naked pain in a child's soul."

"Is there anything we can do to aid her?" Alec asked. Valerie knew that he longed to help, but as with their own daughter, he was sometimes at a loss when it came to the fragile psyche of a little girl. And there would be no helping Evie if Doctor Jacobson's diagnosis proved to be true.

At this point, it was still too early to tell if Kit's leg wound had festered, but they would know for certain by morning, and then a decision would need to be made. Valerie hoped with all her might that Kit's fever and swelling were due to the body's natural effort to heal itself, but she knew better. Edema was normal in injuries of this kind, but not the fever. If Kit's fever didn't break by morning, Doctor Jacobson would want to amputate.

"We can aid Evie by saving Kit," Valerie replied, suddenly pushing Alec's arm away and sitting up in bed.

"What is it, Val?"

"Alec, have two horses saddled first thing in the morning. If Kit is no better, then we have an errand to run," Valerie said. Her heart was thumping in her chest, her earlier fatigue replaced by a surge of adrenaline. She'd been trying so hard to come up with some solution to the problem that she failed to see the one that was right in front of her nose.

"Where are we going?" Alec asked.

"I'll explain everything tomorrow. I just need a little time to work out all the details," Valerie replied absentmindedly. Her mind was going a mile a minute as a plan began to take shape. It had to work. But even if she failed, at least she would have tried rather than just idly stood by and waited for Kit to succumb to his injuries, which he would, if they were left untreated. Surgery was out of the question. It would kill him at worst, leave him a cripple at best; neither being acceptable. But there was another way.

TWENTY-TWO
MARYLAND AUGUST 1781

A glorious summer twilight settled over the forest, replacing dappled sunlight with a dusky purple haze. Scores of light bugs hung above the ground, as if suspended by invisible wires, their little green behinds aglow in the gathering darkness. Finn collected some kindling and a few thicker bits of wood and went about starting a campfire while Sam went to fetch some water from a nearby stream and have a quick wash. They'd been traveling all day and the sweat that had been slick on their skin earlier had dried into salty grime. The heat and humidity of August were nothing new to Sam and Finn, but it was a pleasure to finally feel the cooling breeze that had arrived with the setting of the sun, despite the swarm of mosquitoes that came along with it.

Sam finally returned, handed a pan of water to Finn and shook out his wet hair. "You should have a wash. I feel like a new man. I'll see to the fire and make us some coffee."

"Thanks. Don't mind if I do," Finn replied.

He handed Sam the depleted bundle of food and headed to the stream. They would finish off their supplies tonight, so tomorrow they'd have to find something to eat along the way.

Taverns were few and far between, the only places to buy food the homesteads they passed. More often than not, the farmers were willing to sell some bread, cheese, and even rashers of bacon, but sometimes they refused to part with the food. It was worth more than whatever Finn and Sam were offering in return. Few people had actual coin or paper money, which was sometimes worthless anyway, so the colonists relied on a barter system, trading goods instead. Some were prosperous enough to trade food for information, being so far removed from any town or village, others refused to help.

The water was marvelously cool, and Finn took his time, washing vigorously and scrubbing away the sweat and grime of the past few days. His empty stomach urged him to go back to camp, but he allowed himself a few minutes to float on his back and look up at the darkening sky. He loved these moments of complete peace and tried to create at least one each day. Sometimes he sat on the stile at the farm and gazed up at the sky. At other times, he went for a swim or read a bit of poetry. His mother had taught him that. She called it 'a mental health moment,' which always made his father laugh. People in the seventeenth century, or the eighteenth for that matter, were not particularly concerned with mental health, but evidently this was something people paid a lot of attention to in the future.

These brief moments rejuvenated Finn, especially on days that were particularly difficult and made him think that the war would surely be lost despite his mother's predictions. The intelligence they carried now might alter the events of the next few months and finally turn the tide, if what his mother had said was accurate. The information entrusted to them by John Mallory had been provided by a Negro slave named James Armistead, who served in the British Army and passed on intelligence to his Continental contacts while also relating false facts back to his superiors.

Finn had never met Armistead, but the name inspired awe

and respect among those who knew of his involvement. The man was brave and selfless. If his superiors discovered what he was up to, it would mean certain death, most likely without even the benefit of a trial. Armistead would be shot on the spot or hanged from the nearest tree; no questions asked.

Both Finn and Sam studied the information carefully, memorized it, and then destroyed the scrap of paper for fear of it falling into the wrong hands. It was imperative that they pass on the intelligence to General Washington's staff, and the easiest way of doing that was getting the information to Sam's cousin, Ralph Hewitt, who was an aide-de-camp to General Washington and marching toward Philadelphia with the Continental Army at this very moment. Perhaps Washington was already in Philadelphia, which would be fortuitous. Finn and Sam had to make sure he received their report before leaving Philadelphia, as the information would influence his strategy for the coming weeks.

I should go back, Finn thought as he gazed up at the star-strewn sky but couldn't bring himself to leave just yet. The water was so delicious, and there was no rush to do anything. Once they ate their supper, they would talk for a while and go to sleep, only to get up at dawn and continue their journey. Normally, Finn would enjoy spending a few days on the road with Sam, but he was worried about Mr. Mallory and the women, who were on their own at the farm. Sam didn't say much about his father, turning every attempt to talk about what happened into a joke, but Finn knew Sam was thinking about him day and night.

They had no way to find out if Mr. Mallory had managed to recover from his wound until they returned from this assignment, and that could be a fortnight from now. A lot could happen in a fortnight, but John Mallory was too full of vigor and will to live to succumb to his injury. He would beat the odds; Finn was sure of it.

Finn closed his eyes and pictured Abbie. She would be getting supper on the table right about now, tired from a long day of endless chores and eager to get the children to bed. Finn had been gone for only three days, but he missed his family, his inability to kiss the children and Abbie goodnight an almost physical ache in his belly. Sam missed his brood too, but he relished the brief respite from household duties and screaming children. Finn thought Sam enjoyed a few weeks away from Susanna as well. He had to work hard at being a good husband, a lot harder than Finn ever had to, since Sam had never been a one-woman man.

Sam loved Sue with his whole being, but Finn strongly suspected that if a bit of casual carousing came his way, he might not say no. What Sue didn't know wouldn't hurt her, but Sue was no fool. She knew her husband better than he knew himself and loved him for the man he was rather than the man she wished him to be. Sam needed variety and adventure. A sense of danger made him feel alive.

Finn, on the other hand, loved coming home, always eager for that sense of belonging he felt when reunited with his family. Coming home made Sam feel reined in, although he never said so out loud. Sam actually had more in common with Ralph than with Finn, since Ralph was also a player and a flirt, and thrived on danger, just like Sam.

Finn often wondered if Sam knew of Ralph's involvement in Diana's death. It had been agreed by Mr. Mallory and his brother-in-law, Alfred Hewitt, that Sam must never know what really happened to Diana or who'd been responsible. The story put forth by the innkeeper was that Diana had invited a gentleman into her room, believing him to be a romantic prospect, but the ruffian robbed and killed her, and fled out the back door before anyone knew anything was amiss. The citizens of Williamsburg had been shocked and appalled, but opinion quickly turned against Diana once someone let it slip that she had been a prostitute. The respectable matrons of Williamsburg quickly passed a verdict, claiming that it was God's punishment for lewdness and fornication and Diana was quickly forgotten by all but Sam and by Nathaniel, who still asked about his mother from time to time.

Finn didn't believe Sam to be so naive as to not suspect his uncle's hand in Diana's sad demise. The news of her death had filtered down to them from Williamsburg after a few days, and although Sam had never openly mourned her, he grieved for her in private and blamed himself for her death. Had Diana never followed him to Virginia, she would still be alive. Finn suspected that the only thing that allowed Sam to sleep at night during those first weeks was the knowledge that Diana had blackmailed his father and threatened the cause. She had been the architect of her own death, but the chain of events had begun with Sam. Nat was still young enough to accept Susanna as his mother without question, but in time, he would realize that the four-month age gap between him and Ben required an explanation. Difficult questions would be asked, and terrible awkwardness would ensue once both Nat and Ben learned the truth.

Finn finally forced himself to come out of the water and pull on his clothes. Sam would be wondering what had happened to him, and truth be told, he was starving. They'd stopped at a tavern earlier to get a tankard of ale, but there had been a group of men singing lustily at the next table, believing themselves to be safe in a loyalist town.

> *Yankee Doodle came to town,*
> *For to buy a firelock,*
> *We will tar and feather him,*
> *And so we will John Hancock.*

The song had burned Finn's guts, but Sam shrugged it off. "Let them sing," he said as he gulped down his ale. "Their day will come, and it'll be us singing then. Buck up, Finn. We're on urgent rebel business," Sam whispered with a wink.

TWENTY-THREE

Finn didn't have a towel, so he shook out his hair and pulled on the clothes over his damp skin. He picked up his boots and carried them to keep them from getting wet. He hated walking around in shoes that squelched. He walked slowly toward the camp, his mind on the leftover bread and salted pork that Abbie had packed for them. It took a few moments for him to become aware of the voices that carried on the evening breeze and came from their campsite. Finn stepped behind a tree. It was wiser to remain out of sight until he ascertained whether their visitors were friendly.

"Where is he?" a gruff voice demanded. Finn winced as he heard the dull thud of a punch, followed by a grunt of pain. "Where is the other one?"

"I'm alone," Sam replied, his voice hoarse.

"What kind of fools do you take us for, boy? There are two horses, and two packs. We'll find him anyhow, so you might as well tell us and spare yourself the beating. No point suffering needlessly before you die."

"And why would I die?" Sam asked, earning himself another blow.

"You will die because you are a traitor to your king, just like your misguided sire, who thinks no one knows about his activities. You're all rabble-rousers and deserve to hang for treason, each and every one of you, starting with that upstart arse-wipe, George Washington."

"You are not fit to lick his boots, you pathetic dimwit," Sam snarled. "You just wait and see what happens to the likes of you once the war is won and the British are driven into the sea."

"Too bad you won't be around to see it," the man replied. "We actually thought that British wife of yours might talk some sense into you, but it seems you've suckled her dumplings until she lost all reason. You're good at that, aren't you, you filthy cur? Got every whore in town panting after you."

"My wife's dumplings are very tasty," Sam replied, with a cocky grin, "and if by every whore you mean your wife, then yes, I suppose you're right."

Finn winced as a series of vicious blows left Sam gasping for air. He went quiet long enough to spit out the blood, but of course, Sam being Sam, couldn't remain silent.

"That the best you can do?" he demanded as soon as he could speak again.

Shut up, Sam, Finn nearly screamed. *Just shut up. You'll get yourself killed.*

Finn pinched the bridge of his nose, thinking furiously. Sam wasn't doing himself any favors by provoking his attacker, and it was only a matter of time before matters escalated. There was more than one man, but Finn couldn't see exactly how many there were since the campsite was blocked from view by tree trunks and the wide back of the man who stood before Sam. Finn needed to know precisely what he was up against before deciding on a course of action. He pulled the shirt over his head and threw it to the side. A flash of white would instantly give him away. Finn slid out from behind the tree and inched closer. He was unarmed, but the element of surprise would give him an advantage, so if there were two men, he stood a chance as long as he found a stout piece of wood to wield as a club.

Finn crouched behind a bush and peered at the campsite. There were still only two horses, his and Sam's, which meant that whoever had accosted Sam had followed them on foot, leaving their horses at a safe distance so as not to give their presence away. Finn could make out Sam's white shirt, but the other men wore dark colors and blended into the near darkness. Creeping closer, Finn was finally able to see the entire campsite and the faces of the other men, illuminated by the crimson glow of the fire.

There were three men, all dressed in civilian clothes, so they weren't a British patrol. Finn didn't know the two who held Sam, but he recognized the one who was conducting the interrogation; he'd met him in Williamsburg about a year ago. His name was Leonard Sparks, and he was a cooper by trade. Mr. Mallory had ordered several casks from Sparks to use for storing cider and had complained bitterly about the unreasonable price Sparks had demanded. Finn hadn't given the man much thought since then.

What he knew of the man amounted to very little. The only reason he even remembered him was because of the halo of ginger fuzz that framed his egg-shaped head and gave him a comical appearance. Mr. Mallory had remarked that Sparks looked like an owl in an ivy bush, on account of his frizzy mane.

Sparks was big and muscular, with a pock-marked face and surprisingly beautiful gray eyes, fringed by auburn lashes. He'd been friendly enough, no talk of politics passing his lips during the transaction with Mr. Mallory, but what was happening in the clearing wasn't business; this was personal.

Sparks was a raging Tory, judging by his remarks to Sam, but in Williamsburg, he kept his opinions to himself for fear of destroying his business, which was booming, since Sparks was the only cooper around for miles. He sold barrels to both the

British and the Americans, choosing not to discriminate in the name of profit. Was Leonard Sparks responsible for the attack on John Mallory? Finn wondered as he kept to his hiding place. He supposed that disguising the attempt on Mr. Mallory's life as an Indian attack made sense in Virginia, but now that they were in Maryland, he'd dispensed with all pretense.

"Give over the information you're carrying, and we might spare your life, boy," Sparks said to Sam, who was still bleeding from his mouth. Sparks must have knocked out one of Sam's teeth.

"I'm not carrying anything."

Sparks drew his hand back and punched Sam in the stomach, making him double over with pain. "I repeat, give over the information."

"I don't have any information," Sam insisted.

"So, you're here in Maryland, doing what exactly, taking in the sights?" Sparks snarled.

"That's right."

"I would think you'd want to remain at home by your father's bedside. Is he dead yet? The shit on the arrow was a nice touch, wouldn't you say? Sadly, I can't take credit for it. My wife's idea. Clever woman when she wants to be. Now, where were we? Ah, yes. The intelligence you're on your way to deliver to Washington. Shall I hit you again?" Sparks asked conversationally, a smug smile on his face. He was enjoying torturing Sam and was in no rush whatsoever. Numbers and time were on his side, so he could torment Sam all night if he chose to.

Rage shook Finn to the core. He wanted nothing more than to charge into the clearing, but instead, he forced himself to remain perfectly still. It had been drummed into him by Mr. Mallory that his first priority was to get the intelligence to the Continental Army. If both Finn and Sam perished, then vital information would die with them, and that was unthinkable.

Finn had to think very carefully about what to do. Mr. Mallory would have advised him to get away and deliver the information, but Finn wasn't Mr. Mallory. He wouldn't leave Sam to his fate, and now that Sparks had admitted to the attack on Mr. Mallory, he was certain of what that fate would be. Sparks wasn't bluffing to scare Sam; he intended to carry out his threat once he got what he'd come for.

Leonard Sparks turned to his men. "Right, this one doesn't want to talk, but the other one might. You two, tie him up and search the woods. Whitfield couldn't have gone far. Might have gone to the stream to have a wash. He's probably watching us right now and soiling his breeches like a terrified little girl, unless he's already halfway to Philadelphia, running for his life while we amuse ourselves with his friend. Find Finlay Whitfield."

Finn's name sounded strange on the man's lips. Sparks clearly knew more than anyone in Williamsburg gave him credit for. Did he also know about Alfred Hewitt and Ralph? And were there others who posed a danger to the members of the Committee of Correspondence?

Finn looked around frantically. If he remained in his hiding spot, the two men would find him within minutes. He needed a weapon. All he had was a small knife that he usually carried in his pocket, more for practical purposes than for protection. It had a short blade perfect for cutting food or whittling a stick, but it was useless as a weapon. He would have to be up in someone's face to use it, and the blade was too short to do much damage. All it could do was cause a flesh wound, which might hurt, but not stop an opponent.

Finn looked up at the tree in front of him. It had a thick trunk, nearly bare until the branches fanned out closer to the top. Useless. He continued to look, searching for what he needed. A few feet away, closer to the clearing, was a sprawling beech, with a thick trunk and countless branches reaching toward the sky like stout limbs. Finn crept toward the tree and went up like a cat, lying down on a thick branch that was hidden from view by abundant foliage. He reached out and snapped off a thinner branch, one as thick as two fingers. It was too narrow to use as a club and would probably break as soon as he hit someone, but it was all he could reach. Finn pulled the knife out of his pocket and began to sharpen the branch into a point, making a pike instead. It wouldn't save him from a gunshot or an arrow, but it would be effective in close combat. And it was the only weapon to hand.

Finn stilled as the two men came closer to his tree. They never bothered to look up, assuming that he was hiding on the ground. Finn could hear them speaking to each other, confident they'd find him. One of the men held a pistol, while the other wore a quiver of arrows, just like the ones used on Mr. Mallory. Finn held his breath as the two men passed beneath him and walked in the direction of the stream, then focused his attention on Sam, who was bound hand and foot and sitting on the ground.

"I'm going to give you one more chance to save your life, son," Sparks said, his tone now kind and reasonable. "If you give me the information you are carrying, then your children might still have their daddy come morning. If you don't, then we will first kill you, then Whitfield. That's five children that'll become orphans this night."

Sparks was rewarded by a look of shock on Sam's face. "Oh, we know all about you and your family, sonny. Your prissy British wife, a traitor to her sovereign if I ever saw one, your two children, and your bastard by the whore. And we know about your friend Finn. A girl and a boy, if I recall correctly. His wife, your sister, is quite comely, with those golden curls and large eyes. A man could lose himself in eyes like that. Mrs. Sparks used to be comely, but time takes its toll on all of us, doesn't it?" he mused.

"Shame to make your wife a widow, but I'm sure she'll find herself a new man in no time—that's if she doesn't hang for treason. And with your father, you, and Whitfield gone, it will be all women out there, won't it, except for the little pipsqueaks you call your sons. Your friend's son is too little to even count. Still not breeched, is he?"

"You leave our women alone," Sam growled, but Sparks just laughed.

"Or what? Seems to me that you're in no position to do anything. Why, if something were to happen to those women and children, all alone on the farm, it'd be a real shame."

"Have you no honor?" Sam demanded, furious at his own helplessness. Sparks struck where it hurt this time; that much was obvious.

"Honor? Of course, I have honor. I honor my king and my country. I honor my rights as a British citizen, and I honor the law. You, on the other hand, are nothing but rebel scum, ungrateful vermin who bites the hand that feeds it."

Sparks looked to Sam for a rebuttal, but Sam didn't reply. He looked through Sparks as if he weren't even there. Finn was glad Sam chose not to engage in a political debate. He knew what Sam was doing. He was listening to the silence and praying that Finn got clear away. As long as Finn was free, the message would be delivered, and their women would be safe.

Finn gritted his teeth and willed himself to remain still. He had to bide his time. Sam was bound hand and foot, so if Finn made his presence known, it would be three men against one. Somehow, he had to change the odds. Finn watched as the two men returned to the clearing.

"Well, where is he?" Sparks demanded. His face was illuminated by the fire, his expression one of irritation and derision. "Couldn't find the wood for the trees?" he taunted his companions.

"He's gone, Leonard. Now, keep a civil tongue in your head.

We are not your subordinates, nor do we have to follow your orders."

"Someone's got to be in charge," Sparks protested.

"I don't recall electing you," one of the men said. Finn prayed that a fight would erupt between the men, but the heat had gone out of the man's voice. He didn't want an argument.

"So, this is a democracy now?" Sparks laughed. "All right, I suppose I nominated myself. I do apologize, gentlemen. But there's much at stake, and we need to find Whitfield or this whole thing would have been for naught."

"Right you are, Leonard," the second man said. "Leave off, Bill. Leonard knows what he's about. He may as well be in charge. Better him than you."

"Fine," Bill growled. "Let's get on with it, shall we? What do we do with this one?"

"String him up," Leonard Sparks replied. "We must be on our way. We need to apprehend Whitfield before he has a chance to rendezvous with the Continental Army, and since he's on foot, he couldn't have gone far."

Finn sucked in his breath. They were going to hang Sam. He had to act. The two men pulled a length of rope from a leather satchel and the one named Bill tossed it over a branch, the noose swaying obscenely in the firelight. Finn saw the terror in Sam's eyes as his gaze followed the movement of the rope. The men didn't bother to take the time to tie the rope to the branch, so Bill held it in his hands as Leonard Sparks hauled Sam to his feet and fitted the noose around his neck.

"Any last words?" he guffawed. "No? On your way then."

Bill yanked on the rope and Sam's feet left the ground—his legs jerking wildly as the noose tightened around his neck. There was no time to waste. Finn slithered along the thick branch until he was almost above the clearing and jumped, knocking Leonard Sparks off his feet. Sparks was heavier than Finn by several stone, but the angle gave Finn a momentary advantage and he drove his makeshift pike into Sparks's chest. The pike penetrated the heart, just as Finn had intended, killing him instantly. Finn quickly rolled the dead man on top of himself, using him as a shield to block the shot that rang out. It sounded unnaturally loud, the bang causing several birds to squawk wildly and erupt into the night sky. Sparks's body jerked violently as the bullet penetrated the still-soft flesh, but kept Finn safe, lodging in Sparks's back instead of exiting on the other side. Finn threw off Sparks and charged the man before he had a chance to reload his gun.

Finn's knife wasn't long enough to do much damage if he stabbed the man, so he went for the eye, driving the short blade right through the man's left eye socket and into his brain. The man collapsed in a heap at Finn's feet. Bill let out a squawk of terror before finally letting go of the rope. Sam's body came down like a sack of turnips and hit the ground with a dull thud. Finn looked around wildly. He had to get to Sam, but Bill was already on the offensive, a vicious looking blade in his hand. Finn dove down to the ground and pulled his own knife from the man's eye socket. His pike was firmly stuck in Leonard Sparks, so the pocketknife was the only weapon he had to hand. Finn couldn't hope to defeat Bill in hand-to-hand combat. Bill's knife was much longer, and the man himself was taller, his height giving him greater reach.

Bill expected Finn to get to his feet, but Finn chose a different tactic. He rolled toward Bill and with one swift motion used the knife to slash both ankles, grateful that the man wasn't wearing leather boots. Finn didn't wait to see the blood welling above the buckled shoes and soaking the man's hose as he sank to his knees, unable to put any weight on his legs. Finn continued to roll until he was clear of Bill, then jumped to his feet and grabbed one of the burning logs from the fire. He used the log as a club and knocked the man over the head, setting his hair ablaze in the process.

Bill roared, his eyes bugging out of his head in fear and pain and tried to put out the flame. He rolled around on the ground while Finn took the opportunity to relieve him of his weapon. Finn drove the knife into the man's back, sliding it between the ribs and into the heart. Bill's screaming stopped once the knife found its mark and he finally grew still, lying on his stomach by the fire.

Finn didn't spare Bill another thought as he ran toward Sam and began clawing at the rope still tied about his throat. He loosened it as much as he could and pressed his ear to Sam's chest. The heart was still beating, if sluggishly, but Sam didn't appear to be breathing. Finn put his mouth to Sam's and began to force air into his lungs.

"Come on, Sam," he pleaded as he came up for more oxygen. "Breathe."

Finn continued to blow air into Sam's mouth for what felt like an eternity. He expected a great gasp as Sam came to, but Sam remained completely still, his skin clammy and pale in the glow from the fire. It wasn't until a few moments later that Finn realized Sam's chest was rising and falling as he began to draw breath on his own.

"Oh, thank you, Lord," Finn cried. "Sam, can you hear me? Sam!"

But Sam didn't respond. His heartbeat grew a little stronger and he continued to breathe on his own, but his eyes remained firmly closed, his hand limp in Finn's grasp. "Sam, please," Finn begged. "Wake up. Sam!"

Finn let go of Sam's hand and went to his horse. Mr. Mallory had given him a flask years ago and told him to keep it filled with spirits for emergencies. Well, this was an emergency if Finn ever saw one. He pulled out the flask and held it to Sam's lips, dripping some Madeira into his mouth. He hoped the wine would revive him, but Sam remained unconscious. Finn set aside the flask and removed the noose that looked like some grotesque necklace, throwing the rope onto the fire. He watched the hemp fibers begin to curl in the flames as tears blurred his vision. He wiped them angrily away. This was no time to blub. Finn threw a few more logs on the fire, pushed aside the bodies of the dead men, and returned to Sam. He covered him with a blanket and pushed his wadded coat beneath Sam's head. He would keep vigil over Sam for as long as it took, and if the coded message never made it to Washington, then so be it. Sam was his priority, and always would be.

Finn took a few restorative sips of Madeira and tore off a piece of pork with his teeth. He needed to eat to keep up his strength and prevent the Madeira from making him sleepy. Laying Bill's knife by his side, he settled in for the night. He was fairly certain there'd be no more disturbances tonight, but he had to be prepared in case someone came in search of Sparks and his friends. Finn took hold of Sam's hand and whispered into his ear. "I'm here, Sam. You just sleep."

TWENTY-FOUR

Sunlight filtered through the canopy of leaves, casting shafts of pure gold toward the earth. Patches of clear blue were visible through the gaps in the leafy branches and a few wispy white clouds floated across the sky like swathes of fine wool. The air smelled of pine and earth, the heavenly scent tinged with the bitter smell of ashes from the burnt-out fire. A chorus of birdsong erupted somewhere overhead, and the stream gurgled peacefully in the distance.

Sam stared into the light, afraid to look away. He'd never seen anything so beautiful or awe-inspiring. This was the dawn he wasn't meant to have seen; the day he wasn't supposed to have lived long enough to enjoy. His throat felt swollen and raw, and when he tried to swallow, he felt a pain the likes of which he'd never known. His limbs were as floppy as those of a rag doll and refused to move, but he'd never known the happiness he felt at that moment or had been as grateful to be alive. It was a euphoric, and he took a deep breath, the simple action bringing tears of joy to his eyes.

Sam had no idea what happened after the rope had been placed around his neck and his feet left the ground. The sensation of not being able to breathe or find purchase had been so overwhelming that all he felt was panic and terror. Somewhere at the back of his mind, he'd always known that Sparks meant business, but some foolish part of him believed that it was all a game and he'd find a way out of the situation. As long as Finn was out there, Sam felt safe. But Finn never returned, and when the coarse fibers of the rope bit into Sam's skin, he finally realized that he was about to die, and no eleventh-hour miracle would save him.

Sam had come close to death several times since the start of the war, but never this close, and never in such a gruesome manner. Being shot with a pistol or dying of a bayonet wound somehow didn't seem as awful as having the breath choked out of one's body. It was easier to slip away, the soul free, its shell left behind rather than to gasp for breath and thrash about helplessly, suffocating slowly as the eyes bulged from the unbearable pressure building within and the tongue retracting into the throat in a futile effort to draw breath. Sam experimentally moved his tongue. It felt overly large, but it did move, which was a good sign. Finn had managed to save him after all, for the third time since they'd met. Finn! Sam suddenly felt panicked. Where was Finn?

It took unspeakable effort, but Sam managed to move his head a fraction to the right. Finn's inert body lay close to Sam, his breathing even and deep. A long, evil-looking knife was still in Finn's hand, as if he expected to come under attack at any moment. Sam gently squeezed Finn's hand and he woke with a start. Finn looked momentarily confused, but then the events of last night crystalized and he let go of the knife and bent over Sam, peering into his eyes anxiously.

"Finn," Sam croaked.

"Oh, Sam. Thank God." Sam had never seen Finn cry, but tears rolled down his cheeks, dripping onto Sam's face. Finn angrily wiped the tears away with the back of his hand, shamed by such a display of emotion. "I thought I'd lost you," he mumbled.

"Never. Now, stop blubbing," Sam whispered.

"Are you able to stand?" Finn asked.

"Water," Sam whispered.

"Sure, of course, sorry. I should have thought of it myself. Here, let me get some."

Finn sprang to his feet and ran to the stream to get some fresh water for Sam. Sam gulped it down, ignoring the searing pain. Every swallow hurt like hell, but the cool, sweet water tasted heavenly and soothed his swollen throat.

"Can you eat?"

Sam shook his head. The thought of forcing solid food down his throat seemed inconceivable. Perhaps he'd try to eat something later. Sam wrinkled his nose as a foul smell wafted up, stinging his nostrils. Oh, God, he'd pissed himself last night. Suddenly, Sam was no longer happy, but deeply ashamed. He'd allowed the men to creep up on him and take him completely unawares. There were three of them, they must have made noise, but he'd been daydreaming about meeting General Washington and had paid no attention to the sounds of the forest. He'd assumed he was safe, a terrible mistake given what happened to his own father only a few days ago. Thanks to his carelessness, he'd nearly died, and might have cost Finn his life as well. Thank God for Finn's quick thinking.

What did happen? Sam wondered as he tried to sit up. He couldn't manage it on his own, so Finn eased him into a sitting position and propped him up against the trunk of a tree. Sam flinched when he noticed the corpses littering the clearing. Finn had killed them all. Now Finn would have to carry the weight of last night's work on his conscience because of Sam's idiocy. Finn had killed before, as had Sam, but it didn't make taking a life any easier, and no amount of denial or self-delusion could make the nightmares go away or keep the faces of the dead at bay.

"It comes with the territory, Sam," Finn said, seeing the direction of Sam's gaze. "We can't do what we do if we're not prepared to kill or be killed. I feel no remorse, and neither should you."

Sam nodded. Finn was right, of course. No victory was possible without casualties and they'd think no more on the death of the Tories. Sam supposed it would have been the decent thing to bury them, but he could barely muster the strength to stand up, much less dig a grave. Besides, they didn't have a shovel.

"Sam, I think it's time we were on our way. Eventually, someone will come looking for these men and I want to be far away by the time they find them," Finn said as he helped Sam to his feet. Sam's knees buckled, but Finn held him up and pushed him against the tree for support.

"Can you ride?"

"I'll have to," Sam muttered. "But I need a piss first."

It took Finn a moment to understand what Sam was asking. Sam couldn't manage it himself. His hands shook and his legs seemed on the verge of buckling again. Finn untied Sam's laces and pulled his breeches down a bit. Sam cringed with embarrassment, but Finn looked away, giving Sam a moment of privacy while he did his business, then helped him lace up.

"I'm ready," Sam croaked.

"Give me a few minutes. We can't leave them like this," Finn replied, eyeing the corpses.

He used a leafy branch to sweep away the ashes of the fire, obliterating any sign of a campsite. Then he rolled the corpses into a shallow ravine that might have been a stream bed at some point in the not-so-distant past and threw a few leafy branches over the remains. They'd be found eventually, but he wasn't going to make it easy for whoever came looking.

"Come on." Finn walked Sam to his horse. His limbs felt like lead and Finn was sweating profusely by the time Sam was finally in the saddle. He couldn't seem to remain upright, so he leaned against the horse's neck and hugged it for support. They gingerly made their way toward the road. Sam was in no condition to gallop, or even trot, but as long as they were moving, they were going in the right direction.

Finn cast worried glances in Sam's direction and Sam wished he could assure Finn that he was fine, but last night's ordeal had taken a heavy toll on his body. Sam felt weak and sluggish, and any effort at conversation, which had to be conducted in a whisper, set his throat on fire. It would heal in time, but the next few days would be difficult. Sam pushed his discomfort away and dug his heels into the flanks of his horse. The message wouldn't deliver itself.

TWENTY-FIVE
VIRGINIA AUGUST 1628

Valerie slid out of bed and threw a shawl around her shoulders before tiptoeing to Louisa's room. Louisa had kept her vigil by Kit's bedside all night, refusing to take turns. She'd fallen asleep in her chair, her head lolling to one side and her mouth slightly open. It was hard to tell exactly what time it was without the benefit of a clock, but it had to be close to dawn. Kit appeared to be asleep, but even in his sleep his limbs jerked, and his eyes moved rapidly beneath the closed lids as if he were having a nightmare. Valerie didn't need to touch Kit to see that his fever hadn't abated during the night and the swelling had increased, the mottled skin straining against the bandages and splints. There was an underlying smell of pus beneath the unpleasant aromas of sweat and vomit. A bowl of water stood on the bedside table. Louisa had been applying cool compresses to Kit's forehead to relieve the fever. She looked exhausted and defeated, her hair matted, and her gown soiled and sweat-stained.

"He woke up for a bit," Louisa said quietly, alerted to Valerie's presence by the creaking of a floorboard. "At first, he thought I was his sister. He seemed to be arguing with her about something, but then his tone had changed. He sounded heartbroken and contrite. He kept saying that he was sorry for leaving me in England and that he should have taken me to France where I would have been safe."

"Do you know what he meant?" Valerie asked, horrified by how quickly Kit's condition had deteriorated.

"Not at first, but then I realized it wasn't me he was talking to. It was his first wife, the one who had died while he was in France. He never mentions her, not since that first crossing from England. I thought he was over her," Louisa wailed. Her face was blotchy from crying, and her hair stood on end, having escaped all its pins. Louisa seemed to be coming undone before Valerie's eyes.

"Oh, Lou, of course he is over her. He loves you with all his heart, but he is not himself right now. His mind is playing tricks on him, and perhaps he still feels some residual guilt over her death. That doesn't mean he doesn't love you."

Louisa nodded and blew her nose delicately, but her eyes were still streaming. "I guess. I just can't bear it, Val. He didn't recognize me when I tried to comfort him. He stared at me as if I were a stranger. I gave him some laudanum to ease his suffering and I was glad when he finally stopped talking and fell asleep. I was jealous of a woman who's been dead for over a decade and angry at a man who might not live to see the end of the week," Louisa sobbed. "Oh, Val, I'm so scared. He is going to die; I can feel it." Louisa wrapped her arms about her middle as she rocked back and forth, lost in her misery. "I can't lose him," she moaned over and over. "I can't lose him. I can't bear it. I feel so helpless."

Louisa's whole body shook with here sobs. Valerie swallowed back her own tears as she watched her sister. She could understand what Louisa was going through; she'd lost Finlay after only a few months of marriage, and then two of her children, but this was no time to fall apart. Kit needed her; he needed them all to keep their wits about them.

Valerie grabbed Louisa by the shoulders, forcing her to look to meet her gaze. "Now, you listen to me. Kit needs you, and your children need you. I know you're terrified, but you must pull yourself together. Alec and I will not be here today, so you'll have to hold down the fort."

"What do you mean you won't be here? I need you," Louisa moaned. "I can't do this on my own."

"Lou, I have an idea. It's a long shot, and it might not work, so I don't want to get your hopes up, but I must try. Please, don't ask me any questions. Just do everything you can to bring Kit's fever down. Keep applying cold compresses to his forehead and put some vinegar-soaked rags into his armpits and on the soles of his feet. The vinegar will help to draw the fever out. And get as much liquid as you can into him. He needs to stay hydrated. Do not let Doctor Jacobson near him with that saw. Just give me one day, Lou."

"All right, I won't ask any questions. But please, don't stay away too long." They both remembered what had happened when Valerie lost the time-travel device. They'd been separated for three months at a time when Louisa had needed Valerie the most, and neither of them had known if they'd ever see each other again.

"I won't. Now, let me sit with him for a bit. Get some sleep before you collapse. He needs you to stay strong."

"Okay. I'm bone-weary. I just need an hour. Come get me if I don't wake on my own," Louisa said as she pushed to her feet. She moved like an old woman, her shoulders stooped in defeat and her gait slow, but she wiped her eyes and patted her hair into place, which was a good sign.

"Don't worry, Lou. I'm wide awake. I'll look after him."

Valerie reached for the jug of vinegar and soaked several rags. The room filled with the acrid smell, but Valerie ignored it and went about her task, placing the rags in strategic locations around Kit's body. When she'd lived in the twenty-first century, she'd never used vinegar for anything but salad. Who knew that something as simple and common as vinegar had so many uses? Valerie utilized it not only to preserve certain foods, but to get rid of lice, reduce fevers, disinfect, get stains out, and wash windows. She hated the smell, but a little discomfort was a small price to pay for bringing down Kit's fever by even a few degrees. She'd reapplied the cloths several times before Kit began to breathe a little easier and his color grew healthier in the light of the candle.

Valerie pulled aside the coverlet and examined Kit's leg. Doctor Jacobson had changed the bandage, but the new one was moist with a sickly combination of pus and blood. It was crusted in places, but the spot right over the wound was soaked, which meant that the wound was leaking. Kit's leg was grotesquely swollen, the skin mottled purple. The wound had festered; there was no doubt.

TWENTY-SIX

An unnatural hush hung over the house as Louisa trudged up the stairs in the wake of Doctor Jacobson. Minnie had taken the children outside since they kept asking to see their father and needed to be distracted while Doctor Jacobson conducted his examination. They were tearful and upset, but as much as Louisa longed to comfort them, she felt numb with worry and lack of sleep. They'd gone through a jug of vinegar and had fed Kit at least a gallon of beef tea to keep up his strength and flush out the infection, but these homeopathic remedies were no match for the infection that was raging inside him. Louisa couldn't be sure, but it was possible that his leg had been lacerated by a rusty nail, or something else had gotten into his bloodstream while he lay injured on that dock.

Doctor Jacobson had not bothered with pleasantries this time. Even he realized that anything other than professionalism would be grossly inappropriate on a day when the woman he admired might become a widow. Louisa did not say anything as they entered the room. The smell and Kit's appearance spoke for themselves. Doctor Jacobson turned to Louisa and studied her for a long moment before speaking.

"Lady Sheridan, perhaps you should wait outside," he suggested courteously.

"I would prefer to remain."

"My lady... Louisa, please. This might be too upsetting for you," the doctor insisted.

"Doctor Jacobson, I have been nursing my husband all night. Nothing I see at this juncture will surprise me. Please proceed," Louisa replied.

"As you wish."

Kit was perfectly still, lost in an opium-induced slumber. The laudanum was the only thing keeping him from feeling extreme pain and allowing him to rest. When Kit had come to during the night, he was jolted by a pain so severe that Louisa had immediately administered more laudanum to mitigate his suffering. She was afraid of giving him too much but helping him cope with the pain seemed more urgent. The last dose had been hours ago, and another dose would be needed soon.

Doctor Jacobson pulled back the coverlet and stared at Kit's leg. He then gently pressed his fingers close to the wound and watched as thick pus began to ooze through the linen bandage. The doctor didn't need to see any more. He replaced the blanket and turned his attention to Kit's hand and face. The hand was still swollen, but there was no sign of infection since the skin had never been punctured. The splint kept Kit from moving his wrist, so it was safe to assume that it was in the process of healing. Kit's face was still puffy and flushed, but the cuts on his face had not festered. Doctor Jacobson finished his examination and turned to Louisa.

"Lady Sheridan, the leg needs to come off."

"No."

"Please, listen to me. If I don't operate immediately, the putrefaction will spread and enter his lordship's bloodstream. Once that happens, he will die. Amputation is the only possible way to save his life, if it isn't too late already. I should have insisted on doing it yesterday to prevent further contamination."

Louisa shook her head stubbornly. She knew what the doctor was saying was true. Amputation was the only way to curb the spread of infection in the seventeenth century. There were no medicines strong enough to kill bacteria since penicillin would not be invented for hundreds of years yet. If the doctor operated, Kit would most likely die, but if he didn't, Kit would die for sure. And if Louisa decided to wait until Valerie and Alec came back, it might be too late to try to save Kit. She literally held his life in her hands, and she had to decide. Valerie said that her idea was a long shot. What if it failed? What if Kit's infection turned septic? Could she afford to wait?

Louisa rearranged her face into an expression of calm when Kit opened his eyes. His gaze was unfocused, but his head instantly turned in her direction. Kit was obviously in terrible pain, but he bore it silently as he looked at her.

"Kit?" she called to him gently. "Kit, can you hear me?"

Kit nodded and reached for her. Louisa grasped his good hand and held it tight. It was hot and dry, another indication that the fever was still raging.

"Kit, Doctor Jacobson wants to amputate your leg," Louisa said. Her voice shook, but she tried not to sound as terrified as she felt.

"Where's Alec?" Kit asked.

"Eh, he's not here."

"When will he be back?" Kit mumbled. Louisa wasn't sure why Kit wanted Alec, but this was no time to argue with him.

"He'll be back later. Probably in the afternoon."

"You can amputate then," Kit whispered.

"We can't afford to wait that long, your lordship," Doctor Jacobson interjected, but Kit shook his head.

"Not until Alec is back."

"Kit, please," Louisa pleaded. She'd been prepared to wait

for Valerie and Alec to return, but now all she could think of was saving Kit's life. The doctor was right; they couldn't afford to wait. With every hour that passed the infection grew stronger. Louisa couldn't bear to think of the surgery, so instead tried to focus on the result. Kit would lose a leg, but he'd gain his life. She would not lose him. He would not die.

"Lady Sheridan, I am going to get the saw from my saddlebag. Please administer a strong dose of laudanum to your husband. I will also require the assistance of your cook and maid. We'll need all hands on deck, so to speak," he said, smiling for the first time. "I will not let him die, Louisa," Doctor Jacobson said, as if he were giving Louisa a great gift. He patted her on the hand and left the room.

Louisa reached for the vial of laudanum, but Kit grabbed her by the hand. "Not until Alec returns," he said, his tone forceful.

"Kit, there's no time to lose. I won't let you die."

"And I won't let you watch me get butchered. I won't be able to bear the amputation if you're in the room. I will wait for Alec. And you will take the children and go into Jamestown for a few hours. I will NOT have them hear me scream as my leg is sawed off. Do you hear me? Now, ask Doctor Jacobson to leave."

"I hear you, but I don't agree. We can't afford to wait for Alec. I will not ask Doctor Jacobson to leave." It wasn't until that moment that Louisa realized that she'd made her decision. She wasn't going to wait for Valerie and Alec to return. There was too much at stake.

"Louisa, you will obey me in this," Kit said, his voice rising an octave despite the pain, or maybe because of it. "Send the doctor away."

TWENTY-SEVEN

The day was sunny and bright, last night's wind having died down by morning. The sky was a vast expanse of endless blue, and the trees formed a canopy overhead as Alec and Valerie trotted down a wooded track. Despite the beautiful weather, they were both in a dark mood. Kit's situation was dire, which made Valerie's mission that much more vital.

"So, are you going to tell me where we are going?" Alec asked once they were a mile or so from the house. "You are not normally this secretive."

"I'm not being secretive. I'm just terrified that my idea won't work," Valerie replied as they made their way toward Jamestown. "After living in this century for so long, I've grown superstitious."

Alec looked at her in surprise. "And you think that telling me will somehow invite bad luck?" He looked so hurt that Valerie instantly relented.

"No, I didn't mean it that way. Of course I don't think you'll invite bad luck. I'm just afraid to say it out loud for fear of realizing how far-fetched my plan really is."

Alec brought his horse closer to Valerie's and reached for

her hand. "Valerie, no matter how far-fetched or ridiculous your plan might be, it's motivated by love and a desperate desire to help. Even if you fail, it's still better than doing nothing."

Valerie nodded in acknowledgement, but her insides twisted with unease. Alec was right. It was worth a shot, but would Louisa wait for them to come back? Should she wait? Kit was in a bad way, and perhaps they were condemning him to death by asking Louisa to refuse the amputation. It was time to run the plan past Alec and see if there was any merit to it, since it wasn't too late to turn around and return to Rosewood Manor.

"I am going to try to get antibiotics for Kit," Valerie blurted out.

"In Jamestown?" Alec asked, his eyebrows rising comically.

"No, in Williamsburg."

Alec reined in his horse for a moment and gave Valerie a hard stare. "Williamsburg doesn't exist yet. You mean you are going to the future. You could have told me."

"I am telling you now. I know we agreed that we wouldn't time-travel except to visit Finn, but this is a dire emergency, so I must try," Valerie snapped.

"I understand, and I am in full support, but how do you intend to get antibiotics? Don't you need a prescription from a doctor? Health insurance? Identification? Money? How can you pull this off?"

"I have money," Valerie replied. "I had three hundred dollars left over from the money I withdrew while in 2010. I just couldn't bring myself to dispose of it, so I put it in a safe place, just in case something should ever come up—something like this."

Alec nodded, agreeing with the wisdom of her decision, but he still looked perplexed. "All right, but even if you can bypass the issue of medical insurance and identification and pay for the medication in cash, how will you get a doctor to prescribe an antibiotic? You are not ill."

"No, but I will be," Valerie replied cryptically. She dug her heels into the flanks of her horse, and it took off at a gallop, forestalling any further conversation. Alec followed suit, impressed and mystified in equal parts.

It took them the better part of three hours to get to the point where modern-day Williamsburg would be. It would have been less than a half hour by car, speeding down the Colonial Parkway, but on horseback their progress was slow. There was no direct road, so they had to follow tracks that led them in the general direction of future Williamsburg. Had they had the coordinates, they could have just entered them into the watch and pressed a button, but since Williamsburg wasn't even on the map yet, finding exact coordinates was a problem.

"I think it's right around here," Valerie said as she took in the fragrant meadow surrounded by dense woods. A gentle breeze rippled the tall grass, and the sound of birdsong filled the air. There was nothing nearby, not even a homestead.

"How can you be sure this is the right spot?" Alec asked. They'd gone to Williamsburg once before when his appendix was about to rupture but he couldn't recall precisely where they had left from.

"As long as I wind up somewhere in the center of town, I should be fine." Valerie saved the coordinates of the meadow for the return trip, then began her preparations. She undressed down to her shift and shoes.

"Give me your belt," Valerie demanded.

Alec removed his belt and handed it to her. Valerie belted the shift, then yanked off her cap, pulled out the pins securing her hair, and shook it out until it hung about her shoulders in dark waves.

"Not very fashionable, but at least I don't look like a Colonial housefrau," Valerie joked. "What do you think?"

"I think you look positively disreputable. I know you'll fit right in, but it still shocks me to see a woman strutting around in her undergarments."

Valerie smiled and put on the time-travel watch, checking twice that the strap was secure. She then produced a bundle of food, a book, and the magnifying glass Alec used for reading from the saddlebag and handed the lot to Alec. "I brought you something to eat and read while you wait. I hope to be back in a few hours."

"Are you sure you don't want me to go with you?" Alec asked, reviving the argument they'd been having for the past few hours.

"Alec, if I don't come back by nightfall, you must return home to help Louisa. She'll need you for the surgery. Someone will have to hold Kit down while Doctor Jacobson operates, and I can't bear the thought of Louisa having to witness such savage butchery. If I return and you're not here, I will simply make my way back home, as long as no one helps themselves to my horse. Now, can I go?"

"Valerie, please be careful and come back soon. If you're not back by nightfall, I'll go mad with worry thinking that something terrible has befallen you," Alec said as he accepted the bundle.

"Alec, I promise to return before then. Wish me luck."

"Good luck. Be safe."

"I will." Valerie gave him a sound kiss and set the watch coordinates to the desired time. Alec watched as his wife vanished into thin air.

TWENTY-EIGHT

Alec sat down and leaned against a stout oak, thinking he'd read for a while, but his mind wasn't on the poems of John Dunne. Instead, he studied the sky above, watching the fluffy clouds lazily sail across the deep blue sky and obscure the sun before moving on again. The forest was alive with birdsong, but there were no human sounds and Alec was deeply aware of his solitude. He couldn't recall the last time he'd been on his own like this. The house was always full of people: children laughing and playing, servants going about their business, Valerie and Louisa gossiping and laughing over some private joke, and Charles coming by at all hours as if he still lived at Rosewood Manor. There was always someone about, and truthfully, Alec didn't mind. The noise and activity kept him from becoming too maudlin, as he was right now. Silence forced one to think, and to remember.

Over the past two years, since they'd returned from the future, Alec found himself turning inward and often thinking about the past. He supposed it came with the territory; he was going to be fifty this year. In modern times, fifty was the new forty, as Valerie liked to remind him, but in the seventeenth century, fifty was more like the new seventy. He was in reasonably good health, but he was no longer a young man, as his failing vision reminded him daily. There was so much he still wanted to do, to see, but most of all, he wanted to see Finn and his family.

Alec closed his eyes and tried to picture Finn's face, but instead, he saw another face, another Finn. His brother's green eyes smiled at him from the distant past, his lips curving into a sly smile as he tried to talk Alec into some mischief that would send their father into fits. Alec often found himself talking to Finn in his head, telling him about things that happened and asking for his advice.

After all, Finn should have a say in matters that concerned his son and grandchildren. Oh, how he missed his brother, and Rose, too. Having Jenny about had eased the ache a bit, but Jenny was gone now too, living in far-away Scotland with a man Alec barely knew. Cameron was the type of man he would have chosen for his niece: smart, resourceful, and most of all, loyal. Alec would have welcomed him into the family, had Jenny only spoken up before Cameron had decided to run away after becoming hand-fast with Jenny and promising to send for her.

The family was scattered, with Jenny in Scotland, Kit and Louisa planning to return to England, should Kit recover, Finn and Abbie in the eighteenth century, and Charles over in Jamestown, but somehow further away than everyone else. Alec wished he and Charles could enjoy the kind of relationship he'd had with Finlay, but Charles was just too selfish and self-serving for his own good. And, of course, there was the age difference. They were nearly twenty years apart in age and life experience. There was so much Charles didn't know, so much Alec could never tell him.

Alec had tried so hard to keep the family together, but there was no fighting against the tides of time. And now he wanted to do something for himself. He wanted to go live near his son in the eighteenth century. Given everything that had happened over the past few years, the time was right. The only real obstacle was Louisa. Alec prayed with all his heart that Kit would recover from his injuries, but if he didn't, Louisa would have no reason to remain behind, unless she wished to see her son as the new Lord Sheridan. Perhaps Valerie could be persuaded to part from her sister with the promise that she could use the time-travel watch to visit Louisa once a year.

Alec sighed with frustration. Valerie loved Finn with every fiber of her being, but the bond she shared with her sister surpassed even that love. She needed Louisa in a way that a body needed sustenance. They held each other up, brought each other comfort, and understood each other on a level neither Alec nor Kit could ever hope to achieve. They'd shared a life in the twenty-first century, a life that wasn't as fantastical to Alec as it had once seemed, but still one he couldn't fully understand. Having lived in the future for a few months, he did miss the comforts he'd come to appreciate, especially access to information and modern healthcare. Had Kit had an accident in the future, he would undoubtedly survive. He would have the best medical care, medicines to ease his suffering, and X-rays to check exactly where his bones were broken.

Alec himself was only still alive because Valerie had taken him to a hospital when his appendix had flared up. He'd felt virtually no pain after the surgery, and the doctors and nurses had been kind and knowledgeable. Yes, the future had its benefits, but there was much he didn't miss, like chaos, lack of faith, and a complete absence of morality and discretion. He was content to live in a world where people didn't leak their own sex tapes or post selfies on the Internet in a desperate bid for attention. He liked order and knowing right from wrong. Perhaps his view of the world was a little too black and white, but it made it easier for him to navigate the journey he was on and live with the decisions he'd made and was about to make.

He wasn't sure what would happen, but he could feel it in his bones, change was coming, and it would affect them all.

TWENTY-NINE

Valerie looked around, eager to get her bearings. She was in a small park surrounded by private houses on three sides. The fourth side opened onto a busy thoroughfare, the cars crawling in rush-hour traffic. A city bus rumbled past and belched a cloud of exhaust. Valerie headed toward the street, passing a playground on the way. Several toddlers happily ran around, vigilantly guarded by their parents, and several people hurried past on their way to work. Valerie suddenly felt overwhelmed and sat down on a bench to catch her breath.

She knew she was being silly, but after years of living in the seventeenth century, she felt terribly out of place. She glanced at the passersby, but no one was staring at her, and no one cared where she'd come from or where she was going. That was one major difference between this time and the past. In Jamestown, everyone was like a specimen under a microscope, studied and analyzed until one was practically paralyzed with indecision. The rules of the colony were strict, any transgression judged harshly, and most often, unfairly. How nice it was to be invisible, surrounded by people who didn't care if you'd sinned or blasphemed at the very least. Here, people watched TV for entertainment, not their neighbors, although to some people snooping came naturally. Some things never changed.

Valerie finally summoned the courage to leave the park. She'd walked all over Williamsburg with Alec when they had been stranded two years ago and hoped to see something that looked familiar, but the landmarks didn't ring any bells. She continued to walk toward what she thought might be the center of town, and eventually came upon an intersection she recognized. Valerie had a specific destination in mind and hoped she'd have no trouble finding it now that she knew where she was.

The area became seedier as she continued to walk, prosperous houses and shops giving way to old, clapboard homes fronted by cracked sidewalks and patchy lawns. The businesses and shops were lackluster, and there were fewer major chains and more mom-and-pop establishments that had seen better days. There were more signs in foreign languages, and the people weren't as well-dressed. Children of varying ages played on the sidewalks, running around and laughing as they chased a ball or each other. School would probably start within the next week or two, but for now, the children needed to keep busy while their parents went about the business of earning a living. The older children watched the younger ones, teenage girls acting like moms instead of older sisters. The area reminded Valerie of many such neighborhoods in New York, and she suddenly felt homesick for the city she'd left behind. There was virtually no diversity in Jamestown, which made people that much more convinced of their superiority and even more closed-minded and judgmental than they already were.

Valerie finally spotted the place she was looking for. It was a squat white building with a small parking lot at the back, bordered by a derelict fence held up by several scraggly bushes. The blinds were drawn against the morning sun, but the signs in the window were clearly visible.

Walk-ins welcome
We accept all forms of insurance, Medicaid, and Medicare.
Se Habla Español
Russian, Korean, and Chinese translators Available upon request

Valerie had seen plenty of places like this in New York. They were legitimate medical offices with licensed doctors, but they were in communities where some of the patients weren't strictly legal. As long as the bills were paid, no one asked too many probing questions. After all, if people needed medical help, it would be wrong to turn them away, so instead, the doctors practiced medicine instead of politics. Valerie pulled a handful of ragweed out of her leather pouch and held it to her nose until she began to sneeze, then rubbed some between her fingers and onto her eyes. She'd suffered from hay fever when she'd lived in the future, but it hadn't bothered her as much in the past. Perhaps the ragweed had changed over the centuries but holding it directly to her face did have the desired effect. No doctor would give her an antibiotic for hay fever, but she had a plan.

Tossing away the weeds, Valerie walked into the office. The reception area was half-full. There were several women with young children to whom they spoke to in Spanish. An Asian woman sat in the corner. She looked clammy and pale despite her dark skin, so Valerie made a mental note not to sit anywhere near her; she was clearly ill.

"How can I help you?" a young black receptionist asked. She had long dreadlocks dyed in different shades of blue and purple. *Very artistic*, Valerie thought as she admired the woman's hair.

"I'd like to see a doctor."

"Do you have insurance?"

"No, I'll pay cash." The woman looked her up and down, then pushed a clipboard toward her. "Fill this out. The cost of the visit is fifty dollars."

Valerie took the clipboard and sat down. It asked for some basic information such as name, address, telephone number, and past medical history. Valerie filled out only the name portion and the medical history. It seemed safe enough to put down her name, and the medical history was accurate, as far as she could remember.

The receptionist took back the clipboard, scanned the information and turned to Valerie in dismay. "You left half the form blank."

"I'm sort of in between addresses right now," Valerie replied apologetically.

"Well, do you have a contact number?"

"Not at the moment," Valerie mumbled, hoping the woman would feel sorry for her and stop asking questions.

"I see. All right. The doctor will be with you shortly."

Valerie sat down on a hard, plastic chair in a bright shade of orange and reached for a well-thumbed magazine. It seemed strange to be reading about Botox and diets when she lived in a time when women looked old before they reached thirty. Dieting and beauty regimens were the last thing on their minds as they toiled day and night just to survive and keep their families healthy and sufficiently fed. Valerie reflected on the superficial nature of modern society, but still snuck a peek at herself in the mirror hanging on one of the walls.

Did she look older than her age? Had she still lived in this century, she'd color her hair to hide the gray and have facials, manicures, and a more varied diet, but she didn't think she looked too bad despite the puffiness she'd just induced. In her current life, she consumed no artificial preservatives or sweeteners, her meat wasn't pumped full of hormones, and her eggs were organic, as were the chickens who laid them. She hardly ever ate sweets or foods without nutritional value. Physical work kept her trim and fit without the benefit of going to the gym.

They had few snacks, but Valerie and Louisa had taught Barbara how to make popcorn and granola. Barbara had found it strange at first, but now she often made a bowl of popcorn to take home to Fred, and she quite enjoyed sprinkling granola over the homemade yogurt she often ate for breakfast. The children loved it, too. They'd never had potato chips, candy, or even ice cream. Their only sweet treat was the occasional cake baked with molasses for sweetness.

"Valerie Whitfield," a nurse called out as she came out into reception. Valerie sprang to her feet and followed the nurse into an examining room. The room was a bit shabby, but clean, with several posters taped to the walls, touting the perils of smoking and drinking during pregnancy, the need to practice safe sex to avoid HIV, and reminding the patients that flu shots were available.

"How are you today?" the nurse asked as she invited Valerie to sit on the examining table. She was an older woman with a salt-and-pepper bob that looked out of joint with her youthful face. She had bright blue eyes that looked at Valerie kindly. Perhaps the nurse sensed Valerie's nervousness, or perhaps she just felt like having a chat, but her easy manner helped Valerie relax.

"Beautiful morning. I'm glad the rain has stopped, although my little garden appreciated the watering. I keep meaning to do it, but something always gets in the way, and the next thing you know everything looks sad and dried up. Do you like to garden?"

"Yes," Valerie replied. She had no idea what the weather might have been like until that morning, so didn't comment on it.

"I can't wait for fall. My favorite season," the nurse said as she scribbled something in Valerie's new chart.

"I like fall, too."

"Nothing like sleeping with the windows open," the nurse said as she fitted Valerie with a blood pressure cuff.

"I'll just take your blood pressure, hon." She did, then pointed to the scale in the corner. "On the scale, please." Valerie stepped on with some trepidation. She hadn't weighed herself in two years. She was dismayed to note that she'd gained seven pounds.

"The doctor will be right in."

Thankfully, the doctor didn't make her wait. He came in a few minutes later. He was an attractive man in his fifties, with jet-black hair silvered at the temples, and dark, soulful eyes. He had a slight Spanish accent and spoke in a low, melodious voice that made him sound seductive.

"Good morning, Valerie. I'm Doctor Martinez. How can I help you today? Have you been unwell?"

"I think I have a sinus infection," Valerie replied, trying to sound congested.

"Do you get them often?" the doctor asked as he came over to examine her.

"At least once a year. I have terrible pressure just here," Valerie complained as she touched the sides of her nose.

"Nasal discharge?"

"Yes, thick and mucousy," Valerie replied. The doctor touched her face gently.

"Does it hurt when I touch you here?"

"Yes. And I have terrible headaches and a cough, but mostly when I sleep. Back drip," Valerie added helpfully.

The doctor asked her to open her mouth and peered into the depths of her throat before listening to her lungs.

"Well, your lungs are clear, but your nasal passages are

swollen, and your eyes are puffy. Do you suffer from hay fever?" Doctor Martinez asked.

"No." Valerie hated lying, but this was for Kit, she reminded herself.

The doctor made some notes and turned back to her, prescription in hand. "I'll give you a script for Z-Pack. You only have to take it for five days, but it works for a full ten, like a regular antibiotic regimen."

"Thank you, Doctor."

"If you need the prescription filled quickly, there's a pharmacy just down the block." He gave her a sympathetic look. He wouldn't say it out loud, but he was giving her to understand that they would fill the prescription without asking too many questions as a major drugstore chain might.

"Feel better, Valerie."

Valerie clutched the precious prescription as she sprinted down the block to the pharmacy. The woman behind the counter simply took the script and told her to wait twenty minutes while she filled it. Valerie felt a bit guilty about lying to the doctor, but it had been worth it. She knew from experience that mentioning certain key phrases would manipulate the doctor's diagnosis. A sinus infection always required an antibiotic, and if she complained of pain in her sinuses, headache, pressure, back-drip and congestion, the doctor would buy into it without looking too deeply. He had to take her word for it since there were no obvious physical symptoms other than swelling and congestion.

Valerie paid for the medicine and stored it in her pouch. She was ready to return, but not before she did one more thing. It was almost lunchtime, so Valerie retraced her steps, looking for the McDonald's she'd seen earlier. She would go back to the past soon enough, but not before she had one decadent meal. She had plenty of money left, so she ordered a Big Mac and fries, a Coke, and a hot fudge ice-cream sundae. She'd probably have a terrible stomachache after she ate all that food, but she didn't care. She wanted it so bad it hurt.

Valerie forced herself to eat slowly and enjoy every bite rather than inhaling it as she was tempted to do. It tasted so good after the bland food she'd lived on for the past two years. She was ready to burst after she finished her burger and fries, but she wasn't about to forego the ice cream. She took a few spoonfuls before pushing the sundae away. It tasted sickeningly sweet after a diet of almost no sugar, and she felt a rush that made her heart beat faster. It was time to end her binge and return to Alec, who was probably going mad with worry.

Valerie patted her pouch, smiling at the feel of the medicine box inside it and the other item she'd picked up at the pharmacy —a surprise for Alec. It broke her heart to see him using a magnifying glass to read, and she knew it made him feel self-conscious. He could still see large print, but not the small letters of the books he loved or the figures in his ledger. All he needed was a pair of magnifiers, and she'd picked one up at the drugstore. Valerie had no idea what prescription Alec might need, but she chose glasses that magnified significantly—+4. Better too strong, than too weak. He'd have to hide them from the rest of the household, but at least he'd be able to use them in private. Valerie threw away the remnants of her meal and headed toward the exit. She was ready. She only hoped she wasn't too late.

THIRTY
VIRGINIA AUGUST 1781

Finn's concern for Sam increased as the morning wore on. Sam had been far from well when he woke but considering what he'd endured, he was as well as could be expected, if visibly shaken. Thankfully, Bill hadn't yanked on the rope harder or Sam's neck might have broken, and he would have died instantly. Sam had been spared, but he was in no condition to travel. He could barely stay atop his horse and had become more withdrawn and confused as the hours passed.

Sam's hands shook and his gaze was glazed and unfocused. He hadn't been able to eat anything due to his swollen throat, but Finn did manage to get some ale down him about an hour ago.

"Sam? Are you all right?" Finn asked yet again. Of course Sam wasn't all right, but Finn had no idea what to do or how to help him.

"Right as rain," Sam croaked, his attempt at a smile turning into a grimace of pain.

"Will you take a drink?"

Sam shook his head. "Hurts," he mouthed, then turned his eyes back to the road that wound into the distance like a velvety brown ribbon. They were traveling through the countryside, the pastoral idyll uninterrupted by anything other than the occasional barking of a dog or the bleating of a goat from some distant homestead. The world around them seemed deceptively safe, the landscape undisturbed by the war that had been raging for the past six years. Finn hoped they'd make good time today, but Sam's horse was just ambling along as Sam held the reins in his slack hands and stared at the horizon as if he'd never seen it before.

Finn knew nothing of healing, but it didn't take a medical man to see that Sam was suffering from some sort of aftershock. The euphoria of being alive had worn off and now his body and mind were dealing with the trauma of near-death. Finn had never come as close to dying as Sam had, but he knew what it was like to feel unbearably alive, blood singing in his veins and the possible consequences of his actions nothing more than pesky flies to be shooed away. He also knew what happened once the high wore off. The shakes set in, and the endless thoughts of what could have happened had things gone wrong began to chase each other through the corridors of the mind, like rats trapped in a tiny space.

That first night, after they'd rescued Abbie from the gallows, Finn had been overcome with the enormity of what they'd managed to pull off, not to mention that they'd lost Sam in the process. It took weeks for the nightmares to stop and for his mind to accept that they'd saved Abbie and Sam had survived his injury and managed to escape from the British fort, with Susanna in tow. But the strain of those weeks had left its mark on all of them. Finn couldn't ignore what Sam was going through and pretend that everything was all right now that they were on their way again. Sam needed to come to terms with what had happened, but Finn had no idea how to help him. What he did know was that he couldn't carry out his mission and look after Sam at the same time. He had to make a choice, and he had to make it before they reached the next settlement.

Finn had traveled down this road once before and knew that there was a small Quaker hamlet a few miles north. The Quakers were self-sufficient, only venturing to the nearest town if they needed something they couldn't manufacture themselves. They were kind and peaceful people and had offered Finn a hot meal and bed for the night. They'd even given him a bundle of food for the road, wishing him a good journey and inviting him to come back again should he be passing their way. Finn grabbed the reins of Sam's horse and dug his heels into the flanks of his mare, his decision made.

THIRTY-ONE

Sam hardly noticed when they stopped. It had to be around midday, since the sun was riding high in the sky, but he couldn't be sure; he'd lost all track of time over the past few hours. He tried to focus on what was happening, but his mind wouldn't comply. He felt as if he were drunk, but this sensation was not quite as pleasant. Sam felt removed from both Finn and his surroundings, lost in a fog that refused to lift. At times, he thought he heard Susanna saying something to him, but she wasn't there. His imagination was playing tricks on him. He thought he'd heard his father too, but he was sure his father was at home.

Finn helped Sam to dismount and led him into a house with the help of a young man Sam didn't know. The house was two-storied and spacious, with several outbuildings behind it. There was a woman inside, her forehead creased with anxiety as she took in Sam's appearance and gestured toward a chair. Her husband, if that's who he was, seemed friendly and tried to talk to him, but Sam couldn't grasp the meaning of the words, understanding only that these people meant him no harm. Finn settled Sam into a chair while he spoke to the young couple. He seemed to know them, but Sam couldn't be sure. He battled the fog as he tried to concentrate, needing to understand what was happening.

"Master Hammer, my friend is unwell and can't travel any farther," Finn explained. "I must be on my way as I have urgent business in Philadelphia, but I will be back in three days' time, four at the most. I will pay you to look after him until then," Finn said. He sounded almost as if he were pleading, but the man, who was young and fair but dressed all in black, smiled warmly.

"There's no need to pay us, Friend Finn. It is our Christian duty to help a man in need. We will look after thy friend. He will be safe here with us."

"Don't worry," the young woman chimed in. "I grew up with seven brothers. I know something of caring for young men. I will take good care of him."

"With all due respect, Mistress Hammer, this is a little different. Sam had an accident that nearly killed him. He hasn't been right since. This is not some common ailment."

"Thy friend is in the hands of God, Friend Finn, but a little peace and quiet will soothe his soul, and we will look after his body," the woman replied. "He seems strong and healthy. Perhaps all he needs is a few days' rest."

Sam couldn't quite grasp what they were talking about, but suddenly felt a tightening in his chest. His heart seemed to be beating faster and faster and breathing became even more difficult than before. He gasped for breath as he clutched at the neckcloth that seemed to be choking him. Sam tried to focus, but his thoughts were like mice scurrying in the rafters. He reached out to catch one by the tail, but it eluded him, probably because he was so dizzy.

Sam tried to hold on to even one coherent thought but couldn't. The mice kept running, hundreds of them, making that squeaking sound as they tried to escape from him. Sam tried to stand but felt the kiss of the cold hard floor as he collapsed onto his side and rolled onto his back, still gasping for air. He couldn't breathe, or think, or hold back the darkness that was coming for him.

"He's having a fit," the woman cried as she pushed something soft beneath Sam's head. "Eli, do something."

Sam gagged when something bitter and foul-smelling found its way into his mouth. The woman was speaking, but he couldn't understand a word. All he saw was the opening and closing of her mouth. The bitter liquid made him ill but didn't do anything to stop the convulsions. His legs bounced on the floor, making a terrible racket as the heels of his boots banged against the wood.

"Sam. Sam, listen to me," Finn was saying as he bent over him, but Sam couldn't hear him. He was spinning out of control, his mind a vortex of exploding color and sound.

Sam felt a cool cloth on his forehead as the woman tried to speak to him. "Try to calm down, Friend Sam. Thee is in no danger. I gave thee something to calm thee down. It's an extract of valerian root. It will make thee feel better. Try to relax and allow the fit to pass."

Sam tried to hold on to her words, but they were like bullets, rolling around in his brain the way shot rolled on the table when his father let the girls play with the lead balls after they had cooled.

"Sue," Sam cried out in a hoarse whisper. "Sue, help me."

"'Tis Mary, Friend Sam. Let me help thee."

Mary took his hand in hers and began to massage it gently. The gesture was oddly soothing, and Sam began to calm down. Maybe it was the valerian, but his heartrate gradually slowed down, his thoughts becoming more focused. Mary went to loosen his neckcloth, but Sam gently moved her hand away. She couldn't see the terrible bruising on his neck. Even a Quaker might refuse to help a man who'd just escaped death by hanging. His presence might bring danger to them and their entire community. Sam could hardly tell Mary that they were couriers for the Continental Army and had just killed three supporters of the king, leaving their bodies to rot in the woods. It had been self-defense, but in the eyes of strangers, murder was murder.

"Sam, are you all right?" Finn asked as he knelt next to Sam. "What happened?"

"I don't know. I couldn't stop it, Finn," Sam whispered. "It was blind panic, and it had me in its grip."

"I know. You just rest. Mary and Eli will look after you until I return. Sam, you know what I must do, and I can't manage it if I don't leave you behind."

"Go, Finn. I'll be here when you return."

Finn brushed back Sam's hair and kissed his forehead the way his mother used to do when he was small. "I will be back for you as soon as I can. You will be safe here. This is a Quaker settlement, and they are non-political. They will look after you."

"I understand. I don't want to hold you back. Give my regards to Ralph."

"I will. Now, you just rest. I can't bring you back to Sue in this condition. She'll eat my liver for breakfast."

Sam tried to smile. "Are you saying my wife is unreasonable?"

"I'm saying that your wife will crucify anyone who hurts you or fails to keep you from harm, and I've failed you, Sam."

"You haven't failed me, you idiot. You saved my life. Now go before you make me blub. I feel foolish enough already."

Finn got to his feet and shook hands with the Quaker couple. "I thank you," he said. "I won't forget your kindness."

"Go with God, Friend."

Sam closed his eyes, not because he was upset Finn was leaving but because he didn't want anyone to see his tears. For the first time in his life, he felt completely broken, as if he were beyond repair.

THIRTY-TWO
VIRGINIA AUGUST 1628

It was stifling despite the open window, the air thick with unpleasant odors. Dense clouds blanketed the sky and leached all light from the room as thunder rumbled in the distance. The patch of sky outside the window looked low and threatening, a storm ready to break, but for the moment, everything was still, as if the world were holding its breath. Louisa's upper lip was moist with perspiration and there were damp patches beneath the sleeves of her gown. She crept into the room, kicked off her shoes, and climbed into bed next to Kit, lying next to his uninjured side.

Kit remained immobile, lying there like an effigy on a tombstone, his profile white as marble. Louisa shuddered with fear. He'd still been talking and arguing with her in the morning, but the last few hours saw a marked change. He no longer seemed aware of anything around him. The fever had spiked, and the infection was spreading. Louisa pressed her face to Kit's shoulder, willing him to wake. She shouldn't have listened to him. She should have called for Doctor Jacobson despite Kit's refusal to have the surgery without Alec, and now it might be too late. Doctor Jacobson had left in a huff, angry and humiliated by

Louisa's refusal to defer to his opinion. He might come back if summoned, or he might not. He was a proud man, and his obvious feelings for Louisa made him somewhat irrational and easily wounded.

Kit's only hope lay in Valerie's plan, but Alec and Valerie had been gone for hours, and with every passing minute, Louisa lost a little bit of her hope. They should have been back by now. That they weren't meant one thing—the plan hadn't worked. Precious hours had been lost, and now even an amputation might not save Kit, not if the infection had spread into his bloodstream and he became septic. Doctor Jacobson had warned Louisa that if that happened, Kit's organs would begin to fail.

"Kit," Louisa called softly. "Kit, can you hear me?"

There was no response. Louisa hoped Kit was sleeping, but she knew better. He was hovering somewhere between life and death, his body having no energy to spare for awareness. The fever proved that he was still fighting the infection, but he was losing the battle.

"Kit?" Louisa pleaded. "Kit, please wake up." Louisa listened intently, but all she heard were the voices of the children coming from downstairs. Cook had recruited them to bake bread, using the project to keep them from getting underfoot. Once the bread was ready, Minnie would butter the slices and deliver the afternoon treat to the indentured children, unless the storm broke. Minnie was terrified of thunder and lightning and wouldn't venture outside until the storm had passed.

"Kit, please don't leave me. I can't go on without you. I don't want to," Louisa whispered, but didn't think Kit could hear her.

Kit had heard, but try as he might, couldn't manage to respond. He tried to squeeze Louisa's hand, but even that simple gesture seemed beyond him. His body was no longer his own. A few hours ago, he'd still felt as if he had some control, could make decisions, but now he could barely formulate a thought. The fever was consuming him from within. His leg was on fire, the skin stretched so tight it felt as if it would simply split apart and disgorge muscle and sinew. His heartbeat seemed unnaturally loud, as if the organ were working overtime to keep him alive. Strange and frightening images, all black and red, floated before his closed lids.

Kit tried hard to remember something pleasant, like his estate in England. Gentle spring rain, unfurling leaves, and the first warm days of summer, the sky so blue it hurt his eyes, but the memories were like jelly, refusing to take shape and sliding away. Perhaps he should have agreed to the surgery. He supposed that being crippled was better than being dead, but he didn't believe for a moment that Doctor Jacobson could save him, and perhaps he didn't really want to. Jacobson was in love with Louisa, had been since the trial. With Kit out of the way...

The thought of leaving Louisa tore Kit to shreds. He wasn't ready to leave his children to be brought up by another man, especially not that imbecile Jacobson. He knew Louisa didn't care for the man, but if she became lonely enough, she just might change her mind. There weren't many eligible bachelors in Jamestown. But Louisa couldn't remain in Virginia. She had to go to England, to take Robbie home.

Kit sucked in his breath as a wave of heat washed over him, bringing with it an image of Caro. She looked young, not as he had last seen her when she was dying. Caro had been like a mother to him, and his soul reached out to her, having missed his sister. Caro was smiling and holding out her hands to him. She looked no older than fifteen, her dark tresses falling over her shoulders and her eyes filled with love and compassion.

"Stop fretting, Kitty," she said. She used to call him that when he was a boy and he'd hated it, but now it was comforting. "Come, let's play a game. Remember how you used to love to hide from me? But I always found you in the end because I knew all your hiding places. Come to me, won't you?" she cajoled. "I've missed you so much."

Caro suddenly looked sad. "I miss my Robin, and Walter, but Theo is with me. He is a good boy, Theo, but I never did like that trollop he'd married. You should have stopped that when you had the chance. That girl didn't have a decent bone in her body, no sense of honor or duty," Caro went on.

"Caro," Kit tried to say, but couldn't get the words out. Caro seemed to be getting closer. He could almost feel her hands on his. She was reaching for him, calling him. But he didn't want to talk about Theo. He wanted to see his own son, and Evie. He could almost see their faces, but then they dissolved, leaving behind impenetrable darkness.

THIRTY-THREE

Valerie tossed the reins to Alec and burst into the house. They'd ridden hard, making the journey in less than three hours, desperate to get to Kit in time. A heavy rain began to fall about an hour ago, drenching them in minutes and turning the road from Jamestown into a muddy river, but they had pressed on. The house was quiet, the children unusually subdued as they sat huddled in the parlor, building a pyramid out of the blocks Alec had made for them.

"Grandma," Tom cried when he saw Valerie. "Come here. Look."

"Back in a minute, darling," Valerie replied as she raced up the stairs.

"Are you all right, Mistress?" Minnie called after Valerie, but Valerie didn't answer. She stopped before the door to Louisa's bedroom, reluctant to barge in and knocked softly. There was no answer, so Valerie lifted the latch and inched into the room, praying all the while that she wasn't too late.

Kit was much as they'd left him: fevered, unconscious, and disfigured by ugly welts that had begun to turn a yellowish purple. Valerie held her breath as she watched his chest, letting out a sigh of relief to see that it was rising and falling, if only just. Louisa lay next to Kit, sound asleep, her face gray and haggard in the waning light of the afternoon. Louisa woke up with a start, staring around wild-eyed until she spotted Valerie by the door. She seemed to have aged several years since that morning and her eyes bore into Valerie with an accusing glare.

"Where have you been?" Louisa hissed.

"Lou, I got it," Valerie whispered urgently as she waved the green box in the air.

"What is that?" Louisa peered at the package, still unable to grasp the meaning of Valerie's excitement. She looked completely depleted, an aura of defeat hanging over her.

"Antibiotics!"

Louisa was on her feet in seconds, lunging toward Valerie and snatching the box from her hand, a slow smile spreading across her face as she recognized the name. "How did you get these? Oh God, do you think they will help? They must. Jacobson was ready to saw off Kit's leg, and I almost let him. Oh, Val, I was so desperate to save him, I wasn't thinking straight. I was willing to do anything to give him a chance."

"Thank God you waited. Zithromax is not the strongest antibiotic, but Kit's system has never been exposed to any type of medication, so it should be strong enough for him. Do you think he can swallow a pill?"

"He hasn't responded to anything in the past few hours," Louisa replied, her eyes haunted by unimaginable fear. "We can't risk it dissolving in his mouth."

"Open the capsule," Valerie said as she reached for a cup of water. "We'll mix it with a spoonful of water and pour it down his throat. We have to get it inside him."

Louisa nodded and carefully pulled open the capsule, revealing the powder inside, which quickly dissolved in the water. She opened Kit's mouth and poured a teaspoon of the mixture inside as Valerie held his nose to force him to swallow. Louisa opened Kit's mouth again and peered inside. "I think it went down. How long do you think it will take for the medicine to take effect?"

"At least twenty-four hours. We have to be patient," Valerie replied. Louisa nodded and sat down, suddenly too worn out to stand.

"How's Kit?" Alec asked as he entered the room. He'd already changed into dry clothes, but his hair was still wet from the rain. "Any change?"

"Yes, for the worse," Louisa murmured.

"What about the antibiotic?" he asked, turning to Valerie.

"Alec, it's a miracle drug, but even miracles take time. We have to keep watch over him through the night and pray that he doesn't get any worse," Valerie replied. She suddenly became aware that she was dripping rainwater on the floor and shivered in her wet clothes. A wave of fatigue washed over her, and it didn't go unnoticed by Alec, who instantly took control of the situation.

"Valerie, go change into dry clothes and get a warm drink inside you before you catch a chill. Louisa, spend a few minutes with your children, get something to eat, and go to bed—both of you. I will sit with Kit tonight," Alec said as he gently maneuvered Louisa and Valerie toward the door. "Ask Minnie to bring me some food; I'm starving," he added.

"But what if something changes?" Louisa protested. "I should stay."

"Louisa, I will come and wake you if there's any change, good or bad. You have my word," Alec replied. Louisa smiled wanly and looked up at Alec, grateful for his support.

"Alec, will you do something for me?"

"Anything."

"Pray for him." They both knew that Louisa was apologizing for her earlier outburst. Alec took Louisa by the shoulders and kissed her on the forehead in a gesture of brotherly love.

"I have been praying for him all along, and you as well. Now go. Evie and Robbie are frightened and need to see that at least one of their parents is all right. Leave Kit to me," Alec said.

"Thank you, both of you. I have no words to express my gratitude for what you've done."

"No gratitude is required."

Alec took a seat by the bed and took Kit's uninjured hand in his. "Don't let us down, brother," he said softly. "We are all rooting for you."

Kit didn't respond, but Valerie could have sworn she saw his hand tighten around Alec's fingers.

THIRTY-FOUR

Louisa looked better by the following morning, but Kit didn't. Louisa, Valerie, and Alec gathered by Kit's bedside, searching desperately for any sign of improvement, but saw none. The fever that had been ravaging his body for the past two days had not abated, and the swelling in Kit's leg looked even worse, if such a thing were possible.

"I want to see Papa," a frightened voice whispered from the doorway.

"Evie, I don't think—" Louisa began, but Alec interrupted her, something he seldom did.

"Let her, Louisa. She can't get any more scared than she already is. Sometimes not knowing is worse." Louisa opened her mouth to disagree but saw the validity of Alec's argument.

"All right. Come in," Louisa prompted Evie who still stood by the door, her eyes wide with anxiety.

"Would you like us to leave you alone?" Alec asked, but Evie shook her head. She advanced slowly into the room, her eyes never leaving her father's face. Evie gasped when she saw Kit's leg but didn't say anything. Instead, she sat on the edge of the bed and reached for Kit's hand.

"Would you like to tell him something?" Louisa asked gently. "He can hear you."

"Can he?" Evie asked, her mouth quivering as she tried to hold back the tears.

"I am sure he can."

"Papa, please get better," Evie pleaded. "Robbie and I miss you. He was too scared to come in, but he's waiting by the door. He's such a baby sometimes. He needs you. As do I," she added.

Evie couldn't hold back her tears any longer, so she jumped off the bed and fled, her sobs audible as she pounded down the stairs. Louisa made to go after her, but Alec forestalled her when he saw Robbie's terrified face in the dim corridor.

"Allow me. You see to Robbie."

Alec followed Evie out of the house and toward the pond, which was a favorite spot of hers. Evie didn't sit on the bench but threw herself to the ground and curled into a tight little ball. She was shaking with sobs as she covered her head with her hands. Evie didn't cry often, thinking it was babyish in the extreme, but this was too much even for her. The sight of Kit was enough to devastate an adult, so Alec could only imagine what it had done to a child who'd never seen that kind of physical trauma before.

Alec sat down on the ground next to Evie and pulled her into his arms. "It's all right to cry, sweetheart. I know you're terrified."

"He looks like he's dead already," Evie wailed.

"Evie, your father is still alive, and as long as he is with us there's hope. He needs you to believe that. If we stop believing, then we are as good as allowing him to die."

"It doesn't matter what I believe," Evie screamed, suddenly angry. "Little Louisa died, then Theo, and then Jenny left. Why shouldn't my father leave too? Everyone leaves sooner or later."

They do, Alec thought miserably, but he could hardly admit that to a child. He didn't want to belittle Evie's feelings, but he couldn't let her believe that everyone would either die or leave. What would be the point in living if she thought that?

"Evie, that's an awfully grim view of the world. Yes, Louisa and Theo died, and I know how much you miss them, I miss them too, but Jenny didn't die. She left to be with the man she loves. And the rest of us are still here."

"Jenny said she loved me," Evie retorted, her gaze full of bitterness.

"She does love you, but she married Cameron, and he lives in Scotland. She couldn't be in two places at once, could she?" Alec reasoned, but he could see that his explanation was falling on deaf ears. Evie didn't understand the difference between romantic love and love for a little cousin. In her eyes, Jenny had betrayed her, which was even worse than dying since she'd done it willingly.

How could he explain to Evie that Jenny's choice had not been a simple one? She had wanted to stay, she loved them all, and had felt a sense of belonging that she'd longed for her whole life, but it was either the family or Cameron, and at the end of the day, her love for Cameron won out. Alec stroked Evie's jet-black curls as he considered what other tack he might try. What would make a little girl feel more hopeful in this situation?

"Evie, is there anything that would make you feel better?" Alec asked. She nodded miserably.

"I want to see Millie," she whispered. Alec held her close and smiled into her hair. Of course. They all had each other, but as a child, Evie felt alone. She wanted the company of a friend, someone who could understand her suffering from the same perspective.

"Of course, sweetheart. I will gladly take you to Jamestown to see Millie. Would you like to stay for a few days?"

Evie's head shot up, smacking Alec on the chin. "But what if..." She let the sentence trail off, unable to speak the words.

"I will come and fetch you should there be any change. I promise."

Evie nodded. "Yes, I would like to stay with Millie. Maybe Robbie wants to come too. He misses Harry."

"Go collect your things and I will speak to your mother and see if Robbie would like to come."

Evie smiled, her face transforming from a mask of suffering into an expression of hope. "Thank you, Uncle Alec. I didn't want to bring it up since mama doesn't like Aunt Annabel," she added.

"Evie, you are not being disloyal to your mother. She knows how much you love Millie," Alec replied, glad to see that he was able to help Evie in this small way.

At times, he forgot how perceptive children could be, and although they didn't really understand the reasons for the animosity between Louisa and Annabel, they knew not to mention Annabel in Louisa's presence and vice versa. Clever little mites, Alec thought as he followed Evie back to the house. She sprinted ahead of him, eager to get going as soon as possible.

THIRTY-FIVE

"How's Kit?" Charles asked as he invited Alec into the parlor. Robbie didn't want to leave his mother, but Evie couldn't get to Jamestown fast enough, desperate to see her friend. She clutched her bundle to her chest the whole way, and practically jumped off the bench as soon as the conveyance came to a stop.

"Not well. We're all praying for a miracle," Alec said. He couldn't tell Charles about the medicine, so if Kit improved, his recovery would be attributed to the grace of God rather than modern medicine.

"Well, if anyone is in the business of miracle-making, it would be his dear wife," Annabel quipped, her attempt at humor not fooling anyone since the words dripped with sarcasm. "It took a miracle to clear Kit of the murder charge, and that would never have happened had Lady Sheridan not conjured up witnesses and bewitched the governor with her wiles."

"Do shut up, Belle," Charles hissed, his eyes sliding to Evie, who was standing just behind Annabel, her expression mutinous. Evie didn't really understand what Annabel was implying, but she knew that her mother was under attack and she wasn't having it. Evie walked around to face Annabel, her eyes blazing with contempt. She looked up and held Annabel's gaze, making the older woman visibly nervous. Alec held his breath, quite unable to imagine what a seven-year-old could say to her much older aunt, but Evie didn't say anything at all. She swung her foot back and kicked Annabel in the shin with such force that Annabel cried out in pain and shock as she fell backward onto her behind.

"You little besom," Annabel cried, but Charles interrupted before she had a chance to say any more.

"Don't you dare, Annabel. Apologize to Evangeline for speaking ill of her mother. This minute," Charles roared, visibly frightening his wife. Annabel wasn't often on the receiving end of Charles's anger, but things had been difficult between them since she had testified against Kit and got them thrown out of Rosewood Manor.

Charles held out his hand to help Annabel off the floor, but let go as soon as she was upright, his concern going only as far as her physical well-being. Bright color stained Annabel's cheeks as she caught Alec's eye, but she straightened her shoulders and lifted her head in defiance, letting everyone know she wasn't sorry in the least.

Annabel took her time straightening her skirts and patting her hair into place, all the while watching Evie, in case she decided to kick her again. Evie glared at Annabel with an expression more suited to a woman of thirty than a child. Charles stood with his arms crossed, a scowl of displeasure on his face, and Alec rested his hand on Evie's shoulder in a gesture of silent support. It was clear to Annabel that this tableau wasn't going to come to life until she showed contrition, and she was wise enough to know when she was on the losing end of an argument.

"Evie, I apologize," Annabel finally said. "I hope your father recovers."

"He will recover, no thanks to you," Evie replied, anger staining her cheeks. And it's Lady Evangeline to you," Evie added and walked out of the room, head held high. Alec and Charles did their best not to laugh, but Annabel's expression was priceless.

"Well, that's you put firmly in your place," Charles said, ignoring Annabel's look of outrage. "See that Evie is made comfortable. She will be staying with us for a few days, and you will treat her with the sensitivity and respect she deserves. Is that clear?"

"I will remember your treachery, Charles Whitfield," Annabel hissed as she left the room with whatever dignity she could muster.

"Drink?" Charles asked as he reached for a bottle of rum.

"Yes, please." Alec sat down and watched with some surprise as Charles glanced into the corridor to make sure no one was about before firmly shutting the door.

"I just can't abide her venom lately," Charles said quietly as he took a sip of his rum. "Belle used to be so sweet, but something had snapped inside her after her brother died. I know she worshiped him, but it's been years, and life does go on."

"How does she get along with Cousin Wesley?" Alec asked. Wesley Gaines had inherited the Gaines estate after the death of Tom and Annabel's father, and Annabel never got over the slight, even though Wesley, who was childless, had made Harry his heir. Wesley Gaines had welcomed Annabel and Charles back to the family home in Jamestown and spent as little time in their company as possible. He still had his own modest home on the outskirts of town and preferred to reside there instead of sharing a house with Annabel, who treated him like a usurper, even though he had done nothing illegal or dishonorable.

"She is outwardly polite, but she still resents him, and can't wait for the poor man to do us all a favor and die. I do wish she'd accept things as they are. We have a good life here, and it's a sin to complain and tempt fate. Things could be a lot worse, and probably will be before long," Charles added as he splashed more rum into his cup.

Such a sentiment was so out of character for Charles that Alec gaped at his brother in surprise. They hadn't spent much time together lately, nor did conversation flow effortlessly when they did, but Charles was still Alec's younger brother and there was clearly something weighing on his mind. Charles seemed unusually subdued, his customary self-assurance rattled.

"Is there something wrong?" Alec asked, hoping Charles would swallow his pride and confide in him the way he used to. Alec was more than ready to extend an olive branch, but Charles had to meet him halfway, which wasn't an easy thing to do with Annabel still on the warpath.

"Belle is with child again," Charles replied, looking less than pleased.

"And is that not a blessing?" Alec asked carefully. Charles and Annabel certainly had the means to support another child and had hoped for one as far as Alec knew. What had changed?

Charles drained his cup of rum and beckoned to Alec to join him in the garden, walking purposefully toward the far end, where a bench stood in the shadow of a maple tree. Charles had never been one for garden strolls, so Alec could only assume he had no wish to be overheard. Alec followed and took a seat on the bench. It was a lovely spot that reminded Alec of his daughter, who liked to sit there on summer afternoons when she'd stayed with Charles and Annabel all those years ago and had vied for Tom's affection. Alec supposed that's when the trouble with Louisa had started, but at the time, they'd been ignorant of her feelings for Thomas Gaines or of how far she'd go to get what her heart had desired.

Alec felt a pang of sorrow as he thought of Louisa. What he wouldn't give to see her sitting on this bench again, her needlework in her lap, a dreamy expression on her face. His grief was as raw as it had been when Louisa died, and he looked away for a moment to hide his misery, but Charles was oblivious to Alec's feelings; he was too caught up in his own.

Charles paced back and forth, his expression closed. He turned to Alec, then turned away, clearly unsure how to begin.

"Are you going to tell me what's wrong, Charlie?" Alec finally asked. He wanted nothing more than to get away from this garden and this house. It brought back too many painful memories.

"I've been seeing another woman, Alec. I swore when I married Annabel that I would be true to her but being married to her has been such a trial lately. I needed a diversion, I suppose."

Alec wondered where this was going. He was ashamed to admit that he was surprised Charles had remained faithful to Annabel thus far. There had to be more to this than a mere dalliance.

"Go on," Alec prompted.

"She is also with child," Charles confessed. "She's a widow, you see, so I'm in a bit of a bind. I've spent the past week agonizing over the situation, but I don't know what to do."

"Dear God, Charles," Alec exclaimed. "How could you have been so careless?"

Getting a married woman pregnant was bad enough, but it did happen from time to time, and the woman often passed the child as her husband's in order to avoid public scandal. A pregnant widow was nothing short of disaster. No wonder Charles looked so worried.

"We can't all be the saints you claim to be," Charles retorted, hurt by his brother's reaction. "There's nothing else to occupy the elders of this colony besides their quest for righteousness and a desire to vilify anyone who acts on their desires. I'm only human, Alec."

"Human, is it?" Alec scoffed.

The Colony of Virginia had a litany of laws pertaining to being human. Everything from gossiping to fornication was punishable in the most severe manner. The preachers reminded parishioners of the laws before every sermon, and the sentences were carried out without delay once passed. Fornication was difficult to prove unless someone walked in on the couple, but if the liaison resulted in a pregnancy, the birth was followed by a fornication and bastardy trial. The penalty for the mother could be anything from a hefty fine or being sold into indenture if she couldn't afford to pay to public whipping or branding. Charles's lover would suffer greatly, but Charles, being a married man and the one committing adultery, might be made an example of. If his part in the affair came to light, he could be whipped, branded, or even executed, as had been the case in some of the northern colonies.

"Oh, like you never dipped your quill in someone else's ink," Charles snarled.

"Not while married, no."

"Are you going to help me or not?" Charles demanded, color rising in his cheeks. "Annabel has been difficult enough without learning of my transgressions. She will make my life hell if she finds out, but that will be the least of my problems if I have an 'A' branded on my face or have to suffer a public whipping."

"Charles, I will help you because you are my brother, and because my name is forever linked with yours, but were it up to me, I'd leave you to clean up your own mess. Who is this woman, anyway?"

"Bethany Warren."

"Ah."

"What's that supposed to mean?" Charles demanded.

"It means that the situation is even more complicated than I imagined. Bethany Warren's brother is not a man known for his kindness or capacity for forgiveness."

"He'll be the first to denounce her should he find out," Charles agreed. "He's always ready to cast the first stone, the good Christian that he is."

"Master Abbott is a shrewd and callous man and will very quickly see the benefits of denouncing his sister. Mistress Warren has inherited a sizeable estate from her husband, and her brother would like nothing more than to appropriate it and annex it to his own. Bethany's disgrace will make it that much easier for him to lay claim to what's hers, since she might even get banished from the colony. And make no mistake, Charlie, they will get the name of the father out of her, by any means necessary."

Charles balked. "What are you suggesting?"

"I'm suggesting that it might be wise for Mistress Warren to sell her property and leave the colony before her condition becomes obvious. She can settle someplace else and claim that her husband is recently deceased, or more recently deceased, I should say," Alec suggested.

"Her brother will never allow her to leave. He is her closest male relative and her guardian until she remarries. He has a say in any business transaction she undertakes. He will block the sale of Bethany's land."

Alec nodded. "You are right. He will. I often forget that women have no rights in this colony."

"Alec, what am I to do?" Charles whined. "Bethany's condition will become obvious in a few months, and then all hell will break loose. There hasn't been a fornication and bastardy trial in years, so the people of this colony will lap it up and call for the highest form of punishment. I will be ruined."

Alec threw Charles a look of disgust. It was so like him to think only of himself and what the situation would do to his standing in the community. Anger welled up inside him.

"*You* will be ruined? What about Mistress Warren? She is a good and decent woman, Charles, who recently lost her husband. I can't begin to imagine what made her get into bed with you, other than spectacularly bad judgment and overwhelming loneliness, but you've as good as killed her. She will be branded a whore, and her child—also your child—will forever carry the stain of her sin. Every door will be closed to her, leaving her to live in shame and isolation."

Charles nodded miserably. "You think I haven't considered all that?"

"I'm sure you have, but there aren't many avenues open to you."

"So, what you're saying is that I'm fucked."

Alec cringed at the use of the lewd term, but the summation was accurate. Charles certainly wasn't the first man to have an extramarital affair, and he wasn't the first to sire a child with a woman who wasn't his wife, but Bethany's widowhood certainly made this situation impossible to resolve without the knowledge of the entire colony.

"What do I do?" Charles moaned. He looked as if he were about to burst into tears, making Alec feel sorry for him despite his colossal idiocy. Of all the women he could have fornicated with, he chose the one woman who had the power to ruin him. Alec sprang to his feet, unable to remain immobile any longer. Pacing always helped him to think.

Alec finally stopped and looked at Charles, who gazed at him desperately. "Charles, there is only one way to keep a lid on this scandal. Mistress Warren must marry someone within the next few weeks."

"And pass the child off as her husband's?" Charles asked hopefully.

"No. The man in question must know the truth. I will not allow you to dupe someone."

"And why would someone agree to marry my pregnant mistress?" Charles demanded.

"Because you will make it worth their while. Many a man

has married a widow with children for the sake of her property. You must make Bethany Warren an attractive proposition to a single man. I'll leave the details to you," Alec said and turned toward the house.

"Sometimes I forget how clever you are, Alec," Charles replied. "But what if Bethany refuses?"

"She won't. It's her only choice. You'd best start playing matchmaker, Charles; you don't have much time. Now, I must get going. I'll come back for Evie should anything change with Kit. In the meantime, please make sure your wife doesn't upset her. The child has enough to contend with."

"Don't worry. Evie will be well looked after."

Alec walked out of the house and untied his horse. He had to admit that on some level he could understand Charles's desire to seek the company of someone else. Annabel was a right old shrew at times and living with her couldn't be easy. Had Charles lived in the future, he might have left Annabel or tried some form of marriage counseling, but in the seventeenth century divorce was not an option, at least not for the common folk of Virginia. Charles and Annabel were bound for life, so Charles could either live with a woman he no longer loved or seek happiness elsewhere. Hopefully, Charles would be more prudent in the future.

THIRTY-SIX
SCOTLAND AUGUST 1628

A narrow sliver of light shimmered between the slats of the closed shutters, signaling the arrival of a fine, sunny morning. Cameron rose from the pallet he shared with Jenny and went to check on Ian. The child was fast asleep, wrapped in his blanket, his cheeks rosy with good health. Maybe he would sleep for a wee bit longer and give Jenny a chance to rest. She'd been sleeping poorly this past week, her sleep haunted by nightmares of the fire. The thought of what might have happened had she not woken in time ate away at her, and a terrible guilt weighed heavily on her soul, making her question her worth as wife and mother. Of course, staying in the loft of Cameron's parents' farm with nothing but a pallet to sleep on and Fiona Brody's constant disapproval having over her did little to improve Jenny's spirits.

Cameron climbed down the ladder and went outside, filling his lungs with fresh air. It was only the end of August, but already the warmth of the summer nights was becoming a distant memory as the frosty bite of fall nipped at the heels of summer. Cameron normally loved this time of year, but he wasn't feeling benevolent toward the coming autumn today.

Autumn didn't stick around for long in these parts, not as it had in Virginia, where weeks of golden days and bright-blue skies stretched into months, winter coming gradually and not lasting long. A few more weeks, and it'd be nothing but lashing rain and howling wind, which would soon give way to winter storms and a foot of snow on the ground. Winter was a difficult season at the best of times, but with no house or possessions of their own, this one would surely test their mettle, as well as their marriage.

Things had been rattling about in Cameron's brain, notions he hadn't wanted to think about, but now had no choice. The croft was gone, and to rebuild it would take time since work couldn't begin in earnest until after the harvest was in and the haying done. The site would need to be completely cleared, stones found to replace the ones that couldn't be reused, and thatch would need to be prepared for the roof. By the time all was ready, the winter would be upon them. And once the work finally began, it'd take a month or two to finish the house. Even if Cameron made all the furniture over the winter, realistically, they wouldn't be able to move in until spring or even summer, and Cameron wasn't sure how long Jenny would last under his parents' roof before losing her mind.

Fiona Brody was a strong, competent, no-nonsense woman who could be relied on in any crisis, but sensitivity and compassion did not come easily to her. Jenny's fragility and educated manner irritated her to the point where she picked on Jenny all day long. Fiona admired strength and ability, not fine manners. Had Jenny been a different sort of woman, she would have confronted her mother-in-law and told her to back off. Such brazenness would have earned Fiona's grudging respect and won Jenny an ally for life, but Jenny couldn't bring herself to dress down the older woman, a course of action she believed to be rude and disrespectful.

Cameron sighed as his mother came out of the barn, a pail

of milk in her work-roughened hands. He'd assumed she was still abed, but Fiona never looked to her own comfort, always putting what needed to be done ahead of her own desires.

"What are ye doing up?" Fiona asked as she came closer, her eyes squinting against the bright rays of the morning sun. Not for the first time, Cameron noticed how old and careworn she looked. He'd never given it any thought before being sent down to Virginia, but it occurred to him at some point during his year of servitude that Mistress Whitfield was about the same age as his mother, possibly even older. He was shocked by how young she looked in comparison, and how attractive a woman of that age could still be. His mother never cared for her looks, nor did she think it proper for a married woman to court attention, but it pained Cameron to think that his Jenny might look like this in twenty years' time.

"I couldna sleep. Do ye need help, Ma?"

"Nae. I'll just get breakfast going afore yer grand lady deigns it necessary to wake up."

"Dinna be cruel to Jenny, Ma," Cameron retorted. "She is no grand lady, and she never carries on like one."

"Could have fooled me, her with her fancy foreign ways. To think of all the lassies ye could have chosen, and ye marry that useless wisp of a girl who canna even dry a few clouts without burning the house down."

"We've been through this," Cameron growled. "It was an accident."

"An accident that might have been avoided had she no' fallen asleep instead of making supper for ye, ye dolt. Mary would never have been so useless. She'd have made a fine wife for ye, son, a good wife," his mother sighed.

"Mary is gone, Ma. I love Jenny, and she's the only wife I desire."

"Hmmm," his mother harrumphed as she turned her back on him and went into the house.

This wasn't an argument he would ever win. His mother had practically raised Mary, but Jenny was an unknown quantity. Jenny made his mother feel threatened, which was why Fiona had such a strong aversion to her. She was everything his mother wasn't: educated, well-mannered, and compassionate. Cameron had never realized what a hard woman his mother was until he'd brought Jenny home. But it wasn't just Fiona's attitude toward Jenny that riled Cameron—it was her indifference to Ian. Fiona might not care for his wife, but Ian was still her grandson. Ian took after Jenny in appearance, but he was Cameron's son, and Cameron expected her to love the lad. His father did. He doted on the boy and spent as much time with him as possible, singing to him and bouncing him on his knee. Ian loved his granddad, so at least that was one relationship that hadn't been soured by dislike.

Cameron smiled as Katrina came out. She bounced from foot to foot, desperate for the privy, but still stopped for a moment to wish him a good morning. "Is Jenny still asleep, then?" Katrina asked.

"Oh, not ye too," Cameron replied gruffly.

"I dinna mean nothing by it. She needs her rest, the poor lass. She's so sad these days, even sadder than afore."

Cameron pricked his ears. "She told ye she was sad?"

"She dinna have to, did she? Tis only natural, I reckon. She misses her home and her family, just as ye did when ye were in that primitive place."

Cameron nodded. Perhaps Virginia wasn't as primitive as he had thought. It was still a new colony, but it was a place where progress was possible, unlike this village, which would probably still be the same a hundred years from now. Nothing ever changed here, and nothing ever would. He would spend his life toiling in the fields like his father before him, watch his wife grow old before her time, and then die and be buried in the same churchyard as all his ancestors before him. A few years ago, this seemed like a good life to aspire to, but now, the years ahead stretched like a narrow road through a barren landscape, with low, dark clouds gathering overhead and not a stick of shelter in sight.

Cameron sighed with irritation and went inside, not because he wanted to confront his mother again, but because he needed to be on hand when Jenny made her appearance. The last thing she needed was another tongue-lashing from Fiona Brody. Only a half hour ago, he'd thought a decision needed to be made, but now he realized that he'd made it already. Cameron suddenly felt lighter, as if a great weight had been lifted from his shoulders. It had seemed so complicated, but really, it was the only logical thing to do. He saw that now that he'd come to terms with the idea.

THIRTY-SEVEN
VIRGINIA AUGUST 1628

A steady rain fell outside, lashing the windows with a relentless stream of water that made it impossible to see anything beyond the front yard. The pond had disappeared into the soaked countryside, having burst its banks after two days of continuous rain. It had thundered during the night and the ground was strewn with broken branches, as if they'd fallen from the sky and not been torn off healthy trees by the gusty wind.

The room was nearly dark, only one candle burning as Louisa bent over Kit. They had given him two doses of the antibiotic, but as of last night, his condition had not improved at all. He had been in a state of delirium, his swollen flesh stretched paper thin over the putrid wound. The redness had moved up his thigh, leaving Louisa in no doubt that Kit was living on borrowed time.

Louisa reached out a hand to touch Kit's forehead, but drew it back, terrified of what she'd find. If Kit didn't show any signs of improvement today, then all hope was lost, and the antibiotic wasn't strong enough to vanquish the infection. Perhaps there were other things going on, such as internal bleeding or a collapsed lung, which would explain Kit's labored breathing.

They hadn't given him any more laudanum, wary of mixing opium with the antibiotic, but Kit didn't seem to need it. He hovered between life and death, oblivious to pain.

Louisa breathed a sigh of relief when Valerie stepped into the room. Her face was drawn, her eyes full of fear as she gazed at her sister. "How is he?"

"I don't know," Louisa replied truthfully. "I'm too afraid to find out."

"Would you like me to?" Valerie asked.

"Yes."

She was being a coward, she knew that, but she couldn't bear to discover that her hopes and prayers had been dashed. Louisa held the candle as Valerie bent over Kit and pressed her hand to his forehead. She then pulled back the coverlet and examined his leg. The smell was awful, and the bandage was crusty and soiled, but Valerie nodded in satisfaction and replaced the blanket.

"He's still warm, but not burning up, and the swelling has gone down. We need to get Doctor Jacobson to change the bandage and clean the wound. I'd do it myself, but I'm afraid to shift his bones."

Valerie took the candle from Louisa and set it on the nightstand before pulling Louisa into an embrace. "Lou, I think the medicine is working. There's marked improvement."

"Are you sure?" Louisa whispered. "I'm too afraid to allow myself to believe that he might recover. If I allow hope in and then lose him, I will never mend."

"Lou, I can't guarantee that Kit will recover, but this morning he appears to be doing better, and that's all we can hope for. We still have three pills left, and the medicine will continue to work for another five days after we finish the pack. There is hope."

Louisa and Valerie turned to look at Kit as a low moan

escaped his lips. He hadn't been conscious in two days, so even this was an improvement.

"Kit, can you hear me?" Louisa pleaded with him. "Just squeeze my hand if you do."

Kit didn't squeeze her hand, but slowly opened his eyes instead. "Thirsty," he muttered. "So thirsty."

"Lou, give him some water, and I'll go down and get hot broth," Valerie said. "He needs nourishment. His body must be starving."

Louisa held a cup of water to Kit's lips, and he drank as much as he could, lying back on the pillow and closing his eyes from the effort of holding his head up. "Thank you."

"Kit, how do you feel?" Louisa asked as she sat by him.

"There are no words," he replied. Louisa could barely hear him, but at least he was talking. He did squeeze her hand then, and she nearly cried with relief. He would come back to her; she knew that now.

THIRTY-EIGHT
SCOTLAND AUGUST 1628

Jenny huddled into a corner and put Ian to her breast. She wished she could make herself invisible for a short while to escape Fiona's judgmental looks, but there was nowhere to go besides the barn. Fiona had been mostly civil to her for the past two years, but since the fire, all goodwill seemed to evaporate. Now Fiona believed it was her God-given right to berate Jenny throughout the day, criticizing everything she did for Ian and admonishing her for not being a good enough wife to Cameron. Hamish Brody tried to silence his wife with meaningful looks and occasional reprimands, but the dam had broken, and the tide of disapproval was impossible to stop. Jenny's only ally in the house was Katrina, who often tried to take the blame for whatever Jenny was getting a tongue-lashing for.

"Don't ye protect her," Fiona scolded, hands on hips. "I raised ye, girl, and I taught ye how to do things right and proper. I don't know what those nuns taught her, other than piety, but tis not the way we do things round here."

Jenny swallowed her tears as she buried her nose in Ian's silky curls. He smelled of home and comfort, unlike this house that reeked of disapproval and disappointment. And now

Cameron wasn't there to support her. He left yesterday morning without bothering to tell her where he was going. Cameron constantly assured Jenny that he didn't blame her for the fire, but perhaps his mother's incessant reminders that it was all her fault had finally broken through whatever barrier he'd erected. What if he now saw her through his mother's eyes and regretted having sent for her? Cameron would never leave her or turn his back on his son, but Jenny couldn't bear it if he no longer loved her. Her love for him was stronger than ever and the thought of losing his good opinion wounded her more than anything Fiona could throw at her.

"When's Cameron coming back?" Katrina asked as she sat down next to Jenny.

"I don't know. He didn't say."

"He seemed verra mysterious when he set off. Told me no' to ask any questions."

"He didn't tell me anything at all. Just said he had some business to attend to," Jenny replied. She felt a tiny bit of relief knowing that Cameron hadn't confided in Katrina either. He loved his little sister and liked to tease her about finding a husband. If Cameron were to confide in anyone in his family, it would be Katrina. He rarely saw his older sister, Laren, since she'd moved to a neighboring village after her marriage, and although he loved and honored his parents, Jenny didn't think he shared much of his soul with them. Not anymore. Cameron was close to his father, but Jenny thought that at times he wished Hamish would stand up to his wife and tell her to "shut her gob." Hamish didn't like confrontations and allowed his wife to rule the roost, something she did with relish.

Jenny pulled up her bodice and hugged Ian, nearly bursting into tears as his pudgy little arms came around her neck. Ian pressed his lips to her cheek in an imitation of a kiss.

"Mama," he suddenly said, and Jenny promptly dissolved into the tears she'd been holding back for so long. Ian had been making sounds for months but had never said an actual word, especially not intentionally. Jenny talked to him all day long, partly because she was lonely and partly because she thought it might help Ian develop spoken language sooner. It seemed her efforts had paid off. Ian smiled happily and repeated the word.

"Mama."

"Oh, Lord. His first word," Katrina exclaimed. "And so clear. Ian, gaol mo chridhe, say it again."

"Mama," Ian said again. Then he pointed to Katrina. "Ka Ka."

"Well, no' the name I was hoping for, but I'll take it," Katrina laughed. "Can you say 'Dada'?"

"Da," Ian proudly replied.

"You clever boy," Jenny said as she lifted Ian up into the air, making him giggle.

"Mama," he said again, bringing on a fresh flow of tears.

Katrina reached over and put her arm around Jenny. "Don't cry, Jenny. I know my brother, and he'll not allow ye to suffer."

I'm suffering already, Jenny thought, but she forced herself to smile as she looked at Katrina. "I know."

* * *

Cameron didn't return until nightfall of the following day. He looked tired and travel-stained, but there was a twinkle in his eye as he kissed Jenny and ruffled Ian's hair. Fiona instantly launched into a litany of complaints.

"Nice of ye to come back to us. Yer father could have used yer help with the broken stile but seems ye have more important things to do. And where, pray tell, have ye been these two days?"

"Oh, Mam, leave off," Katrina cut across her mother. She didn't usually show her mother disrespect, but she was bursting to tell Cameron the news.

"Ian said 'Mama' and 'Da'," Katrina said proudly, leaving out her own unappealing name.

"Did ye, my wee angel?" Cameron crooned to Ian and lifted him out of Jenny's arms. "Which did he say first?"

"Mama," Jenny and Katrina replied in unison.

"Tis as it should be. Mama is more important, at least as long as ye get to enjoy her bountiful breast several times a day," Cameron said, making Jenny blush and Fiona snort with disapproval.

"Mam, why don't ye take yer grandson for a moment, so that I can talk to my wife?"

"And why can't ye talk to her while she's holding yer son?" Fiona demanded, but reached out for the boy. She had not been excited about Ian's first words. It was natural for a boy to start talking. No great miracle there.

Cameron grabbed Jenny by the hand and pulled her outside, holding her hand as they walked away from the house. There was a particularly picturesque spot where the trees parted to reveal the shimmering loch, the water a silvery purple in the summer twilight. The evening was cool and fresh, and wonderfully still. The first stars of the evening twinkled faintly in the dusky sky and the outline of the crescent moon was already visible above the trees.

Cameron sat down on the ground and pulled Jenny onto his lap, making her giggle as he nuzzled her neck. "I missed ye," he said. "I never wish to be away from ye again."

"Where did you go, Cam?" Jenny asked, suddenly afraid he wouldn't tell her. He'd been distant and secretive the past few days, something important occupying his mind.

"I went to Glasgow, lass."

"Why?"

"I had a dual purpose there, and I accomplished both feats," Cameron replied as he smiled cryptically and turned his attention back to her neck, but Jenny gently pushed him away.

"Are you going to tell me, or do I have to guess?"

"I'll have to tell ye, because ye'll never guess," Cameron said happily. "Are ye ready?"

"As ready as I'll ever be."

Jenny looked at Cameron fearfully. He seemed very pleased with himself, but what if his news came as a blow to her? What if whatever it was didn't have the desired effect on Jenny? She suddenly wished he wouldn't tell her. That way, she could enjoy his good mood and not fret about what had brought it on.

"Jenny, I went to Glasgow to sell the farm. There's no' croft left, but the land is worth quite a bit. I was able to fetch a good price. There's a man I'd heard of, Master McCollough, who buys up land and leases it to farmers. They work the land and pay him rent and a percentage of the profits."

Jenny balked and stared at Cameron. Dear God, did he intend to live with his parents for good? His father was getting on in years, so perhaps he thought it'd be a good idea to farm the land together until he inherited the lot. Hamish always talked of what would happen once he passed, but Cameron refused to humor him and told him that he'd just have to live forever to look after his property and wife, since Cameron refused to live with more than one woman in the house ever again.

"Why, Cameron?" Jenny moaned. She was horrified. This was even worse than she'd feared.

"Because we no longer need it, lass," Cameron replied, his expression careful.

"Why don't we need it?"

"I'm taking ye home, Jenny," Cameron said, his face breaking into a huge smile. "I'm taking ye to Virginia. I booked us passage on a ship bound for the colonies."

Jenny felt as if her heart might stop beating. Home. Family. People who cared for her. Was he truly willing to go back after everything that had happened?

"Cameron, you are coming with me, aren't you?" Jenny asked, suddenly fearful that Cameron was sending her away. He did say 'us' and 'we', but perhaps meant to say 'you'.

"Of course, I am. Ye didn't think I'd remain here with my parents, did ye? Ye're my family, Jenny—ye and Ian."

"But why? Why do you want to go back?"

"Jenny, it was a mistake to bring ye here. Ye've never been happy, and it's not for any lack of trying on yer part. This place is just not ready for someone like ye. I thought that perhaps, in time, ye'd get used to it and everyone would get used to ye but seeing how my own mam treats ye made me realize that I were just dreaming. Ye belong with yer family. Yer uncle loves ye like his own daughter, and he will welcome ye back with open arms. I've settled my debt with him, so I hope that he might welcome me as well, as yer husband. The money I received for the farm will be enough to buy a small property in Virginia. We'll grow tobacco. We'll prosper," Cameron promised.

"Oh, Cam." Jenny clapped her hands with joy. "What a wonderful surprise. When are we to go?"

"At the end of the week, lass, so ye'd better start getting ready."

Jenny looked deep into Cameron's blue eyes. "Cam, but what about the other business?"

"Deverell, ye mean?" Cameron shrugged. "Jenny, I've done wrong by taking a man's life, and I've prayed and asked the good Lord for forgiveness, but I will not turn myself in to the law, if that's what ye're asking. Deverell got what was coming to him. Justice was done. Can ye live with that?"

"Yes," Jenny replied simply. She had learned since leaving the convent that life was never straightforward, nor were things ever black and white. Everything in life was a shade of gray, even murder. The law murdered people in the name of justice every day. Was administering your own justice when the law had failed really that different? Aloysius Deverell had killed

Cameron's betrothed and had nearly been responsible for Cameron's death by hanging. Cameron had meted out his own justice, and she was all right with that.

"Funny, isn't it?" Cameron said, his tone thoughtful. "I thought that Deverell had stolen my life, but in a way, he gave me a whole new life instead."

"It wasn't Deverell who gave you a new life, Cameron Brody, it was me," Jenny giggled.

"Hmm, that is true, lass. Ye are my life. Ye and Ian. And hopefully before long they'll be four of us," he added meaningfully as he pushed Jenny down onto the grass and ran his hand up her leg, making her shiver with anticipation. They hadn't made love since before the fire and Jenny thrilled to his touch. It would be nice if she got with child again, but if she didn't right away, she'd enjoy trying. It'd been a long time since she felt so aroused, and it made her glow with happiness to know that she could be. She thought she'd never feel such yearning again, not with all the unhappiness that had been weighing her down of late.

Jenny yanked up her skirt and spread her legs as Cameron tore at his laces. She gasped when Cameron pushed inside her, grateful for the privacy the trees afforded them. It felt so right when they came together like this, so perfect. Jenny wrapped her bare legs around Cameron's waist, bringing him even closer. It only took a few thrusts for her to reach her peak and she cried out, not only from pleasure, but from the sheer joy of being alive, adored, and understood by the man she loved.

THIRTY-NINE
VIRGINIA AUGUST 1628

Charles peeked out into the garden. Harry was drawing something in the dirt using a pointy stick. Evie and Millie sat on a blanket on the grass, their heads close together as they whispered secrets to each other, and Annabel sat on the bench, her sewing forgotten in her lap. She had dozed off in the midafternoon sun, and her fair head drooped, her chin nearly resting on her ample bosom. This picture of domestic bliss did nothing to lift Charles's spirits. He tiptoed away and left the house, leading his horse well away before mounting it. He knew that as soon as Annabel heard hoofbeats, she'd wake up and wonder where he'd disappeared to.

Charles trotted away from Jamestown, nodding to various acquaintances he passed in the street and pretending that he was in no great hurry. He wasn't really, but he needed to speak to Bethany and hoped that he'd be able to get her on her own. Given the size of Master Abbott's family, catching Bethany alone at the farm was impossible, not to mention inadvisable, since he had no business being there and being seen with her given the current situation could only be detrimental to them both. The only thing he could do was go past the farm, as if he were on his way to Rosewood Manor, to the glade where they met for their trysts, and hope that Bethany had spotted him and would show up. No doubt Bethany had been on the lookout for him these past few days and would come as soon as she was able.

The thought of Bethany caused Charles some discomfort, making his breeches uncomfortably snug in the groin area. He still desired her despite their predicament, perhaps even more so. Bethany had always been forbidden fruit, but now she was not only forbidden, but extremely dangerous. If she carried the child to term, she'd be tried and punished, but he would be brought to justice only if Bethany revealed his name to the magistrate and the church leaders. As long as Bethany kept quiet, he was safe, but Charles couldn't be sure that Bethany could be prevailed upon to keep her mouth shut, not if she didn't want to. She might choose to punish him rather than bear the brunt of the situation alone, and who could blame her.

Charles wasn't even sure what had drawn him to Bethany in the first place, other than his annoyance with Annabel. Bethany was as different from Annabel as could be. Whereas Annabel was fair, short, and pleasantly plump, Bethany was dark, lean, and nearly as tall as Charles himself. Her legs were surprisingly muscular, and her breasts were firm and round, unlike Annabel's, which were large, pillowy, and tipped with delicious rosy nipples. Charles had always liked plump, buxom women, and still found his wife attractive. He lay with her regularly and would have continued to do so had her increasingly foul temper not driven him into the arms of another woman. Bethany was so desperate for affection that she'd been willing to come to Charles on any terms he set forth and hadn't asked him for anything in return. The arrangement had suited them both, until now.

Charles finally reached the glade. He dismounted, tied up his horse and walked toward Bethany, who was sitting beneath a shady tree, her arms wrapped around her legs. She'd removed her cap, and her hair framed her face and moved in the gentle breeze, reminding Charles that she was still very young, years younger than his own wife. She was barely older than nineteen, and had already been widowed for over a year, longer than she'd been married.

Bethany's head shot up when she heard a noise and she sprang to her feet, a pensive expression on her face. She didn't smile as Charles drew nearer, but watched him with narrowed eyes, as if trying to gauge what he'd come to tell her.

"Are you really with child?" Charles demanded without preamble. Bethany wasn't the type of woman to lie about such a serious matter, but for some reason, Charles wanted to put her on the defensive.

"Why would I lie?" Bethany asked, clearly shocked.

"Because faking pregnancy would be a good way to extort money from me," Charles retorted. "Your brother has full control of your inheritance, perhaps you'd like some funds of your own."

He could see in the widening of Bethany's eyes that she was stung by the accusation, but he wasn't ready to relent. He needed to know the truth before outlining his plan.

"And what would I do with these funds, Charles?" Bethany retorted. "My brother and his wife watch my every move. I'm not allowed out on my own. Money is of no use to me. Besides, if you don't believe me, just wait a few months," Bethany replied bitterly.

"And how do I know it's mine?" he goaded her.

"Do you think I lie with every man I know?" Bethany cried, tears spilling down her cheeks.

"I don't know what you do, Bethany. You gave yourself to me willingly enough." That wasn't true, and he knew it, but he wished to hurt her.

"Well, let me tell you what I do, Master Whitfield. I wake

up before dawn and work until nightfall, taking care of a family that isn't my own. As a widowed woman, I have nothing that belongs to me, since it's not proper for me to live alone or manage my own affairs. I am forced to reside with my brother and endure being treated like a servant while he dips into the inheritance from my husband. I share a bed with three of his daughters and cannot do anything without my brother's blessing, since, as a woman, I apparently have no more sense than a sheep. The few hours I spent with you were the only happy moments I have known since my husband died, and now you've ruined that as well by calling me a harlot to my face and questioning my motives."

Bethany's cheeks were stained with an angry flush and her hands were balled into fists. She was no longer crying. Instead, she looked like she wanted to punch him.

"Bethany, I am a married man, so it isn't within my power to resolve this situation. I can't marry you, and I must think of my own reputation and standing in the community."

"Funny, you didn't seem to be too concerned with your reputation when you decided to pursue me."

"I was selfish, and my lust got the better of me, but I didn't force you. You came to me of your own free will, and fully aware of the consequences."

"Are you saying you won't help me?" Bethany demanded. She looked at him as if he were the lowest form of scum on earth and it stung.

"No, I'm not saying that. I wish to propose a plan."

"Then why are you taunting me this way?" Bethany asked, losing some of her righteous anger.

"I'm taunting you because I need you to understand the reality of what you're facing. This is nothing compared to what you will have to endure. You'll be branded a whore once the truth comes out, so you must be willing to do whatever it takes to keep that from happening. And you must refrain from naming me as the father of your child."

"I'm listening," Bethany said quietly. She sounded defeated, and Charles wanted to go to her and take her in his arms, but now wasn't the time to show weakness.

"The only way to avoid a scandal and a trial is for you to marry as soon as possible."

"Who am I meant to marry? Do you think I wouldn't already be married if I had a suitor? Marriage is the only way out for me, not only because of the coming babe, but because if I live with my brother any longer, I will lose any chance of ever having a life of my own. My brother will have spent everything, and I will have nothing left to bring to my husband. No one will want me."

"Bethany, you will marry whomever I put forth."

"I don't understand," Bethany cried. "Who would be willing to take me when I'm already full in the belly?"

"Don't worry about that. Just act normally and don't give your brother or his wife any reason to suspect that you're with child."

Bethany threw Charles a dubious look, and he suddenly realized that she didn't believe him. She thought he was stalling for time, not that time would solve the problem, but if Charles decided to pick up stakes and leave the colony, as some men did when caught in a similar situation, Bethany would be left to deal with the consequences on her own.

"I welcome your help, Charles, but allow me to give you an additional bit of incentive," Bethany said, tears forgotten, hands on hips. "If you don't find me a husband within the next two weeks, I will go to your wife. I might not tell the whole of Jamestown who fathered my child until after it's born, but I will tell her. If I must suffer for my actions, then so do you."

Bethany turned and walked away, her back ramrod straight since she knew Charles was watching her. She'd allow her shoulders to slump once she was out of sight, but Bethany was a proud woman and wouldn't give him the satisfaction of seeing her vulnerability ever again.

Charles had every intention of returning to Jamestown immediately, but instead, sat on a fallen log and contemplated the situation. He really did feel sympathy for Bethany. She was a comely young woman who would wind up an old, embittered shrew, thanks to the laws of the colony and her brother's indifference. Noah Abbott was a hard man, whose wife looked twenty years older than her true age after bearing the man more than a dozen children, nine of whom still lived. Having Bethany under his roof was no hardship for Abbott, but it didn't bode well for Bethany, not if the man was helping himself to what was rightfully hers. Marriage was the only way out for her, but to find a suitable husband would take more than two weeks. Charles thought he'd had the upper hand when he came to meet her today, but Bethany had effectively turned the tables on him with her threat.

Charles got to his feet and sighed. He'd need to give this some thought, but just then, he had to go home. Annabel would question his absence and he could hardly tell her he'd gone to visit Alec, since Alec had just delivered Evie only the day before.

As he rode back to town, he thought of the coming child. If it lived, he would have another son or daughter, a child he would not be able to acknowledge or ever get to know. He wasn't always a good or a kind man, but he did love his children, and the knowledge that the child would be a stranger to him made him feel angry and disappointed. He had no one to blame but himself, but it was too late for recriminations. He had to act, and quickly.

FORTY

VIRGINIA AUGUST 1781

Abbie brought the trap to a stop just outside the house. John Mallory sat next to her, his back erect, his expression alert. He'd made a miraculous recovery, according to Sue, and was finally ready to home. Hannah had remained behind while Abbie went to fetch her father, taking the time to make an extra-special welcome home meal for her husband. She came running out, her hands covered with flour and her face aglow with joy.

"John!" she exclaimed. "Well, aren't you a sight for sore eyes."

"As are you, m'dear," John Mallory said as he carefully climbed down from the trap. His shoulder was still bandaged beneath the shirt and there was some residual swelling and pain, but for the most part, the wound seemed to be healing nicely. "Is that venison stew I smell?"

"It certainly is, with buttermilk biscuits, corn pudding, and an apple pie baked by your loving daughters," Hannah added proudly. Sarah, Annie, and Martha spilled outside, eager to welcome their father. And Sue stood off to the side, smiling happily.

"And where are all my grandchildren?" John cried as he

looked around. "I see Ben, Nat, and Rachel, but I don't see anyone else. Now, I'm just going to cover my eyes for a quick moment and see who shows up when I open them."

Of course, John saw the children hiding behind their mothers, but this was a favorite game of theirs, so he covered his eyes and smiled at the mad giggling that erupted from the children. Diana, Edward, and Joe tried to elbow their way through Ben, Nat, and Rachel, and little Daisy, who was perched on Martha's hip, reached out her arms toward her cousins, not wishing to be left behind. Martha brought her closer but didn't set her on the ground, fearful that the children would shove her out of the way in their excitement.

"Ready or not!" John cried and opened his eyes. He was surrounded by children, who were hugging his legs and pulling on his hands.

"We're here. We're all here," Diana cried. "Come inside, Granddad. There's pie."

"Oh, I know there's pie. I can smell it from here. Who picked the apples?"

"I did," Joe replied, since he was the only one tall enough to reach the lower branches.

"And who made the crust?" John asked.

"We did," Sarah and Annie replied in unison.

"Then it will be the tastiest pie I've ever had. Lead the way," John said to Diana, who was tugging on his hand.

Abbie followed the crowd inside. She was happy to have her father home, but she was still worried about Finn. A persistent nagging in her gut kept her from focusing on the children or her chores.

"Quit moping, Abbie," Martha said as she hoisted Daisy higher on her hip. "Pa has recovered, and our men will come back. Gil went off with the militia again, but you don't see me going around with a face like a lemon."

"There's safety in numbers, Martha, and the militia is

armed. Finn and Sam are on their own, with nothing but a knife between them."

"When did you become such a scaredy-cat?" Martha asked. "Look, even Ma is not fretting as much as usual. Just enjoy this moment; it so easily might not have come."

"You're right," Abbie conceded. "And that pie does smell awfully good. We should have baked one more in case anyone wants seconds."

"I have a sneaking suspicion that if there was enough for seconds, Sarah would be squirreling a piece away for that boy. What's his name?"

"Derek. Derek Johnson. It's so strange to see our little sister sweet on a boy," Abbie said as she settled Edward on a bench next to Rachel. Sarah was busy dishing out stew and hadn't heard her.

"You were just about that age when you set your cap at Finn," Martha observed.

"But I seemed so much older," Abbie protested, recalling that summer.

"You weren't," Martha replied as she disentangled herself from her daughter and plopped the child onto her lap. "Gosh, she's getting heavy," Martha sighed.

"Anyway, Finn and I had to wait to get married," Abbie said, feeling a bit defensive.

"You'd have married him then and there if Pa had allowed it," Martha reminded her. "You had practically proposed to Finn yourself."

"Nothing wrong with that. Men need to be told what's good for them," Hannah chimed in. "Why, if we waited for them to come to their senses, we'd never make it to the church. Just look at your father and me. He'd still be hemming and hawing if I didn't tell him I wished to get married."

"As if," John Mallory chuckled. "Good thing you did though, Hannah, or you would have been an old maid at the ripe old age of seventeen. I saved you from a life of loneliness and hardship."

Hannah Mallory laughed. "I'll never be lonely as long as I have you, you old rascal."

"Good, because I'm not going anywhere. Now, give me some food, woman. I'm starving."

"Here you are, Pa," Annie said shyly as she placed a bowl of stew in front of her father. "And have some corn pudding. Sarah and I made it ourselves."

"Don't mind if I do. I love me some corn pudding. And do you know what we are going to do after supper?" John asked, addressing all the children.

"No, what?" Ben asked.

"I'm going to play the fiddle, and we are going to have a singalong. How does that sound?"

"Yeah!" the children roared.

"Now we'll never get them to bed on time," Sue said, sighing with resignation. "But I suppose this is a special occasion."

"Nothing wrong with a little bit of fun," Hannah said. She was beaming, so Sue hastily agreed.

Abbie looked around the table as everyone tucked into their food and breathed a sigh of contentment. Martha was right, and everything would be all right. Their father was home, and Finn and Sam should be back in a week or so. She just had to buck up till then.

FORTY-ONE

SOMEWHERE IN THE ATLANTIC AUGUST 1628

The darkness was impenetrable, even after her eyes had a moment to adjust. Jenny dressed hastily, using the tips of her fingers to see, then crept toward the door and let herself out of the cabin as quietly as she could. Cameron was sound asleep with Ian lying in the crook of his arm, his little head resting against Cameron's side. They might have looked beatific had Jenny been able to make out their features. She walked carefully, holding on to the wall with one hand, then climbed the ladder to the deck. She woke before dawn no matter how tired she got the day before, and instead of tossing and turning on her narrow berth usually came up on deck to get a bit of fresh air and an hour of peace.

The still-dark sky was strewn with thousands of stars, their light surprisingly bright against the velvety darkness. A quarter moon hung just above the main mast, or so it seemed from Jenny's vantage point. She walked toward the prow and took her customary spot, staring into the black waters of the Atlantic. A lantern burned on the bridge where the quartermaster, Master Ingalls stood at the wheel. The captain was in his cabin, probably still asleep. Captain Rogers rarely emerged before eight, looking bleary-eyed and disgruntled after an evening alone with his port. A few sailors were on deck, but the rest of the crew were slumbering in their hammocks below deck, enjoying their well-deserved rest.

Jenny leaned against the railing and breathed in the briny tang of the ocean. It was warm on deck during the day, but at night, the air was fresh and cool, scented with just a hint of wood and oil from the lanterns. Jenny liked this time of day. It was still dark, but dawn wasn't too far off. She had been at her post for about a quarter of an hour when the sky began to lighten ever so slightly, and the stars lost some of their luster. Jenny peered into the distance, waiting for the moment when the first sliver of shimmering crimson sunlight appeared above the horizon, marking the spot where the sky met the sea and casting out darkness and doubt. She knew it was pointless to doubt, especially now when they were en route to Virginia, but that little nagging voice in her head never left her alone.

She supposed that after two decades of feeling unloved and unwanted, it was natural for her to question people's feelings for her, but she knew, as sure as she knew the sun would rise this day, that Uncle Alec loved her and would welcome her with open arms. She wasn't as sure of Uncle Charles or his haughty wife, but the thought of seeing Alec and Valerie made her breath catch with longing. How was it possible to miss people you'd known for only a short while this much? But she did. She secretly thought of Alec and Valerie as her parents and wholeheartedly wished that they were.

Her natural parents had been faceless specters for most of her life, but at least now she knew something of her mother, Rose, and cherished every morsel that Uncle Alec had shared with her. Charles didn't remember much about his sister, having been a small child when Rose had run off to France to join a convent, but he remembered that she had been kind and loving, and had always found time to play with the little brother who'd made her the butt of his mischievous jokes.

Whenever Jenny thought of what her mother might have been like had she lived, her imagination strayed to Valerie, who was everything a mother should be. Jenny missed Valerie's tactful advice and easygoing attitude. She wasn't like most women she'd met in Jamestown. Valerie, as well as Louisa, were different somehow—more enlightened, more open to change and progress. Valerie and Louisa secretly (or perhaps not so secretly) championed the rights of women, and always told Jenny that she had the right to choose her own path rather than blindly obey her male relatives, not that Uncle Alec had ever tried to force anything on her. It had been Jenny's decision to follow Cameron halfway across the world, and she hadn't regretted her choice for a moment.

The thought of Cameron still made her heart flutter with joy and her secret parts grow moist with longing, and the little secret she'd decided to keep from him felt like a warm glow inside her belly. Jenny laid her hand over her still-flat stomach, smiling happily to herself. Perhaps this one would be a girl, a daughter to love and cherish, and to do all the things with that she'd missed out on doing with her own mother. Cameron would be thrilled, but she wanted to wait before telling him, to be sure the pregnancy took.

She was only a few weeks late, but already she felt the same fatigue she'd felt when first pregnant with Ian. Her breasts were tender to the touch, and she fought nausea every morning, feeling better only after eating some bread. Ale turned her stomach, but there wasn't much else onboard to drink, so she forced herself to gulp it down, knowing that she needed every bit of nourishment for the child.

Jenny sucked in her breath, overcome with wonder, when a crimson dot appeared on the horizon. The murky darkness vanished almost instantaneously, replaced by an inferno of color, the sun rising majestically out of the sea and painting a shimmering pathway across the water. It seemed to lead directly to Jenny, and she turned her face to the sun, not wishing to miss a moment of the glorious sunrise.

"Aurora," Jenny whispered to herself. Dawn. "I'll call you Aurora if you're a girl," she said to the tiny being growing inside her. "If your father agrees, of course," she added, feeling too bold for her own good.

"I think Aurora is a fine name," Cameron whispered in her ear as he wrapped his arm around her shoulders. "What do you think, Ian?"

Ian stuck his thumb in his mouth and looked at Jenny adoringly before remembering that it was time for breakfast. He reached out his arms to Jenny, eyeing her breasts with undisguised lust. Jenny felt a pang of anxiety. Her milk was less plentiful, and she worried that he wasn't getting enough to eat. He had several teeth and was able to gnaw on a hard biscuit and eat some gruel, but Jenny didn't think that was enough to sustain a growing boy. Ian seemed content though and felt even heavier in her arms than only a week ago. He was thriving, there was no doubt, so she pushed her worry aside.

"Come on, little man. Time to eat," Jenny said as she planted a kiss on his nose and turned to go back to their cabin where she could nurse him in private. The last thing she saw before returning to their cabin was Cameron's joyful grin.

FORTY-TWO
VIRGINIA AUGUST 1628

Charles let himself into the house and set his purchases down on the carved mahogany cabinet. He was nearly out of ink and paper, and Annabel had asked for candles. Most people made their own candles, as well as ink, using soot or oak galls, but Annabel preferred to purchase whatever possible since they only had one servant and the poor woman was run off her feet. Charles shrugged off his coat and walked into the parlor, ready to face his wife, who had been in a hell of a mood earlier. Her two previous pregnancies had been fairly easy, but this time, she felt ill well into the afternoon and suffered from fatigue and headaches. Charles advised her to have a lie-down every afternoon, more for his own sake than for hers because by that time she was angry and unreasonable.

He'd come back to the house now because he knew this was the time Annabel liked to rest and the children took an afternoon nap. The house would be quiet, for once, and he would have an hour to himself. Charles stopped short when he walked into the parlor. Annabel was sitting on the edge of the settle, applying a compress to someone's head. All Charles could see of the woman were homespun skirts and well-worn shoes.

"Belle? What happened?" Charles asked. He assumed the woman was their servant Nan, but then caught sight of dark hair spilling from beneath a linen cap and a sun-kissed cheek. Nan was fair-haired and white as buttermilk.

"Mistress Warren felt unwell in the street," Annabel replied, leaving out the part of the explanation where she enlightened Charles as to how exactly Mistress Warren had ended up in his house. "I find that a cool compress always helps."

"I feel much improved. Thank you, Mistress Whitfield," Bethany said from her place on the settle. "I really should be going. I've imposed on you for far too long already."

"Nonsense. You just rest for as long as you need, and then my husband will take you home in the trap. You can't walk all that way by yourself."

"That's really not necessary," Bethany protested, but Charles saw a gleam of amusement in her dark eyes. Not only was she enjoying this, but she'd likely staged the whole thing just to gain entry to his house and access to his wife. He never thought of Bethany as being devious, but suddenly he saw a whole new side to her and realized that he knew little of her nature.

"It would be my pleasure to escort you home, Mistress Warren," Charles said with a slight bow. "You just let me know when you feel ready."

Charles retrieved his purchases from the cabinet and went to deposit them in his makeshift study. Their house was large by Jamestown standards, with two bedchambers on the upper story, a parlor, dining room, and a tiny study at the back of the house, where Charles liked to hide from Annabel when she was in a state. He stored the paper in a drawer, refilled the ink pot, and filled the small wooden cup with new quills, but his mind was on Bethany. Had she said anything to Annabel? She didn't seem to have done since Annabel didn't appear hostile toward him, but this was no coincidence. This was a warning that if he didn't help her, she would speak to Annabel and tell her all.

Of course, under the law of the Virginia Colony, Annabel was powerless to do anything. The most she could do was accuse Bethany Warren of wanton behavior and hope that she was punished, but in doing so, she would also be exposing Charles and shaming herself. No, Annabel would never do such a thing. She would rage at him, make threats, and do her utmost to make his life difficult, but it would all blow over soon enough.

Charles left his sanctuary and went to fetch the trap. Annabel might be without legal rights, but he would be a fool to let things get that far. The situation could get out of hand before Bethany had even begun to show. Annabel might torture him privately for his part in the affair but wouldn't wish to see him punished for lewd behavior before all of Jamestown. Instead, Annabel could publicly accuse Bethany of slander, since she had no way of proving her baby's paternity. To some degree, being accused of slander was even worse than being accused of fornication since it carried a severe punishment, and Charles would hate to see Bethany subjected to any kind of cruelty.

"Charles, if you would take Mistress Warren home now. She's feeling well enough to travel," Annabel called to him through the open door.

"Of course."

Charles handed Bethany into the trap before setting off at a stately pace. Many people would see them together, but he was being a Good Samaritan, not a faithless husband, and that's the image he wanted to put forth. He called out greetings to several people but didn't speak to Bethany until they left Jamestown behind. Then he allowed the smile to slide off his face.

"I hope you're pleased with yourself," he said as he picked up the pace a bit. "That was rather clever, pretending to feel unwell and taking advantage of my wife's good nature."

Bethany shrugged. "I felt you needed a reminder of what's at stake. I haven't seen you in days."

"Oh, I haven't forgotten."

"Good," Bethany replied. "I would hate to think that you would get a woman with child and wash your hands of her."

Charles gave Bethany a sidelong look. She'd tucked her hair back into the cap, but a few stray tendrils escaped, framing her oval face. Her pert nose was up in the air, quivering with righteous indignation, and her eyes blazed with determination. He shifted in his seat, irritated by his body's reaction to his blackmailer. He supposed that Bethany had the same quality he'd once found so attractive in Annabel. She'd managed to remain spirited in a colony where women had virtually no rights and no voice. Bethany was brave and resourceful, and he found that most arousing.

Charles reached over and took Bethany's hand, squeezing her fingers lightly. That surprised her out of her sulk. She turned to look at him, and suddenly her face broke into a smile. She'd been putting on a brave face, but she was desperate for a bit of affection and reassurance that he hadn't simply discarded her now that she was with child. Charles turned the trap off the road and hid it in a clump of trees as he handed Bethany down. She spread an old blanket on the ground and reclined on it, pulling her skirts up just enough to reveal her hose-clad legs, which were lean and shapely. Charles pushed her down on the blanket and kissed her hard, his hand sliding between her legs. Bethany pulled down her bodice and arched her back, offering him her breasts. They'd grown rounder since the last time he'd seen them and were now swollen and tender.

Charles pushed down his breeches and plunged into Bethany's warm depths, gasping with the intensity of the feeling. It never felt this way with Annabel, not anymore. She allowed him to take her, but she no longer enjoyed it, nor did she care enough to even pretend. She pulled her nightdress down as soon as Charles was finished and rolled over to face the wall. Gone were the days of cuddling and sweet pillow talk. He supposed that was the nature of marriage, but he doubted that Valerie treated his brother the same way. She still adored him after all these years, and the feeling was mutual. Alec would never betray his marriage vows; he had too much to lose.

Bethany cried out as he brought her to a climax. Her body felt different now that she was with child, languid and soft. He used to have to tease her for a bit before she was ready for him, but this time, she'd been so moist that he slid right in with no resistance. She had been as aroused as he was, unlike Annabel who forbade relations whenever she was pregnant, saying it wasn't good for the child.

Bethany got to her feet, adjusted her skirts, and tucked her hair back into her cap. "Shall we?" she asked.

"Of course."

They climbed back into the trap and continued on their way as if nothing had happened. Bethany slid further away from Charles as they neared the Abbott farm, where Mistress Abbott was hanging out the washing in the yard.

"Thank you, good sir," Bethany said as Charles handed her down from the trap. "I felt unwell, and Master Whitfield was kind enough to offer me a ride home," Bethany explained to her good-sister, who was watching them with narrowed eyes, laundry forgotten.

Charles tipped his hat to Bethany's brother, who was coming out of the barn, then drove off before the man had a chance to come up to the trap and speak to him. He disliked Noah Abbott, and not only because he was Bethany's brother. There was something shifty about the man and Charles felt a pang of sympathy for Bethany. Any husband would be an improvement on living with this sanctimonious turd.

FORTY-THREE

Charles did not rush home. Instead, he found a secluded spot and settled beneath a leafy tree. It was a glorious afternoon, and the slanted rays of the sun cast a golden light on the clearing. Charles removed his hat and turned his face toward the sky, drinking in the warmth and the church-like silence. He so rarely got any peace these days. It was heavenly to just sit beneath the tree with no one asking anything of him, complaining, crying, or sulking. He'd always thought that it must be awful to be alone, but in small doses it was bliss.

He enjoyed a brief nap before turning his mind to the problem at hand. He would feel an absolute villain if he allowed Bethany to be disgraced and punished. Even if his name was never bandied about in connection with hers, he was a man of honor and owed her a debt. Charles rested his arms behind his head and watched the clouds floating above. Finding a husband in Jamestown was no simple matter. There were plenty of unmarried men among the indentures, but they were in no position to marry, legally or financially. Charles mentally cast his eye over the church congregation. Doctor Jacobson would be a desirable candidate, having recently lost his wife, but being a medical man, he'd suspect that Bethany was already with child, and that simply wouldn't do. Despite his promise to Alec, Charles had no intention of revealing Bethany's pregnancy unless he absolutely had to.

The man Bethany married had to believe that the child was his and had simply come a bit earlier than expected. Bethany wasn't that far along, so at this point, the scheme could still work. But how could he entice someone to marry his mistress without telling them the truth of the situation? Why would a man who is not in any way connected to Bethany Warren be trying to arrange a marriage for her and offering a financial incentive? Tongues would start to wag within five minutes of his approaching the first would-be bridegroom, making the situation even worse. Charles had to be very discreet, and only approach anyone he thought would be open to his proposal. Charles closed his eyes and tried to envision the single men he knew.

There were two men in their seventies, so Charles crossed them off the list, along with a dozen teenage boys who were too young for Bethany. Their parents would not wish them to marry a widow several years their senior. No, it had to be a widower. *Cousin Wesley?* Charles thought, but instantly dismissed Wesley Gaines as a candidate. Wesley had made Harry his heir, but if he married Bethany and she was delivered of a boy, Harry would no longer inherit his grandfather's estate.

David Strong? No, there was talk that he'd beaten his wife to death. He was a violent man who liked his drink, and he had three teenage sons who were as brutish as their sire.

Ethan Bartlett? Charles sat up, suddenly hopeful. He'd forgotten all about Bartlett, probably because the man was new to the colony. Ethan Bartlett had arrived in late spring. He'd lost his wife on the crossing from England and had disembarked at Jamestown with a three-year-old daughter, whom he'd had to foster with a neighboring family since he couldn't manage to care for her himself and work a farm at the same time. He was in his late twenties, with thick dark hair and light eyes, blue or green, Charles couldn't say with any certainty. Bartlett wasn't very tall, but he gave the appearance of strength and resilience.

Charles knew little of his character, but he seemed like a good man. Charles didn't know why Ethan Bartlett had chosen to leave England, but he did know that he was working his farm alone, so he likely had no means to hire help. Whatever profit he made went to pay for his daughter's upkeep and his own survival. Perhaps he would be open to a little monetary incentive, but Charles had to proceed carefully. Bartlett gave the impression of being a proud, independent man. He would not appreciate being duped or manipulated.

Charles finally got to his feet and climbed onto the bench. He would need an excuse to approach Bartlett, but at least he had a candidate. This was welcome news, but Charles's stomach soured at the thought of Bethany lying with Ethan Bartlett.

"You absolute prick," Charles said aloud to himself. "Can't have her for yourself but can't bear anyone else to have her either."

FORTY-FOUR
VIRGINIA SEPTEMBER 1628

Morning light streamed through the window, outlining Alec's profile as he gazed at something beyond the horizon. Kit smiled ruefully, feeling guilty for all the anxiety he'd caused. Someone always kept a vigil by his bed, even though he was on the mend. The miracle drug Valerie had brought back from the future seemed to stop the putrefaction from spreading and allowed his body to begin the process of healing. His leg was still swollen and felt more like a wooden log than a limb, but it was much improved, and the skin was no longer stretched so painfully. The swelling in his hand had gone down, and he was able to move his fingers, if not his wrist. And he was hungry, which was always a good sign.

Louisa brought him something small to eat every few hours, explaining that his body would have a difficult time digesting a large meal when he was bedbound. She'd moved her spinning wheel into the room and sat with him for hours, talking to him when he was awake and spinning quietly when he was asleep. She fed him, washed him, and kept him up to date on the activities of everyone in the house. Kit missed Evie. He hadn't seen her in days, but she was in Jamestown.

He was glad she was with Millie, who was always a positive influence on his wayward daughter. Millie was a sweet, gentle girl, who delighted in making herself useful and craved praise, unlike Evie, who had no use for compliments or approval.

Alec turned toward Kit, his face breaking into a warm smile. "You're awake. Is there anything I can get you? Are you hungry?"

"No, thank you, but I would welcome a game of chess. I could use a distraction. Perhaps Fred could be convinced to visit me. He's a worthy opponent."

"And I'm not?" Alec demanded, clearly wounded by the slight.

"Of course, you are, but you have a plantation to run, and Master Taylor so enjoys reminding me who's the stronger player. Have you decided what to do with those children yet?" Kit asked, earning himself a scowl from Alec.

"Not really. I've turned them over to Master Worthing, who's put them to work clearing a new field, but I don't feel good about exploiting children."

"You can hardly sell them on," Kit observed, knowing that their situation might be worse with a different master.

"No, but I wish Charles would just mind his own business," Alec replied hotly.

"He feels angry, Alec, and useless. He was your partner for years, and now he has nothing more to do than supervise the loading and unloading of your ships. He gets a healthy profit from the rum trade, but he needs something to keep him occupied, and being in the house with Annabel certainly doesn't help matters."

"No, I don't suppose it does," Alec chuckled.

"Alec, don't punish Charles for the actions of his wife. I know you don't always see eye to eye, but he's your only surviving brother, and he does love you and look up to you."

"You're becoming very philosophical in your old age," Alec quipped.

"You know I'm right," Kit replied.

"You are, and Charles might be in for a pleasant surprise one day soon," Alec said.

Kit's smile slid off his face as he absorbed what Alec had said. He could mean only one thing by that comment, as far as Kit could see.

"Are you really going to leave?" Kit asked.

"I miss Finn, Kit. It's like there's a hole in my heart that seems to get bigger with every passing year. I want to be near him. I want to be a part of his life. If it weren't for Valerie's attachment to Louisa, we would have left already, I think, but I don't want to be responsible for tearing those two apart."

Kit nodded. He understood only too well. He was faced with the same dilemma now that he was to live.

"Alec, can I ask you something?"

"Of course."

Kit hesitated. He had to choose his words carefully. "Alec, will I be a cripple?"

"No," Alec replied instantly. "You will not. It will take time for your bones to knit properly, but you will walk again, Kit. You will be every inch the man you were before this catastrophe."

"Are you just saying that to make me feel better? I can't bear the thought of being a burden to Louisa."

"You could never be a burden to her. She loves you. But I am telling you the truth. You will fully recover."

Kit exhaled loudly, feeling as if a great weight had been lifted from his shoulders. "In that case, will you help me shave? I'm afraid Louisa will slit my throat if I ask her to help me. She's good at everything she does, but wielding a razor is not her strong suit."

Alec laughed and got to his feet. "I was wondering when

you would get tired of that forest on your face. I'll get hot water."

"Thank you. It's so itchy."

"Would you like it the way it was before?"

"No. I think I want it all off. I haven't had a clean-shaven face since I was twenty. I hope Louisa will like it."

"Anything is better than that," Alec replied, giving Kit a look of mock disgust. "If I grew a beard like that, Valerie would have nothing more to do with me."

"Well, it wasn't by choice, was it?" Kit replied. He wouldn't be able to use his hand for weeks yet, much less handle a razor.

Alec smiled and left to get the shaving implements.

FORTY-FIVE

Charles woke with a start, certain that he'd heard the creak of an opening door. Normally, he'd just go back to sleep, attributing the sound to Nan going to the privy, but there was an escaped Negro slave on the loose, so it would be imprudent not to investigate. The man would be a fool to come to Jamestown, but who knew how those people thought. Maybe he'd assumed that it would be easier to get his hands on food or valuables rather than taking his chances with the Indians in the woods, or maybe he was biding his time until a loaded ship was ready to leave port, like that Scotsman Jenny had married.

It was pitch dark in the room, but a sliver of lighter darkness could be seen between the shutters, so dawn probably wasn't far off. Charles armed himself with a heavy candlestick and stepped into the corridor, where he nearly collided with Evie, who resembled a restless spirit in her flowing white nightdress.

"What are you doing up, petal? Are you ill?" Charles asked.

"I couldn't sleep," Evie replied. Charles could hear the tears in her voice, so he set aside his weapon and lifted Evie into his arms. "Come, let's go sit in the parlor and you can tell me all about it."

Charles settled Evie on his lap and pushed the hair out of her face to better see her expression. "Did you have a bad dream?"

"No," Evie moaned.

"Then what?"

"I was bad," Evie confessed. Charles tried to keep from smiling. Evie was always bad. She was a mischievous, clever little minx, but whatever she'd done this time must be really special if she couldn't sleep.

"I'm sure it's not as bad as you imagine. What did you do?"

"I let my papa down. I let him think that I don't love him," Evie wailed, finally giving way to her tears.

That took Charles utterly by surprise. "I don't understand, Evie."

"Seeing him in pain made me cry, so I ran away. I didn't want to stay at home where I had to look at him, and now he'll think that I don't love him."

Charles twisted one of Evie's ebony curls around his finger, lost in thought. He had to say something to make her feel better, but it had to make sense to a child. "Evie," he began, "parents who love their children, as your papa loves you, suffer terribly when their children are hurting. So, your papa feels much better because he knows that you are not crying for him. You helped him by leaving."

Evie stared at Charles in the silvery darkness of the moonlit parlor. "That's sound reasoning, Uncle Charles," Evie said wisely. Was she mocking him?

"So, you feel better?"

"I suppose, but I still wish to return home. Now."

"Evie, it's the middle of the night."

"No, it's not." Evie pointed to the window where a peachy ribbon of light wound just above the tree line. "It's morning."

"Wouldn't you like some breakfast?" Charles asked.

He would like some breakfast, but Evie's determined little

face told him he wasn't about to get any. She was already sliding off his lap and heading to the room she shared with Millie and Harry to get dressed and get her things. Charles hoped Nan would be up by the time they were ready to leave and would pack him something for the journey. It would take him at least two hours, and his stomach was growling with hunger, since he hadn't eaten much for supper the night before. Maybe Valerie would invite him to stay for breakfast. Mistress Taylor was a far better cook than Nan and brewed chicory coffee every morning for Valerie and Louisa, who loved the stuff. He thought it was foul at first, but had developed a taste for it, and wouldn't say no to a cup.

By the time the fiery globe of the sun began to rise in the morning sky, Charles and Evie were already on their way to Rosewood Manor. Evie clutched her bundle like a drowning man holding on to a piece of flotsam, her eyes fixed on the road ahead.

"We'll be there soon, petal," Charles assured her. "Did you say goodbye to Millie?"

"No, she was still asleep. Millie is a baby," Evie said haughtily.

Charles smiled to himself. Harry and Robbie were such simple souls, but Millie and Evie were already women through and through. Whoever said that women were inferior to men? Their emotions spanned a much greater range of feeling, even at such a young age, and they felt things so deeply that it seared their souls. Evie and Millie were of an age, but they were so different, and had been from birth. Charles suddenly wondered what his child with Bethany would be like if it were a daughter. Would she be sweet and compliant like Millie or temperamental and fiery like Evie? He hoped she would be like Millicent. Women like Millie found life easier, since they didn't chafe against their limitations so much. They found contentment in what they had rather than focusing on what they didn't.

Evie would not have an easy time of it once she came of age, Charles was sure of that. She was too much like her cousin Louisa, who'd managed to stir up trouble everywhere she went.

Charles pushed thoughts of Bethany Warren and their future child from his mind as Rosewood Manor came into view. Evie sat up straighter and leaned forward, desperate to be home. Charles hoped Kit knew how lucky he was to have a daughter who loved him so dearly. Evie jumped into Charles's arms as soon as he came around to help her down from the trap and sprinted toward the house, screaming, "Papa, I'm back." Charles chuckled and followed her inside, his mouth watering at the smell of freshly baked bread and coffee.

FORTY-SIX

Despite the early hour, the house was humming with activity. Cook was dishing out breakfast, Minnie was feeding the children, and Alec was on his way to the tobacco fields, which he had neglected since Kit's accident. Charles happily accepted a cup of coffee and a slice of bread liberally spread with butter and Valerie's strawberry jam. He sighed with pleasure as the sweetness settled on his tongue. Nan didn't know how to make jam, nor was there anywhere for her to pick strawberries.

Valerie spread butter and jam on two more slices of bread and placed them on a plate to be taken up to Kit. Louisa reached for the plate and handed it to Evie.

"Here, why don't you take breakfast up to Papa? He will be so happy to see you. He's been asking for you."

Evie carefully balanced the plate in her hands as she headed toward the stairs. "Bye, Uncle Charles," she called over her shoulder.

"Thank you for bringing her home," Louisa said as she poured a cup of coffee for herself. "She can be unbearable when she sets her mind to something."

"It was no trouble," Charles replied.

He still felt awkward around Louisa. She was outwardly polite, but sometimes the way she looked at him made his blood run cold. Charles finished his breakfast and stood to leave. He'd hoped to see Kit but didn't want to interrupt his reunion with Evie. Charles felt a pang of sadness as he said his goodbyes and left the house. He missed living at Rosewood Manor, and he missed the people in it. If it weren't for Annabel, relations would not be strained, and things could go back normal. But Louisa would never forgive Annabel for what she'd done, and although Kit remained politely tight-lipped, he resented Annabel as well, and some of that resentment was reserved for Charles.

He couldn't blame Kit and Louisa. He should have tried harder to stop Annabel. He should have locked her in the house and exercised his husbandly right to forbid her to testify. He'd been a fool, and now he was paying the price. He was still welcome at Rosewood Manor, but just barely, and things would never be the same.

Alec was leading his horse out of the stable but stopped to speak with Charles. "Are you any closer to resolving the matter we discussed?" Alec asked, referring to Bethany. There was no one about, but Alec still preferred to be discreet, which, for some reason, annoyed Charles.

"No, but Bethany decided to pay Annabel a visit, just to spur me on," Charles complained.

"She's scared, Charles, and with good reason."

"I know, and I am scared for her, and for myself, but I can't conjure up a husband out of thin air."

"Have you come up with any suitable prospects?" Alec asked.

"I might have. How are the orphans working out?" Charles asked, desperate to change the subject. He was suddenly sorry he'd shared his troubles with Alec. It made him feel small and dirty to be in this position when his brother was a veritable saint.

Alec threw him a look of derision. "Don't talk to me about that, Charles. Every time I send those children into the fields, I feel like a monster. Some of them are as young as Evie and Robbie. But what am I supposed to do with them if I don't put them to work? I must still clothe and feed them, and there are twelve of them, not two. I do wish you would have consulted me before making this decision."

"And what would you have said?"

"You know what I would have said."

"You used to value my input, Alec, and now you treat me like a pariah," Charles retorted, feeling defensive and humiliated.

Alec and his holier-than-thou attitude always annoyed him. If Charles were running the plantation, as he should have been, things would be different. Charles jumped onto the bench of the trap and grabbed the reins. It was time to go. He obviously wasn't welcome here, not today.

"Thank you for breakfast, Valerie," Charles called out as Valerie came to the door.

"Anytime, Charlie."

Charles gave a halfhearted wave and drove away. It was time to go see Ethan Bartlett and put his plan into action, but he needed something to fall back on. Bartlett might reject his proposal out of hand, and then he'd be back where he'd started. Charles, once again, cast his mind over the bachelors of Jamestown. There was one person he'd overlooked. Baxter Healy. Healy lived in town and was a whitesmith, who supplied Jamestown with pewter and tin products. He did a brisk trade, since there was always a demand for cups, plates, and lanterns. Healy had been in Jamestown for at least a decade and had buried three wives during that time. Now he lived alone, with not even a child to comfort him.

Charles considered this odd situation. Three wives and not a single child between them. The wives did not die in childbirth, as far as he was aware, so it was possible that Healy had not been able to get any of them with child. Usually, when a couple failed to produce an offspring, the woman was blamed and accused of being barren, but if all three women had failed to conceive, it stood to reason that it was the man who was to blame. Perhaps Healy would welcome a child, even if it weren't his own. He'd built a successful business over the past decade and might want someone to leave it to. Charles brightened at this idea. Yes, Healy was a definite possibility. He was nearing fifty, stocky, and bald, but beggars couldn't be choosers. He would approach Healy if Bartlett refused.

Charles found Ethan Bartlett in the barn, milking a cow. If the man was surprised by Charles's unexpected visit, he was too polite to say so and invited Charles into his home for a cup of beer. Charles accepted and followed Bartlett into the house. The place was surprisingly tidy for a man with no wife. There was no dirty crockery stacked high, no unmade bed, and no sign of rodents. In fact, the floor was swept, the bed was neatly made, and all the wooden surfaces gleamed as if Bartlett polished them as soon as he woke in the morning. Charles accepted a seat at the table and thanked Bartlett for the beer.

Ethan Bartlett poured a cup for himself and sat across from Charles, his expression one of mild curiosity. Charles had prepared a speech on his way over but looking into the man's eyes made him change tack. The only way forward was to tell the truth, unpalatable though it might be. If Ethan Bartlett accepted his terms, he'd be doing so after full disclosure.

"How can I help you, Master Whitfield?" Bartlett asked politely.

"I was hoping I might be able to help you," Charles replied. He set down his empty cup and pinned Bartlett with his stare.

THE TIES THAT BIND

"Look, I'm going to get straight to the point. Some time ago, I took up with a woman who is not my wife," Charles began.

"And now she is with child, and you're looking for someone to make an honest woman of her," Bartlett completed the sentence. "Please, leave my house, Master Whitfield. I'm not your man."

"Look, Bartlett, I am offering something in return. You need help on the farm, and I will secure an indenture of your choice. Also, having a wife will enable you to get your daughter back. The lady in question is a beautiful, kind woman. Her only misstep has been to allow herself to be seduced by the likes of me. Won't you at least think about it?"

"No. Do you honestly think that I would marry someone's cast-offs? My daughter and I deserve better than that, and I'm deeply offended that you would even put this proposition before me. Now, go."

"I'm sorry, Master Bartlett. I shouldn't have come." Charles stood and held out a hand to Ethan Bartlett, but the man refused to shake it.

"Who else will you be offering this to?" Bartlett asked as he walked Charles to the door. He didn't sound angry, just mildly curious.

"I have several candidates in mind, but truthfully, you were my first choice."

"Why? Because you think me gullible, or because you imagine that I can't manage on my own and would jump at the chance?"

"No, because you're handsome," Charles replied with a guilty smile. It felt strange to say that to another man, but it was the truth. Bartlett was a good-looking man, with a pleasant demeanor and open manner, well, at least when he wasn't being insulted.

"What?" Bartlett looked stunned by Charles's answer, but

then he laughed. "You think me handsome? Was that your only criteria?"

"I just thought that the lady deserves some happiness in her life. She lost her husband after being married less than a year. She is young and beautiful, and I thought that if I found her an attractive man she might eventually fall in love with him and be happy."

Charles walked out the door, but Bartlett followed him outside. "You really care for her, don't you?"

"I do. And I care for the child she's carrying. Were I free to marry, I would wed her in a heartbeat, but I have a wife and children, and my life is no longer my own."

"I've met your wife, Whitfield. She's a handsome woman," Bartlett said as he walked Charles to the trap. He didn't say anything more, but Charles could see the question in his eyes.

"Yes, she is, but sometimes things happen in a marriage that taint everything that had come before."

"Are you referring to that murder trial? I heard about that, although it'd happened before I arrived in the colony."

"Yes, my wife insisted on testifying and her obstinacy tore the family apart," Charles replied. He hadn't intended to be so open with Bartlett, but there was something about the man's easygoing manner that invited confidences.

"You could have stopped her," Bartlett said as he looked at Charles with newfound interest.

"Yes, I suppose I could have, and should have, but I tend to believe that women have minds of their own and deserve respect. I didn't prevent her from testifying because she genuinely believed she was doing the right thing, and now I'm about as welcome at my brother's house as Judas."

"I must admit, you surprise me, Whitfield. I didn't take you for a liberal, nor did I think you'd care about the fate of a woman you'd used to lessen your marital dissatisfaction. You always struck me as something of a selfish bastard," Bartlett said with a disarming grin.

"A few years ago, I wouldn't have cared," Charles replied as he took hold of the reins. "Please keep what I asked of you in confidence, Master Bartlett."

"Wait," Bartlett called after Charles as he pulled away from the yard. "Can I have some time to think about your offer?"

"You have until tomorrow," Charles called out over his shoulder. He was glad that Bartlett couldn't see his smug smile.

FORTY-SEVEN
PENNSYLVANIA SEPTEMBER 1781

Finn grew angrier with every mile he put between himself and Sam. He had a mind to turn back, but deep down, he knew he wouldn't. He had a mission to complete, and had no choice but to see it through, but oh how he wished he didn't feel so helpless. When his parents had described the wondrous inventions of the future, he'd listened with great interest and wished that he could see these miracles for himself, since he simply couldn't envision them, but he'd never longed for one in his real life. Tales of the future were fascinating, but to him, they were nothing more than science fiction, as his dad referred to stories that took place in realms that were made up by imaginative authors.

A cell phone. What he wouldn't give for one of those now. To be able to speak to someone who was far away, even on another continent, was a notion so miraculous he couldn't quite believe his parents hadn't made up the whole thing to astound him for their own amusement. Finn could almost believe that hot water came out of pipes or that a moving picture could be shown in a flat box, but a communication device that wasn't attached to anything and could fit into the palm of a hand was beyond his comprehension. He couldn't believe it was real, but it was, and at this moment, he wished for nothing more than to be able to have access to one. He knew that having the apparatus wasn't enough. The people he was trying to reach would need one too, and there was something called a cell tower that sent signals and made communication possible, but he didn't care about the logistics of the thing, he just wanted to call Sam and Abbie.

Finn gritted his teeth as he tried to get a handle on his emotions. He had no way of knowing if Abbie, the children, and the Mallory women were safe, any more than he could find out if Mr. Mallory was on the road to recovery or had succumbed to his wounds. And Sam. Poor Sam. He'd left his best friend in the world with virtual strangers less than twenty-four hours after he'd been hanged and nearly died. Sam wasn't himself; he needed help, but Finn had left him to deliver a message that might no longer be relevant by the time he finally got it to Washington's camp. Information changed daily, and the intelligence he carried might already be worthless. But how could he know? How could he make the choice between the future of his country and his own feelings? He tried to tell himself that Sam understood and was in good hands with the Hammers, but the nagging voice of guilt wouldn't be silenced.

And Abbie. Dear God, what he wouldn't give to know that Abbie was safe. If only he could make a call to Washington's headquarters and relay what he'd memorized so carefully, then he could turn around, fetch Sam and return home to his family. Finn dug his heels into the flanks of his horse, urging the tired animal to go faster. He had to get to Philadelphia no later than tomorrow. In the meantime, he had to trust that everyone was all right, but his innards twisted with apprehension. They weren't. He just knew it.

FORTY-EIGHT

Sam woke with a start, snatched from a deep sleep by a jolt that seemed to start in his chest and reverberate all through his body. He'd seen a deer get struck by lightning once and watched the helpless animal as it shuddered and convulsed, its eyes rolling wildly in its head. The unbridled power of the lightning bolt went through it and burned it from the inside, leaving it in a lifeless heap on the forest floor, the air smelling of charred flesh and ozone. That was the only comparison he could make to what this felt like.

The house was quiet, the darkness absolute. Sam tried to make out the outline of the shutters, hoping it was almost morning, but couldn't discern even a sliver of lighter black where the window should be. He sucked in his breath, bracing for another attack. He'd suffered one the night Finn left. Mary Hammer had tried to help by talking gently to him and administering some decoction meant to calm him down, but although he appreciated her efforts, they hadn't worked. Sam had continued to convulse, gasping for breath as his heart hammered in his chest, his body seemingly being torn apart. After a time, the attack had passed, leaving him eviscerated and trembling with fatigue. He'd fallen into a deep sleep that lasted well into the next day.

The Hammers normally rose at dawn, but Friend Mary allowed Sam to sleep for as long as he needed, and he began to feel marginally better over the course of the next few days. His throat was still on fire and he couldn't speak above a whisper, but he'd helped Eli Hammer with some chores and had spent an hour chopping wood, something he found strangely cathartic.

Sam thought he might finally be on the mend, but as his heart began to race and all thought was driven from his mind, he tried to hold on to the only thing he could in the face of such an assault – Susanna. But the tempest that raged within him had the power to obliterate all thought. His body shuddered and his mind seemed to shatter into a million pieces, each fragment a tail-end of a thought, or a feeling—he couldn't tell which. Sam gasped for breath and grabbed on to the sides of the straw mattress as he tried to hold on to the here and now despite the vortex of sensation he was experiencing.

The Hammers remained blissfully unaware of his suffering as they slumbered on in the next room. Sam fought for breath as bursts of color detonated inside his head, the explosions blinding against his closed eyelids. The frame of the cot rattled as his body shook, but eventually the intensity of the attack began to ebb, and Sam was able to draw breath again. He was soaked with sweat but freezing at the same time. He reached out a hand to feel his breeches. Thankfully, he hadn't wet himself.

Sam waited a few minutes before sitting up on his cot. He was dizzy and thought he might throw up, but he forced himself to stand and held on to the wall as he made for the door. The air outside was balmy and thick with the smells of vegetation and muck from the barn. The stars were obscured by a thick haze that blanketed the sky like cotton wool, the humidity making it hard to breathe. Sam focused on staying upright as he walked toward the barn and found the stall housing his horse. He ran his hand gently along the horse's back, talking to it as if it were an old friend as he led it from the stall. He couldn't stay in that house a moment longer. He needed to get away. He had to get home.

Sam walked the horse toward the chopping block he'd used earlier that day. Normally, he would have vaulted into the saddle, but his legs felt weak and he needed a leg-up. He leaned forward and rested his face against the warm neck of the horse, grateful for that small physical contact. It helped him to feel more himself somehow, and he wrapped his arms around the powerful neck of the animal, drawing comfort from it. The horse responded by pressing its ears back, as it often did when the children gave it an apple or a piece of carrot, and Sam smiled, suddenly feeling less vulnerable.

A gentle rain began to fall, coating Sam's hair and skin in a fine mist. He lifted his face to the heavens and allowed the rain to fall into his eyes and mouth as the horse walked on, oblivious to the weather. Sam was soaked within minutes, but the cool wetness of his shirt and the intoxicating smell of rain-soaked earth and pine were exhilarating.

"Let's go home, boy," Sam said to the horse as he picked up the pace to a trot. "Let's go home."

FORTY-NINE
VIRGINIA SEPTEMBER 1628

Charles blew out the candle and got into bed. Annabel was snoring lightly, her face relaxed in repose. No one could tell she was pregnant when she was fully dressed, but now, clad only in her nightdress, all the signs were there. Her breasts were fuller, and her normally flat belly was rounded, reminding Charles of a half moon. She was about five months along, so the babe should start moving any day now, perhaps it already had, but Annabel hadn't told him.

Charles reached out and put his hand on Annabel's stomach. She didn't wake, so he left his palm resting on her belly in the hope that the child would make its presence known. He was excited about the new baby and hoped it would be another boy. He adored his Millie, but in his mind, boys were easier for a father to connect with. Millie would always be his little darling, but in a few short years, she would start developing into a woman and then their bond would be tested. He would have to guide and control her, especially once she became old enough for marriage. He hated the thought of losing Millie to some man, but that was the way of the world. He only hoped that she would find happiness in her future union.

Charles finally removed his hand. The child must be sleeping, he concluded as he turned over onto his side. Tomorrow he would have to go see Baxter Healy. Charles had hoped that he'd convinced Bartlett to go along with his plan, but the day had come and gone and with no word from Ethan Bartlett. Charles sighed irritably. He didn't want Bethany to marry Healy, and besides, what incentive could he offer the man? Healy was comfortably off, and in a position to marry again if he chose to. Why would he wish to marry Charles's pregnant mistress?

Charles cringed with disgust as he imagined Baxter Healy panting and groaning atop his Bethany. Funny, but only a few weeks ago, Charles had taken Bethany completely for granted, thinking of her only when he felt the urge to lie with her, but now that she was almost out of his reach, he suddenly felt melancholy and—for lack of a better word—jealous. Yes, he was jealous of the man who'd marry Bethany, and resentful that someone else would bring up his child. If only he could have two wives, he mused as he stared up at the embroidered canopy. Then again, it would be double the aggravation. He'd loved Annabel once and hadn't been able to wait to come home to her, but over the years, his sweet girl had become angry and bitter, and at times, vengeful. She'd been devastated by the loss of her father and brother, but everyone lost people. They were blessed not to have lost any children. Mortality was so high for children, especially in this colony where the only medical man was Doctor Jacobson.

The colonists called Jacobson names behind his back and made cruel jokes at his expense, but Charles thought they were being unfair. The man had little to work with. He was far removed from the medical advances of Europe and had no access to new medicines or surgical implements. He did his best with what he had to hand. The natives had some knowledge of local plants and healing potions, but Doctor Jacobson would never permit himself to learn from the savages or admit that they might not be entirely ignorant when it came to healing.

Doctor Jacobson seemed to have helped Kit, who was on the mend. Perhaps bringing Kit back from the brink of death would improve his standing in the community. Kit's recovery was nothing short of miraculous, so perhaps the Sheridans would leave for England before long. With Kit and Louisa out of the way, the path to a full reconciliation with Alec and Valerie would be clear, and perhaps they could even move back into Rosewood Manor. Charles smiled as he imagined such an outcome. He and Annabel back at the house, Bethany married to a good man, and two new babies to mark a new beginning.

Charles closed his eyes and tried to sleep, but all he could see was the broad back of Baxter Healy as he labored between the legs of his lover, his unborn babe squirming between them. Charles's stomach soured, his lovely dream shattering into a million pieces.

FIFTY

Alec shut the door to the study and pulled his glasses from their hiding place. He never used to keep the door closed, but since Valerie brought him the glasses, he could no longer afford for someone to just walk in. He still marveled at how the glasses improved his eyesight. He could see as well as he did when he was a young man. Suddenly, the print and the numbers were crystal clear, and he no longer got headaches from trying to balance a ledger or reading a passage in a book.

He was just about to add up a column of figures when there was a knock at the door. He whipped off the glasses and shoved them in a drawer before inviting his visitor to come in. He was surprised to see Louisa. She never came to his study, and especially not looking as sheepish as she did at that moment. The color had returned to her cheeks, and she no longer had the haunted look of someone whose worst possible fears were about to come true. Louisa still spent much of her day with Kit, but now that he was feeling better, she was once again involved in the running of the household and the schooling of the children.

"Alec, may I have a word?" Louisa asked as she shut the door behind her.

"Of course. Is Kit all right?"

"Kit is going mad with boredom and inactivity, but he is feeling better. I've even asked around Jamestown if anyone might be willing to lend him a few books to aid his recovery. Reading is about the only thing he can manage right now, and our library is so limited. Oh, I do wish there was a bookshop in this God-forsaken colony."

"As do I. I've read all our books cover to cover and back again. The *Morning Star* is not due back until sometime in December. There will be new reading material then," Alec said, hoping that the captain had purchased everything on his list.

"That's actually not why I'm here," Louisa said shyly. "I would like your permission for something."

"My permission?" Alec asked, utterly taken aback. As a rule, Valerie and Louisa presented him with their fully formulated plans, but never asked for permission to put any of them into action. "What are you up to, Louisa?"

Louisa grew flustered for a moment, as if searching for the best way to present her idea to him, then finally spoke.

"Alec, I would like to start a school."

The notion of opening a school in the colony was radical, since most colonists were virtually illiterate, but a school run by a woman was tantamount to suggesting a trip to the moon.

"In town?" Alex asked carefully, hoping to buy himself time to formulate a gentle refusal.

"No," Louisa chuckled. She understood only too well how unrealistic such an undertaking would be. "I'd like to start a school right here on the plantation."

Alec leaned back in his chair and studied Louisa for a moment. He wasn't sure what he'd expected, but it wasn't this.

"Go on," he prompted.

"I know that the townspeople would never send their children to school. They need them to help with the chores, and in any case, most of them are illiterate and would see no point in learning to read and write. The ones who aren't, teach their children at home. I am talking about the children on the plantation. I know that this is the way things are done now and that these orphans are lucky to end up in your care, but I can't help wondering what will happen to them once their indenture is up. What skills will they have to help them succeed in this colony? How will they support themselves?"

"So, what exactly are you proposing?" Alec asked, intrigued.

"I propose that the children finish work by noon on Saturdays and then have lessons after lunch. I can start with teaching them how to read, and if I'm successful, I can move on to writing and simple arithmetic. It would be once a week, for no more than two hours. I know that reading and writing won't solve all their problems, but it will give them something they would otherwise never have—options."

"I think that's a wonderful idea, Louisa, but we don't have enough paper, quills, and ink for a dozen pupils. Supplies are always short."

Louisa gave Alec a triumphant smile. "I've thought of that, and I already have a solution. All I will need is about seven sheets of paper."

Alec gaped at her. "How can you possibly teach twelve children to read with seven sheets of paper?"

"I will cut the paper into eighths and make cards, two cards per letter. Once I've taught the children to recognize the letters, I will use the cue cards to spell out simple words."

"And then?"

"And then I will write out simple sentences and have the children read them. Once they can do that, we can use one of your books to practice."

Alec nodded, agreeing to this plan. "Louisa, that's brilliant. I will talk to the children today at supper and tell them of your plan. But what if some of the other workers wish to participate?"

"Perhaps we can start after the harvest. There won't be as much work, so everyone might be spared for two hours once a week. I think our school should be open to anyone who wishes to learn."

"I agree. You make the cards, and I will find a book with the simplest wording for you to use."

Louisa beamed. "Thank you, Alec. It's not just for the children, you know. It's for me as well. I know that there's always plenty to do but carding wool or darning stockings doesn't give me a sense of accomplishment. I long make a difference, even in some small way. I suppose that's the modern woman in me talking, but I feel so useless at times."

"Louisa, you are anything but useless, but I understand what you mean. I might not have before my sojourn to the future, but I do now. Women have come a long way, and for you and Valerie to have to live with the limitations imposed on you by this society must be more difficult than I can imagine. Start your school and make a success of it. I'm behind you all the way."

Louisa came around and planted a kiss on Alec's cheek. "You know, you're all right, Alec Whitfield."

"I'm glad you think so."

FIFTY-ONE

It was nearly noon by the time the ship from England finally docked, and another two hours before the indentures were released from its bowels and led to the center of town where potential buyers already milled about, ready to inspect the latest crop. The new arrivals were a sorry bunch: dirty, smelly, and infested with vermin. There were four women and nine men, all likely sent down for some minor crime against the Crown. Charles wasn't planning on making any bids today, but he liked to come and watch the proceedings, having little else to do since he wasn't needed or wanted at the plantation, and neither of the Whitfield ships were due to come in for a while. It was also a welcome distraction, since today was the day Bethany had set as the deadline for him. Charles didn't blame her for trying to force his hand, but nothing had come out of his attempt at finding her a husband.

Charles had approached Baxter Healy after all, but the man refused to hear him out. He had no wish to marry again, and if he did, he'd find his own wife, thank you very much. Charles was careful not to reveal the name of the woman in question, fearful that the news would get out and Bethany would be persecuted, but the truth would become obvious soon enough. Bethany was naturally slim, so her condition would become apparent sooner rather than later. Perhaps she could keep it a secret for a few more months, but by the time she was six months gone, all of Jamestown would know, and she would become a target for abuse and derision. He had to protect her at all cost, even if he couldn't fulfill his side of the bargain and find her a safe haven. He'd go see her later today. Perhaps he could convince her to leave Jamestown and travel to a neighboring colony where she could claim to be a widow, but a pregnant woman traveling alone with a sum of money was a dangerous proposition, and Bethany might never make it to her destination alive.

And truth be told, Charles didn't want Bethany to leave. He wanted to see his child, even if he couldn't be a part of its life. Charles clasped his hands behind his back and fixed his attention on the indentures, mentally choosing the ones he would buy if he were shopping today. Two of the men looked promising. They were young and strong and had years of hard work in them. But Alec had forbidden him to purchase any more workers, claiming that he had more than enough to work the tobacco fields and the corn and wheat fields. Had it been up to Charles, he would have expanded the plantation and added at least one more tobacco field to make the estate more profitable, but Alec seemed to have no interest in increasing their profits. He was content with the way things were, claiming that between the tobacco crop and the trade with England and the West Indies, he earned more than enough to support everyone at Rosewood Manor and give his share to Charles.

Alec had grown old and soft, and Charles felt the old resentment welling within him as he thought of the injustice done to him first by their uncle, who left the entire estate to Alec, and then by Alec himself. Perhaps it was time for him to break with the family business and begin a venture of his own.

To hell with Alec. Charles needed to buy some land and start growing tobacco. He could start small, just one field, but if he reinvested all his profit into the business, he could expand his operation to several fields and eventually become a competitor to Alec and the rest of the tobacco growers in the colony.

And he could demand that Alec surrender the ownership of one of the ships to Charles. After all, why did Alec get to control everything? Yes, he was the elder, but there were two brothers and two ships. It made sense that each brother should own one ship. It made for healthy competition. Their imports of rum to the colony had increased tenfold since Valerie suggested that they start bringing the cane liquor from the West Indies. That had been a brilliant idea, more so because it had been put forth by a woman. Perhaps it was time to start importing rum not only to Virginia, but to England. The number of taverns in London alone was staggering, so why limit imports to the two small inns in Jamestown.

The thought made Charles smile. Why hadn't he considered this before? He'd been moping around and licking his wounds for the past two years, feeling sorry for himself, when he should have been planning his future. He would have to wait and see what happened with Bethany, but in the meantime, he needed to plan and save toward buying his first tract of land. Charles studied the indentures with new interest. He couldn't start buying workers before he had land for them to work, but now it wasn't just idle curiosity, it was research.

"I'll take that one," a voice behind him said quietly. Charles turned around, surprised to find Ethan Bartlett behind him. Bartlett had his hat pulled low over his eyes to block out the sun, but Charles could still see the smug smile playing about his lips.

"Which one?"

"The tall, fair one. He looks strong and able," Bartlett replied, moving to stand shoulder to shoulder with Charles.

"Does this mean you accept my terms?" Charles asked, his heart swelling with hope.

"It does."

"What changed your mind?" Charles asked as he stealthily passed Bartlett several coins. It wouldn't do for anyone to suspect that Charles had paid for the man. There'd be talk and speculation among the townsfolk, and that was the last thing either Charles or Ethan Bartlett needed under the circumstances. The bid had to come from Bartlett himself, and the indenture contract signed by him.

"My wife changed my mind," Ethan Bartlett replied as he waited for the man's turn at the block.

"Pardon?"

"My wife and I had known each other since we were children," Ethan Bartlett said, his voice trembling with sorrow. "There had never been anyone else for either of us. It was her dream to come to Virginia and start a new life where we would have more opportunities and freedom. But, as you know, she died during the crossing, never having laid eyes on the New World she had so looked forward to seeing. If I allow my farm to fail and see our daughter raised by strangers, I would have failed my Kathy, so I accept your offer. I will marry your woman, get my daughter back, and use the additional help to make my farm prosper. Perhaps in time, I will also learn to care for my new wife and her baby. I know that Kathy would want me to help a young woman in need and give shelter to a child who might not otherwise know love or security."

"You're a good man, Bartlett," Charles said as he clapped Ethan Bartlett on the shoulder.

"Pity I can't say the same for you, Whitfield. There is one condition," Bartlett added, his eyes narrowing as he stared at Charles. "If I see you anywhere near my wife, I will appeal to have the marriage annulled, and name you as the father of her child. You will both be disgraced, and your family will suffer."

"You wouldn't dare," Charles retorted, furious at being manipulated by Bartlett, who now had the upper hand in the negotiation.

"Oh, I would. You and your mistress have a lot more to lose than I do. Everyone will pity me for being duped, and I will still get to keep the indenture and, in time, reclaim my child. Do we have a deal, Whitfield?"

"We do." Charles knew when he was over a barrel and made no attempt to dissuade Bartlett. He would have imposed the same condition were he in the man's shoes. Charles held out his hand and Bartlett shook it, smiling broadly.

"Let's inform the bride then."

FIFTY-TWO

PENNSYLVANIA SEPTEMBER 1781

Finn's misery dissipated somewhat by the time he reached Philadelphia. His mother said that the name meant "The City of Brotherly Love," and he could certainly see why it had inspired such a romantic name. The biggest city Finn had seen to date had been Williamsburg, but Philadelphia was like nothing he'd ever experienced. It was a sprawling metropolis with wide streets flanked by imposing brick mansions. Did one family really need that much room? Finn supposed that they did if they had to house a staff of servants. Everything about Philadelphia seemed bigger and grander, and even the people who walked the streets or passed by in open carriages were more sophisticated.

Finn watched a woman come out of a mansion followed by a turbaned Negro servant who walked a few steps behind her mistress. The woman was dressed in an exquisite gown of peacock-blue with accents of gold, her hair swept back from her forehead and arranged in a mass of curls atop her head, with one long curl snaking over her shoulder and resting on her ample breast. Finn stopped and watched as the woman made her way toward a waiting carriage. A gentleman in a Continental uniform, a high-ranking officer by the looks of it, bent over her hand and kissed it before helping the lady into the carriage.

Finn felt a pang of irritation. Americans wanted to throw off the yoke of British rule and everything that went with it, such as titles and the king himself, but even without the accoutrements of a monarchy, there would always be rich and poor. Abbie, who worked from dawn to dusk, would never own such a beautiful gown or have a lady's maid to style her hair. She wore homespun every day of her life and covered her own lovely curls with a lace-trimmed mob cap to keep it from getting dusty and tangled as she went about the myriad tasks that needed to be done every single day. Finn wanted more for his family than never-ending toil. Abbie deserved to feel luxurious fabric against her skin and have her hair fashionably styled.

Perhaps it was wrong to nurse his dissatisfaction, but his father had grown up a gentleman and his mother had owned beautiful gowns before coming to Virginia in the beginning of the seventeenth century. There was nothing wrong with wanting to better one's lot. Was there? Was there a moral line between ambition and greed? And what man didn't wish for a house of his own? He'd been promised one, but now, two years later, he and Abbie still lived in the loft of the Mallory farm. There never seemed to be enough time or sufficient resources to build them a home of their own.

"Once this blasted war is over and we are victorious, then we will build you a house, Finn," Mr. Mallory said often, especially when his normally gruff exterior was mellowed by drink. "And a fine house it will be."

Finn stopped short, his heart thumping in his breast. He'd heard that phrase so often, but it'd just dawned on him that the end of the war was less than six weeks away. October 19th, 1781—the date of British surrender at Yorktown. Perhaps the information he carried would play a vital role in the outcome after all. Finn pushed silk gowns and spacious rooms from his mind and hurried down the street. He had a job to do. He'd do it and leave immediately to return to Sam. He was in no doubt that Mary and Eli Hammer were taking good care of his friend, but Sam needed him, and he needed his family. No one would care for him like Susanna, and he would recover in no time.

It took Finn the better part of an hour to locate the house where Ralph Hewitt was quartered, but he finally found himself in front of an imposing mansion on Filbert Street. There seemed to be a lot of activity as people came and went, some in uniform, others in civilian attire. Finn approached the door and was stopped by a uniformed soldier who demanded to know his business.

"I'm looking for Ralph Hewitt. I have important information for him," Finn replied, squaring his shoulders. He wasn't sure why he felt defensive, but the soldier made him feel like a country bumpkin who'd lost his way.

"You mean, General Hewitt?" the soldier retorted with a sneer.

"Ah yes, General Hewitt."

"This way," the soldier replied and led Finn into the foyer. "Wait here. And don't touch anything."

Finn walked slowly toward a tall clock positioned between the windows that faced the street. He'd never seen anything so fine in his life. The body of the clock was made of polished dark wood, naval scenes depicted on the base and up the column. The clock itself was made of metal, its face glowing in the light as intricately wrought hands pointed to large Roman numerals. Finn nearly jumped out of his skin when the clock began to chime the hour, the sound deep and somber.

"That's a pendulum clock," Ralph said as he joined Finn in the foyer. "Beautiful, isn't it? Came with the house. It belonged to a wealthy Tory family. They fled Philadelphia when the

British pulled out and left most of their possessions behind. Their loss is our gain."

Finn turned to face Ralph. He'd never seen him in uniform, and the effect was intimidating. Ralph wore a dark-blue coat with a buff collar, lapels, and cuffs, the row of metal buttons gleaming in the sunlight. His waistcoat and breeches were white, as was the neckcloth that was a stark contrast to Ralph's tanned face, but what impressed Finn most were the golden epaulets on Ralph's shoulders, a symbol of his high rank.

"You look splendid, Ralph," Finn said as he followed Ralph into a receiving room where they could speak privately.

"I feel like a glorified peacock, but the ladies find our uniforms hard to resist," he joked. "It's strange, but we attend more balls than battles. I never expected dancing to be a valuable skill in a soldier. Good thing my mother had taught me. Father never did hold with all that frivolity."

Finn laughed. Ralph's father, Alfred Hewitt, always looked like a crow. He wasn't a Quaker, but he dressed like one, favoring black and dark gray. He was a modest man who didn't like to attract attention, especially in his line of work. And an image of Alfred Hewitt dancing was enough to make Finn chuckle with mirth.

"Are you partnering all the eligible ladies of Philadelphia or is there someone special?" Finn asked as he accepted a seat and a glass of brandy from Ralph. It was cut crystal. No pewter cups here. Ralph settled across from Finn.

"I haven't had time to partner the ladies of Philadelphia just yet. We've been on the march for the past few weeks and arrived here only last night. We are continuing our march tomorrow, but tonight there's a reception to honor General Washington."

"Where are you marching to?" Finn asked, curious if his intelligence corresponded with Washington's plans.

"Sorry, Finn, but I can't tell you that. The British believe we are planning a siege of New York, and that suits General Washington just fine."

"Why would they think that?" Finn asked. What would be the point of marching from Rhode Island to Pennsylvania if New York City was the ultimate destination? Was the Continental Army intending to double back and return to New York? That didn't make sense, but of course, Finn didn't have all the information.

"They think we're planning an attack on New York because that's what we want them to think. False dispatches are sent all the time with the intention of misleading the British. So, what intelligence do you have for me?"

"Admiral de Grasse's fleet has arrived and is at anchor just off the Virginia Capes," Finn said. He hadn't understood why that information was so important when he was entrusted with it, but now it all made sense.

"You're marching to Virginia to rendezvous with de Grasse's fleet. The Continental Army will strike Cornwallis, who at this moment believes that the army will be heading the other way to New York."

Ralph smiled. "I can neither confirm nor deny that, but you are free to formulate your own conclusions, Finlay."

Finn smiled back. General Washington had been waiting for this news, so his intelligence was neither dated nor useless. The Battle of Yorktown would end the war, and it was Finn's information that would allow General Washington to order the march to Virginia. Finn stared into his brandy to hide his excitement. He wished he could tell Ralph what he knew, but that was out of the question. Ralph would find out soon enough. Today was September 5th, and the Continental Army would leave Philadelphia tomorrow, according to his mother. The rest was, as they say, history.

"I'll be right back, Finn," Ralph said as he sprang to his feet. "I must relay the information immediately."

Ralph returned a few moments later, his face now more relaxed. "Good man," he said as he refilled Finn's glass. "Now, tell me, how's the family? How's Sam?"

Finn opened his mouth to tell Ralph about Sam but stopped himself just in time. There was nothing Ralph could do to help in his present situation, and he already felt guilty enough about his role in Diana's death.

"Everyone is fine. Well, except for Mr. Mallory. He was ambushed by Tories about two weeks back. He was shot through the shoulder with an Indian arrow smeared with shit."

"Is he...?" Ralph couldn't finish the question. He was too shocked.

"He was still alive when I left."

Ralph shook his head. "I would never have imagined that the Tories would stoop to such low tactics, but people will do terrible things when they feel desperate. Why, just yesterday the soldiers announced that they won't budge until they get paid in actual coin. They are frustrated and angry and have no way of supporting their families while they are away fighting. I can't wait for this war to end," Ralph added. "I'm tired, Finn."

"What will you do once it's over?" Finn asked.

The war had been raging for so long that people had forgotten how to lead normal lives, especially people like Ralph and Jonah, who'd joined the Continental Army at the outbreak of the conflict and had spent the past six years in the thick of it. The men were battle-weary and angry. Ralph had to be nearing thirty now, an age when most men were already settled and had families of their own.

"I'd like to open a tavern," Ralph said, shocking Finn into silence. Finn didn't see Ralph as a publican, but then again, he didn't see him as anything but a soldier.

"Really?"

"Yes. And I'd like to marry and have children. Soon."

"Have you anyone in mind?" Finn asked.

Ralph smiled shyly. "I might. Don't know if she'll accept me, seeing as I have nothing to my name save this uniform, but I am hopeful. You'll meet her tonight."

"Tonight?"

"I have a surprise for you. Two, in fact."

"Ralph, I can't stay. I must leave right away. Well, maybe after I have something to eat," Finn added, suddenly remembering that he hadn't eaten anything since the day before. "I'm famished."

"I'll have some food sent up to your room. You can't leave tonight, Finn. There is a ball in honor of General Washington, and you are coming as my guest."

Finn slumped in his chair as he stared at Ralph in awe. "I will get to meet General Washington?"

"Yes. He will be glad to make your acquaintance."

"My acquaintance?" Finn echoed stupidly.

"He knows about you, Finn, just as he knows about my uncle and Sam. General Washington knows everything and values every man who's risked his life for the cause and to provide invaluable information that will help us defeat the British once and for all. What's the matter?" Ralph asked, noticing Finn's scowl.

"Ralph, Sam is not well. I have to go back."

Ralph waved his hand in a dismissive manner that reminded Finn of Sam. He had the same cavalier attitude and Ralph's reaction made Finn feel marginally better. Neither Sam nor Ralph spent much time worrying, and somehow everything always turned out all right for them in the end. Ralph put his arm around Finn's shoulders as he steered him toward the door.

"Sam's got nine lives, Finn. He will be all right. You must stay. I have a suit of navy velvet that will do nicely, I think," Ralph mused as he measured Finn with his gaze. "You'll need a bath, of course. Now, stop dawdling and come upstairs."

Ralph led the way to a spacious bedroom at the top of the

stairs that was decorated in shades of dark blue and cream. The room was distinctly masculine but had clearly been decorated by a woman of good taste. There was a dressing room accessible by a connecting door, where a copper tub gleamed in the light from the narrow window.

"This is a beautiful house," Finn remarked as he took in his surroundings. Abbie would have never seen anything so grand in all her days. What would it feel like to have a bedroom like this one, and not to have to take a weekly bath in a communal tub dragged before the hearth?

"This house was built by a famous privateer, John Macpherson, around 1761, but the decoration you see was commissioned by Margaret Shippen—Mrs. Benedict Arnold."

Finn spun on his heels and gaped at Ralph. "This is the home of Benedict Arnold?" he gasped. "The traitor?"

"It is. The man liked luxury, as did his wife. She had the entire house redecorated before moving in. Pity they didn't live here for very long. Perhaps things might have turned out differently for all involved had the Arnolds remained in Philadelphia. General Washington took the news of Arnold's treachery very badly. He genuinely liked and trusted the man and had given him his support when others questioned his motives and loyalty to the cause. Anyway, enough of that. I'll send Winnie up with hot water and she'll bring you a tray. There's some boiled beef with horseradish sauce and freshly baked bread. That should tide you over until supper, which will be sumptuous, I'm sure. Rest up before the ball, and stop fretting about Sam. He'll be fine."

Ralph let himself out of the room and left Finn to await his luncheon. Finn pulled off his dusty boots and sat down carefully on a silk-upholstered chair. He did fret about Sam, but he'd been traveling for days and hadn't had a proper meal since leaving the Hammers. He was hungry, tired, and filthy. By the time he ate, bathed, and rested, it'd be too late to leave anyway, and the prospect of meeting George Washington left him speechless with awe. How could he turn his back on such an opportunity? One more day wouldn't change anything for Sam, and he would bring a present for the Hammers as a thank you for their help. They wouldn't accept money, but they might accept a token of his gratitude. He would consult Ralph as to what might be an appropriate gift for the Quaker couple.

Finn leaned back in the chair, forgetting his soiled clothes, and smiled to himself. He was to attend a ball with the highest military personnel. He only wished Abbie could join him. She would look beautiful in mauve, or maybe apple-green silk. The smile slid off Finn's face as he allowed himself a moment to dwell on his failings. It was true that he'd come to the eighteenth century with nothing but his wits, but he'd been here for some time now, and what did he have to show for it? Even once the war ended, he'd need time to sort things out. While working the Mallory farm, he'd had no opportunity to earn anything for himself, so his dream of opening a shop would have to be put on hold yet again until he could think of a way to raise enough capital.

Finn wished, as he so often did, that he could talk to his father. Alec would know how to go about raising cash. He was a man of business and had been since he was a young man, unlike Mr. Mallory, who was a farmer. Finn respected Alec's business acumen and would consult him the next time he saw him. *Whenever that might be,* Finn thought pessimistically.

He jumped to his feet when a Negro woman entered the room balancing a tray in her hands. A boy of about twelve, who judging by his resemblance to the woman, could only be her son, carried two buckets of steaming water. He made straight for the dressing room while the woman shut the door with her hip without upsetting the tray.

"Here, let me help," Finn exclaimed as he reached for the tray, but the woman looked shocked by the suggestion.

"You just let me do my job, Master Finlay. My Saul will have your bath ready in no time at all. Until then, you can enjoy your luncheon. General Hewitt said to feed you well," she said with a dimpled smile. "And feed you I shall. Now, sit yourself down and I will serve you."

"Thank you," Finn mumbled as he settled at a small table by the window. He felt a bit awkward, but bit back any further comments and inhaled the heavenly scent of beef and horseradish. His stomach growled at the sight of the food, so he lifted the knife and fork and tucked in. Winnie poured him a cup of beer and set the jug on the table should he want more.

"Now, you enjoy your meal, Master Finlay, and I will bring you fresh towels. General Hewitt asked me to lay out his navy suit for you for tonight's festivities. Just leave your own clothes outside the dressing room before you get into the bath and I will have them laundered and pressed in time for you to leave tomorrow. Is there anything else I can do for you?" she asked.

"No, thank you. You've been very kind."

"If you want seconds, you just let me know. There's plenty more where this came from." She gave him an encouraging nod and Finn smiled happily.

"Yes, please. I would love some more."

"Be back in a tic," Winnie replied and left the room.

Finn turned his attention back to his meal. It wasn't often that he got to eat beef. Mrs. Mallory mostly made stews, using whatever meat was available. There was venison, rabbit, duck, and sometimes even possum, but they never had beef. Cows were too valuable to slaughter for meat since they were the source of all the milk, butter, and cheese. Finn sat back and allowed the tender meat to dissolve on his tongue. It was delicious, and he felt a pang of guilt at enjoying such bounty, then chuckled to himself. He could just see Abbie standing there with her hands on her hips, staring at him as if he were a dimwitted child, and he knew exactly what she would say.

"Now, you just stop this nonsense and enjoy yourself, Finlay Whitfield. You deserve a decent meal, and you deserve recognition for your work on behalf of the Committee of Correspondence even more. So, stop feeling sorry for yourself and ruining this moment. Just you make sure to remember every detail so that you can tell me all about it when you return."

Finn felt as if a great weight had been lifted off his shoulders. Abbie would say just that, and she would be right. He was acting like a fool. He might not be a decorated officer, but he'd made his contribution to the war effort and had risked his life as often as any soldier. There was no shame in taking a moment to acknowledge that.

Gratefully accepting more beef from Winnie, Finn savored every bite. She'd even brought him a slice of cherry tart for dessert. He finished his meal, then stripped off his clothes, dumped them in a pile on the floor outside the dressing room, and got into the steaming tub. Finn sank into the hot water, grateful for the opportunity to wash away the grime of the road. He hadn't had a proper bath in at least two weeks, and the water quickly turned a murky brown once he began to scrub his skin with the pumice stone Winnie had left for him.

Finn often wondered how his mother and Aunt Louisa managed to live in the seventeenth century after the wonders they had grown up with. Even his father had been to the future twice and could talk himself blue about the glory of cars, trains, and airplanes. Finn felt distinctly left out when his parents began to reminisce about the miracles of the twenty-first century. He'd never seriously entertained the idea of time-traveling himself, but what if he could? His parents had the device built for them by Isaac Bloom, and although they used it only to visit him, that little bracelet with a square screen had the power to whisk one anywhere they wished to go.

What if he were to borrow it one day and visit the future? Of course, that would probably mean that he'd have to tell

Abbie the family secret, but perhaps she wouldn't be as shocked as one might imagine. After all, Kit had accepted his wife's strange origins, although, come to think of it, he'd never asked to visit the future, according to his parents. Was he afraid? Was the prospect too intimidating, or was he simply not interested in seeing it for himself?

Finn sank deeper into the tub and closed his eyes, trying to picture the future he'd only heard of. He would certainly enjoy seeing a film. He didn't think he'd enjoy science fiction, like his father, who'd spent a futile hour trying to describe spaceships and alien invasions to a bemused Finn, but the idea of seeing a moving picture, in color, telling him a story seemed like something he could go in for. He'd never so much as seen a play, having lived most of his life in Colonial Virginia, where people's idea of entertainment was a quick gossip after church on Sunday.

Finn shut his eyes, enjoying his fantasy. He would borrow the time-travel device from his parents and take Abbie to the twenty-first century for a few days. Of course, they would be well-versed in the ways of the future, dressed in modern clothes, and flush with coin. The thought of Abbie in breeches gave Finn momentary pause, but he thought he'd be able to handle it if other women were similarly dressed. Of course, as soon as Finn and Abbie arrived in his imaginary future, Finn's mind went blank. Even with all the stories he'd heard from his parents, he couldn't quite envision what that world was like. His mind couldn't formulate the necessary images, nor could he imagine himself going about like he belonged and not like some country bumpkin out in the big city, kind of like he'd felt today.

Finn's fantasy fizzled as glanced toward the window. It was late afternoon, the sun already making its descent and lengthening shadows heralding the coming evening. Finn reluctantly got out of the tub, dried off, and dressed in the fine suit Winnie had laid out for him. He tied a snowy neckcloth around his throat and pulled his damp hair into a ponytail, tying it with a black ribbon.

"You almost look good," Ralph joked as he came to collect Finn. "Come downstairs. I have a surprise for you."

"I thought the surprise was meeting General Washington," Finn said as they descended the wide staircase.

"It is, but I told you there were two surprises, did I not?"

Finn whooped with delight when he saw the surprise that awaited him at the bottom of the stairs. "Jonah!" he cried as he enveloped Jonah in a bear hug. "I never expected to see you here. Ralph didn't tell me you were in Philadelphia."

Jonah laughed happily as he clapped Finn on the shoulder. "I wanted to come earlier, but Ralphie here said you needed time to freshen up."

"That's General Hewitt to you, you insolent pup," Ralph laughed as he ushered them into the parlor. "Come on. One drink before we go."

Ralph poured them glasses of Madeira and invited them to sit down. Finn accepted his drink, but his eyes never left Jonah. He hadn't seen him in nearly two years and was glad that Jonah looked a lot better than he had the last time they'd met. The dreadful pallor he'd acquired after his bout of malaria was gone, and although he was still whippet-thin, he looked healthy and strong, his face cleanly shaven and youthful.

"You've been promoted, I see," Finn said, eyeing the insignia on Jonah's coat.

"Captain Mallory, at your service," Jonah replied, giving Finn a sweeping bow before taking a seat and accepting the wine from his cousin.

"Congratulations. Augusta must be very proud. And how's Gemma?" Finn asked, referring to Jonah's baby girl.

A cloud passed over Jonah's face, and Finn nearly kicked himself for asking. Most likely, Johan had no idea. With Augusta living in Georgia, a letter might take months to reach

Jonah, if it reached him at all. Augusta wasn't much of a correspondent, and although she'd promised to write to Mr. and Mrs. Mallory, they'd received only one letter in the past two years, apprising them of Gemma's birth.

"I've only seen her twice, Finn. She's a fine little thing, or so Augusta tells me. She walks and talks, and asks for her papa, whom she can't even remember. What if I never see her again?" Jonah asked, his voice anguished. So many men had died without seeing the children who'd been born in their absence. Perhaps seeing Gemma twice was even worse than never having seen her at all. Now Jonah knew exactly what he was missing.

"Who does she look like?" Finn asked, in order to distract Jonah from his morbid thoughts.

"She looks like Augusta for the most part, but she has my eyes," Jonah replied proudly.

"She must be beautiful then. And how are the other children?" Augusta had two children from her first husband.

"Oh, they are well. Thankfully, they help on the farm and dote on Gemma. Ruth loves being an older sister, and Reggie fancies himself the man of the house. I suppose he is," Jonah added. "Imagine being the man of the house at nine. I never realized how safe and loved Pa made us feel while we were growing up. I hope to do the same for my children, if I get the chance."

"Jonah, quit moaning," Ralph cut in. "You will live to be a grumpy old man and drive everyone to insanity with your unreasonable demands, just like my father. I tell you, sometimes I wish he'd find himself a woman and enjoy what's left of his life. My mother's been gone for years now, and that man can seriously use the attentions of a lady, if you know what I mean. Perhaps it would wipe that scowl off his face."

They all laughed. The notion of Alfred Hewitt happy and in love was about as likely as the British Army simply packing

THE TIES THAT BIND

up and wishing the colonists much luck with their new country before sailing home.

"And speaking of fathers. How's Pa?" Jonah asked.

Finn considered telling Jonah about Mr. Mallory's condition, but decided to refrain. He wasn't lying, simply omitting the truth. If Mr. Mallory pulled through, then there was no reason to worry Jonah needlessly, and if he hadn't, then Jonah would find out soon enough. He seemed forlorn enough already.

"Stubborn as ever, and ruling us all with an iron fist," Finn joked.

"How's everyone back home?" Jonah asked. "I haven't had word from Ma in nearly three months."

"Everyone is well. Sarah's in love, or so Abbie tells me."

"Is that so? Who's the lucky fellow?"

"A local lad named Derek Johnson."

"Dudley Johnson's son? I know him." Jonah sounded wistful. "My God, I still think of Sarah and Annie as children, but they are not, are they? Sarah might be married by the time I see her again."

"I doubt it. Your father has put his foot down. Sarah is not to marry until she turns eighteen, and your mother is watching her like a hawk to ensure that there's no reason to marry sooner. It's safe to say that you'll see her before her wedding."

"And Sam?" Jonah asked. "I miss Sam."

Finn was grateful for Ralph's silence. "Sam is fine. Driving Sue to distraction, as usual," he replied with what he hoped was a reassuring smile.

"Come, boys. Time to go. It's rude to be late," Ralph cut in, just in time to rescue Finn from more questions he had no wish to answer.

Jonah drained the rest of his wine and set the glass on the table. He gave Finn a sad smile. "I miss everyone so much."

"I know, Jonah. They miss you too."

FIFTY-THREE

VIRGINIA SEPTEMBER 1781

John Mallory pushed away his plate, sighing with satisfaction. He shouldn't have indulged in that second helping of stew, especially since it had been followed by a slice of blackberry crumble, but he hadn't been able to resist. Now he felt pleasantly full and at peace with the world. He'd been in a remarkably benevolent mood since coming home several days ago, suddenly appreciating all the small things that he'd always taken for granted, like Hannah's excellent cooking. John had always considered himself a lucky man, but these past few days had been some of the happiest he'd ever known. Perhaps looking death squarely in the face reminded a man of what was truly important.

Regardless of the outcome of the war, he had a loving wife, children who'd make any man proud, and a brood of grandchildren that made him feel the kind of unconditional love he'd never felt for his own children when they were young. It was a parent's duty to teach and discipline, but a grandfather's duty to love and spoil. He had to admit that he had a soft spot for the little ones. Diana, Ben, Joe, and Nat were great fun, but it was Rachel, Daisy, and Edward that truly held his heart in their little hands. They were still soft and vulnerable, and always happy to be cuddled and kissed. Diana allowed herself to be kissed from time to time, but Ben and Nat squirmed away and made faces.

"We're not babies, Granddad," Ben protested when John tried to give him a hug.

"Sorry, I forgot, you're practically grown men," John replied, enjoying the look on his grandsons' faces. "You are just about ready to join me in the fields. Think you can manage a plow?"

Ben and Nat exchanged loaded glances. "We can't reach that high, Granddad," Ben replied. He usually spoke for them both, but Nat nodded in agreement.

"Well, maybe we'll give it one more year, and then I'm putting you two to work. Now that you are all grown up."

"Not to me, you're not," Hannah cut in as she chased the giggling boys around the table. "I'll catch you yet, and then I'll hug and kiss you to my heart's content."

John caught Hannah's eye and smiled. She'd never been so playful with their own children but becoming a grandmother had softened her. She was no longer afraid of spoiling the children by showering them with affection, and she certainly had more energy these days. When Hannah was a young woman, there were always small children underfoot and usually a baby in her belly, and still she'd worked from dawn till dusk, taking care of everything singlehandedly. John smiled as he remembered those days. He'd loved it when Hannah was pregnant. She'd always been beautiful, but when she was with child, she practically glowed. She was as ripe as summer fruit, her breasts heavy and her belly rounded with new life. If only they weren't too old to have another. He'd love to see her that way again, to have her press her enormous belly against his back as they slept and feel the child moving between them.

Hannah had Sam when she was just seventeen, only a year

older than Sarah. He'd thought her a grown woman then, but when he looked at Sarah, he realized that she'd been nothing more than a girl. His girl. She was forty-seven now, too old for babies, but not too old to welcome her husband back into her bed. Hannah had refused his advances since he'd returned home, but tonight he would insist. His shoulder hardly pained him anymore and he felt better than he had in years. A newfound energy surged through him, and he meant to take advantage of it.

"I'll get you some water for the dishes," John said as he pushed to his feet.

"There's no need, John. Annie can do it. You just rest."

"I'm tired of resting, woman. Stop treating me like an invalid."

Hannah threw a meaningful look over her shoulder but said nothing. She knew he wouldn't appreciate being dressed down in front of his children.

"Tell us a story, Granddad," Diana begged, but Abbie put an end to that idea.

"You are off to bed, young lady, as is your brother. Up you go."

Diana shrugged and gave John a sad smile. "Off to bed," she said, mimicking Abbie's tone exactly and making John laugh.

"Say goodnight," Abbie said, hands on hips as she glared at her children.

"Goodnight," Diana and Edward said in unison and reluctantly turned toward the ladder to the loft. "See you tomorrow, Granddad."

"Sleep well."

"You should go to bed as well," Hannah said as she began to clear plates off the table.

"I'm not tired. I think I'll just go outside for a few minutes, get some fresh air." John considered taking his pipe but changed his mind. He felt restless. Perhaps he'd take a walk instead, to the stile and back. He felt a need to be in motion, and to release some of this energy that seemed to be coursing through his veins.

The evening was lovely, with the pleasant smell of wood smoke and cut grass in the air. John loved this time of year, the sense of anticipation at the start of the harvest and the satisfaction of a job well done when it was all in and the haying done. He hoped the boys would be back before the harvest was ready to be brought in. He felt good for an old codger, but still needed their help. Perhaps this year he would hold off on clearing the maize field and make a corn maze for the children. He hadn't made one since Annie was little, but the children were old enough to enjoy it, and it would be nice to see them running around, calling to each other and laughing as they searched for a way out.

John flexed his shoulder, testing for pain. It still felt a bit sore where the arrow had pierced it, but the infection was gone, and the wound was healing nicely. Susanna had worked a miracle with her salves and potions. He would have to thank her again. She was a good sort, for an Englishwoman. Sam was lucky.

John was about to set off toward the stile when his gaze fell on the wood pile. It had diminished significantly since the boys had left for Philadelphia. There was still plenty left, but you could never have too much firewood. They would spend the months after the harvest preparing for winter: chopping wood, pickling vegetables, curing bacon, making jams and jellies, and making sure that everyone had enough woolens to keep them warm during the cold months.

John walked over to the chopping block and reached for the ax. It felt good in his hands, the worn handle smooth and elegant. John set a piece of wood on the block and split it in two, enjoying the thwack of the blade as it met with wood. He lifted another log and then another. Before he knew it, there was a sizeable pile at his feet. He'd need to stack the wood before going back inside. He'd split a few more logs, then put away the chopped wood. John positioned the hunk of wood on the chopping block and hefted the ax, ready to strike.

A white-hot pain tore through his chest, leaving him breathless, and his entire left side went numb. The ax slipped from his hand and fell to the ground, just barely missing his foot, but John hadn't even noticed. A hot coal had replaced his heart. He clutched at his chest with his good arm, trying to push the pain away, but the coal morphed into a blazing inferno, searing him with its intensity. The world tilted as John fell forward, hitting his head on the chopping block.

"Pa!" Annie screamed as she stepped outside to fetch the water. "Oh, Pa!"

FIFTY-FOUR
VIRGINIA SEPTEMBER 1628

Charles whistled happily as he headed back to Jamestown. It had been a very productive day to say the least, and he felt a sense of well-being the likes of which he hadn't experienced in months. The slanting rays of the sun warmed his shoulders, and the smell of hay was pleasantly sweet, overlaid by the tangy smell of the James River. There was not a cloud in the sky, the heavens above an expanse of endless blue.

He'd been away from home longer than he should have and knew Annabel would be angry with him, but he'd had to take care of business, and now it was done. It had taken over an hour to finalize the purchase of Timothy Bell's indenture contract. Charles thought the man was in his thirties, but on closer inspection he discovered that he was no older than twenty. The young man was filthy and weak from weeks of inadequate food and lack of exercise, but he would recover quickly once he got settled on Bartlett's farm. Bartlett signed the contract but wished for Charles to remain on hand should he have any questions.

"What do I do with him now?" Ethan Bartlett asked once

he was in possession of the scroll giving him power over Bell's life for the next seven years. Charles wrinkled his nose.

"You take the man back to your farm. There he can bathe, shave, and wash his clothes. Do you have any old garments you can spare?"

"I'll find something," Bartlett replied. He still looked uncertain, as if he couldn't believe that he suddenly had a human being at his disposal.

"Bell needs a good meal and a place to sleep. You can put him to work once he's had a chance to rest a bit. He can barely stand," Charles remarked as he helped Timothy Bell into Bartlett's wagon. The young man had trouble remaining upright and still hadn't uttered a word. He looked around in dismay, taking in the low wooden buildings and the town square with its stockade and whipping post.

"Master Bell," Charles addressed the man. "For what crime were you sent down to Virginia?"

The man gaped at the question and Charles wondered if he might be simple, but the young man finally pulled himself together.

"Stealing, sir."

"And from where do you hail?" Bartlett asked, curious about the man who would share his home for the next seven years.

"London town, sir."

"So, this must look very primitive to you," Charles commented as he mounted his horse to follow Bartlett back to his farm.

"Just a bit, sir."

"You'll get used to it," Bartlett assured him as the wagon lurched, making Bell grasp the sides for balance. Bell remained silent throughout the ride, but looked around with interest, eager to see something of his new surroundings.

"It doesn't look that different from England," Charles observed.

"I wouldn't know, sir. Never been outside the city walls, before being sent down that is."

Bartlett threw Charles an annoyed look. Bell might be young and potentially strong, but he clearly knew nothing whatsoever of farming and would need to be taught everything.

"I'm a quick study," Bell said, noting Bartlett's look. "You won't be sorry, Master Bartlett."

"I sincerely hope not," Bartlett grumbled.

Getting Timothy Bell situated took a bit of time since Bartlett had reservations about leaving the man alone at the farm. Bartlett wasn't a rich man, but he worried about Bell robbing him and taking off at the first opportunity. Once a thief, always a thief. Charles waited until Bell had washed, donned some of Bartlett's old clothes, and eaten his fill before addressing the man.

"Bell, your master and I must leave you for a time as we have some urgent business to attend to. You are to sleep in the hayloft for now and not set foot in the house. Just in case you're contemplating running away, be aware that should you do so, you will be caught and severely punished. There's nowhere to run. There are Indians in the woods, who will happily scalp you and leave your carcass for the animals. No Virginian will give you shelter or help you find a passage home, so consider yourself fortunate to have a place with a good, kind man for a master. If you work hard, you will work off your indenture and have a chance at a desirable future here in Virginia," Charles finished, satisfied with Bell's frightened expression.

"There are natives, sir?"

Ethan Bartlett was about to reassure the young man that he was quite safe, but Charles cut him off.

"You will remain unharmed as long as you remain on the farm."

"Yes, sir," Bell replied.

"Now, get some rest," Ethan Bartlett told him. "Here's a blanket. I'll be back before dark."

Timothy Bell meekly walked to the barn and climbed the ladder to the hayloft.

"He's scared to death," Bartlett said to Charles as they set off. "Probably thinks there's a savage behind every tree."

Charles shrugged, irritated by Bartlett's naiveté. "No man wants to be a slave, Bartlett. As soon as your new servant gets his bearings, he will begin to evaluate his options. He must understand that running away will result in either capture and punishment or death. That is the only way he will be content to work off his indenture until the end."

"I have no wish to be cruel," Bartlett ventured.

"And you don't need to be. But he is not a relative or a friend. He's your property for the next seven years, and you must maintain your distance if you wish to be treated as his master and not his crony."

"I suppose you'd know," Bartlett agreed. "How many men work on your brother's plantation?"

"More than two dozen. My brother and I don't always see eye to eye on the running of things though," Charles confessed.

"Your brother is a good man. I have great respect for him," Ethan Bartlett replied.

He didn't say any more, but Charles felt a pang of animosity toward the man. He was implying that Charles could never be the man Alec was, and perhaps he was right. Alec would never find himself in this situation, nor would he break a promise, something Charles planned to do as soon as possible. He had no intention of giving up Bethany for good or staying out of the life of his child. Bethany would have more children after this one, of that Charles was sure, but no one would know if they were sired by her husband or her lover.

It was well past dinnertime by the time Charles and Ethan

Bartlett arrived at Noah Abbott's farm. His wife was sitting on the stoop and grinding corn into flour as the younger children played close to her, their game making them shriek with laughter.

"We would like to speak with your husband, Mistress Abbott," Bartlett said as he removed his hat and bowed stiffly.

"You'll find him in the barn, gentlemen," she replied. She was clearly curious as to the purpose of their visit but couldn't come out and ask.

"Is Mistress Warren about?" Bartlett asked. His voice shook with nerves, but his expression betrayed nothing but polite interest.

"I'm afraid she isn't. She had an errand in town and has not returned yet. I expect her back shortly."

Charles noticed the frown on Mrs. Abbott's face. She understood and wasn't best pleased. Having Bethany live with her family provided her with an unpaid servant. Bethany helped with housework, minded the children, and at times drew the wrath of Noah Abbott, redirecting it from his wife. Losing Bethany would be much more of a blow to Esther Abbott than it would be to her husband.

"I'll fetch my husband if you'd like to wait inside," Mrs. Abbott offered as she set aside the bowl.

Charles and Ethan Bartlett accepted a cup of beer from a young girl who curtsied awkwardly and left them alone. The beer was cool and went down easily after the dusty ride to the farm.

"Stay calm, man," Charles advised Bartlett, who looked like an errant boy awaiting his punishment. "Abbott has no reason to refuse."

Both men rose to their feet when Noah Abbott entered the house. He was a stern-looking man with a lush gray beard and hard eyes. "A Bible thumper," Valerie had called him, and it hadn't been a compliment to his piety.

"Good afternoon, sirs. How can I help?" Abbott asked as he poured himself a cup of beer. "Make yourself scarce," he barked at his daughter who came in after him.

"Master Abbott, I have come to make an offer of marriage to your sister, Mistress Warren. I hold her in very high regard and would give her a comfortable life should she agree to become my wife," Ethan Bartlett said. He was about to add something when the door flew open and Bethany stood on the threshold, her eyes huge in her pale face.

"Bethany, it seems you've an admirer," Abbott said, his tone heavy with sarcasm. He gazed upon his sister with undisguised dislike, apparently glad to see her discomfiture. Bethany nodded to Charles and Ethan Bartlett but did not advance into the room.

"Mistress Bartlett, I have come to make you an offer of marriage," Bartlett said as he smiled at Bethany. "You need not look so frightened."

"I will have to consider your offer, sir," Abbott cut in. "I will not have my sister wed to a man I consider unfit for her, and I know very little of your character."

"I accept," Bethany said firmly. "I will be honored to be your wife, sir."

"You will accept nothing without my blessing," Noah Abbott snarled, his mouth tightening with suppressed fury.

"I am a grown woman, married and widowed. I do not require your permission, but I would welcome your blessing," Bethany said evenly, her eyes challenging her brother to refuse. He opened his mouth to retort but realized that he would only humiliate himself. Bethany's mind was made up.

"Very well then. You are to be married as soon as possible, and after the nuptials, you will no longer be welcome in my house, you insolent wretch."

Noah Abbott turned on his heel and walked out of the

house, leaving the three of them alone, unless there were children spying on them from the loft above.

"Thank you, Master Bartlett. I will be a good and devoted wife to you," Bethany said as her eyes slid to Charles.

"Master Bartlett knows the truth of the matter," Charles replied to her unspoken question. "He's willing to take you on."

Bethany's cheeks reddened, but she remained mute.

"I will have the banns read this Sunday, and then we can marry in three weeks' time," Ethan Bartlett said. "Perhaps you can visit me after church on Sunday, with a chaperone, of course, and see your future home and meet my daughter. I see her after church on Sundays, but I trust I will be able to fetch her home once we are wed."

"Indeed, you will, sir. I will love her as my own," Bethany added.

"Then our business is done," Bartlett said, bowing to Bethany. "I will see you at church."

Bethany looked shaken as the two men bid her goodbye and let themselves out. Charles turned to glance at her, but Bethany lowered her eyes, unwilling to meet his gaze.

FIFTY-FIVE

Charles was glad to finally get home. He was hungry, not having had anything but the beer at Noah Abbott's house. He'd had a hearty breakfast, but that was hours ago, and he was ready for a good meal. He inhaled deeply as he entered the house, hoping that something delicious was cooking for supper. The house seemed unusually quiet, and Nan scurried past him with her head down and her arms full of soiled linen.

"Nan, is there anything to eat?" Charles called out after her, but she didn't reply.

He followed Nan into the kitchen and froze at the sight of the sheets she'd just immersed in a tub of cold water. Blood bloomed on the surface, forming intricate red patterns. Nan still avoided looking at him but had pulled her hands out of the tub and clasped them in front of her, staining her apron with blood.

"Nan, what's happened?" Charles gasped. "Is it Harry?" Harry was so mischievous. Perhaps he'd hurt himself climbing a tree or whittling a stick.

"No, Master Charles. Tis the mistress."

Charles hurried to the bedchamber, his heart pounding in

his panic. He erupted into the room, desperate for reassurance that Annabel was alive. She lay against the pillows, her face ashen and her eyes closed, but he could see the rise and fall of her chest. Thank the Lord she was still living. Charles turned to Elizabeth Goodall, who was washing her hands in a basin of water. Mistress Goodall was young, but she was an experienced midwife, having worked with her mother since an early age. Elizabeth's mother, Mavis, still attended births, but swelling in her joints, especially during the colder months, had curtailed her efforts.

"Mistress Goodall, what happened?" Charles pleaded.

"Your wife lost the babe, sir. She's suffered greatly and lost much blood. She needs rest. I have instructed your servant to have her drink cow's blood mixed with milk once a day for a week."

"And the child?" Charles asked. There was a catch in his throat, but he needed to know.

"A boy, Master Whitfield."

"Where is he?"

Elizabeth Goodall's eyes slid to a tightly wrapped bundle resting next to the basin. It was stained with blood and no bigger than Charles's hand. "Don't open it, sir," Elizabeth Goodall warned. "Tis a difficult thing to gaze upon, especially for a parent."

Charles nodded. He didn't think he could bring himself to look at the child anyhow. "What will you do with it?" he asked. The child would not be buried in a churchyard since it hadn't been carried to term or baptized, but Charles had no idea what happened to the remains of children who were miscarried or stillborn.

"You may bury it in the garden," Mistress Goodall said gently. "But bury it deep enough that it won't be rooted out by pigs. They'll eat it if they dig it up."

Charles felt a wave of nausea assail him but nodded in understanding. "Thank you, Mistress Goodall."

The midwife collected her things and let herself out, leaving Charles alone with Annabel. He briefly wondered where the children had got to but figured that Nan had sent them out into the garden to play.

"Belle," Charles called out softly. "Can you hear me, Belle?"

Annabel forced her eyes open. They looked sunken, and her flushed face was all sharp lines and angles, not pale and soft as he was used to seeing it. Her hair was in disarray, and her nightdress was crumpled and stained.

"Belle, I'm sorry," Charles said as he reached for her hand, but Annabel yanked it away.

"Are you?"

"Of course. It was a boy," he added, nearly choking on the words.

Annabel threw him a look of such hatred; it took his breath away. "As a woman, I have no rights, and cannot apply to have the marriage dissolved, but mark me, Charles Whitfield, I will never forgive you for what you've done, and I will never be a willing wife to you again. You may exercise your husbandly rights if you see fit to do so, but I will never welcome you into my bed, nor will I ever give you another child."

"Belle, what are you talking about? Why are you so angry?" Was Annabel lashing out at him because she was heartbroken or was there another reason for this outburst?

"She was here this afternoon, your whore. She told me that she's carrying your child, and you have turned your back on her."

"Did she cause this?"

Annabel turned away from him and squeezed her eyes shut. When she made up her mind to something, she rarely changed it. Charles felt a wall of ice rising between them and knew that he could never scale it. Annabel was a proud woman, and she would never forgive his betrayal, nor would she forget that it was his perfidy that caused her to lose their son.

He tried to take her hand, but she yanked it away. "Get out," she hissed.

Charles stumbled from the room.

FIFTY-SIX

VIRGINIA SEPTEMBER 1781

Susanna wiped her brow on the sleeve of her dress. She was perspiring freely, but John Mallory was cold as ice, his face gray, except for the livid bruise on his forehead. Sue had been summoned by Abbie last night, who'd managed to tell her what was wrong between sobs. Sue had roused the children, who'd just fallen asleep, grabbed her medicine box, and rushed to the Mallory farm. The children would spend the night with their cousins, since it'd be too late to return home, and Susanna would keep vigil over John. Hannah, Abbie, and the girls had managed to bring him into the house and settle him on the bed, but he was still unconscious.

Based on Mrs. Mallory's account, Susanna thought that Mr. Mallory had suffered what her father referred to as a myocardial infarction, which basically meant a failure of the heart, most likely brought on by vigorous activity following a serious injury. John Mallory should have been resting as much as possible since he'd lost a great deal of blood and his body was weakened. There was nothing she could do for him now. He would either rally or his damaged heart would wear itself out and stop.

Susanna took John's wrist between two fingers to check his

pulse. It was slow and erratic, his wrist limp and cold. She tucked a blanket around John and stepped into the other room where Hannah and the girls were waiting for news. Hannah looked at Susanna and blanched, interpreting the look on her face correctly.

"I'm so sorry, but there's nothing I can do. If he makes it through the night, there's hope of him waking up," Susanna added to soften the blow. "Someone should stay with him."

"I will stay with him. Susanna, I'll come and get you should anything change," Hannah said, taking charge as usual. "Girls, go to bed. It's late."

Abbie and Susanna headed up to the loft, while Sarah and Annie retired to their room. Abbie undressed silently and got into bed, leaving room for Susanna to lie down next to her. Neither one of them could sleep, but they remained silent, lost in their own thoughts as the hours ticked by. Eventually, Abbie drifted off, but Sue remained wide awake. Sue slipped out of bed and descended the ladder. Hannah was sitting by the bed, her gaze fixed on her husband. Hannah hadn't cried or uttered a word of complaint, but it was obvious she was hanging on by a thread. John Mallory was her world.

Some marriages were held together by shared experience and children, and then there were those rare unions built on genuine love and respect, and John and Hannah Mallory had one of those. Their life together was like a tapestry, worked in vibrant colors that wove through the fabric beneath, the foundation and the backdrop created by years of devotion. Hannah would be stoic in the face of loss and grief, but she would never recover fully once her heart was lost.

"I can sit with him for a while," Susanna offered. "You must get some rest."

Hannah shook her head. "I'm weary, but I can't sleep. You can sit with me if you like," she added.

Susanna sat on the trunk at the foot of the bed, since Hannah occupied the only chair.

"He's not going to recover, is he?" Hannah asked, her voice barely above a whisper.

Susanna could soften the truth or lie altogether, but she knew that Hannah Mallory needed to hear the truth, at least the truth as Susanna knew it.

"I don't know, Hannah. Sometimes recovery depends on the person, at least that's what my father used to say. Some patients have a stronger will to live than others."

"Even if their heart is damaged?" Hannah asked, her tone hopeful.

"I don't have much experience with afflictions of the heart. I helped my father operate on and nurse soldiers who were wounded on the battlefield. There was one major who'd suffered an apoplexy during a battle. He recovered, but lost mobility in the right side of his face and his right hand."

"But he had lived," Hannah said.

"Yes, he had lived."

"If recovery has anything to do with the will to live, then I know my John will live. He's strong and determined. He will not willingly succumb to death," Hannah stated. It was bravado speaking, but Susanna nodded in agreement. What could she say? Time would tell, but the longer John Mallory remained unconscious, the less chance he'd come to.

It was a relief to see the pink rays of the rising sun dispel the gloom of the sickroom. It had been a long night for all of them. Abbie and the girls filed into the main room, looking pale and tired and started on their daily chores. Annie went out to get water, Sarah laid the fire in the hearth, and Abbie reached for the skillet, ready to fry some bacon. The children would be up soon, and they'd need to be fed, even if the adults weren't that hungry.

"The smell of bacon will wake Pa up," Annie said. "He loves bacon."

"I love bacon too," Ben said as he climbed down the ladder in his nightshirt. "I'm hungry, Mama."

"Me too," Diana called down. The children all came down, ready for their breakfast.

"Come on, then. Wash your face and hands and sit yourselves down," Abbie said as she sliced bread and placed a piece on each plate. Sarah poured cups of milk for the children as they settled themselves at the table.

"Sarah, today promises to be a hot day," Hannah said as they finished breakfast. "Perhaps you can take the children to the stream for a little while. They'll enjoy splashing in the cool water."

"I want to go swimming," Ben declared.

"Me too," Rachel cried, always fearful of being left behind by her brothers. "Me too."

"Of course, you too," Susanna said as she lifted Rachel into her arms. "I'll take you."

"Woo-hoo," Ben cried as he pushed away his plate and made for the door, still clad in his nightshirt. The others followed.

"Don't go in the water before I get there," Sarah called after them, but they were already halfway to the stream. Sarah threw a worried look at her mother, but Hannah waved her away. "Go. Your father needs quiet and rest. Keep them occupied for as long as you can."

"Yes, Ma," Sarah replied and took off after the kids, followed by Susanna. There was nothing more she could do for John, and she felt an overwhelming desire to get out of the house and get some fresh air. Besides, she wanted to give Hannah some privacy. She needed to be alone with John since it might be for the last time.

Susanna grabbed Rachel by the hand before she ran off and catapulted herself into the stream where the rest of the children were already splashing under the watchful eye of Sarah, who sat on the bank. Susanna was forever astounded by Rachel's fearlessness. Perhaps it was because she had two older brothers, unlike Susanna who only had one younger sister. They had always been terribly fearful growing up, afraid to set a foot wrong for fear of earning their father's disapproval or getting into trouble. They were model children, who'd grown into model adults, well at least one of them had.

Laura had followed the roadmap drawn by their father. She'd married well, had remained in England, and had at least one child, as far as Susanna knew. Susanna had written countless letters, both to Laura and her father, Doctor Freeman, but they'd severed all contact with her when she ran away from a British fort in Staten Island with a rebel spy. The ache of losing her family still dwelled in her heart and was as acute today as it had been when the rift first occurred. Perhaps seeing the death struggle of John Mallory served to remind her how important it was to forgive and make amends before it was too late, but she had nothing to make amends for.

Running away with Sam was the most exciting thing she'd ever done, and she would do it again in a heartbeat. He'd woken her from a deep slumber, and she'd been astounded to realize what she'd been missing. Of course, life with Sam hadn't been all rainbows and butterflies. Susanna still burned with anger when she recalled Diana's ploy to take Sam away from her, but Diana was now sleeping in a graveyard, her scheming forever at an end. Susanna didn't believe for a moment that Diana's spirit was at rest, but she didn't much care. She'd managed to hold on to her love, and she genuinely loved Nat. He was a part of Sam, and that was all that mattered. They were a family, a single unit but part of a greater whole, a whole that was about to be torn apart by the death of its patriarch.

Susanna smiled when she heard the joyful shrieks of her

boys. Rachel yanked her hand out of Susanna's and sprinted toward the stream, her bare heels pink against the lush green of the summer grass. Ben opened his arms and Rachel flew into them, crying with excitement as he lifted her up then plunged her beneath the water for a few seconds. Rachel's eyes were round with fear when she came up, but also with the fun of it, and she cried, "Again, Ben. Again."

Susanna stood on the bank for a moment, debating the wisdom of joining the children, then tore off her own dress and waded into the stream in her shift. There was no one about, she was hot, and nothing could lift her spirits more than playing with the children and stealing a few moments of joy from an otherwise depressing day. Sarah followed suit. It was hot for September and the water was deliciously cool against their skin as they immersed themselves, the children swimming around them like a school of fish.

Eventually, everyone got out and reclined on the grass to dry off. The sun was warm, and the children became drowsy as they lounged on the bank, watching the clouds float overhead. Even Ben and Nat were quiet, enjoying the moment. Another few weeks and it'd be too cold to swim and they would have to wait until next summer.

"Can we go in again?" Diana asked.

Sarah looked like she was about to say no, but then remembered her mother's orders. "All right. But I'm staying right here," she said, shaking out her wet hair. The children plunged into the creek again, squealing with delight.

"I'm going to take Rachel back to the house. She looks done in," Susanna said as she pulled on her dress. "Don't rush back. The children are having a good time, and your father needs his rest."

Sarah nodded and turned her gaze toward the stream, intent on the children. Susanna scooped up Rachel, who immediately rested her head on her mother's shoulder and closed her eyes.

She was due for a nap. Susanna walked slowly toward the house, wishing she could turn around and go home. She couldn't bear to be on this death watch, because that's what it was.

Hannah was sitting on the bench outside the house, her head against the wall and her eyes closed. She looked peaceful, sitting there in the sunshine, but it wasn't until Susanna drew closer that she noticed the silent tears sliding down the older woman's cheeks.

"Hannah?" she called softly.

Hannah opened her eyes and the pain Susanna saw in them told her everything she needed to know.

"He's gone," Hannah said. "He's left me."

Susanna sat down next to Hannah, careful not to wake up Rachel. Hannah leaned against Susanna's shoulder as held her in a one-armed embrace.

"I'm so sorry, Hannah," Susanna said as she tried to hold back her own tears.

"He put up a good fight. John was never one to give up easily. We've had a wonderful life together. I know I should be grateful for that, but right now all I feel is anger and sorrow at having lost him so soon."

"It's all right to be angry. I was angry when my mother died. I felt as if she had abandoned me. I know that she had no choice, but it was easier to be angry than give in to grief."

The grief would come later; Susanna knew that. Hannah and John Mallory had enjoyed an exemplary marriage, the type of marriage she hoped to have with Sam. Sam wasn't exactly like his father, but if she were honest with herself, she liked his wild streak. Perhaps John Mallory had been a bit wild himself in his youth, she mused. Susanna knew she should go inside and offer her condolences to Abbie and Annie, but she couldn't seem to find the strength to get up. Rachel slept on, and the two women just sat side by side, lost in their memories of John Mallory.

"You should eat something," Susanna finally said. She hadn't had any breakfast, and her hands shook slightly in her lap.

"I'm not hungry."

"I know, but you must stay strong, Hannah. For John."

Hannah stubbornly shook her head. "There are arrangements to be made. I must go into the village and order a coffin from Mr. Pitt, then see Reverend Greene about a funeral. I'd like Sam and Finn to be there for the funeral, but there's no telling when they'll be back, and the body won't keep in this heat. We mustn't delay. Oh, and I must break the news to Sarah and the children," Hannah sighed. "They'll be heartbroken about their granddad."

"Would you like me to do that?" Susanna asked.

"Thank you, dear, but it has to come from me," Hannah said quietly.

"If there's anything at all I can do...."

"Just be there for Abbie. The younger girls will lean on me, but Abbie is at the age where she's torn between independence and a need for her mother. Sometimes having a friend helps. She can find comfort in sharing with you without allowing her grief to overwhelm her. She was very close with John, and he had doted on her, especially after we lost Luke. They were twins, you know."

"Yes, Abbie told me about Luke. I think she still mourns him."

"As do I. Every night before I go to sleep, I try to picture his face, but the image is blurred, and I can no longer hear his voice in my head. Time erodes our memories, but not the sense of loss. You never get over losing a child. And I suppose you never get over losing a husband either, as I'm soon to find out."

Sue didn't say anything. Hannah would mourn John for the

rest of her days. She wasn't the type of woman to remarry as soon as someone worthy came along. No one would ever take John's place in her heart, and Sue suspected that Hannah would be all right with that. She'd had her great love, and in time, she would rejoice in the love they had shared.

Hannah patted Susanna's hand. "Don't fret, Sue. I'll be all right. And when I get lonely, well, there are my grandchildren to make me happy. God has certainly blessed me in that regard, and I hope he continues to be generous. It won't be long now until Sarah is ready to wed. John wanted her to wait until she turned eighteen, and I will respect his wishes, but time goes so quickly."

"Yes, it certainly does."

"Derek is a good boy, if a bit wild." Hannah smiled wistfully, realizing what she'd just said. "I suppose I can't expect her to object to a bit of wildness. Just look at Sam. Sarah has always idolized him. And John was a right card when I met him. So handsome, and so unpredictable. There never was anyone else for me from the day I set eyes on him."

"No, I imagine not."

"My poor man," Hannah sighed as she got to her feet. "I just need to be alone for a bit before I start planning the funeral. You understand, don't you?"

"Of course, I do."

Susanna watched Hannah Mallory walk away. She had aged ten years in the past few hours, and Susanna felt a searing pain in her heart. She couldn't share what the older woman was feeling, but the thought of losing Sam left Susanna so paralyzed with terror that she understood only too well what it must be like to have your worst fears realized.

FIFTY-SEVEN
VIRGINIA SEPTEMBER 1628

Soft morning light streamed through the window, casting a golden halo around Louisa's head. Robbie's shirt rested on her lap, the needle suspended in her fingers. She had a faraway look in her eyes and was probably thinking about her life in the twenty-first century. Kit had noticed that look several times over the past few days as Louisa sat sewing by the window, taking her work into their bedroom to keep him company. He'd have liked to go downstairs and spend some time with the family, but Doctor Jacobson had strictly forbidden him to get out of bed for several more weeks at least, and getting down the stairs would be tricky since he wasn't able to bend his leg. His day consisted of three meals and several visits from various family members. The rest of the time was spent alone.

Kit looked forward to seeing the children. Robbie and Evie came by every morning, but Robbie only stayed for a few minutes. He didn't have the patience to sit and talk to Kit and kept asking when they would be able to go fishing. Evie, on the other hand, often climbed into bed with Kit and asked him to tell her stories of times gone by. She liked to hear about life aboard a ship and about all the places Kit had visited, particularly the Caribbean islands. Evie could listen for hours, eager to hear about the sandy beaches, the turquoise sea, and the swaying palm trees that cast a shaggy shadow onto the sizzling sand.

Kit enjoyed spending time with Evie and was gratified by her interest, but he strongly suspected that Evie simply wanted to be near him and craved reassurance that the adults weren't deceiving her, and he was truly on his way to recovery. His little Evie. Strange how men always longed for sons but lost their hearts to their daughters. Kit knew how much Alec still mourned his own wayward girl. Alec loved Finn, but it had been Louisa who'd held his heart in her hands and had broken it into a thousand pieces. Kit prayed that he wouldn't lose his little lady, not even once she married.

Louisa finally emerged from her reverie and poked the needle into the fabric as if it were the shirt's fault that she had stopped sewing. Louisa hated sewing, just as she hated carding wool, spinning, weaving, and anything else that had to do with the production or maintenance of clothing. Laundry day was the bane of her existence. She preferred being outdoors and kept a vigilant eye on the vegetable patch and her ever-expanding orchard, which yielded more fruit with every passing year. Louisa had a real sweet tooth and used stewed fruit and jams to sweeten cakes and porridge.

Setting the sewing aside, Louisa looked at Kit. She had that little furrow between her brows, the one she got when she was concentrating, or thinking how to best phrase something. Over the years, Kit had learned not to get too anxious when Louisa brought up her old life in the future. She missed it, which was natural, but had no desire to go back, fully accepting that her life was in the here and now. So he simply heard her out, recognizing her need to speak to him of her past life. Valerie and Alec often spoke of their time in the twenty-first century, and sometimes Kit felt a pang of envy, wishing he could join in the conversation. The three people closest to him had experienced something he couldn't even imagine, but no one had ever suggested that he visit the future himself. He often wondered how it would feel to finally see the things he'd only heard about and understand those inside jokes at last.

Truth be told, he hadn't wished to go before. He didn't think himself a coward, but the stories Alec told him about speeding cars, metal birds full of people traveling from place to place through the sky, and the speed of everyday life, left him feeling secretly grateful that he didn't have to test his mettle against the threat of modern life. He had no desire to embarrass himself in front of his wife or feel like a newborn babe entirely dependent on others for its survival. But having spent the better part of the last month in bed, the idea of time travel suddenly seemed a lot more appealing, as did any kind of travel. He was going mad lying there day after day like a fish that had been tossed out by the ocean and left to suffocate on the beach with lifesaving water only inches away. Just the fact that he was even thinking of himself as a beached fish was cause for concern. He was feeling sorry for himself, and self-pity was not to be tolerated. Kit turned to Louisa and gave her an encouraging smile. If she wished to talk, he was more than ready to listen.

"What were you thinking about?" Kit asked, noting Louisa's guilty look.

"The future."

"Anything in particular?"

"I was just thinking how there was always talk of inferior education, lack of affordable health care, and a woman's right to have an abortion."

"Well, you know how I feel about the abortion part," Kit said carefully, wondering what had brought this on. Could it be that Louisa was with child? He would love to have more children, but Louisa was in her late thirties; the risk was too great. Louisa had assured him that women bore children well into their forties in the twenty-first century, but those women had advanced medical care, vitamins for mother and child, and doctors whose names weren't associated with butchery. Louisa had safely delivered two healthy children. He was thankful and didn't dare ask for more.

Louisa shook her head, as if brushing off his comment. "It's just that people never realize how fortunate they are. If they could see what life is like now, they would thank their lucky stars for having education, healthcare, and life choices. Every child goes to school, gets immunized against major diseases, and has parents or guardians to care for them. I look at those children in the barracks and my heart breaks. Some of them are so achingly young, and they've never known anything but the streets."

"Lou, you are doing something to better their lives," Kit said, hoping that he could break through her melancholy. "You are teaching them, which is something no one had bothered to do before."

"Am I bettering their lives? I thought they'd jump at the chance to learn to read and write, but most of them only attend my class because they are afraid to be punished if they don't, and stare at me with blank faces, refusing to absorb what I'm trying to tell them."

Kit smiled. Louisa was eager to help and make a difference, but she didn't fully understand what she was up against. These children were not the boys and girls who went to school in her time, coddled by their parents and encouraged by their teachers. These children were orphans who'd lived on the streets and survived by their wits alone. They viewed Louisa's efforts as some sort of trick rather than a sincere attempt to help them.

"You must win the trust of the older children," Kit said, considering how best to phrase his advice. "The younger ones look to the older children, having cast them into the role of parents. Perhaps if you could somehow make learning relevant to their own lives."

"And how do I do that? Who wouldn't want to read and write?" Louisa asked. She sounded defensive. Having had an education, Louisa couldn't imagine a world in which she wasn't literate, so it was difficult for her to understand that for some people illiteracy was the norm and would be for centuries to come.

"These children don't imagine that they will ever do anything more than manual labor. Many of them don't even expect to survive into adulthood. They see learning as something that has nothing to do with them or their future."

"So, how do I engage them? I couldn't even get them to learn something as simple as the first three letters of the alphabet. They repeated after me but forgot everything I said the moment I was done," Louisa complained. She'd been so excited about her project, but now, two weeks into the lessons, she was frustrated and upset.

Kit considered the situation. He had experience of tenants on this estate and the sailors he'd captained, but he had little experience of children. His own children were loved and well cared for, so he'd never had to break through the wall of self-protective defiance urchins tended to erect to guard their hearts. And then he thought of Evie, and an idea began to take shape in his mind.

"Why don't you hold off on teaching them their letters for a bit and tell them stories instead? Pique their curiosity. Teach them to trust you and reassure them that they don't have to do anything but listen."

"What kind of stories?" Louisa asked, instantly intrigued.

"Remember how you told me about Dickens? Well, what if you tailor *Oliver Twist* to this century and tell the children the story bit by bit. Get them interested enough to want to come back for more. After all, who could they relate to if not an orphan boy who is hungry and scared?"

"You really think that will work?" Louisa asked, excitement seeping into her voice. Kit could already see the gears turning in her brain as she tried to recall the story of Oliver Twist with more clarity.

"I think it's worth a try. Tell them something they can relate to, win their trust, and then try teaching them again. Perhaps they'll be more open to learning once they feel that you understand them and know something of their plight."

"I'm not sure that I remember the story exactly as it was written," Louisa mused. "I read it eons ago."

"You don't need to. It's not as if they'll be reading it for themselves. It hasn't even been written yet. Alter it to suit your needs and just think of it as a teaching tool."

"Kit, you really are a genius sometimes," Louisa exclaimed as she planted a kiss on his lips.

"Only sometimes?" Kit quipped, happy to have been able to help.

"Well, most times."

"If you need any help, I'm at your disposal. It's not as if I'm going anywhere," Kit grumbled.

"Yes, you are. We'll have you out of this bed by the end of October."

"That's nearly two more months," Kit groaned, making Louisa smile.

"The time will go by quickly. You'll see."

"You try lying in bed all day long and see how quickly the time goes," Kit complained.

"How about I ask Mr. Taylor to come visit and bring his beloved chess set? A game or two will cheer you up."

"Yes, I'd like that. I haven't seen Mr. Taylor in weeks," Kit said, suddenly realizing that Fred hadn't been to visit him much, which was out of character for the old man since he liked to be part of everything that went on at Rosewood Manor.

"He's been unwell. He thinks he has an ulcer."

"And what would that be?" Kit asked. He was always fascinated by how much Louisa and Valerie knew of the human body and various diseases without having had any sort of medical education. It seemed that the people of the future were very well informed.

"It's a sort of festering boil on the lining of the stomach. It can be very painful."

"Is there a cure for this ulcer?" Kit asked.

"There is medicine for it in the future, but the only thing Fred can do right now is mind his diet. Basically, he can't eat anything greasy, spicy, acidic, or difficult to digest."

Kit gaped at Louisa. "So, what can he eat, the poor man?"

"Barbara's been making him beef tea, and he can still stomach most milk products and bread. He can have apples too, but not berries of any kind."

"Is he improving?"

"I think so. In the meantime, I think you can both use a distraction. I'll ask Fred to come see you tomorrow."

"I'll look forward to it." *And let Fred win. Winning always makes him feel better*, Kit thought.

FIFTY-EIGHT

Valerie slung the basket over her arm and stepped outside into the warm September sunshine. Alec was already in the trap, Tom in his lap, holding on to the reins. He loved to pretend he was driving. Valerie had intended to leave Tom with Minnie, but the little boy cried and begged to come along, eager for an outing. He was normally such an undemanding child that to deny him such a simple request seemed unkind.

Valerie deposited the basket full of strawberry jam, homemade peanut butter, and fresh muffins into the back and climbed onto the bench next to Alec and Tom. "Don't drive too fast now, Tom," she said with a smile.

Tom gave her a look that clearly said, "I'll drive as fast as I want to."

His expression nearly undid Valerie. He looked so much like his mother. She loved seeing these little things that reminded her of Louisa and hoped that someday they would no longer hurt so much, but Louisa's death was still too fresh. Valerie often wondered what sort of parent Louisa would have been had she lived. Would she have doted on Tom as his grandparents did or would she have seen him as an obstacle to her happiness and always worry that his true parentage would come to light? With Louisa one never knew, but Valerie wanted to believe that she would have loved this little boy with all her heart, the way Valerie and Alec had loved her, and still did.

Alec covered Tom's hands with his own and took hold of the reins. The trap began to move, and Tom squealed with delight.

"Myself," he protested. "Drive myself."

Once the trap was moving at a steady pace, Alec withdrew his hands and allowed Tom to drive. Tom was glowing with pride as he held on to the reins with intense concentration.

"Does Louisa know we're going to visit Annabel?" Alec asked over Tom's head.

"She does," Valerie replied.

She'd considered not telling Louisa, but they'd never had secrets from each other and weren't about to start now. Since the trial, relations had been glacial, but Valerie was still cordial to Annabel for Charles's sake. They were family, after all, and the children loved each other and begged to spend time together. And who could blame them? They had few entertainments in seventeenth-century Virginia and their cousins were the only playmates they had.

"I'll never forgive Annabel for what she had tried to do," Valerie said, "but I do feel sympathy for her. She must have suffered terribly. She was nearly six months gone, wasn't she?"

"Just about," Alec replied. He looked pensive as he kept an eye on the road.

"What? You're not telling me something," Valerie demanded. "I can see it in your face."

Alec glanced over at her and smiled ruefully. "Can't hide anything from you, can I?"

"Don't even bother to try. What happened?"

Alec gave Tom a meaningful look, but Valerie nodded for him to go on. Tom was too young to understand most of what they talked about and he was so absorbed in driving the trap that he wouldn't notice if an actual car overtook them.

"Annabel didn't just miscarry," Alec confessed. "She had a visit from Bethany Warren just before it happened."

Valerie's eyebrows rose higher, waiting for Alec to elaborate. "Bethany is with child, Val, and it's Charlie's. She's about two months gone, according to my brother. She'd threatened to tell Annabel if Charles didn't do something to safeguard her reputation and allow her to escape prosecution once the truth came out."

"Bethany Warren was sleeping with Charles?" Valerie gasped. "And she's pregnant? She's always as quiet as a mouse when I see her in church, eyes downcast and hands demurely folded in her lap. I would have never taken her for a scarlet woman. Just shows you how little we know of someone's true nature."

"Scarlet woman?" Alec asked, turning away from the road to give Valerie a look of disapproval.

"It's from a book, *The Scarlet Letter*."

"What's it about?"

"It's about a woman in seventeenth-century Massachusetts who has an affair and gets with child. She must wear a scarlet letter 'A' pinned to her bodice to show that she is an adulteress. She's imprisoned and humiliated in every possible way when she refuses to name the father of her child. Bethany Warren has every reason to be afraid, but I can't imagine what Charles can do to safeguard her reputation. She's an unmarried woman who is pregnant with a child conceived out of wedlock. No amount of money can save her from the consequences once word gets out," Valerie said.

When she read *The Scarlet Letter* in school she'd been bored. What modern teenage girl could relate to the mental and physical suffering of Hester Prynne? But now Valerie understood only too well and felt an overwhelming pity for Bethany

Warren. Virginia was not a Puritan colony, but Bethany Warren would still face some form of punishment, and the derision and judgment of the other women would probably be the worst part of it. She would survive the punishment but be ostracized and treated like a pariah for the rest of her life, as would her child.

She'd always known that Charles was a philanderer, but to get a recently widowed young woman with child was low even for him. Bethany Warren would be crucified once her condition became obvious, and the first one to accuse her of wanton behavior would be her righteous brother and his wife.

"Charles bribed Ethan Bartlett to marry Bethany. Everyone will assume the babe came early once her time comes," Alec explained.

Valerie grabbed the bench, she nearly tumbling off the trap in her shock. "He bribed Ethan Bartlett to marry his pregnant mistress? Alec, that's absolutely Machiavellian."

"My brother *is* Machiavellian. I've often wondered how it is that four children of the same parents came to be so different, but then again, I suppose we are not that different after all."

"Aren't you?"

Alec shrugged as he covered Tom's hands with his own, urging the horse that had slowed down considerably to go faster. "Finlay and Charles took after my father. He was a good man, but a product of his time, whereas Rose and I favored our mother in temperament."

"You've never said anything critical about your father before," Valerie said, eager to hear more family gossip. Alec spoke of his life before her so rarely that she savored every morsel, interested in learning anything she could about Alec's childhood and youth.

"I suppose I had never thought about it before visiting the twenty-first century. Finlay and I were raised with the idea that a man can do as he pleases. My father loved our mother and showed her great respect, but I know for a fact that he wasn't faithful to her, nor did he often consider her feelings or health. When I was a child, I rarely spent time with my mother. She was worn out by pregnancies and childbirth, so my grandmother had stepped into the breach. She spent a lot of time with me, telling me stories of her childhood in Hungary. She felt sorry for me, I think, since I was the oldest and received the least amount of attention from our mother. It wasn't until after Charles was weaned that my mother had begun to recover some of her vitality, and by then she had her hands full with Rose. She was always so sensitive and excitable. My mother tried her best to prepare Rose for what was to come."

"You mean marriage?" Valerie asked, trying to imagine what Alec's sister had been like before running off to a French convent just after the death of their parents from the bloody flux.

"Rose was terrified of marriage and childbirth. She'd seen and heard too much when our mother was in labor. My mother saw each living child as a gift from God, but Rose saw it only as a punishment for the sins of Eve and prayed to be spared. I think my mother had tried to tell her otherwise, but Rose saw the marriage bed as a type of sacrificial altar on which she would be defiled."

"Poor girl," Valerie said as she thought of their own daughter. Louisa had been born with a sensuality that was as much a part of her as her willfulness. She didn't wish to broach the subject with Alec, but she sometimes wondered whether it was best for a woman of this time to own her sexuality or deny it like Rose had tried to do. She supposed neither, but at least Louisa had chosen her own fate, whereas poor Rose had indeed turned out to be the sacrificial lamb on the altar of lust, being raped at the convent and impregnated with a child she didn't want. Would she have been able to be a mother to Jenny had she lived, or would she have rejected her and seen her only as a product of sin?

"I miss Jenny," Alec suddenly said, as if reading her thoughts. "I thought that in time I would get used to her not being here. After all, I hadn't even been aware of her existence until she'd showed up in London, but there is a hollow spot in my heart that will never be filled."

Valerie patted Alec's hand, choosing not to voice her thoughts. She missed her too, but to Alec Jenny was more than a niece. Jenny was the girl who should have been his daughter. She was gentle, humble, and kind, a woman who gave her love freely, with no agenda in mind. Jenny was someone Alec understood, unlike their own Louisa who had been proud, ambitious, and ruthless. Louisa had taken the life of Tom's father, had planned a murder and carried it out without a smidgeon of remorse. She would have likely destroyed her husband as well, had she not died in childbirth. Valerie had loved her daughter fiercely but knew Louisa for the sort of woman she was. She had left a trail of destruction in her wake and had never looked back. She simply hadn't cared.

Valerie draped an arm around Tom, who was still absorbed in driving the trap. This little boy held her heart, and Alec's too, but what would he be like once he grew up? Louisa and Thomas Gaines had both been willful, often cruel, and given to scheming. Would Tom take after them? Valerie wondered as she planted a kiss atop Tom's blond head. Would they be able to save Tom from himself, and would they have a better chance if they took him to a different time?

Valerie tried to ignore the ache in her heart and not to think of what was coming, but the Battle of Yorktown was only weeks away. Logically, she knew that Finn wouldn't be on the front lines, but he was close enough, and the not knowing was the hardest to bear. She longed to be with her son, to see his face and look into those green eyes, so like his father's. She longed to protect him from harm. She knew he was in good hands with John and Hannah Mallory. They loved her boy, but he was hers, not theirs, and she wanted to be a part of his life, and the lives of his children. The ache had become so acute, she could no longer bear it.

"Alec, I want to go," she heard herself saying. "I want to go to Finn."

"We'll visit as soon as Kit is on his feet again."

"No, I want to *go*."

Alec gazed at her over Tom's head, his expression one of pleasant surprise. "Are you saying that you are ready to be parted from Louisa? Are you sure, Valerie? I know you worry about Finn, but this separation would almost certainly be permanent. You and Louisa would never share a house again, or even a century."

"It seems that it's not possible for me to have everyone I love around me. It's the only thing I've ever wanted, and the only thing I can't seem to will into being. I will miss Louisa and Kit every day of my life, but I am ready to go to our son, Alec."

Alec nodded. He'd been waiting for Valerie to decide. He would never force a separation between her and Louisa, but she was ready at last. She had chosen.

"We must wait until Kit's recovered. We can't possibly leave Louisa to cope on her own. And landing in the middle of an epic battle is probably not a good plan. Beginning of November?" Alec asked, his tone hopeful.

"Yes." It was a simple word, a simple promise, but it held so much hope, love, and despair in its three letters. Alec covered Valerie's hand with his own. He knew what this meant to her; he understood.

"There will be much to work out," Alec said as he took the reins from Tom. They were nearing Jamestown and the conversation would have to wait, but no move was easy, especially one where you simply fell off the face of the earth in one century and reappeared in another.

FIFTY-NINE

Fred Taylor took his cup outside and sat in his favorite spot on the porch. He'd added the porch to the tiny cabin himself, his first real carpentry project, and made sure it faced west to catch the sunset. He'd never had much of a view from his flat over the antique shop, despite living in a picturesque village. The front of the building had faced the marina, but his rooms overlooked several other houses, and he'd often kept the curtains closed to avoid prying eyes. Now he took advantage of the view whenever the weather was fine. Fred normally had supper with the family and waited around to walk Barbara home after she set the kitchen to rights, but lately, he preferred to enjoy the blissful peace of the Virginia evenings since eating supper was no longer an option.

Fred stared at the blood-orange orb of the sun as it brushed the treetops in the distance, totally mesmerized. It was such an awesome sight, one that had happened since the beginning of time, long before there were people on this land, or any other. The continuity of nature always reminded him how insignificant man was compared to all that wild beauty and how brief a time he spent on this earth. Fred sighed and leaned back in his chair, refusing to squint in the face of all that crimson glory. Funny that it wasn't until he was in his seventies that he had found contentment at last.

For the first time in his life, he had love and companionship with his dear Barbara, and he also had the girls and their families. Fred viewed Valerie and Louisa as the daughters he never had and couldn't care for them more had they been his biological children. What brave, beautiful women they were, and how generous to allow him into their lives, despite his many failings. Would they miss him when he was gone? He hoped so.

Fred finally tore his gaze away from the setting sun and glanced at the cup. A few more minutes. He'd known for some time now that he was ill. At first, he'd attributed the constipation, bloating, and stomach pains to advancing age and tried to adjust his diet, choosing blander, easier to digest foods. It wasn't until he'd noticed dark-red blood every time he moved his bowels that he'd begun to suspect that his discomfort wasn't mere indigestion. The bleeding had increased, and so had the pain every time he went to the privy. He often vomited, his body finding a way to evacuate the toxins from his system.

Desperate for relief, Fred had even consulted Doctor Jacobson. The doctor had received him in his Jamestown surgery.

"How may I help you, Master Taylor?" Jacobson had asked.

Fred had explained the symptoms, wondering how much Jacobson really knew of the inner workings of the human body. He could be trusted to set a broken bone or lance a boil, but when it came to internal organs, all he had to go on was supposition and instinct, since he could only base his diagnosis on the obvious symptoms. Had Fred gone to the doctor in the future, there would have been blood work, scans, and a possible biopsy, but Doctor Jacobson had only the most primitive medical tools at his disposal. Still, he had to try. A small part of Fred had still hoped that his condition was something manageable, like an ulcer, but he had his doubts.

Fred had looked on with amusement as Doctor Jacobson pulled on a cleaned sheath of animal intestine over his fingers, for lack of a latex glove, unprepared for the pain he'd feel when Dr. Jacobson probed him. The doctor had pulled off his bloodied glove and thrown it into the fire before palpating the abdomen, his expression thoughtful.

"So, what say you, Doctor?" Fred had asked as he'd pulled his breeches back on. He'd tried to sound cavalier, but his insides were quivering with fear, mostly due to the grave look on the doctor's face.

"You appear to have a rather large mass in your rectum, Master Taylor, and one in your lower abdomen. Perhaps there are other tumors deeper inside, but I can't say for certain."

"I see. Is there anything you can do to help me, Doctor?"

Doctor Jacobson was a brusque man who always opted for the truth when it came to dealing with his patients. Bedside manner was not something he considered important, but Fred believed it took a certain amount of courage to look a person in the face and tell them the truth rather than placate them with euphemisms. In a time when people rarely recovered from serious illnesses, it was important for them to know the truth so that they could make provisions for their families or make any last-minute wishes known.

"To be perfectly honest, I would gladly cut you open and try to remove the tumors, but the surgery would benefit me a lot more than it would benefit you. I would learn more about the human body and the cancer that's spreading inside you, but you are not likely to survive the procedure, even if it proved successful, which is highly unlikely."

"You will forgive me, Doctor, if I decide against donating my body to science," Fred quipped in an effort to hide his despair. "Is there anything you can recommend that would ease my suffering?"

Doctor Jacobson had rooted through his medicine chest and

extracted a small pouch. "This is dried cassia senna and rhubarb. Brew this into a tea and drink daily. It will help you move your bowels, but it's not a cure, not by any means."

"How long do I have?"

"I can't say with any certainty. Several months, perhaps. The pain and bleeding will get worse as the mass continues to grow."

Fred had paid Doctor Jacobson with a jar of jam he'd pilfered from Barbara's pantry and left. He didn't know much about colon cancer, but from what he recalled, the symptoms did not become obvious until the cancer had spread. If Jacobson could feel a growth in his rectum and one in his gut, then there were probably others along the way. A few months, Fred had mused as he mounted his mule and set off for home. That would bring him into early fall and allow him to enjoy one more summer. He would not say anything to Barbara other than he was suffering from a stomach ulcer, nor would he wait for the pain to become unbearable. No, he'd know when the time was right.

And the time was right now. He awoke this morning in a pool of blood. Thankfully, Barbara had already left for the big house, so Fred was able to strip the bed and wash out the sheet and his shirt before hanging them out to dry. The sheet was back on the bed, and his shirt was neatly folded on his pillow. He didn't wish for Barbara to suffer, nor did he want to be a burden to anyone. And once his illness became common knowledge, he wouldn't be able to do what he'd planned to do all along. Alec would not allow it, being the good Catholic that he was. At times, Fred envied Alec his faith. It helped him through the hard times, and God knows, he'd had many.

Fred looked back toward the sun. It had nearly set, the ribbons of color unfurled along the horizon a startling contrast to the darkness of the trees. Another few minutes and the sun would drop below the horizon, dusk settling over the distant hills. Fred raised his cup to the sun in a toast.

"Good night, sweet prince," he said and gulped down the mixture of beer and wolfsbane. He then hurled the cup into a nearby bush, certain that Barbara would never find it there. She couldn't know the truth. All she needed to know was that her husband had died peacefully. After all, by seventeenth-century standards, he was not only elderly, he was ancient. It was time to go.

Fred doubled over as a sharp pain bloomed in his bowels but refused to give in to it. Instead, he focused his gaze on the last rays of the setting sun, his eyes no longer seeing anything by the time it vanished below the horizon.

SIXTY

"So how did she seem?" Louisa asked Valerie as they walked away from the little cemetery on the hill. Louisa was referring to Annabel, but Valerie wasn't sure why she wanted to talk about her now. The funeral had left Valerie feeling gutted and desperate for a little solitude to deal with her grief. Alec had performed the service, as he always did, and Valerie had cried quietly as she watched Barbara Taylor toss the first clump of earth into the yawning grave. Barbara had done her best to remain composed, but Valerie could see the pain in her eyes and almost feel the older woman's bewilderment. She was alone once again, torn from the devoted partner of her old age.

Valerie had her own theory about Fred's death, but wasn't about to share it with anyone. She was sure Fred had been more seriously ill than he let on, putting about the story about his ulcer to keep them from guessing the truth. Fred had been a shrewd and practical man and would not have wanted to suffer or cause unnecessary grief to those around him. But what good did it do to speculate? Even if Fred had helped speed matters along, he deserved a Christian burial and the grief of those who'd cared for him. Louisa had remained stonily dry-eyed, but

Valerie wept when Alec spoke, and especially when the coffin was lowered into the ground by two indentures.

Perhaps she was transferring her feelings about her own parents onto Fred, but she really had cared about the old man, despite the role he'd played in sending her to the past. She had forgiven him a long time ago and made sure that he'd known it. His failure to get her back, and Alec's grandmother before her, had gnawed at him, and Valerie thought it important to grant him peace. Fred's relationship with Louisa had been different from the start, since he'd helped her to find Valerie, so he never sought her forgiveness as he had Valerie's. Louisa had held Fred in high regard and treated him as a father. Valerie supposed that Fred had become a father of sorts to her as well, and now he'd just slipped out of their lives as suddenly as he had appeared, quietly and without a fuss.

"Well?" Louisa nudged her. "How was Annabel?"

"Desolate. Broken. I've never seen her look so vulnerable."

Valerie had been shocked by Annabel's appearance. Gone was the usual defiance and sense of righteousness. Annabel was a shell of her former self, and Valerie felt nothing but sympathy toward the other woman. It was hard enough to lose a baby early in the pregnancy, but Annabel had been in her third trimester, and the baby was as real to her as if it had already been born.

"I still despise her, but I do feel for her. I'm not sure what's worse, losing a child so late in the pregnancy or finding out that your husband has been at it with someone else and is expecting another child by his mistress. Do you think they'll ever come back from this?" Louisa asked.

It wasn't that long ago that Louisa had found out about Kit's affair with Buckingham, so she understood only too well how Annabel must be feeling.

"I suppose they'll have to. Annabel is a proud woman and would never consider divorce under any circumstances. And if

Bethany Warren marries Ethan Bartlett the whole affair can be swept under the rug. I think she'll come around, but she'll make Charles's life a living hell," Valerie mused. "He looks like he's halfway there already."

"Not that he doesn't deserve it. And to think that Charles had been sneaking around with Bethany Warren all this time. That's one woman I'd never have imagined succumbing to his charms. She always seemed so—what's the word—upstanding."

"I think she was just terribly lonely, and Charles took advantage of that," Valerie replied.

"Perhaps, but why did she tell Annabel? That was unnecessarily cruel," Louisa remarked as they walked toward the house.

"I think she was frightened of what would happen to her and her child and wanted to impress on Charles the seriousness of her situation. I'm sure she never meant for Annabel to miscarry. She just wasn't thinking straight. Her life would have been made unbearable had the truth come out."

"I suppose she was desperate, but taking down another woman is never the right decision, is it?" Louisa sighed. "There are times when I still can't believe that we went from living in "The Land of the Free" to this moral prison of well-meant tyranny."

Valerie sighed. She'd been dreading this moment for longer than she realized, but it had to be done, and there would be no right time to tell Louisa. Valerie stopped walking and turned to face her sister. She was grateful that they had taken the long way back and were alone on the path, with no one to interrupt what she had to say.

"Lou, there's something I have to tell you," Valerie began. She saw Louisa's eyes brim with tears, her face turning pale as she wrapped her arms about her middle, as if to ward off a blow. She nodded as tears spilled down her cheeks.

"I know what you're going to tell me. You've hinted at it often enough. I've lived this moment a thousand times, and it never gets easier. Oh, Val, how am I supposed to live without you? How can I survive?"

Valerie had promised herself that she would stay strong, but that resolution went out the window as soon as she saw Louisa's tears. She'd practiced her speech, made a list of reasons why she had to tear their lives apart, but now she'd forgotten everything she'd planned to say. She wrapped her arms about Louisa, and they just stood there, enveloped in their grief.

"How long?" Louisa sobbed. "How long until you leave me?"

"We'll wait until Kit's recovered. We won't leave you in the lurch. He'll want to sail for England come spring anyway."

"I thought I could talk him out of it," Louisa cried. "I thought I could buy us a few more years. Oh Val, I don't want to go to England. I want to be with you. You are my only link to that other life, to our parents. Without you, I will never be whole again. And I'm scared for Kit."

"Why? He is getting better every day."

"I know, but what will happen once we return? Who's to say that Buckingham won't try to reclaim what was once his? Kit will be vulnerable and a target for blackmail. If Deverell knew, then others might know as well. Will this nightmare never end?" Louisa exclaimed as she tore herself from Valerie's arms and stomped toward the house.

Valerie made to follow, then stopped. She needed a few moments to compose herself, and Louisa needed time to think. As painful as it had been telling her sister, Valerie felt a sense of relief. She was over the biggest hurdle, and now it was real. They were really going.

SIXTY-ONE

Kit used his good arm to pull the blanket over Louisa. She'd cried herself to sleep, and no amount of sweet-talking would make her feel less wretched. Louisa was a woman who turned to sex to work through her feelings and Kit wished that he'd been able to pound her into oblivion, but he couldn't move his leg, and even if she'd straddled him, he'd still have to move his hips and possibly do damage to his knitting bones. He had to get out of this bed—now more than ever. Kit sighed and pushed a lock of hair out of Louisa's eyes. She'd dreaded this day for a long time, and now it had finally come. Valerie's news wasn't really a bombshell, more of a confirmation of his wife's worst fears. He'd known it was coming sooner rather than later but hadn't told Louisa. It had to come from Valerie. Their bond was the strongest he'd ever known, and he could understand Louisa's pain and bewilderment. It wouldn't be easy for him either.

Kit stared at the ceiling. He thought he was prepared for Valerie's news, but now that Louisa was finally asleep, he could drop the façade and allow himself a moment of grief. He'd been close to his sister once, but not until meeting Alec Whitfield had he found a true friend. Alec was—in a word—decent, and decency wasn't something Kit had seen much of in his life. Having grown up at the Court of James I, Kit understood the value of loyalty only too well. He'd learned early on that to trust anyone completely was a leap of such blind faith that it wasn't worth taking. The scheming, gossiping, and maneuvering of the nobles was more appropriate to a snake pit than the court of one of the greatest monarchies in the world. No wonder Louisa had hated every moment she'd spent at court.

And now James was dead, and there was a new monarch on the throne. Charles I was a vainglorious, selfish man who believed that no one, not even Parliament had the right to curb the power of God's representative on Earth. Perhaps Kit had spent too much time with Louisa and Valerie, but his view of the world had changed dramatically over the past decade. He found himself questioning the old ways and longing for a life where democracy wasn't something that only philosophers discussed in old, dusty tomes.

Louisa was right, adjusting to life in England wasn't going to be easy, and truthfully, Kit did not relish the prospect of going back. He needed to go, he'd planned to, but the reality was that he was just as shattered as Louisa. Kit tried to imagine a life without the Whitfields, and his heart contracted with acute misery. Losing Alec and Valerie was like losing a limb, and he should know, he'd nearly lost two already. Life without them would never be the same, and Kit suddenly feared for the future, and for his marriage.

SIXTY-TWO
VIRGINIA SEPTEMBER 1781

Slanted rays of the late-afternoon sun striped the narrow path, the warmth of the day finally abating as evening drew near. A chorus of birdsong and the clip-clop of hoofbeats were the only sounds to disturb the peace of the lonely road. Sam looked around in dismay. He was fairly certain he was in Virginia, but he'd been traveling all day and hadn't come upon any settlements or even lone homesteads. He thought he knew where he was going when he'd left the Hammers, but after nearly three days in the saddle, he had to admit that he was lost. He'd stopped at several farms along the way to ask for food but hadn't recognized the names of the nearby towns or seen anything even remotely familiar. Sam sighed, feeling defeated. He must have taken a wrong turn somewhere, and although he was traveling in the right direction, he had no way of knowing exactly where he was. He'd have to stop and make camp soon. He was starving, exhausted, and frustrated.

His last decent meal had been the night before when he'd stopped at a small homestead. The woman had been frightened at first, but seeing his condition took pity on him. She'd fed him and allowed him to bed down in the barn, even going so far as to give him a blanket and some milk and bread for breakfast. Her husband was with the militia and she had three children under the age of six all peering at Sam from the loft, their curious little faces pressed against the wooden slats. Seeing the children made him miss his own kids. There were times when he felt overwhelmed by the responsibility of being a husband and father and dreamed of having some time to himself. Before he married, and before the war, he'd often spent his nights drinking and wenching or the day fishing with Jonah. Sam missed those days.

But being away from home and nearly dying at the end of a rope had made him realize how much he loved his family. He'd promised himself that he would never take Sue for granted again, and never lose his temper with the children, especially the boys, who tended to try to show each other up by making mischief. And he missed his Rachel. If there was one person in this world who loved him unconditionally it was his baby girl. Rachel loved birds, so he would carve her a pretty bird once he got back and stain it with indigo to make it look like a bluebird.

Sam squinted up at the sun, which was now peeking playfully through the thick canopy of the trees that lined the track. There was no point in stopping just yet. It's not as if he had anything to prepare for supper, so he might as well keep going for a little while longer. He'd stop when it grew dark and just go to sleep. He didn't even have the strength to gather wood for a fire. If he got lucky, perhaps he'd come upon a homestead and ask for some food and a place to bed down for the night.

Sam tried to whistle, but his throat was still raw and swollen, so he stopped after a few bars. He hadn't had another panic attack since leaving the Hammers, which was good he supposed, but he didn't feel at all well. He'd always taken his good health and vitality for granted, but these last few days had been a humbling experience. He was so uncoordinated he could barely mount his horse, much less do anything that required real effort. He felt weak and confused, and unbearably tired. And his back ached like the devil after days without anything to rest it against.

Sam stared ahead as his horse staggered on, but his eyelids grew heavy, and the birdsong started to blend into a low hum as he leaned forward and rested his forehead against the horse's warm neck. He'd close his eyes for just a moment. It felt so good to let go and not think about what awaited him when he got home. Sue would make a terrible fuss, especially once she saw his neck. Sam smiled dreamily. Perhaps being fussed over wasn't such a terrible thing. At this moment, he would give his eyeteeth for someone to feed and water his horse and give him a hot meal with several cups of cool beer. And a clean bed. He'd give a lot for a bed, especially his own bed. Sam felt as if he could go to sleep and never wake up. He could almost feel himself stretched out between the cool sheets, his head resting on a soft pillow. What a pleasure that would be.

Sam hit the ground hard, his eyes flying open as a sharp pain tore through his lower back. He was on his back, staring up at the dusky sky, his horse glaring at him with obvious displeasure. He must have fallen asleep and slid off. Sam tried to get up, but the pain was so intense that he immediately lay back down. He reached up and grabbed onto the reins. If the horse bolted, he'd be stranded in the middle of nowhere. The horse didn't seem intent on leaving, but it did appreciate the opportunity to graze. The poor animal was as tired and hungry as Sam was, but at least it could find food anywhere in the form of grass. Sam tried to use the reins to lift himself, but when the leather nearly snapped, gave up. Even if he managed to get to his feet, he wouldn't be able to mount the horse. Holding on to the reins, he closed his eyes and allowed his mind to drift until he fell into an uneasy sleep.

By the time he awoke at dawn, he was stiff and shivering from the cold. His clothes were damp with dew and his back hurt as much as it had last night. Sam ran his hand along the wet grass and used the moisture to wipe his face. He was thirsty, and terribly hungry. His stomach growled in protest at not having been fed in more than twenty-four hours, and his lips were dry and chapped. He needed to get up and get going or he would die out here. Sam tried to sit up, but a scream of agony tore from deep inside him. He couldn't move. He must have broken something in the fall and was doomed to lie here until either someone came upon him or he was attacked by a pack of hungry wolves. Were there wolves in Virginia? Was he even in Virginia or had he gone the wrong way and wound up in Delaware instead? Sam's eyes filled with tears of frustration and pain. What would become of him if no one came?

Calm down, you idiot, Sam told himself. *You're carrying on like a hysterical maiden. What you need is a plan.*

Sam forced himself to relax and looked around. He was lying on the side of the road, but a few feet away were several fallen branches. If he could manage to scoot across and get hold of a stout stick, he could use it to help himself to his feet. What he would do after that was anyone's guess, but at least he wouldn't feel as helpless, and even if he couldn't get up, he could at least use the stick as a weapon against animals.

Sam tried to shift his hips in the direction of the tree line. It hurt like hell, but he did manage to move several inches before giving up. He needed to rest for a bit and allow the pain to recede before attempting to move again. It might take him an hour or two to reach the branches, but he had to keep trying. If only he weren't so hungry. Sam waited a few minutes, then tried moving again. The pain was so severe, it left him breathless, but he did manage to get a little closer. At this rate, he'd get there by noon, he mused.

About an hour later, Sam was still nowhere near the trees. He was panting with exertion and his face glistened with sweat, but he'd managed to move only about a foot. Sam froze when he heard a familiar sound. Someone was coming, but he couldn't see anything without twisting his back. Sam felt around for a stone. He needed a weapon in case the person meant him harm. Finding a medium-sized rock, he closed his fingers around it. It wasn't much, but it was better than nothing. Enough to crack someone's skull if the situation called for it.

Sam tensed when he saw a horse come into view, followed by a small trap, the bench hardly wide enough for one person to sit on. The man pulled on the reins to stop the trap and got down. Sam couldn't see his face, since it was shadowed by the wide brim of his hat, but he did see the rest of him. He was of medium height and build, and his clothes, although dusty and travel-stained were of good quality, not the homespun usually worn by farmers. This was someone who came from the city. But which city? Sam wondered as he gripped his rock.

The man walked toward Sam and squatted next to him. "My dear fellow, are you hurt?" the man asked, his British accent putting Sam's hackles up. He didn't appear to be a soldier though, so Sam forced himself to resist the urge to brain him.

"Yes, I fell off my horse and hurt my back," Sam replied in a whisper.

"I see. And what happened to your neck?"

Sam realized that he'd untied his neckcloth earlier and the man could see the horrible bruises on his swollen throat.

"Nothing. An accident." That was a blatant lie, but he didn't owe this stranger any explanation. The man didn't persist with his questioning but moved back just a bit when he noticed the rock in Sam's hand.

"I'd like to help you, but I would appreciate it if you didn't bash me over the head. It would serve little purpose."

Sam released the rock and let it fall from his hand just as the man pushed up his hat and a ray of sunshine illuminated his face. Sam stared, the spark of recognition igniting in both their faces at once.

"You!" the man said as he stared at Sam, his demeanor transforming from benevolence to outrage. He jumped to his feet and took a step back from Sam as an angry flush stained his cheeks. "Why? I ought to—" he began, but stopped, unsure of what he meant to say.

"Won't you help me, Doctor Freeman?" Sam asked. "I'll die out here if you don't." He sounded pitiful, and the man nodded.

"Of course, I'll help you. I'm a physician, after all. I can't walk away from an injured man, no matter how much I'd like to. So, what should I call you, Corporal Johnson or Samuel Mallory?" the doctor asked bitterly. "As I recall, the last time I helped you, you repaid me by running off with my daughter."

"Sir, with all due respect, your daughter is a smart and headstrong woman. Had she not wanted to leave with me, an army of soldiers would not have been able to shift her."

Sam wanted to say more, but the long speech made his throat burn and he began to cough, the spasms forcing his back to seize.

"All right, son, we'll clear the air at a later date. Now, I need to examine you."

"Water. Please," Sam mumbled.

"Good Lord, how long have you been lying here?" Doctor Freeman exclaimed, suddenly realizing that Sam hadn't just fallen off, but had been there for some time.

"Since yesterday."

Doctor Freeman jumped to his feet and went to retrieve a satchel from the trap. He held a bottle of warm ale to Sam's lips and Sam drank greedily, some of the ale running down his chin and onto his shirt.

"Easy now. Have you eaten anything?"

"No."

"Let me take a look at you, and then I'll feed you." Doctor

Freeman set aside the leather bottle and gently touched Sam's neck, pulling the neckcloth even looser to see the extent of his injuries.

"Did someone try to hang you?" he asked as he worked.

"Is it that obvious?" Sam whispered. It hurt to talk, but he found it difficult not to answer.

"How long before you were cut down?"

"I don't know."

"Have you been experiencing any unusual symptoms since the hanging?" Sam nodded miserably.

"And then you fell off your horse and hurt your back," Doctor Freeman tut-tutted with disapproval. "You really must take better care of yourself."

Sam grunted at that. It's not as if he'd gotten himself strung up and fell on purpose.

"Sam, put your arm around me, and use me as a crutch. We need to get you into the trap. There isn't much room, but if you lift your knees, you should be able to lie down. This is going to hurt, but it's the only way."

"I'm ready."

Sam screamed with pain as Doctor Freeman lifted him to his feet and dragged him over to the trap. If getting to his feet was painful, climbing into the trap and lying down on his back hurt even more. Sam was covered in sweat and shaking by the time he was finally in position. Doctor Freeman climbed into the cart with Sam and covered him with a blanket.

"I'm sorry. I know that must have hurt terribly. Undue pressure was put on your spine when your neck was in that noose, and you surely kicked your legs when you found yourself short of oxygen. Sometimes it takes a few days for the full extent of the injury to become apparent. Falling off the horse aggravated the situation, causing something in your already weakened back to snap out of its proper place. It will get better, but you need complete rest."

"I can't rest. I'm too hungry," Sam whispered miserably.

Doctor Freeman pulled a bundle out of his satchel and produced some bread and cheese, which he began to feed to Sam very slowly, giving him time to chew and swallow. Each bite was followed by a sip of ale. Sam ate despite the pain, feeling as if he would never get full.

"Sam, after you've eaten, I will give you a few drops of laudanum. It will help you sleep and relieve some of the pain."

"I have attacks," Sam whispered. "Dreadful attacks."

"You mean you feel an overwhelming sense of panic and think that you're dying?" Doctor Freeman asked, his eyes aglow with interest.

"Yes."

"I've had soldiers complaining of that very same thing, especially after a battle. It's a nervous condition, to be sure, not physical, but I haven't found anything that helps except a period of rest. It does get better in time, although going back into battle soon after is not advisable," he rambled on, obviously fascinated by the subject. "I've made that recommendation to my superiors, but they said the men suffer from nothing more than a bout of cowardice."

Sam stiffened. "Where are you taking me? Are you going to hand me over to the British?" Panic attacks would be the least of his problems if he wound up in a British camp.

"No, dear boy. I'm taking you home to your wife. I was on my way to see my daughter and meet my grandchildren. I've resigned my post, you see."

"Have you become sympathetic to the cause?" Sam asked, with a small smile.

"You know, I believe I have."

SIXTY-THREE

Finn breathed a sigh of relief when the peaked roof of the Hammer homestead finally came into view. He'd ridden hell-for-leather for the past few days, barely giving his horse time to rest, to get back to Sam. He'd hardly noticed the miles as his mind still reeled from the evening he'd spent in Philadelphia. Finn wished more than anything that he could share his experience with Sam, but to tell him would be cruel, especially after what he'd suffered for the cause.

Finn smiled for the umpteenth time as he recalled meeting General Washington. He'd always thought of the man as larger than life, almost infallible, but the real man had been something of a surprise. General Washington didn't come off as brusque and decisive, cutting a swath through the crowd at the ball and commanding everyone's attention. He was gracious, soft-spoken, and well-mannered. He'd done nothing to draw undue attention to himself, nor did he spend the whole evening discussing the progress of the war. He was the model guest and spent the evening dancing, dining, and indulging in polite conversation.

The evening was well on the way by the time Finn had

been introduced to General Washington. A telltale blush had crept up his cheeks as the general shook his hand and smiled as if he were meeting an old friend, his dark eyes shining with warmth and good humor.

"It's an honor to meet you, General Washington," Finn had mumbled, suddenly tongue-tied.

"The honor is all mine. I've heard much about you, Mr. Whitfield, and about your ring. John Mallory is an inspiration to us all, and his son Samuel deserves a commendation as well. Why, that stunt you two pulled in New York," Washington said, smiling broadly. "Stuff of legend."

"You heard about that?" Finn asked, suddenly feeling more at ease.

"Of course. And Sam's escape from the British fort as well. Brave lad. Is he here tonight?"

"Ah, no, sir."

"Well, be sure to give him and his father my regards. Their contribution is noted and appreciated, as is the intelligence you brought us today. Very timely, Mr. Whitfield. It might very well alter the course of the war."

"I'm glad to hear that, sir."

George Washington bowed from the neck as his attention was captured by a late arrival.

"If you will excuse me, Mr. Whitfield, but a dear friend of mine has just arrived, and I must say hello."

"Of course."

Ralph clapped Finn on the back after Washington left their little group. "I hope that was worth staying for, Finn. Now, you can start breathing again, and maybe even take a turn about the dance floor. There's a young lady who's been eyeing you all evening."

"I can't," Finn protested. "Abbie wouldn't like it."

"My dear boy, in polite society men and women dance with partners who are not their spouses. It's all part of social intercourse. Have you not seen General Washington dancing with several different ladies? Now, stop acting like the country mouse that you are and ask the young lady to dance."

Finn snuck a peek at the dance floor where Jonah was dancing with a middle-aged woman who was gazing up at him adoringly. Finn supposed there was no harm in a dance or two. It'd been so long since he'd had an opportunity to dance. The young lady blushed prettily as he approached her and bowed from the neck.

"May I have the next dance, Miss?"

"Miss Osbourne," the girl replied. "Thank you, Mr. Whitfield. It would be my pleasure."

Finn didn't ask how the woman knew his name as she placed her hand in his and allowed him to escort her onto the floor. Finn hoped he remembered the steps to the minuet, which had just started up. He would have preferred a spirited country dance, but this wasn't a barn dance. The women were no farmer's wives, and at least half the men were in uniform. Finn felt privileged to be in such company. He got through the dance without embarrassing himself and asked another young lady to partner him in the next dance. Ralph was right; he might as well make the most of the evening. The euphoria he'd felt after General Washington's praise had left him unable to stand still.

It wasn't until well after midnight that Ralph finally took him home. Finn had enjoyed the supper that followed the dancing, the food so beautifully presented it was almost a shame to eat it. His gaze had strayed to General Washington several times, but the general was engaged in conversation with his dinner companions. It would have been nice if Jonah or Ralph were seated next to him, but both men were on the opposite side, seated next to attractive young women, who kept them occupied throughout the meal.

Finn spurred his horse on as he neared the house. He

wouldn't tell Sam everything, but he would certainly tell him about his conversation with General Washington. Sam deserved to know that his contribution had been acknowledged and would love to know that General Washington thought his heroics in New York worth mentioning. Now that the fear of those days was behind them, they could reminisce about their miraculous escape.

Finn slowed down when he saw Eli Hammer watching him as he stepped out of the barn. Finn waved and Hammer waved back, but the expression on his face gave Finn pause. Something wasn't right. Finn dismounted and strode toward the man.

"Friend Eli, I hope you're well," Finn began. "I do apologize for taking longer than I had anticipated."

"Thank thee, Friend Finn. Mary and I are well. There's no need for thee to apologize, but I'm afraid Friend Sam is no longer with us."

The world tilted when Finn heard Eli Hammer's words. Had Sam died while he was dancing and socializing in Philadelphia? Finn felt as if a horse had just kicked him in the gut. He knew Sam wasn't well, but he didn't think he was dying, just in need of a few days' rest.

"Friend Finn, I didn't mean... that is to say that Friend Sam left."

Finn stared at Eli Hammer, confused. "He left? So, he'd recovered then?"

Mary Hammer came out of the house, wiping her hands on her apron. "I'm afraid Friend Sam was very unwell. We looked after him as best we could, but he just left in the middle of the night without a word. We assumed he'd followed thee."

"No, he didn't," Finn replied.

Had Sam followed him, he'd either made it to Philadelphia too late to meet up with Finn or had met with trouble on the road. Once in Philadelphia, Same would have found that the Continental Army had moved out the day after the ball and was headed south toward Virginia instead of north toward New York.

"Perhaps he's gone home," Mary suggested. "Might he have done that?"

"I hope so, Friend Mary. I really hope so," Finn said. "I best be on my way then."

"Wait, stay for dinner. We've got plenty, and thou must be hungry."

"Thank you," Finn replied and headed into the house. He was hungry, and his horse needed a rest and some oats.

Sam, you'd better be all right, Finn thought as he accepted a cup of beer from Mary Hammer.

SIXTY-FOUR
VIRGINIA SEPTEMBER 1628

Louisa finished the story and gazed at the enraptured faces around her. She'd thrown herself into teaching the children to alleviate some of the pain she felt at the thought of the upcoming separation. For two hours a week, she didn't think about anything but the pupils before her. They loved the story of Oliver Twist, just as Kit had predicted, but Louisa had tailored the story to suit her own ends. Her Oliver never got adopted by a wealthy benefactor. Instead, he learned to read and write, and having bettered himself, found a position that lifted him out of the quagmire of poverty and gave him new hope for the future. After all, what was the point of sowing fantasies of rescue in the minds of these orphans? No one was coming for them, were they?

Louisa was shocked to find that most of the children weren't even sure how old they were or know their surnames. Some of them had had families once, but their parents were long gone, and any remaining kin didn't know of their existence. The oldest, although he didn't look it, was a boy named Irish Mick. He was about thirteen and had stepped into a leadership position among the children. He was a tough lad, but Louisa could see that he genuinely cared about the others. They were the only family he had, and he tried to look after them, which endeared Mick to her. The youngest was Sally. She was a waif of a girl, with wide blue eyes and reddish hair. Louisa guessed Sally to be around seven, but she looked younger due to years of malnutrition.

Louisa had to admit that the children looked better than when they'd first arrived. After a month on the plantation, they'd filled out, were fairly clean, and had lost the haunted look that nearly broke her heart the first time she saw them. Alec had them clearing a new field for the spring planting, but it wasn't an overly grueling task, and the children took plenty of breaks to sit in the sun and talk among themselves while they enjoyed a cool drink.

Louisa turned to a girl of about ten, whose name was Aggie, and showed her a card. "Aggie, can you tell me what letter this is?" she asked.

"Tis a C, yer ladyship," Aggie replied proudly.

"Indeed, it is. And Mick, what letter am I holding up now?"

"I don't rightly know, yer ladyship," Mick replied. He looked sheepish as he looked around the room. "Why don't yer ask Sally," he suggested. Louisa knew what Mick was doing. He was trying to build up Sally's confidence, since the little girl rarely spoke.

Louisa saw a look of anxiety cross Sally's features, but she seemed to overcome it when Louisa held up the card. "Sally, I bet you know this one," she prompted.

"B, yer ladyship," Sally whispered, her cheeks turning a deep red.

"You are absolutely right. And can anyone think of a word that starts with the letter B?" Louisa asked, hoping someone would volunteer.

"Buns. Baked buns," a boy named Styx called out from the back.

"Double right. Both words start with the letter B. Good job, Styx. Well, I think we are done for today. I will see you all Saturday next."

"Will yer tell us another story?" Mick asked after much whispering. The children had nominated him to ask.

"Would you like one?" They all nodded in unison.

"I will gladly tell you another story. I know lots of them."

"What will it be about?" a girl whose name Louisa couldn't quite remember asked.

"It will be about a man who stole a loaf of bread to feed his sister's son and went to prison for his crime."

"That sounds like a right sad story, ma'am," Mick chimed in.

"You might think that, but the outcome is quite unpredictable." Louisa thought back to reading *Les Miserables* and then seeing the musical on Broadway. How she wished the children could see the show, or at least hear some of the songs, which were fantastic. None of the children had ever seen a play.

"What's 'unpredictable'?" Styx asked, unfamiliar with the word.

"It means that you can't easily figure out how it will end."

"Fancy word," Mick mumbled, but smiled, nonetheless.

"So, what's the name o' this man as stole a loaf o' bread?" Aggie asked.

Louisa was about to say Jean Valjean, then stopped herself. These children had an inherent fear of foreigners and might not be able to relate to someone they thought of as being different. Besides, she could hardly tell them about a revolution that hadn't happened yet. She would tailor this story as well. No one said it had to be accurate.

"His name is John Johnson," Louisa replied, pleased with herself. She might change the name, the place, and the time, but the story would still appeal to the children. Most of them had been sent down for theft and had to pay with years of their life just for trying to survive. They were the English version of *Les Miserables*, and she hoped that Jean Valjean's plight might inspire them to aspire to greater things.

Louisa collected her cards and said goodbye to the children. She needed to make sure that by the time she was ready to leave for England all the children could read. She doubted that Charles, if left in charge, would agree to see to their education, but once she had taught them, no one would be able to take the knowledge away from them.

Louisa stepped out into the warm September afternoon and saw Valerie walking from the spring house toward her.

"How did it go today?" Valerie asked. She carried a pitcher of buttermilk, which meant that Cook was going to make biscuits.

"It went well. They are really engaged now. They've asked for another story."

"Which one will you tell?" Valerie asked, smiling at Louisa.

"*Les Miserables*, but with some alterations."

"Makes sense. You always look happy after a lesson," Valerie remarked as they neared the house. Louisa had been subdued since Fred Taylor's death and Valerie's news, but teaching the children seemed to lift some of that melancholy, at least temporarily.

"You know something, Val, for the first time since leaving modern life, I feel like I'm doing something that matters. I know that it matters to be Kit's wife and a mother to my children, but this is different. I feel a sense of accomplishment that I haven't felt since I had an actual job. Oh, I do miss working sometimes."

"So do I. Finn made me a proposition the last time we saw him," Valerie confessed. Louisa knew that Valerie was usually careful when speaking about the future. She didn't wish to upset Louisa, but it was impossible to avoid the subject altogether.

"What kind of proposition?"

"He wants me to write and illustrate books for children."

"And do what with them?" Louisa asked, surprised to see the spark in Valerie's eyes. She loved to draw, but there wasn't much call for artwork in colonial Virginia unless it was for portraiture or painting landscapes.

"He wants to open a shop and devote a part of it to selling books and toys for children. Very few people consider making anything especially for children, so Finn hopes to corner the market."

"That's a clever idea, but you can't utilize the stories you already know. Most of the fairy tales haven't even been written yet, and you can hardly predate Hans Christian Andersen and the Brothers Grimm."

"Hmm, that's a valid point. I haven't thought of that. I suppose I'll have to make up my own stories. How hard can it be? My first story can be about an orphan who comes to Virginia from England and has some interesting adventures."

"I hope this story will have a happy ending."

"Of course, it will. There will be a beautiful benefactress, like the Fairy Godmother, named Louisa." Valerie meant to make Louisa smile, but instead her face crumpled, and a desperate sob tore from her chest.

"Oh, Val, don't say that. I'm the one in need of a Fairy Godmother that can whisk me to see you every time I feel lonely. I can't bear the thought of this separation."

Valerie set down the pitcher of buttermilk on the porch and wrapped her arms around Louisa. "Oh, Lou, I can hardly bear to think about it myself. I will try to visit. I promise."

"But it won't be the same. We will no longer be a part of each other's daily lives. The best we can hope for is seeing each other maybe once a year, and as the children get older, there'll be more and more explaining to do."

"I know, but we will make it work. We must."

Louisa nodded, tears sliding down her face. She'd been

happy and pleased only a few minutes ago, but the pleasure of her lesson was already forgotten, the familiar ache settling in her heart. Perhaps Kit was right, and it'd get easier once Alec and Valerie actually left. This waiting for the other shoe to drop was absolute torture.

SIXTY-FIVE

VIRGINIA SEPTEMBER 1781

Abbie wiped the sweat from her brow, leaving a streak of flour on her cheek. She'd been baking since noon in preparation for the wake that was to take place tomorrow after the burial. Her mother wished for the funeral to take place as soon as possible, but the carpenter had been ill, and his apprentice, although skilled, needed time to finish an order that was already past due. The coffin had finally been delivered that morning, and her mother had gone off to the spring house where they'd been keeping the body to dress her husband and prepare him for his final journey. Abbie was in charge of preparing the food.

"Come on, girls," she said to Sarah and Annie, who were preparing the corn bread. "Let's get these in while the oven is hot. This will be the last batch for today. I think we have enough baked goods to feed an army."

The girls were silent, their faces streaked with tears, but they poured the mixture into pans, glad to have something useful to do. It was hard to accept that their father was gone. John Mallory had always seemed larger than life, a man who could be counted on to get any job done and still find time to soothe his daughters' fears and sing them a song when they couldn't sleep. He'd loved all his children and had doted on his grandkids, especially the younger ones. His only regret had been that he'd never got to spend time with Jonah's Gemma, and now he never would. Gemma would have no memory of her grandfather at all. Abbie hoped that Edward, Daisy, and Rachel would remember him. They were still so little, but perhaps they would retain some glimmer of memory, helped along by stories of their grandfather.

Abbie sighed as she pushed the pans into the oven and went to check on the children. They were playing outside, their shrieks giving her a massive headache. It was time for their supper. On fine days, Abbie took the kids to the creek for a wash before supper, but today, she was too tired. She'd been on her feet for hours, taking a break only to go to the privy. The table was almost completely covered with pies, fritters, and fruit crumbles. Water from the rain barrel would have to do for the children today. She scooped up Edward and washed his face. He squealed like a piglet and tried to keep the water from getting into his eyes. For someone who loved to swim, he sure hated being washed.

"Want to play," he cried as Abbie washed his filthy hands.

"Aren't you hungry?"

Edward considered this for a moment. Unlike Diana, he was always hungry, and always begging for another helping. He was a sturdy boy, his build similar John Mallory's, who'd been barrel-chested and wide in the shoulders. The thought of Edward resembling her father made Abbie cry, but she wiped her tears away angrily and turned to Diana.

"Come on. Your turn," she said. Diana liked being clean, so she washed her own face and hands as Abbie held her up to the barrel.

"When's Grandma coming back?" Diana asked. "She promised to help me make a skirt for my dolly."

"Grandma will help you after the funeral, Di."

"What's a funeral?" Diana asked.

She hadn't attended the funeral for her namesake, who died two years ago under mysterious circumstances, leaving her son to be raised by Sue and Sam. Abbie had a fairly good idea what happened to Diana, but the truth was never spoken out loud, and she preferred to believe that her father hadn't ordered Diana to be killed.

"A funeral is when you say goodbye to someone who has died and put their body in the ground."

"Is Grandpa going to Heaven?" Diana asked. She was always asking questions about God and Heaven and Hell.

"He most certainly is," Abbie replied.

Was there a Heaven? she wondered as she set slices of rabbit pie before the children. Reverend Greene said there was, but sometimes she wasn't so sure. Finn said that Heaven was an imaginary place, invented by the Church to make death easier to accept. Sometimes Finn's ideas shocked her, but Abbie secretly believed that her father had shared Finn's theories. John Mallory had gone to church for the sake of his wife and children, and to maintain his standing in the community, but he was more of an atheist, if Abbie were honest.

She'd heard that word only once, but it had stayed with her, as had the crazy idea that God did not exist. The notion of a world without God was terrifying. That would mean that everything that happened was utterly random, and there was no one looking out for them or waiting for them in the next life. Was it possible that life was just a form of chaos, a world full of people running amok without the guidance of a heavenly father?

"Granddad is going to Heaven," Abbie said again, more to herself than to her daughter.

She needed to believe that her father, who had committed sins in the name of the cause and had been responsible for the deaths of others, would still go to a better place, where he would be forgiven for his transgressions and seen for the good and loyal man he really was. Was it a sin to kill during wartime, and was it a mortal sin to kill the mother of a young boy? Abbie didn't care to dwell on this question, but every so often she thought of Diana, especially when she saw Nat. He favored Sam in his looks, but there were times when he looked up at Abbie in a certain way, or smiled that slow, secret smile that reminded Abbie of the woman who'd given birth to him. Had Diana gone to Heaven? Abbie wondered.

She supposed it was natural to question her beliefs on the eve of her father's funeral. It was all part of the grieving process, or so Sue had said. Sue had her own theories about the world and Abbie found that she liked Sue's view of things.

"All right, off to bed," Abbie said once the children finished their meal.

They were both drooping, having played outside for the better part of the day. Abbie watched them through the window to make sure they were safe but had to admit that it was liberating not to have a child attached to her skirts or her breasts. She'd weaned Eddie over a year ago and relished the freedom of not having to nurse him several times a day. Abbie sighed. Finn wanted more children, but she absolutely refused to have another baby until they had a home of their own. Now, with her father gone, everything would be up in the air yet again. Her mother and sisters couldn't manage the farm on their own, and Sam couldn't possibly do all the work himself. Finn would be needed here.

By the time Abbie finally got the children settled, it was fully dark outside. She wondered where her mother was but figured she must have decided to stop at Sue's before coming home, or maybe she couldn't bear to leave her husband on his last night above ground. Hannah had been stoic and philosophical in the face of loss, but she was shattered on the inside, only keeping up the façade for the benefit of her children.

Abbie descended the ladder and looked in on Sarah and

Annie. They were sitting on their bed, brushing their hair before plaiting it for the night. Abbie went to clear away the supper dishes. She was exhausted, but the dishes had to be washed before she went up to bed. She stopped what she was doing and listened intently. She thought she heard the neighing of a horse. Her mother had gone on foot, so it wouldn't be her.

Abbie's heart swelled with joy. Finn. It had to be Finn. She ran to the door and yanked it open, shocked to find two strange men on the doorstep. Abbie took an involuntary step back as the men pushed their way into the house and shut the door behind them. Abbie stared at their faces. She knew one of them. His name was Leo Sparks, but the other man was a stranger to her. He was short and wiry with long, lanky dark hair, unlike his companion who was tall and broad, his rust-colored hair falling in shiny waves. He had wide gray eyes that were full of malice.

"What do you want?" Abbie demanded. She tried to sound outraged, but her insides quivered with fear. The men looked threatening as they advanced farther into the house.

"We'd like a word with your husband, Mistress Whitfield," Sparks said.

"My husband isn't here," Abbie replied, wondering if telling them was a mistake.

"No, he isn't, is he? You'd better tell me where he is then."

"I don't know," Abbie replied as she backed away from Sparks.

"Don't you? I wager you know exactly where he is, or is meant to be, that is."

"I told you; I don't know," Abbie stammered. She hadn't turned around, but she could sense Sarah and Annie behind her, their fear palpable.

"Well, look at that, George," Leo Sparks said to his companion. "Three lovely ladies with nary a father, brother, or husband to protect them. How lucky for us."

George looked momentarily abashed but agreed with his friend. "Yeh Leo, luck's on our side."

"What do you want with us?" Abbie asked again. She had no one to turn to for help, so her only hope of getting the men to leave was to reason with them. The longer she spoke, the more time they'd have to cool down and reconsider whatever it was they meant to do.

"My brother went after your husband," Leo finally said. "He wished to... eh... reason with him... shall we say. But my brother never came back, so I went looking for him at the request of his wife, who was worried."

Abbie swallowed hard, terrified of what Leo Sparks was about to tell her.

"I found him, or what was left of him, with a pike in his chest, left to rot in a ravine. Found his companions, too. Both dead, and half-eaten by animals."

Leo Sparks grew red in the face and was now panting with fury. "Oh, and you know what else I found? I found a rope slung over a tree and cut halfway through. Looks like a hanging took place in that clearing, so one of yours is dead. Either your brother or your husband, take your pick," Leo laughed harshly. "Now, little lady, I'm going to find whichever one of them survived long enough to cut the other one down, and I'm going to kill him, and you're going to tell me where he is."

Abbie began to cry, huge racking sobs tearing her apart. The thought of losing Finn or Sam was devastating, as was the realization that these men wouldn't just leave. They were out for vengeance, and she was it, as well as her sisters and her children. Abbie trembled with fear as Leo Sparks bore down on her.

"If you don't tell me, I'll make you tell me. Do we understand each other?" Abbie cried harder as she continued to back away from him. She prayed that her sisters would do something, but what could two young girls do?

"I don't know where Finn is. He didn't tell me where he was going."

"Now what kind of husband doesn't tell his wife where he's off to?" Leo asked sweetly.

Abbie stared in horror as he lifted a poker and held the tip over the flame. "You're too trusting, my girl, is what you are," Leo said as he twirled the poker in the flames.

Leo Sparks suddenly reached out and grabbed her arm, making her cry out. His grip on her wrist was like a vice, and she squeezed her legs so as not to wet herself. Sparks took the poker out of the fire, admiring the glowing red tip.

"Last chance," he said, his voice cajoling. "I'm going to kill the surviving one either way, so you might as well avoid getting hurt. I hate to see a woman that's scarred."

Abbie's teeth chattered as she tried to speak, but no words would come out. She was terrified and knew that nothing she said would stop what was about to happen.

"Well, have it your way," Sparks said and pressed the hot poker to the tender skin of Abbie's forearm. Abbie screamed as her flesh sizzled beneath the burning metal. A sickening smell filled the room, making her gag. Leo let go of her arm and she held it against her body to protect it from further harm as a wave of nausea overwhelmed her and she was sick all over the front of her skirt.

Sarah and Annie were crying, but she couldn't spare them any attention. Her arm throbbed, the flesh so tender that even the slightest contact caused her agony. She stared at the man who had branded her, unable to believe that he would do that to a helpless woman.

"Shall we have another go?" Sparks asked pleasantly. "I'm ready if you are."

Abbie let out an inhuman wail as she heard the children crying upstairs. What would he do to them if she didn't tell him where Finn had gone? Abbie began to scream when she saw Sparks putting the poker back into the flames.

"Please! I don't know. I really don't. Don't hurt me."

Sparks shook his head while he waited for the poker to heat up. His companion looked horrified, but said nothing, so Abbie tried to appeal to him.

"How can you let him do this? What kind of man are you? We are alone and helpless."

The man looked uncomfortable and mumbled something unintelligible, but his feeble protest did nothing to deter Sparks. He grabbed Abbie's arm again and smiled evilly.

"Please!" Abbie cried.

Sparks held up the poker for her to see. "Shall I make a pretty pattern?" he asked, laughing uproariously at his own wit.

Abbie tried to yank her arm away, but Sparks held it in his grip. "No, you don't."

Abbie closed her eyes when she saw the poker advancing toward her arm slowly, Sparks grinning with the pleasure of torturing her. She tensed and sucked in her breath, but nothing happened. Instead, there was a loud crash as the door flew open. Sarah and Annie screamed as two men burst into the house, their faces covered with kerchiefs and shadowed by hats. Abbie let out a shriek of terror when she saw the muzzle of a gun pointed at her. Leo Sparks froze, the hot poker forgotten as he took in the new arrivals.

"What the hell do you want?" he growled.

"Put that poker down and get out," the taller man hissed. Abbie thought she recognized his voice, but it was barely above a whisper, and she couldn't be sure.

"Or what? You gonna shoot me?" Sparks demanded as he flipped the poker in his hand to go from a method of torture to a weapon.

The man fired. It must have happened quickly, but to Abbie, everything seemed to be taking place in slow motion.

The lead ball erupted from the barrel of the gun and whizzed through the air, hitting Leo Sparks just above the heart. He screamed and dropped the poker, the metal making a mighty clatter as it bounced off the stones of the hearth. Abbie saw the bullet emerge through Spark's back and lodge itself in the wall above the sideboard, the wood splintering with the force of the shot. A bloody stain bloomed on Sparks' shirt, spreading and soaking the fabric with surprising speed. Sparks clutched at his chest as blood spurted between his thick fingers, then fell to his knees.

Abbie leaned against the wall, her skirt reeking of urine as her bladder let go. She slid to the floor, laughing hysterically, on the verge of a breakdown. Sarah and Annie clung to each other as they stared at the wounded man at their feet.

"Get him out of here before I shoot him again," the man said hoarsely to the one named George. He didn't need to be told twice. George pulled Sparks to his feet and dragged him out of the house and into the night.

"Abbie, are you all right?" Sam whispered as he pulled down his kerchief. He looked ashen, and his face was contorted with pain, but he hobbled toward Abbie, who was still laughing, tears pouring down her face.

"Sam," she whispered. "Oh, Sam."

Sam's hand went to his back as he leaned against the wall, moaning with pain. The second man pulled off his mask as well and bowed formally to the girls. "Doctor Joseph Freeman, at your service."

Abbie wrapped her arms around her middle as she tried to calm down. She couldn't begin to understand what this all meant. Everything had been all right only a quarter of an hour ago, but now her arm throbbed with terrible pain and blood spread across the wooden planks of the floor, seeping into the crevices between the slats.

"Finn," was all she managed to croak. If Sam was alive, then

Finn must be dead. Her Finn was dead, his body left in the woods to be ravaged by wild animals.

"Finn is fine, Abs. Finn went to Philadelphia."

Abbie cried with relief but grew silent when she noticed the horrible scars on Sam's neck and realized that he was still speaking in a whisper.

"Oh, Sam," she moaned.

"I can't stand," Sam croaked as he slid to the floor. "My back."

Abbie looked up at her mother, who had materialized in the doorway, looking like an avenging angel. She took in the scene and began to roll up her sleeves.

"We'd better clean this mess up. Sam, you're just in time for your father's funeral. And who are you?" she said to Doctor Freeman, although her voice held no heat. She was grateful to the man, whoever he was.

"I'm Susanna's father, Doctor Freeman. An honor to meet you, Mrs. Mallory."

"The honor is all mine, by the looks of it. I just saw George Kilmer helping a wounded Leo Sparks onto his horse."

"I shot him," Sam supplied from the floor. "He was torturing Abbie with a hot poker."

"Should have killed him then. Your father would have done without any reservation," Hannah Mallory said viciously as she went to help Abbie up. She didn't ask any questions. Answers would have to wait. All her attention was on Abbie.

Sam moaned. "I can't get up."

"Girls, can you help me get Sam to bed?" Doctor Freeman asked. "I'm afraid he's rather heavy."

Sarah and Annie came forward obediently, their eyes still huge with terror. They helped Dr. Freeman lift Sam off the floor and walked him to the nearest bed, where he reclined with a gasp of pain.

"Come on, my girl," Hannah cajoled Abbie as she lifted her

off the floor and applied a cool cloth to her injured arm. "Why don't you sit down for a moment and I'll get some salve. It will help with the pain and allow the burn to heal faster. Are the children all right?"

Abbie nodded. She felt as if she were underwater, voices distorted and lights swimming before her eyes. She sighed and fainted dead away, prevented from falling off the chair by Doctor Freeman, who caught her just in time.

"She needs to lie down. She's had quite a shock. Would you have any brandy, my dear lady?"

"Of course." Hannah took down a flask from a high shelf and handed it to Doctor Freeman. "You look after Abbie while I check on the children."

The children had stopped crying but were clearly still frightened. Hannah scooped up Eddie and took Diana by the hand. "Now, it's back to bed with you two. Nothing to see here."

"But Gran, that man," Diana whispered. "He hurt Ma, and then Uncle Sam shot him."

"Don't you worry about the man. Just a misunderstanding between grown-ups."

Diana threw her a look laced with disbelief, but Hannah was in no mood to assuage her fears. Instead, she tucked both children into bed and kissed them tenderly, silently thanking the Good Lord that they hadn't been hurt.

"Now, go to sleep, and when you wake up, I'll make you a wonderful breakfast."

"Can we have biscuits?" Diana whined from her cot. "I like biscuits."

"I know, love. I'll make you an extra one for being such a good girl."

"All right," Diana sighed and turned onto her side. "Goodnight, Granny."

SIXTY-SIX

When Abbie came to, she found herself lying on her parents' bed. She felt weak and confused, and her arm burned and throbbed. She tasted brandy on her lips but couldn't recall drinking any. There was also the herbal smell of the salve her mother had applied to her wound before bandaging it. Someone had changed her out of her wet skirt. Abbie's heart began to race as the events of the evening returned with full force. What if Leo Sparks meant to come back with more men to finish what he'd started? What happened to Sam, and where was Finn? If Sam was back, how come Finn wasn't? And what in the name of all that was holy was Susanna's estranged father doing with Sam, whom he'd blamed for his daughter's betrayal?

Abbie shook with fear and delayed shock as she tried to make sense of what had happened that evening. She needed to go to the privy, but her limbs felt as if they were weighted down with stones, and she felt woozy when she tried to lift her head. A few more minutes, Abbie thought drowsily, a few more minutes and she would get up. It was dark, but she could see candlelight in the other room and hear the slap of a wet rag against a wooden floor. Sarah and Annie were cleaning up, but there was none of their usual banter as they went about their task. The girls were silent. Abbie strained to hear anything else, but the house was quiet. The children must have gone to sleep, and her mother and Doctor Freeman were clearly not there.

Abbie stifled a scream as a hand closed around her wrist. "It's only me, Abs."

Abbie hadn't realized that Sam was lying next to her. His profile was shadowed, but she could see the lines of pain etched into his face and recalled the horrible scars she'd glimpsed on his neck.

"Sam, are you all right?" Abbie asked. It was a silly question, but she wasn't sure how to phrase what was really in her heart.

"No."

"What happened to you?"

"I was hanged," Sam whispered. "Oh, Abbie, I've never felt such terror in my life. I was suffocating. Finn saved me just in time."

"Thank God."

Sam grew quiet for a moment before speaking again. "You know, I've gone to church every Sunday for as long as I can remember, but I've never given God much thought. I repeated the words, sang the hymns, and made eyes at all the pretty girls, but I never really took any of it seriously."

"And now you've found God?" Abbie asked, a smile in her voice. She felt calmer with Sam there, even if he seemed unable to move without pain.

"No, I think he found me."

"Sam, what are you talking about?" Abbie asked. This wasn't Sam; this was some stranger talking. Sam never took anything seriously, least of all religion, and Sue often threw him evil looks in church when he made faces at the children instead of listening to the sermon. And now this.

"Abs, I saw something."

"So now you're having visions?" Abbie scoffed, but she felt sorry for him. He must have suffered greatly to be talking like this.

"Abs, I saw Luke."

That got her attention. Luke died years ago, but not a day went by that Abbie didn't remember him in some small way. He had been her twin, her best friend, and her soul mate. His death had devastated her, and she still missed him every time she looked around the dinner table.

"Tell me," she whispered.

"I was struggling for breath, desperate to free my hands so that I could get even a finger between my throat and the rope. If I could loosen it just a bit, I might be able to breathe, but it was too late. I was dying. I felt myself blacking out and knew that my time was up. And then I saw it. It was so bright and warm."

"What was?"

"There was this light. It made me feel safe and calm. I began to move toward it, but something held me back, and then I saw Luke. He looked just as I remembered him, with that forelock falling into his face. He was smiling at me but shaking his head at the same time. He spoke to me."

"What did he say?" Abbie whispered.

"He said, 'Sam, go back. It isn't your time. God doesn't want you yet.' And then the next thing I knew, I was awake, and everything was so beautiful."

Abbie considered this for a moment. Perhaps Sam had some sort of a dream when he lost consciousness. It was possible, wasn't it?

"So, what does this have to do with God? You think you were on your way to Heaven?"

"All my life I thought that things happened randomly and that we make the decision what to do and when. But having Luke tell me that it wasn't my time and then finding myself alive, I suddenly thought that maybe nothing is random at all and maybe everything happens when it should."

"Tell that to Pa. Was this his time to go?" Abbie asked, suddenly feeling defensive. Sam hadn't shown much grief upon learning of their father's death, but in all fairness, he hadn't had much time to deal with his loss.

"Maybe it was. Who are we to know when the right time is?" Sam asked. "There was something else."

"What? You can now walk on water and perform miracles?"

Abbie wasn't sure why she was baiting Sam. He was sharing something special with her, something that clearly meant a lot to him, but for some reason she had a hard time taking him seriously. This was Sam, her older brother, who liked to clown around and cause mischief. This wasn't someone she'd ever call pious or even God-fearing. What on earth was he ranting about?

"Abs, I fell off my horse and couldn't move. Doctor Freeman said that while I was hanging I must have bucked so hard that I hurt my back, and when I fell, something snapped. I couldn't move, couldn't get up. I spent the whole night just lying there, on my own. But then I felt a presence and I was no longer alone. Maybe it was Luke's spirit, or maybe it was God, but I knew I wouldn't die on the side of that road. It wasn't my time, and someone would come along to help me."

"Well, it being a road and all, it would make sense that someone would come along," Abbie retorted.

"Yes, but the person who came along was not only my father-in-law, whom I hadn't seen since escaping from the British fort, but also a doctor. He was able to help me. I was feeling much better by the time we got closer to home, but I seem to have suffered a bit of a setback."

"Sam, how did you know?" Abbie asked, suddenly realizing that Sam and Doctor Freeman had come out of nowhere, materializing when she needed help most. Had they not come when they did, Abbie might not be lying here talking about God and Heaven. She might have been dead, or more badly hurt than she already was. And the girls might have suffered as well. She didn't think Sparks would have hurt the children, but he wasn't above using her sisters to get to her.

"We saw two men ahead of us on the road. Doctor Freeman commented on it. I didn't recognize them from a distance, especially since it was nearly dark. I didn't think much of it until they turned toward the farm. They were strangers, and they had no business at the house after dark. We were bound for my house, but I asked Doctor Freeman to go to the farm instead. I wanted to make sure that you were all safe. Doctor Freeman had a pistol, and he'd primed it before entering the house, just in case. He said he's not much of a shot, so I took it. I never meant to use it, but when I saw what that man was doing to you... I'm sorry, Abs. I should have helped you sooner."

"Sam, you did what you could and I'm so grateful. I don't think they meant to kill us, but they would have hurt us very badly if you hadn't come in time. I saw the other one looking at Sarah and licking his lips. He might have assaulted her."

Abbie forced herself to sit up. "I must check on the children," she said.

"They're asleep. Ma saw to them before leaving with Doctor Freeman."

"Where did they go?"

"She took Doctor Freeman to see Sue. He did not want to wait till morning. Don't worry, Abs, we're safe for tonight."

Were they safe? Leo Sparks had claimed that Finn and Sam killed his brother and his brother's companions and had taken justice into his own hands, but Abbie couldn't involve the local authorities and alert them to the fact that Sam and Finn were spying for the Continental Army. There could be repercussions and that wasn't something any of them could afford, not even Leo Sparks. He would go home and nurse his wound, but he wouldn't report the shooting; Abbie was sure of that. Not unless he wished to explain his reasons for torturing an innocent woman in a house full of children at the time.

Abbie shuddered as she recalled the kiss of the hot iron against her skin. She would never forget the agonizing pain or the stench of sizzling flesh. Not even when she'd awaited her execution in New York had she felt as frightened as she had last night, having come face to face with someone who meant her harm and was willing to cause her any amount of suffering to get what he was after. Even a hanging would be considered more humane compared to what Sparks had planned for her. Hot tears ran down her cheeks. She was still shaken and terrified. And she wanted Finn.

"Sam, where is Finn?" Abbie asked, trying not to let Sam see her tears. "He should have been back by now. I want my husband."

"Abs, I have no way of knowing exactly where Finn is, but he'll be back. Now, I must get some sleep. I'm exhausted, and my back feels as if a draft horse has just walked over it, twice. And you should sleep too. You've had a terrible shock. Everything will seem better in the morning."

"Pa's funeral is in the morning," Abbie replied, her voice quivering. She'd nearly forgotten all about the funeral in the aftermath of the evening's events.

"I know," Sam breathed. "And I mean to be there even if I have to crawl."

"Get some rest, Sam. You've earned it," Abbie said, her heart going out to Sam.

Abbie couldn't be sure, but she thought Sam was crying. She patted his hand, but remained silent, giving him a moment of privacy.

SIXTY-SEVEN

A heavy rain fell from a leaden sky, rivulets of water turning the road into a mud bath. It had cooled too, and Finn's clothes stuck uncomfortably to his back, making him shiver with a sudden chill. He'd been traveling for nearly ten hours, desperate to get home, especially since finding out that Sam had absconded from the Hammer's farm in the night. It wasn't like Sam to leave without a word of thanks, and Finn was worried for his safety. Sam clearly hadn't been himself, so who knew what his thought process might have been? Finn prayed that Mary was right and Sam had gone home instead of setting off for Philadelphia.

Finn felt a spark of happiness when he finally saw the Mallory farm in the distance. It looked small and gray beneath the thunderous sky, but it was home, and it would be dry and warm. He was exhausted and starving. Mary Hammer had given him some bread and sausage for the journey, but he'd finished the food last night and hadn't eaten anything since, not wanting to stop for the night. Finn was near collapse by the time he finally cantered into the yard and slid off his tired horse.

"I'm sorry, boy. I know you're done in," Finn said to the animal as he walked it into the stable and gave it some water and hay. The horse began to chew hungrily, reminding Finn how hungry he was. He ran across the yard, splashing his breeches with mud and sliding on the slippery ground, and burst into the house, ready for a warm welcome, but the house was deserted, the hearth cold. There were pies and breads on the sideboard, their rich aroma making Finn salivate. Where was everyone, and was there to be a party?

Finn approached the sideboard and stared at the ugly scar a few inches above the wooden surface. Was that a bullet hole? He reached out and touched the splintered wood, then pushed his finger into the hole. The tip of his finger found the smooth curve of a lead ball. He turned around slowly, searching for other signs of violence, but found none. Perhaps the hole was the result of an accident. Abbie wasn't much of a shot, but why would she be discharging a gun inside the house and pointing it at the sideboard of all things? It didn't make any sense.

Finn's head ached and his stomach growled loudly, reminding him that he needed to eat before doing anything else. He didn't dare touch the pies but found a half-eaten loaf of bread and some cold pork and ate quickly, inhaling the food before washing it down with cold buttermilk. He could have eaten a whole pie had he allowed himself to raid the sideboard, but Mrs. Mallory would have his head if she'd prepared the pies for a party. Hunger satisfied, Finn looked around. The house was clean and tidy, the floor had been recently washed, but now it was covered with his muddy footprints. The ashes in the hearth were still warm, but someone had deliberately put out the fire.

Setting down his cup, Finn sank into a chair. There was only one place everyone could be on a rainy weekday. A funeral. He couldn't think of any other reason why the house would be empty and there would be ready-made pies waiting to be eaten later. A wake. And not just any wake, but a wake for a member of the family. Mrs. Mallory might bring an offering of food to someone else's house as a gesture of sympathy, but the number of baked goods on the sideboard meant only one thing— a Mallory was dead.

Finn was paralyzed by momentary panic, then sprang into action. He climbed to the loft and changed out of his wet clothes, putting on a woolen coat over his shirt. The coat would get wet in the rain, but at least the shirt would remain dry. He ran across to the stable and chose a fresh horse, allowing his mare to rest after the long journey, then galloped out of the yard, hoping he'd be in time for the burial.

Finn dismounted and ran through the windswept cemetery. The door of the church was firmly shut against the weather, its spire obscured by the threatening clouds. A small party congregated around an open grave as Reverend Greene spoke about the deceased. Mrs. Mallory was crying softly, Annie and Sarah flanking her like pillars of support. Abbie stood next to Sarah. Eddie was in her arms and Diana was holding onto her hand. Sam stood next to Susanna, leaning heavily on a walking stick. Their children were huddled around an older man Finn had never met, who had his arms around their shoulders. The man's round spectacles were fogged up from the rain, but Finn could see the warmth in his eyes as he glanced at Sue. Several friends and neighbors were gathered behind the family.

Finn removed his hat and walked up to the grave. Abbie let go of Diana, set Eddie down, and flew into his arms, sobbing pitifully. She looked exhausted and frightened, and there were dark smudges beneath her red-rimmed eyes. Her forearm was bandaged just below the elbow. Finn reached for her arm, but Abbie yanked it away, a grimace of pain twisting her features when he accidentally brushed against the wound.

"I'm sorry, love," Finn murmured in Abbie's ear. "I'm so sorry about your father."

Abbie raised her tearstained face to his. She looked like she wanted to say something but changed her mind.

"What is it?" Finn asked, sensing that something momentous had happened while he was away.

"Later."

Finn lifted Eddie into his arms and took his place by the grave. Diana rested her capped head against his thigh, and he placed his palm on her shoulder to comfort her. Reverend Greene finished reading the burial service, but no one moved. Everyone continued to stare into the grave as two gravediggers began to shovel the earth on top of the coffin, the clumps hitting the wood with sickening finality.

"I'm very sorry," Finn said to Hannah, who gave him a wan smile.

Hannah moved away, followed by her children. Martha, who always had something to say but remained ominously silent on this occasion, walked behind her mother, Daisy in her arms. Even Gil was there, looking glum as he trailed behind his wife with Joe. The villagers filed past Finn, eager to go back to the house and partake of the spread that awaited them.

Finn turned to Sam, whose knuckles were white on the walking stick. He looked ill and shaky, and Sue kept close to him as if to catch him should he fall. Sam's neckcloth hid the swelling and bruising on his throat, but Finn could tell that it was still there.

"Sam, are you all right?" Finn asked as he took in his miserable appearance.

"I will be. Doctor Freeman is setting me to rights."

Finn turned to greet the man who'd approached him with Sam's children in tow. The boys looked frightened, but Rachel was smiling happily at her grandfather, too young to understand the loss the family had suffered.

"Doctor Freeman," the man said, bowing stiffly to Finn. "It's a pleasure to finally meet you, Finlay."

"The pleasure is all mine," Finn replied, feeling slightly bemused. Last he'd heard, Doctor Freeman was a surgeon with the British Army. What was he doing here? Finn watched as Susanna threaded her arm through her father's. She looked happy for such a somber occasion and Finn was glad that at least a part of her family had been restored to her. There was a sister in England, but he doubted very much that they'd see each other anytime soon.

Finn followed the sad little party out of the cemetery and toward the waiting wagon. He helped Mrs. Mallory, then handed Abbie into the wagon and passed her the children. Sam and Sue had a wagon of their own, and Finn watched with trepidation as Sam struggled to climb onto the bench. He longed to give him a hand but didn't want to embarrass him in front of his family. Sam finally managed to sit down and took up the reins. Finn mounted his horse and followed behind, eager to get back to the house. He had a sinking feeling in the pit of his stomach, and it had nothing to do with the grief he felt at losing Mr. Mallory. He would deal with that later, but now he had to help the family get through this day because something had happened in his absence—something awful.

SIXTY-EIGHT
VIRGINIA OCTOBER 1628

The shutters were still tightly shut against the impending dawn, but a sliver of gray appeared around the wooden panels, signaling the arrival of morning. Annabel slid out of bed and dressed hastily, mindful of waking Charles, who was a light sleeper. She slipped from the room and let herself out of the house. The air was fresh and cool, and a misty haze hung in the air, coating Annabel's skin with a sheen of moisture. She walked slowly, enjoying the peaceful silence of the pre-dawn hour. All the windows were still shuttered, and even the dogs were still asleep, not bothering to bark when she passed.

This was the first time she'd left the house since losing the baby a fortnight ago. Annabel was physically recovered, but there was a gaping emptiness, not only in her womb but in her heart. She mourned the baby, a boy, every moment of the day. Sometimes she forgot the baby was gone and placed her hand on her stomach, waiting for the child within to stir. He had been moving and kicking, a little person just waiting to be born and fill the arms that had been empty for so long. She'd prayed for another child, and God had granted her one, only to take it away in such a cruel manner.

Annabel sighed. She was unhappy long before Bethany Warren had come to enlighten her about her husband's perfidy. Testifying against Kit in that farce of a trial had been the biggest mistake she'd ever made. She'd thought of herself as an avenging angel, an instrument of justice, but the reality was she'd been a spiteful shrew. She'd wanted to punish the Whitfields for the loss of her beloved brother and had thought that somehow Tom might be restored to her, not in physical custody, but as a nephew, but instead, she'd made an enemy of Louisa and lost Valerie's friendship as a result. It wasn't until they had been banished from Rosewood Manor that Annabel understood what it meant to be alone. She had never appreciated the friendship and support of other women, but she sorely lacked it now. Louisa and Valerie had been like sisters to her and she had betrayed them and set out to hurt them by making an accusation against Kit. What had possessed her?

Annabel stopped on the riverbank and looked up at the peachy haze shimmering above the dark water as the sun began to rise. She had lost her family, her friends, and her baby. Even her children were angry with her. They longed for their cousins and hated living in Jamestown. Millie and Harry missed the open spaces of Rosewood, swimming in the pond on hot days, and catching frogs with Robbie and Evie. They missed Tom and their aunts and uncles. They'd never warmed to Cousin Wesley and he didn't have much of a way with children, never having had any of his own. They'd lost so much, thanks to her.

And she'd lost Charles. She'd been sure of his love. Charles had been a part of her life since she was barely fifteen, but he'd been carrying on with Bethany Warren behind her back and had gotten her with child. Annabel wasn't Charles's love; she was his chattel, his property. He could do with her as he pleased and exercise his husbandly rights even if she didn't wish him to. Already, he was getting impatient, demanding that she submit to him, but she couldn't, not anymore. He'd betrayed and humiliated her, and in the process, he'd destroyed everything that was dear to her and demolished everything she believed in.

Losing the respect and support of the Whitfields and Sheridans was bearable as long as she had the love and support of her husband, but that was no longer the case. She had prayed that Charles would deny the accusation and tell her that Bethany Warren had some sort of hidden agenda or grievance against him. She would have believed him had he told her that Bethany lied, but he'd averted his eyes and squared his shoulders, silently letting her know it was true.

Charles had been lying with Bethany for months, and she was carrying his child, but it was all taken care of, according to Charles. Bethany Warren would be married soon, tomorrow, as a matter of fact, to a man who'd sold his soul for thirty pieces of silver. What kind of man married someone else's pregnant mistress? Perhaps a man who was kind and generous of spirit, unlike her own husband who'd always been selfish and self-serving. Perhaps Bethany Warren hadn't been the first, and Annabel was certain she wouldn't be the last.

There were always vulnerable, lonely women to be had. They arrived by the boatload, some as indentures and others as slaves. And there were plenty of women who were not alone but still lonely and searching for someone to remind them that they were worth noticing. Annabel had been worth noticing once, but now she was nothing but an empty shell. Even her baby had left her.

Annabel never stopped watching the rising sun as she picked up a few large stones and dropped them into the pockets of her skirt. She knew what this meant and what the repercussions would be, but it felt so very right. She'd made up her mind a few days ago, but gave herself time to change her mind, to feel fear. She felt none. What she felt was peace—wonderful, all-encompassing peace, and a sense of resolution such as she hadn't felt since announcing to her father that she would marry Charles Whitfield whether he approved or not.

Annabel lifted her face to the glowing sun and closed her eyes. She thought she should pray, but for some reason, God was the furthest thing from her mind. She felt glorious, at peace with the world and herself at last. She took a step forward, then another, and sighed with relief as the waters of the James swirled around her ankles. She continued to wade in, her eyes still closed, the warmth of the sun on her face until the greedy water closed over her head, leaving nothing behind but a ripple that continued to spread outward as the woman beneath sank to the bottom, weighed down by her heartbreak and the stones.

SIXTY-NINE

"Where's your mother?" Charles asked as he walked into the kitchen where Millie and Harry were having breakfast.

Millie shrugged and continued to eat her porridge, but Harry looked around uncertainly. Annabel hadn't left the house since the miscarriage, but she did venture out into the garden from time to time, and just sat on the bench, staring into nothingness. She needed time to recover from her loss; Charles understood that, but it was time to get back to the business of living. People lost babies every day. He mourned the loss of his son as well, but Annabel was still of child-bearing age and they would have more children. They would get past this unfortunate episode and go on as before.

Once Louisa and Kit left for England, Valerie would be in need of companionship, and Alec would be a friend short. Perhaps that would be an opportune moment to try and bridge the gap that had only widened since the trial. And Bethany and Ethan were to be married tomorrow. Another chapter closed. Annabel had to be patient; that was all.

"I'll check outside," Charles said as he stepped into the weed-choked garden. He'd have to talk to the stable boy about doing some weeding in his spare time. Nan simply didn't have enough free time to clean, launder, cook, and look after the garden. She tended the vegetable patch; that was enough. Besides, her indenture contract would be up in six months' time, and they would have to find a new servant, unless Nan decided to stay on of her own free will. They were used to her, but she was still a young woman and might wish to find a husband. She wasn't an attractive girl, which was part of the reason Charles had chosen her, needing to keep temptation at bay, but there were enough men who would gladly settle for a hardworking, obedient woman who'd be grateful for a home of her own and a man to look after her.

The garden was empty, the leaves and flowers weighed down by morning dew, the moisture sparkling in the sun and making the little garden look almost magical. The mist of the early morning had burned off, leaving behind a cloudless autumn sky. Charles inhaled deeply, enjoying the scent of late-summer roses. Another few weeks and the cold would be upon them, but this morning one could still believe that it was summer. Charles turned around and went back into the house. He checked every room and then went out back to the privy.

"Annabel, are you in there?" Charles called, but all he heard was the chatter of insects and the trilling of birds overhead.

A twinge of worry was starting to flutter in his gut, but he ignored it. There was nowhere Annabel could have gone. Jamestown was a small place, and aside from the town square, which would still be deserted at this time of the morning, there was nowhere to be. Perhaps she'd gone to church, but surely it was too early for prayer. She'd had a lot on her mind though, and he should have been more sensitive. Instead of begging for Annabel's forgiveness and promising her his unwavering devotion, he'd been unkind and brusque, all but blaming her for his need to take a mistress. The accusation had come from a place of guilt and remorse, but she didn't know that.

I'll make it up to her, Charles thought as he grabbed his coat and hat and left the house. *I'll make her forget all about Bethany Warren.* Charles sighed as he walked toward the river. What was wrong with him? Why couldn't he be content with what he had? He loved his wife, had done since she was hardly more than a girl, and he treasured their family. He'd gone and ruined everything simply because he was bored and annoyed with Annabel. That happened in the best of marriages, but people forgave each other and soldiered on. That was the very nature of marriage. Perhaps that was the lesson. Alec always banged on about learning from your mistakes and rising above. Well, he had learned, and he would rise above despite all the things that had previously caused him discontent.

Marital relations with Annabel had grown stale and predictable, and he'd longed to feel young and alive. He wasn't even thirty yet, not for another few months, but his life had become stagnant and regimented. He'd rebelled and paid the price for his thoughtless behavior. Charles made two circles around Jamestown and turned for home. Where in the world could Annabel have gone so early in the morning?

SEVENTY

Alec ran his hand over the smooth wood, then tested the strength of the crutch by leaning heavily on it. He'd made it for Kit based on the ones he'd seen in the hospital. The crutches there were metal, but a wooden one would do. It would allow Kit to finally get out of bed. The poor man was becoming desperate, and with a crutch to lean on, he would be able to get down the stairs and spend time with the rest of the family. Alec smiled as he envisioned Kit's reaction. Walking with a crutch would take some getting used to, but it would make things easier for both Kit and Louisa. According to Doctor Jacobson, Kit needed at least one more month until his bones were sufficiently knitted, but Kit felt well enough to get up and would be fine as long as he didn't bend his leg.

Alec stepped out of the shed and nearly collided with his estate manager. The man looked upset, his cheeks burning with an angry flush and his forehead glistening with sweat. He removed his hat as soon as he saw Alec, a guilty look flitting across his face.

"What is it, Mr. Worthing?" Alec asked. "Is something amiss?"

The man looked glum as he stepped from foot to foot, as if he simply couldn't bear to stand still.

"Mr. Worthing?" Alec prompted.

"It's Mistress Whitfield, sir."

Alec felt a cold dread settle over his heart. "What about Mistress Whitfield?" He'd seen Valerie only two hours ago. Valerie and Evie had been in the vegetable garden, weeding and watering the plants.

"One of the men was by the river, sir, and he came upon her."

"What?" Alec exclaimed. "What are you saying, man? Where is my wife?"

Mr. Worthing looked momentarily confused, then pulled himself together long enough to explain. "It's not Mistress Valerie, sir. It's Mr. Charles's wife—Mistress Annabel. She drowned, sir."

Alec set aside the crutch and ran toward the river. It was some distance away, and Alec felt a stitch in his side, but he couldn't stop. Perhaps Annabel was still alive and could be saved with mouth-to-mouth resuscitation, but deep down, he knew that wasn't the case. Worthing knew a dead body when he saw one. Had Annabel really drowned? And what had she been doing this far from Jamestown?

The overseer was running after Alec, huffing and puffing as he tried to speak. "Her body must have been carried on the current, sir. It's strong round these parts. The man saw her floating and pulled her in."

Alec finally reached the riverbank and stopped. Several men were standing around, staring at the sodden mess on the ground. Alec approached slowly, steeling himself for what he was about to see. He took one look at Annabel's bloated, greenish face and felt sick to his stomach. Annabel had been so attractive, so lively when he'd first met her. She'd been a spirited girl who'd grown into a difficult, opinionated woman, but no matter how much he'd disliked her at times, she was still his brother's wife and the mother of his niece and nephew. She didn't deserve this kind of end. No one did.

"She must have fallen into the river," Alec said, forcing himself to look at the corpse.

The manager pulled him aside. "It seems she had some stones in her pockets," he whispered so the other men wouldn't hear.

"The stones must have slipped in when she was carried along by the current and scraped the bottom of the riverbed," Alec replied. He knew the suggestion was absurd, but this was his one chance to protect Charles and the children from what was to come. Should Annabel be branded a suicide, they would face disgrace and condemnation. Alec could spare them that at least, if not the grief of their loss.

"Send someone to fetch my brother, Mr. Worthing," Alec said. "And, please, tell them not to break the news to him in front of his children."

"Yes, Mr. Whitfield."

Alec turned to the workers who were still milling around, waiting for instructions. "Wrap Mistress Whitfield's body in some sacking and take her into one of the sheds. She can't be left out here in the sun."

Annabel's body smelled of the river, but after a few hours on the bank, she would start to reek of decomposition and decay. *She would have hated that*, Alec thought as he adjusted her skirts to cover her legs. He removed the stones from Annabel's pockets and threw them away. Then, he waited until the men returned with the sacking and carefully wrapped Annabel's body before taking it away. It would be cool and shady in the shed and keep the corpse fresh until Charles had a chance to identify her and say his goodbyes.

Alec went back to retrieve the crutch and walked slowly toward the house. Valerie and Louisa had been angry with

Annabel and wished her gone from Rosewood Manor, but her death would still tear them up. Annabel had been a friend once, and any death was heartbreaking, especially that of a woman in her twenties. Millie and Harry would be heartbroken. Alec suddenly realized that he wasn't at all sure how Charles would feel. He didn't wish to judge or lay blame, but if Annabel had really killed herself, it might be Charles's fault. She'd recently learned about his mistress and coming child and had lost her own baby. That must have pushed her over the edge, and there was no one to blame for that but Charles.

Alec shook his head in dismay. Would Charles never learn that every action had a consequence? He always assumed that things would work themselves out, or someone, like Alec, would step in to resolve the crisis, but this time there was nothing Alec could do but try to squash speculation as to how Annabel died. He could remove the stones and make sure Annabel received a Christian burial, but he couldn't fool God. If Annabel had really taken her own life, there would be a reckoning. He wished he could spare her that, but there was nothing more he could do.

"Rest in peace, Annabel," Alec said under his breath as he went inside to break the news.

SEVENTY-ONE

The shed was cool, and mercifully dark. Charles didn't have the heart to look at Annabel. He didn't want to see her this way, bloated and disfigured. He preferred to remember her as she had been, beautiful and full of life. Alec said that Annabel must have fallen into the river. Charles was grateful to Alec for trying to spare his feelings, but he knew the truth. Annabel had killed herself, driven to despair by his infidelity and the loss of their child. Charles felt sorrow, and anger. How could she leave him and abandon her children? What was he to do now? The children would be devastated, especially Millie. She'd always been close with her mother. Of course, he'd tell them that it was an accident and their mother had fought to stay alive, but he would have to live with the truth for the rest of his days.

Charles leaned against the wall and shut his eyes. Annabel's death had presented him with another dilemma. Bethany was still carrying his child, and he was free to marry, but to marry so soon after the death of his wife would appear callous and indecent. But how could he let her marry Bartlett tomorrow when he could have her for himself? Had Bethany not been pregnant, he could have asked her to wait until he'd completed his year of mourning, but time was not on his side. Bethany was about three months gone. There was no time to lose.

"Goodbye, Annabel," Charles said to the still figure at his feet. "I hope you can forgive me."

He exited the shed and nodded to Alec, who was waiting outside. Valerie had offered to prepare Annabel's body for burial. Her kindness was unexpected, and it brought tears to Charles's eyes. Annabel didn't have any other female relatives, but she wouldn't want the townswomen to handle her body. She'd wish to retain her dignity, even in death. Once Annabel was ready and wrapped in a shroud, Charles would allow the children to come and say goodbye to their mother. There was no need for them to see her like this. It would frighten them. He could still recall the terror he'd felt after the death of his own parents and Alec's first wife and newborn son.

All those years ago, Finlay had allowed Charles to sleep in his bed because he was frightened. Charles would have preferred to stay with Alec or Rose, but Finlay wouldn't let him go near them. Rose had locked herself in her room, and Alec had been piss drunk, unable to accept the loss of his family. A short time later, Rose had run off to the convent, and Alec and Finn had shipped Charles off to live with their aunt and uncle, not up to the task of bringing up a small child by themselves. Charles hadn't thought of that time in nearly twenty-two years, but the memory suddenly rushed in, reminding him how quickly life could change and how irrevocable death was.

"Are you all right?" Alec asked.

"Not really. I can't believe she's done this."

"It was an accident," Alec countered stubbornly.

"It wasn't, and you know it. She had found out about Bethany, and the distress caused her to lose the baby," Charles said, his voice flat. "It was all my doing. She blamed me, and this is her way of punishing me."

"Not everything is about you, Charles," Alec replied.

"Isn't it? I find myself suddenly widowed, with another woman carrying my child and getting ready to wed a man I'd purchased for her. What am I to do, Alec?"

Alec threw Charles a look of pure loathing. "Figure it out for yourself," he retorted and walked away.

Alec was disgusted with him. He was too much of a saint to ever get himself into such a predicament. *Alec has milk in his veins*, Charles thought angrily. That's why they never really saw eye to eye. He was more like Finlay, who'd been as hot-blooded as Charles, if the stories about his brother could be believed. Finlay would never have remained faithful to Valerie had he not died; he'd been incapable of such commitment. Valerie had lucked out when Alec had inherited her after his brother's death. She'd got the better deal, and the more decent man. Charles spat into the dirt and went to fetch his horse. He had to speak to Bethany before she heard the news from the town gossips.

Having convinced himself that he was doing the right thing, Charles had calmed down a bit by the time he presented himself at the Abbott farm. If Noah Abbott was surprised to find Charles on his doorstep, he didn't say so. He invited Charles inside, but Charles politely refused, asking to speak to Mistress Warren privately. At any other time, Abbott would have refused, but now that Bethany was about to marry, he was more lenient. Maybe he hoped that the betrothal would fall apart so that his sister would continue to help his wife with the housework while he remained in charge of her assets.

Bethany stepped outside. She looked well, her dark hair glossy beneath her cap and her skin glowing in the autumn sunshine, but her eyes betrayed her apprehension. There was no good reason for Charles to be visiting her the day before her wedding, and she feared that he might be the bearer of bad news. If Ethan Bartlett wished to pull out at this late stage, Bethany was as good as ruined.

"Why are you here?" she asked as soon as the door closed behind Abbott, who was now watching them through the window, no doubt hoping to overhear their conversation.

"My wife is dead," Charles cried. He hadn't meant to blurt it out like that, but his mind was addled by grief and the urgency of the situation.

"I'm sorry. What happened?" Bethany asked, her eyes softening.

"She seems to have fallen into the river."

Their eyes met and Charles silently confirmed what Bethany had already deduced for herself. She paled, her guilt getting the better of her. She wasn't a cruel woman by nature, only a desperate one.

"I really am sorry, Charles. Please accept my condolences."

"Thank you. Bethany, I'm free to marry," Charles said, surprised that Bethany hadn't grasped the purpose of his visit.

Bethany's eyes widened in surprise. "Are you asking me to marry you?" she asked. Her shock was evident, but Charles plowed on.

"I am. I know it will look unseemly, but once we're wed, everyone will forget about the impropriety of our haste soon enough. The scandal will die down."

Bethany continued to stare at Charles, her head cocked to the side. She seemed to be considering his offer, which was encouraging. Why would she refuse him, anyway? She was carrying his child, and it's not as if she felt anything toward Bartlett. Their betrothal was a business transaction, nothing more.

"The banns have been called, Charles. I'm due to marry Ethan Bartlett tomorrow. Will you rescind your offer to him now?"

"No, I won't. He can keep Timothy Bell for seven years, as agreed."

"Then, if it's all the same to you, I'd rather marry Master Bartlett," Bethany said.

"Are you mad, woman? He doesn't love you."

"And you do?" Bethany hissed. "Your wife's body is not even in the ground, and already you're proposing marriage to me. She loved you, and you had failed her. I will pray for forgiveness every day of my life for what I did to that woman. Now, please leave."

"Bethany, I don't understand," Charles implored. "I care for you. I wish to marry you and give our child the legitimacy it deserves. What's wrong with that?"

"Charles, I've gotten to know Ethan these past weeks, and I'm sorry to say, but he is a much better man than you are. I don't want to be the next Mistress Whitfield, considering what happened to the first one. I'd rather take my chances with Ethan. He's a good and decent man and he will cherish me and take care of the child."

"So sure, are you?" Charles sneered. He could go to Ethan Bartlett and undo their arrangement within minutes, and Bethany was well aware of that. She recognized the threat in his eyes.

"Are you really so spiteful and callous that you would expose me and your child to ruin and ridicule just to punish me for not wishing to marry you?" Bethany asked, hands on hips. She turned on her heel and walked into the house, leaving Charles to stare at the closed door.

No, I'm not, Charles thought as he mounted his horse. He wouldn't do anything to spoil Bethany's wedding. If she preferred Bartlett, then he was welcome to her. There were plenty of women in Jamestown, and new ones arrived every month. Charles smiled to himself as he cantered out of the yard. He would observe his year of mourning, and then he would find love again.

SEVENTY-TWO

A shimmering golden haze enveloped the orchard. It was one of those rare afternoons that come around every so often just before the chill of autumn sets in. Valerie stood in the sun-dappled shade of the apple tree, its branches laden with fruit. She set her basket on the ground and began to pluck the apples from the lowest branches. She'd make an apple cake for dessert to lift everyone's sagging spirits. A pall of melancholy had settled over the house, brought on by two unexpected deaths. They mourned Fred, but Annabel's death had devastated them all, since she had been young and healthy. Annabel had been buried in the church cemetery with all the customary funerary rites, but all the adults at Rosewood Manor knew the truth.

Charles had asked Alec to take the children but had not been to the house himself. He said he needed some time alone, which was understandable. The children were currently by the pond with Alec and Louisa, hunting for frogs. Shrieks of dismay erupted every time a frog managed to elude them and hop away. Several minutes later, there was a triumphant cry as Tom managed to capture a frog with Alec's help.

Valerie filled the basket and returned to the house. Kit was sitting on the porch, his leg outstretched, watching the fun at the pond from a distance. He'd been coming down every day, using the crutch Alec had made for him. The descent down the stairs was awkward, but at least it afforded Kit the opportunity to spend time with the family and get some fresh air. He looked pale and drawn after weeks in bed, but the splints would come off in a few weeks and he'd be able to walk on his own. Kit's face was healing nicely. Soon the scars would fade altogether, leaving behind faint lines. Valerie felt a pang of sadness. In a few weeks, they would be ready to leave for the eighteenth century. Alec had set November first as their departure date— All Souls Day. Somehow it seemed appropriate. They'd decided to wait until after the battle of Yorktown to arrive, since it wouldn't do to turn up in the middle of such chaos. The conflict wouldn't end with the battle, but it would finally turn Parliament against the war and within two years the British would leave the colonies for good. Valerie prayed every night that the battle wouldn't affect Finn or his immediate family, since the engagement would be taking place virtually on their doorstep.

Valerie was just about to go in when both Alec and Kit turned toward the road, becoming aware of the conveyance that was heading toward Rosewood Manor. Valerie couldn't make out who their visitor was, but thought it might be Charles, coming to see the children. As the trap drew closer, Valerie realized that there were two people sitting on the bench. So not Charles then. She couldn't make out any distinguishing features, since she was too far away, but Alec stiffened, his face going from simple curiosity to shock and disbelief. He set Tom on the ground, said something to Louisa, who was peering toward the road as well, then took off at a run.

Valerie went after him, eager to find out what all the excitement was about. She watched as Alec approached the wagon, waited for it to come to a stop, then enveloped the woman in his arms with a whoop of pure joy. The woman hugged Alec awkwardly on account of the child in her arms, but the man swept off his hat, revealing a mane of copper hair that glowed in the sun.

"Cameron," Valerie breathed as she broke into a run.

"Jenny!" Valerie cried. "Oh, Jenny." Jenny handed the child to Alec and ran toward her, tears streaming down her face as she swept Valerie into a huge hug.

"Aunt Valerie," Jenny gasped. She tried to say something, but nothing came out since she was laughing and crying at the same time.

"Why didn't you write?" Valerie cried. "We would have been so happy to know you were coming."

"There was no time. It all happened so fast. The letter would have gotten here at about the same time as us."

They finally broke apart when Louisa arrived, followed by the children, who were shrieking happily. Valerie turned toward Alec and Cameron. The man looked ill at ease as he climbed down from the cart, clearly unsure what to expect. Valerie laughed when she saw Alec ignore Cameron's outstretched hand and draw him into a manly hug, the child squealing with delight between them.

Louisa released Jenny to allow her to greet the children. The boys and Millie hung back, but Evie wrapped her arms around Jenny's middle, her eyes aglow with happiness.

"Jenny, I thought I'd never see you again. I've missed you," Evie cried.

"And I you. Oh, Evie, I thought about you every day. I thought about all of you," Jenny added, blushing.

"And who is this young man?" Valerie asked as she took Ian from Alec. Ian was looking around curiously, his eyes round with interest.

"Ian," Jenny said simply. "My wee Ian."

"Our wee Ian," Cameron said as he approached the group and allowed Valerie to pull him into a hug.

"Cameron, I'm so glad you are here," Valerie gushed. "Come into the house. Cook will prepare some refreshments. You must be tired after your journey."

"I'll just see to the trap," Cameron replied. "Ye go on in, Jenny," he said to his wife.

"Jenny, how do you come to be here?" Valerie asked carefully, worried she might upset Jenny.

Jenny smiled hugely, her eyes dancing with delight. "I burned the house down," she said, as if that explained everything.

"Well, try not to burn down ours," Alec said as he shepherded the children toward the house. They were curious about the new arrivals and excited at the prospect of refreshments.

Everyone filed inside. Cook and Minnie erupted from the kitchen, eager to see Jenny. Minnie, in particular, was thrilled, having once shared a room with Jenny. They had been good friends, and Minnie had missed Jenny terribly since she left.

Minnie hung back, but Jenny put her arms around the girl and gave her a kiss on the cheek. "Oh, I did miss you, Minnie."

"Are you here to stay?" Minnie asked happily.

"I hope so," Jenny replied shyly, looking at Alec. "Can we stay, Uncle Alec?"

"What a question! Of course, you can stay. You must stay. We wouldn't have it any other way."

"If you all give me a half hour, I will serve supper. I think I've enough to go around," Cook said as she executed a head count. "We'll just need two more seats. Minnie, fetch the bench from outside. That will do the trick."

"I'll do it," Cameron said. "It must be too heavy for a wee lass like her."

"This is Ian," Jenny said proudly as she showed the child to Cook and Minnie, who was already making faces at the little boy. He giggled as he grabbed a lock of hair that had escaped from Minnie's cap.

"You are a big boy, aren't you?" Cook cooed to him. "And you look just like your daddy, except for the hair."

"He's a sweet laddie," Cameron interjected as he brought in the bench. "He was almost an angel on the crossing," he added with an amused smile.

"Almost," Jenny repeated, dimpling at her son.

It took a few minutes for everyone to finally settle down. Minnie took Ian to eat with the other children, and a welcome quiet settled upon the dining room. Alec looked around the table, but his eyes kept returning to Jenny. Valerie hadn't seen him look this happy in a long time.

"Have you come to stay for good?" Alec asked once Cook had served a meat pie with roasted potatoes and a salad of greens.

"Yes. We plan to buy a farm of our own, but we need some time to get things settled."

"There's no rush," Alec replied. "We'll put you in the attic room since the house is full to the bursting. Millie and Harry are staying with us at present," he added.

"And how's Uncle Charles and Aunt Annabel?" Jenny asked as she tucked into her pie. She'd never been a big eater, but she seemed ravenous.

"Charles has had a bereavement," Alec replied tactfully. "We've lost Mr. Taylor as well."

Jenny's face fell. She'd been close with Fred Taylor when she'd lived with them before. He and Barbara had been like the grandparents Jenny never had, and she often visited them at their cottage. Jenny never really got into chess, as Fred had hoped, but she liked to listen to his stories and to talk about her time in France.

"Was he ill?"

"Yes, he was," Alec replied, leaving out the details.

"And Aunt Annabel?" Jenny whispered.

"Annabel fell into the river and drowned."

Jenny's hand flew to her mouth as her eyes filled with tears. "She was so young. And those poor children. They must be devastated."

"They are, but we are trying to keep them from brooding. Millie especially is having a hard time of it," Louisa said. "It helps her to be with Evie. They're very close."

No one mentioned that Evie would be leaving for England in the spring, or that Alec and Valerie had plans of their own. Alec turned to Cameron, engaging him in conversation about farming and the crossing. He was trying to make Cameron feel welcome and reassure him that his escape was forgiven and forgotten. He was now Jenny's husband and part of their family.

Cameron smiled broadly as he replied to Alec's questions. Valerie liked him and admired his courage. Jenny had done well for herself, and she was thrilled for her. No one deserved a happy marriage more. Valerie stifled a smile when she saw Jenny accept a second helping of pie from Cook. She could be wrong, but she thought that before long there'd be another little Brody running around. She gave Jenny a conspiratorial smile and Jenny smiled back, her cheeks turning beet red.

The exchange wasn't lost on Alec, who set down his cup and looked at his niece.

"Yes," Jenny whispered, crimson with embarrassment. "I am with child."

"Jenny, what wonderful news. When is the child due?" Alec asked. Valerie could see the pain in his eyes. He would no longer be here when the child was born, but he couldn't just blurt that out to a smiling Jenny.

"Sometime in May, I think."

"We're hoping for a lassie this time around," Cameron said. "Aurora."

"What a lovely name," Louisa said. "What made you think of it?"

"I couldn't sleep on the crossing and went up on deck to watch the sunrise every morning. There's nothing more wonderful than seeing the sun come up and light replace darkness. That's how I felt about coming back to you," Jenny added, eyes downcast.

Alec reached over and squeezed her hand. It pained him to know that Jenny thought of her time in Scotland as a time of darkness, but she appeared to be healthy and happy, so he didn't comment.

By the time they finished supper, Jenny looked ready for bed. Minnie had already prepared a room for the new arrivals, so Jenny took Ian from her and wished everyone a good night before retiring. Valerie helped Cook and Minnie clean up the remains of their meal and made her own way upstairs. Her thoughts were in turmoil and she was almost afraid to speak to Alec about this unexpected development. What if he changed his mind? He loved Jenny as he would his own child and felt an obligation to her. Would he wish to postpone their departure?

Valerie undressed, brushed out her hair, and climbed into bed. Alec had stepped outside for a breath of fresh air with Kit before helping him upstairs to his own bed. She could hear the thumping of Kit's crutch as he crossed the room. Alec entered their bedroom but didn't say a word as he pulled off his boots and undressed before getting into bed and pulling Valerie into his arms. "I know what you're thinking," he said as he kissed her temple.

"Unfortunately, I can't make the same claim about you," Valerie replied. She hadn't realized how nervous she was, but now she felt somewhat more at ease. Alec wasn't someone who changed his mind unless he had a very good reason, and although Jenny's arrival was probably the best kind of reason, he wouldn't just scrap their plans without discussing his decision with her.

"Alec, what now?" Valerie asked, looking up at him.

"I've been thinking about that, and I've spoken to Kit."

"And?"

"And I have an idea, but I need some time to think things through. I promise that we will still go to Finn. Now, go to sleep. Or don't go to sleep," he said with a wicked grin. "I'm too worked up to sleep," he added as he pulled Valerie closer. "I bet you are too."

Valerie had to admit that sleep would not come easily, so she smiled into Alec's eyes. "I could be persuaded to stay up for a bit."

"Oh, really?" Alec was already moving downward, his hands pushing up her nightdress. Valerie spread her legs with a quivering sigh. She liked it when Alec was in a playful mood, since she was the beneficiary of his ardor. She gasped as his tongue slid into her, forgetting all about Jenny and this new dilemma.

SEVENTY-THREE
VIRGINIA OCTOBER 1628

The sun shone brightly onto the grassy bank, but there was a chill in the air, signaling the approach of winter. September had been unseasonably warm, but now it was the third week of October and autumn had taken hold, the leaves turning brilliant shades of orange and yellow and the fields looking barren and shorn after the harvest and the haying. The James River flowed lazily past, the sparkling surface concealing the strong currents below. Fluffy white clouds scuttled overhead, casting passing shadows onto the group gathered on the bank. Valerie handed out sandwiches and Alec poured cups of ale, looking for all the world like a family enjoying a picnic, alas one without children.

Kit sat on an upturned bucket, his leg stretched out in front of him since he couldn't sit on the ground. Everyone tucked into their meal with relish, but the mood was expectant, and somewhat subdued. Alec had let it be known that this was an important family meeting, one that needed to be held away from the house for fear of the servants and the children overhearing what was discussed. Jenny picked at her sandwich, while Cameron gulped his ale and held out his cup for a refill, the two of them clearly nervous. Louisa and Kit had a fairly good idea of why Alec had called this meeting, but they looked just as glum.

Alec set his own food aside and stared pensively at the river. He knew that at some point he would have to reveal the reason for this gathering, but the painful knot in his gut told him that his news wouldn't be met with acceptance or even an open mind. However, the time had come, and he had to be honest. There was no choice. He turned to watch as Charles strode toward them, his face set in harsh lines. Charles looked as if he'd indulged in some hard drinking over the past few weeks. His eyes were bloodshot, and his jaw was covered with several days' growth of beard. Even his clothes were untidy, something completely out of character for Alec's fastidious brother.

"I got your summons," Charles said as he towered over everyone. "At your service, dear brother."

He tried to sound sarcastic, but there was something pitiful in his attempt at nonchalance. He had the look of a man who needed a reason to go on, otherwise he would apply himself to drinking until he forgot himself permanently. Perhaps the grief of losing Annabel had finally gotten the better of him, or perhaps it was anger at losing Bethany just when he'd thought he might have her at last.

Valerie had seen Bethany in town several times and at church with her new husband. Bethany was thriving and had taken on the role of stepmother with relish. The Bartletts looked like a happy family, and although there were those who made snide comments about Bethany's expanding waistline, no one could make them too loudly since she was now a married woman. There would be talk once the child was born, and Valerie hoped that Charles wouldn't do anything foolish, like try to see the baby or make a loaded comment within the hearing of others.

"Would you like a sandwich, Charles?" Valerie asked once

Charles finally sat down. Charles shook his head but accepted a cup of ale.

"What's this all about?" he demanded.

Alec stood and faced the group. "I've asked you to come here today so that we could speak privately, for what I have to say to you cannot be overheard," Alec began. "Some of you already know what this is about, but for the rest of you, this will come as quite a surprise. Please, bear with me, and know that I speak the truth, no matter how unbelievable it might sound. First, I must tell you a story. It starts with a man who lived far in the future, in the twentieth century to be exact, a man who studied physics and with the help of his partner had invented a time-travel device."

"Alec, are you drunk?" Charles demanded as he stared at him in utter disbelief. "Or have you been eating those mushrooms that Fred Taylor forever warned us about, the ones that Indians use to cause visions?"

"I'm not drunk, nor am I under the influence of mushrooms, Charles."

"Go on then," Charles conceded.

"The man I speak of is Mr. Taylor. He created a time-travel device that he had carelessly left on a shelf in his shop. The first person to use it accidentally had been a young Hungarian student named Erzsebet. She was later known as Elizabeth, and she was our grandmother."

"Now, wait just a second, Alec," Charles cut in angrily. "What are you talking about? I remember Grandmother Elizabeth, and there was nothing about her to suggest that she wasn't a woman of her time."

"Be quiet, Charles," Alec replied. "And listen."

"Mr. Taylor had intended get rid of the device but couldn't bring himself to destroy it and left it sitting on a shelf. It was years later that a young American woman—yes, I said American, as this land will become a new country in the not-so-distant future—walked into his shop and unwittingly turned the hands of the time travel clock, winding up in 1605. Confused and frightened, she arrived at Yealm Castle, since that was the only place she could reach on foot."

"So, who was it that time?" Charles asked, his voice dripping sarcasm.

"It was Valerie," Alec replied, earning shocked looks from Cameron and Jenny. "Valerie had come from the year 2010, from a place called the United States of America. I have been to this place and I have seen it with my own eyes, and it's glorious," Alec said before Charles could interrupt him again.

"Please, go on, Uncle Alec," Jenny pleaded. Her eyes were huge with shock, but she seemed eager to hear the rest.

"Sometime later, Valerie's sister, Louisa, followed her to the past. We thought our time-travel adventures were over, but Mr. Taylor had decided to pay Valerie and Louisa a visit. He felt guilty and thought they might wish to return to their own time. When he arrived, he brought along a new, smaller, and more portable device."

"Well, clearly they stayed, because this is the only time that exists right now," Charles cut in again. "You're delusional, Alec."

Alec ignored Charles's outburst and continued. "Mr. Taylor had been careless in the past, and he was careless again. He left the device in his room where it was discovered by our teenage son. Finn transported himself to the eighteenth century and landed in the middle of the Revolutionary War, fought between the colonists and the British."

"Ridiculous," Charles spat out. "What war? We are all subjects of the king."

"Charles, you're beginning to try my patience," Alec replied. "You are free to leave if you are not interested in what I have to say."

Charles looked as if he were about to take Alec up on his

offer, but curiosity won out. "Go on, Alec. I won't interrupt you again."

"Finn has been living in the eighteenth century since. He has a wife and two children. And this week, in October 1781, the War of Independence will take a drastic turn in favor of the colonists. A new country will be born, a country that will go from thirteen colonies to fifty states and become one of the world's greatest superpowers."

"Pardon me, Master Whitfield, but why are ye telling us all this?" Cameron asked. "Even if we accept it as the truth, which I admit is not an easy thing to do, what will change if we ken?"

Alec looked around and sighed. This was it; this was the reason for this meeting. "The reason I'm telling you this after all this time is because Valerie and I are leaving. We wish to be close to our son and grandchildren. We care for you all deeply, but we've made our choice. Finn is our only living child and we want to be near him and his family."

Jenny began to cry softly, but Alec held up his hand. "Jenny, I wasn't finished."

"Sorry, Uncle Alec," Jenny mumbled as Cameron put his arm around her. They had just crossed the world to be with her family, and now the family was about to leave.

"Louisa and Kit will be leaving for England shortly. If Kit is physically up to it, they might even leave next month and not wait until the spring. I'm asking you to come with us," Alec announced, looking at Charles and then Jenny.

"We have enough savings to finance our life in the eighteenth century. We can sell the plantation and go. Cameron, the eighteenth century will offer you opportunities that you would never have here. It's a place of democracy and liberty. There will no longer be a monarch, or a class system. Everyone will be considered equal under the law of the land, and there will be religious tolerance. We will no longer need to pretend to be Protestant or attend Protestant services in order to fool our neighbors. For the first time in our lives, we will be free to live as we see fit. And Charles, your children are still young enough that they won't remember what happened. You can simply tell them that we are moving to a different place. With their mother gone, there's nothing to keep you here. What do you say?"

"I say you're mad, Brother," Charles snarled. "Thanks, but no thanks. I will stay right here where I belong, and if you are going time traveling, or whatever it is you think you're doing, please leave me the deed to the plantation. You owe me that much."

"Charles, the plantation will indeed be yours after we leave, but I must have your promise that you will treat the indentures decently and with respect and look after the children. Louisa has invested a lot of her time into teaching them to read and write. Don't let her work go to waste. Those children deserve a chance at a better future."

"Yes, Alec, I will be a good owner. Contrary to popular belief, I'm not a monster," Charles said defensively. He would gladly honor Alec's wishes if he would really leave and sign the plantation over.

"No one says you're a monster, Charles, but you can be a bit mercenary, if you'll pardon me saying so," Alec replied. Charles inclined his head, refusing to argue the point.

"Jenny, Cameron, what say you?"

Cameron gazed at his wife, whose eyes were sending him silent pleas, then turned to Alec. "If indeed ye're telling the truth and such a thing is possible, then I for one would like to see the future. Canna be worse than what I've experienced in this accursed century. Equality, liberty, and religious freedom sound verra appealing to someone like me."

"We have been preparing and turning some of our assets into gold to be used for our life in the eighteenth century. I have designated November first as our departure date."

"All Souls Day," Cameron chuckled. "Wouldn't ye prefer All Hallows' Eve, since we'll be dead to this world?"

The mention of death brought angry tears to Louisa's eyes, but she wiped them away and glared at Kit, who looked away, his mouth set in a stern line.

"It's settled then. Jenny and Cameron will come with us, Kit and Louisa will leave for England, and Charles will assume control of the estate. November first," Alec reiterated.

"November first," everyone mumbled as they brushed crumbs from their clothes and got to their feet. It was a subdued group that walked back to Rosewood Manor. Valerie and Jenny fell behind, and Alec heard Jenny asking, her voice full of awe. "Is it really true, Aunt Valerie? Is such a thing possible?"

"I never thought so, until I found myself terrified and alone in a time I'd only read about in books. Finlay and Alec took me in and offered me a future. I don't know what would have happened to me had they not. I don't imagine I would have survived on my own. I had nothing and knew little of the realities of life in the seventeenth century. It wasn't an easy adjustment. I still miss my life in the future, as does Louisa."

Jenny nodded in understanding and walked on silently. It would take time for Jenny and Cameron to fully comprehend what they'd agreed to, but their trust in Alec and Valerie would help. Charles, on the other hand, would be a problem, Alec thought. He didn't believe a word of what had Alec said, but he yearned for the plantation, so he would bide his time and see what happened come November.

Alec walked on ahead, his mind on practical details. Transporting this many people at the same time would not be easy, nor would they be able to appear in the future unnoticed. He would have to select a time and a place that would allow them to arrive undetected and not arouse suspicion. For all the progress of the eighteenth century, people would still not take kindly to four adults and two children appearing out of thin air.

Alec's thoughts were interrupted by Charles, who came up alongside him. Charles looked intrigued, which Alec supposed was not a bad thing, considering the state he'd been in for the past few weeks. He blamed himself for Annabel's death, and if Alec were honest with himself, he blamed Charles as well. Bethany had called on Annabel just before she'd suffered the miscarriage that led to her downward spiral. It wasn't for Alec to pass judgment on his brother, but neither was it for him to assuage Charles's guilt.

"I want to see it," Charles said without preamble.

"See what?"

"I want to see the device," Charles clarified.

"All right, I'll show it to you when we get back to the house. It's a very sophisticated piece of equipment, so you have to promise not to touch it."

Charles gave a bark of laughter. "I'm not a child, Alec. I won't break your toy. I just want to see it with my own eyes."

"Will seeing it change your mind?" Alec asked, his tone casual.

He wasn't sure he wanted Charles to come with them. Charles was too brash and too stubborn to make the changes needed to fit in. He would make trouble. He always did. Besides, someone had to take over the plantation and the people on it. If Charles decided to come along, Alec would have to sell up first. He suddenly recalled something Finn had mentioned a long time ago, when they'd first found him after his time-traveling escapade. He said that when he'd found himself in the eighteenth century, there were no longer Whitfields at Rosewood Manor.

Was it possible that they'd all gone to the future, or had the seventeenth-century line died out over the ensuing years? With only Harry left to carry on the Whitfield line, it was entirely possible that over the next few generations the Whitfield name would die out. If Harry failed to produce a son, it could happen as soon as the next generation. But that wasn't something Alec needed to worry about. Even with a gap in the family tree, their family would go on.

Charles stomped into the house after Alec and followed him to the study where Alec kept the time-travel device under lock and key. He stepped from foot to foot impatiently while Alec retrieved the key from its secret place and unlocked the drawer, laying the watch on the desk. Charles reached out but then snatched back his hand before it made contact with the strange object.

"I've never seen anything like this before," Charles said as he bent lower to study the device. "What's it made of?"

"Plastic. It won't be invented until the twentieth century. It's durable, flexible, and comes in a variety of colors," Alec said with an amused grin. He liked seeing Charles baffled.

"And the buttons?"

"The buttons are for setting the time and the coordinates, and there's a 'Menu' button that allows the traveler to review previously activated destinations. We have saved Finn's coordinates, since we use them frequently. If we use the destination preprogrammed for Finn, it takes us to the same place, but not to the same date as before. The time corresponds to our own, so if for example we had traveled to see Finn in April of this year, our next trip will correspond to our own time and bring us into November 1st, 1781."

"That's ingenious," Charles said as he continued to stare at the watch. "So, if it's so precise, how in the world did Valerie and our grandmother just end up somewhere without their consent?"

"This is not the original device. The original time-travel device was in the form of a French ormolu clock where the hands had to be turned to a specific location. Valerie turned the hands to 4:05, because that was the correct time. 4:05 translates to 1605, so she wound up in the same spot only in the seventeenth century."

"What kind of cretin would leave something so powerful out in the open?" Charles asked with derision. He'd never really taken to Mr. Taylor and had thought him a foolish old man. This clearly confirmed his poor opinion.

"Mr. Taylor was a good man, Charles, if a bit absentminded and careless at times. You will be respectful of his memory."

Charles gave Alec a sarcastic bow, not in the mood to argue. Alec could see the curiosity in his eyes, but there was another dominant emotion—greed. With Alec gone, Charles would be lord and master of the Whitfield estate. His avarice outweighed his desire to see the future.

"So, will you be joining us?" Alec asked with a slight smile. He already knew the answer.

"I thank you for your offer, Alec, and under different circumstances perhaps I would have, but someone has to take care of the estate, and I have another child on the way, a child I will not raise, but will still love. I will remain here, where I belong. I will miss you, all of you."

"And I will miss you," Alec replied as he locked the watch in a drawer and put the key away.

SEVENTY-FOUR

Gentle sunshine shone through the trees, setting the autumn foliage ablaze. Normally, Louisa loved this time of year, but today, the beauty around her only served to annoy her. She couldn't bear to return to the house with the others, so she went for a walk instead. Valerie had offered to come along, but Louisa politely declined. She often went off on her own when she had a headache, desperate to get away from the noise and overcrowding of the house. The peaceful quiet of the forest always helped, curing the headache and restoring her to a positive state of mind. But today, she didn't have a headache—it was her heart that was in pain. She'd known of the plan all along and nothing Alec said had come as a surprise, but the words still took her breath away when she heard them spoken out loud.

November first was less than two weeks away, the day when Valerie would be torn from her forever. The first time they'd been separated had been traumatic, terrifying, and confusing, but this time the separation was planned, and it would be permanent. Valerie would not return. They might see each other a handful of times in the future, but never again would they be a part of each other's daily lives. Perhaps this would be easier for Valerie, since she was losing Louisa but gaining Finn and his family, but for Louisa, it felt like a scheduled amputation of a limb. She wasn't gaining anything. She was losing her sister, the basic freedoms she would no longer be able to enjoy in England, and possibly her husband, whose very liberty would depend on the whims of one man.

Louisa had never actively wished harm on anyone, but if there was one person in the world whose grave she'd like to dance on, it would be the final resting place of George Villiers, 1st Duke of Buckingham, who'd blackmailed and sodomized Kit. Buckingham had been in love with Kit and seeing him again might rekindle the flames of Buckingham's passion. The consequences didn't bear thinking about. Louisa had been able to forgive Kit once, knowing that he'd genuinely suffered at the hands of Buckingham and had not gone to his bed willingly, but Louisa would not be able to forgive again. Except that if the worst happened, she'd have no way to leave, and no way to summon Valerie to her aid.

She had still hoped that Alec and Valerie would change their minds about going, but there was no turning back now, not after Alec had told everyone the truth. She didn't blame them in the least. Had it been one of her children, she would go in a heartbeat, but the thought of losing them tore her apart. Had their circumstances been different, she would have begged and pleaded with Kit, but she couldn't ask him to give up everything he'd been born to. She couldn't make the decision to deny her son the estate and title that were his due. And there was Evie to consider as well.

Evie was Lady Evangeline Sheridan, daughter of Lord Christopher Sheridan and granddaughter of Admiral Sheridan, member of the Privy Council and war hero. Evie would have her pick of eligible suitors when the time came. With her beauty and charm, she would be the jewel of the court, an opportunity Louisa couldn't bear to deny her. Kit dreamed of

SEVENTY-SIX

Alec was overcome with tenderness when he saw Robbie's face. The little boy looked terrified, his cheeks wet with tears as he looked imploringly at his father, desperate to be told that what happened hadn't been his fault.

Kit gathered Robbie to him and held him close. "It's all right, son," he whispered, even though his own eyes were damp. "It's all right. No one is blaming you. Just tell us what happened."

Alec knelt in front of Robbie and took him by the shoulders. "Robbie, it wasn't your fault, but we need to know exactly what Evie did." It wouldn't make all that much of a difference, but for some reason, it was important to have all the facts.

Robbie buried his face in Alec's shoulder. "I don't know what she did. She just disappeared. She was there one moment, gone the next. I was afraid to go in. I thought I would disappear too."

"Did you go into the study?" Alec asked him gently.

Robbie nodded miserably. "I thought I could save her."

"And what did you do?"

"I looked around, but Evie wasn't there. She wasn't hiding or playing a trick on me. She was truly gone."

"Why didn't you tell anyone?" Alec asked. He tried not to look at Kit who was leaning against a stall, looking as if he might pass out.

"I was scared, Uncle Alec. I thought everyone would blame me."

"Why would they blame you?" Alec asked, wondering if Robbie was telling them the whole truth.

"Because I'm her brother, and I should have protected her."

"Robbie, you couldn't have protected her."

But Robbie wasn't listening. He was sobbing, his face contorted with grief.

"I could have. I should have stopped her."

"Did you see exactly what Evie did?" Alec asked.

"She said that you kept a wonderful toy in your desk. She'd seen you showing it to Uncle Charles. Evie said she knew where you kept the key, and she'd found it. I told her to put it back before she got in trouble, but she wouldn't listen. She wanted to see the toy."

"What did she do then?"

"She unlocked the drawer and took something out. I don't know what it was. It was black with a little window on it. Evie made it light up. The light was strange. Green. I ran from the room. I was frightened." Robbie began to wail.

"It's all right, son," Kit mumbled, but he seemed to be drawing on the very last reserves of his strength.

"Kit, do you need to sit down?" Alec asked, concerned about his friend.

"No."

"Robbie, what happened then?" Alec asked.

"Evie pressed something and then she was gone. She just vanished," Robbie moaned. "I thought she was playing a trick on me, but she was really gone. Just like that."

"Did she take toy with her?" Alec asked. He hadn't realized it, but he was holding his breath in anticipation of Robbie's answer.

"No, it fell to the floor."

"Where is it?" Alec cried, feeling hopeful for the first time that afternoon.

"I picked it up after it went black again and put it back in the drawer, then I locked it away and put the key back. I didn't want to get in trouble or have someone else find it and vanish."

"Oh, dear God," Kit moaned. His face was ghostly in the dim light and his hand was shaking on the crutch.

"You did well, Robbie," Alec said. "Go play with Tom." Robbie ran off, glad to have shed the weight of responsibility for Evie's disappearance.

"Kit, let me help you back to the house. If Robbie did as he said, then I will be able to get Evie back. We just need to figure out exactly where she went."

Kit hobbled out of the stable and glanced at the setting sun. It would be dark in less than an hour, and his daughter was out there somewhere, alone and scared.

"Alec, I'm coming with you," Kit said, his face set in grim lines.

"No, you're not. You can barely stand, let alone traipse around the countryside in your condition."

But Kit shook his head. "Alec, Evie is my daughter, and I will do what I must. I will remove the splints and walk."

"You're not ready," Alec protested, but knew it to be useless. Kit was determined and nothing would stop him from going in pursuit of Evie. Alec hoped that his bones were sufficiently healed, or Kit would only hold him back at a time when every moment was crucial. Taking Cameron would have been the wiser choice, given his physical strength and ability to adapt, but Alec didn't have the heart to argue. Had it been his child, he'd do the same.

"All right, Kit. We should leave as soon as possible, but first, we must retrieve the device and tell Louisa the good news."

They found Louisa and Valerie in the parlor. Louisa was sitting up, her face swollen from crying. She made a whimpering sound when she saw Alec and Kit. Alec held up the time-travel watch. "Lou, she'd dropped it. There's hope. We are going after her."

"Kit, you can't—" Louisa began, but stopped upon seeing Kit's expression. "Please be careful and bring her back," she whispered. "Oh, please bring her back."

Evie making a grand marriage and possibly uniting the Sheridans with another great English family. He was ambitious, her husband, and shrewd. He had to be. He'd been born and bred to this life, and despite his voluntary hiatus from life at court, he was still a nobleman.

Louisa thanked God every day that Kit had been spared, but there was nothing God could do to spare her the painful separation that was coming closer every day. She'd lived in the seventeenth century long enough to understand that she had a duty to her husband and children and couldn't simply do what her heart desired, as she might have done in her modern life. She was no longer a free agent, a woman who could decide to leave everything behind and travel through time at a moment's notice. She was a wife and a mother, and her own needs had to come last. It would break her heart to say goodbye, but she would do it, and she would put on a brave face for Kit's sake. He felt awful enough already.

Louisa wiped away the tears and turned toward home. Kit would be tired after the walk to the river, and perhaps she would join him in bed for an hour of rest. They hadn't made love since his accident, but sometimes just lying next to him with his arm safely around her made up for the lack of sex. He was alive, he was on the mend, he loved her, and she wouldn't change that for the world.

SEVENTY-FIVE

Louisa walked into the house and called out a greeting, but it was met with an ominous silence. She poked her head into the parlor, but found it empty, then went to the kitchen. Cook turned to face her, her face creased with worry. Minnie wasn't there, but Robbie and Tom sat at the table, eating bread with butter and drinking cider. Robbie's eyes slid away from her when she looked at him, his eyes welling with tears.

"Barbara, where's everyone?" Louisa asked. She couldn't be sure something was wrong, but a telltale jolt of anxiety was already coursing through her, her instincts well ahead of her brain.

"It's Evie, your ladyship. She's gone missing. Everyone is out searching for her."

Louisa looked around wildly. Where could Evie have gone? She wasn't allowed to go out by herself. A sinking feeling nearly brought Louisa to her knees. Evie loved the pond. She was always in competition with Robbie for who could catch more frogs or dragonflies. What if she had snuck out and fallen into the water? The pond wasn't that deep, but it was deep enough for a seven-year-old child to drown in.

Louisa picked up her skirts and ran outside. She could see Alec and Kit standing by the pond, clearly having come to the same conclusion. Valerie was coming from the direction of the spring house, and Minnie was checking the outbuildings. Louisa could see Cameron off in the distance, Ian in his arms, striding from the Taylor's cottage, while Jenny was in the garden. Evie loved the vegetable patch and always went to check on the produce, eager to be the one to pick a ripe marrow or a bunch of radishes. But Louisa could tell from everyone's body language that there was no sign of her daughter. A desperate sob escaped from her chest as she raced toward the pond.

"Kit, has she been here?" she cried.

"I don't think so. She always brings her basket and a jar for the dragonflies. And she always takes off her shoes," he added. Kit's tone was even, but Louisa could see the deathly pallor of his skin. He was terrified, as they all were. There was nowhere Evie could have gone where they wouldn't be able to find her. Louisa had the mad idea that Evie had left with Charles, who'd taken Millie and Harry home after the meeting, but Alec assured her that Charles would never take Evie along without telling someone.

"So, where is she?" Louisa sobbed. "Where's my girl?"

The search continued for another two hours. Every tree, bush, outbuilding, hidden corner, and hiding place had been checked more than once. Alec and Cameron thoroughly checked the barracks where the indentures lived, having thought that perhaps Evie had gone to visit the children, but no one had seen her. She seemed to have vanished into thin air.

"It will be dark in a few hours," Louisa wailed when she saw Alec and Cameron returning and ran to meet them. "Alec, she can't be out there alone after dark."

"I know," Alec said gently as he took Louisa by the shoulders. "We must remain calm. There's no indication that Evie was taken by someone. She must have wandered off and will return once it starts to grow dark."

"You don't believe that for a minute," Louisa sobbed. "We've looked everywhere."

Louisa froze when Valerie came outside and strode toward them, her face ashen, her mouth set in a grim line.

"Val, what is it?" Louisa pleaded. "Please, tell me."

"Robbie just confessed," Valerie said. Her voice shook as she looked at Alec, her eyes wide and frightened.

"To what?" Alec demanded, already striding toward the house.

Valerie took a deep breath, and Louisa thought she might faint. Whatever Valerie was about to say was going to shatter her universe.

"Evie watched through the keyhole when Alec showed Charles the time-travel device. She saw Alec put it away in the drawer, lock it, and hide the key. She went into the study after Alec and Charles had left and retrieved the watch. Robbie saw her disappear."

"I've searched the study twice," Alec exclaimed, his face going from worry to unbridled panic. "Nothing looked out of place. Oh, dear God, if she still has the watch, we won't be able to get her back."

The world began to spin as black orbs appeared before Louisa's eyes, blurring her vision and sucking her into a vortex of darkness. Evie was gone. She was lost to her forever. Louisa collapsed, Alec's arms the only thing keeping her tethered to this world. She'd lost her baby, and it was all because of that goddamned, accursed device that had started everything in the first place. They should have smashed it to bits when they'd had the chance.

"Lou, can you hear me?" Valerie was asking. "Alec, let's get her in the house. She needs to lie down. I have some valerian drops I can give her. It will calm her down."

Alec carried Louisa toward the house. "She fainted," Alec explained to Kit, who'd just come out of the stables. "She'll be all right. Valerie will look after her. We need to speak to Robbie," Alec said. "Cameron, can you kindly bring Robbie to the stables. We can't speak to him in the house."

Alec settled Louisa on the settee in the parlor where Valerie was already waiting with an infusion of valerian root. The concoction smelled terrible, the foul odor filling the room, but it was the only thing Valerie could administer to Louisa without resorting to laudanum, which she kept under lock and key in her medicine chest.

Louisa, who was just beginning to come to, obediently took a few sips, grimacing with distaste. Valerie held a cup of water to her lips and she took a swallow before sinking deeper into the settee.

"Perhaps a cool compress, Mistress Valerie," Minnie offered as she came in with a wet towel.

"Yes, thank you, Minnie." Valerie used the towel to sponge Louisa's face, then folded it and pressed it to her forehead. She focused on Louisa, too distraught to wonder where Evie might be. The idea that Evie might be lost to them was inconceivable. Memories of Finn's disappearance forced their way into Valerie's mind, making her tremble with fear. Finn had been sixteen, a grown man by seventeenth-century standards. He'd known how to hunt, track, and could generally take care of himself. Evie was just a little girl. She'd spent most of her life at Rosewood Manor, with occasional visits to Jamestown. She possessed no survival skills, nor would she be able to comprehend what had happened to her or how to get back. The device was too complicated for her to set, even if she came to realize its significance. The coordinates for Rosewood Manor were programmed into the memory, but Evie would have no idea how to activate the device for a return trip. She would be trapped wherever and whenever she wound up, terrified, alone, and with no way to get home.

Valerie began to cry softly, her hand over her mouth to stifle her sobs. Louisa would never recover from this, none of them would. Alec would blame himself, and now they would never see Finn and his family again. All their lives had changed irrevocably, destroyed by the curiosity of a clever little girl.

SEVENTY-SEVEN

Alec breathed a sigh of relief when he saw Evie's destination. She'd pressed 'Menu 1', the address programmed for Finn. Had she chosen the last used coordinates, she would have wound up in twenty-first century Williamsburg, and to find her in such a large modern metropolis would be a lot more difficult. Alec changed into his eighteenth-century garb and produced a pair of more suitable breeches for Kit. Kit carefully removed the splints, and Alec helped him change. Kit looked nervous as he put weight on his leg for the first time since the accident.

"How is it?"

"All right, I think," Kit said. "Can I take the crutch with me in case I have need of it?"

"Yes, of course. Kit, are you sure you want to come? I can take Cameron."

"Alec, Evie is my child," Kit replied through gritted teeth. "I'm going with you."

"All right, let's go then."

Cameron drove them some way away from the plantation and watched as the two men vanished into the coming night, his stunned expression the last thing either of them saw. Alec had adjusted the coordinates to bring them closer to Williamsburg, since Kit was in no position to walk for any length of time. At this time of the evening, the appearance of two men would draw little attention since it was dark enough to believe they'd stepped out of the shadows rather than appeared out of thin air.

Alec drew Kit along the Duke of Gloucester Street. At any other time, he would have enjoyed watching Kit's reaction to the busy thoroughfare and the elegant outlines of the Capitol building and the college just visible in the gathering dusk, but today, all Alec could think of was where Evie might have gone had she gotten as far as Williamsburg. The coordinates she'd used would have brought her halfway between the city and the Mallory farm, which meant that Evie would have found herself in the middle of a forested area bisected by a road. Alec hoped that she'd walked toward Williamsburg, but it was impossible to tell what a little girl might do. What if she was somewhere in the woods, waiting for rescue? She wouldn't last long on her own.

"Where shall we start?" Kit asked once he got his bearings.

"Let's split up. You take the left side of the street, and I'll take the right. We'll meet in an hour's time at the end of the street. How does that sound?"

Kit nodded and set off. Alec hoped and prayed that by the time they reconvened they'd have something to share. He began by walking into the nearest tavern and questioning the publican and the patrons. Then on to the next one when his enquiry yielded no results. Alec spoke to nearly every person he passed in the street and everyone he could find at that time of evening. There weren't many women about, but there were plenty of men, nursing their tankards of ale and enjoying an hour of bonhomie with their friends before going home for the night. Alec ran into a few people he'd met on his previous visits to Williamsburg. They invited him to join them for a drink and promised to get in touch should they hear anything. Alec gave his contact information as the White Hart Inn, realizing very quickly that they would have to spend the night.

Kit looked exhausted and glum by the time Alec met him an hour later. He hadn't had any luck in tracing Evie's whereabouts and looked as if he were close to his physical breaking point.

"What now?" Kit asked, his eyes fixed on Alec as if he had all the answers.

"Now we go to the White Hart Inn. You need to rest, and some food and a drink wouldn't go amiss. We've put the word out; that's all we can do for tonight. We'll start again first thing in the morning."

"No," Kit retorted. "I can't eat and drink when Evie is out there somewhere all alone."

"So, what do you propose?" Alec asked calmly. He'd anticipated Kit's reaction, but realistically, there was nothing more they could do at this time of night short of knocking on people's doors.

"Kit, I told everyone that we're staying at the White Hart Inn. Should they see something or remember some pertinent detail, they will let us know. People are not unkind. A lost child is something that tugs at everyone's heartstrings, and there's not a person who hadn't promised to alert us should they hear something. All we can do now is wait."

Kit inclined his head in surrender and followed Alec toward the inn. He walked slowly, leaning heavily on his crutch and Alec felt guilty for not being able to help him. The only thing he could reasonably do was get him to bed, where he could get some rest before they started again tomorrow. They would most likely have to hire horses from the livery and start searching the surrounding area. They would stop at every farm on every road leading into Williamsburg until they picked up Evie's trail.

Once back at the inn, Alec settled Kit at a corner table and went to speak to the landlord. He knew the man from before, and they exchanged a few pleasantries before Alec ordered a meal and some ale.

"Don't you worry, Mr. Whitfield," the publican promised. "If any message comes in for you, I will personally deliver it. A little girl. My word. I do hope she found shelter for the night, the poor mite. I remember when my own daughter was that age, frightened of her own shadow, she was, bless her heart. Now I can barely keep her from following the army. Got herself engaged to a young captain and wants to be with him no matter what. You wait until this blasted war is over, I told her, then you can marry your captain. At any other time, I'd be in favor, but I won't allow her to be a widow before she can be a wife, if you know what I mean."

"Yes, of course," Alec said amicably, eager to get away from the man and back to Kit. The war would be over soon. Unless the young captain was unlucky enough to die so close to the end, the young woman would be a bride in no time.

"Anything?" Kit asked miserably as Alec joined him at the table.

"No, but he will pass on any messages he receives. Now, I've ordered some roast beef with potatoes, and you will eat your meal, for Evie's sake."

"You sound like you're talking to Tom. I'm not three years old, Alec."

"I'm sorry. I just want to make sure that you're all right."

Kit gave Alec a look that said that there was no way he could be all right when his daughter was missing, but then tried for a tired smile instead. "I will eat my supper."

"Good. The food here is rather good."

Alec had to admit that despite the knot of worry in his gut, he was hungry. He'd barely eaten anything earlier, having been too wound up. He tucked into his roast beef, eager to have something to do other than fret. Tomorrow was a new day, and he hoped that they'd have better luck.

SEVENTY-EIGHT
VIRGINIA OCTOBER 1781

Evie curled into a ball and pulled the blanket up to her chin. The chiming of the clock scared her. It sounded like the tolling of a church bell when someone died. The room was too big, the ceiling too high, and the huge window wider than most doors in their house. The bed was surprisingly comfortable though, the mattress soft and not lumpy at all. There was enough room for several girls, and she wished with all her heart that Millie were there. Evie closed her eyes and began to pray. The only other time she'd prayed outside of church was when her father had nearly died, but tonight she prayed with a fervor born of pure terror. She was lucky to have a place to sleep, or she would still be out on her own in the woods at night. The thought made her yank the blanket over her head and pull her legs up until her chin pressed against her knees.

Evie had found herself on the side of a road a moment after pressing the button on that strange toy Uncle Alec kept locked in his drawer. She had no idea what happened, or how she'd wound up outside, but when she'd looked to the right and left, she'd seen no signs of habitation. She was nowhere near Rosewood Manor and had no idea which way to go. She had stood there for a good long while, hoping that someone would come for her, but no one had, so she began to walk. Even if she went the wrong way, she would wind up in Jamestown and seek out Uncle Charles. He would take her home or allow her to spend the night with Millie.

As she walked, she wondered if Robbie had told anyone she'd gone. He'd warned her about playing with the toy. He'd been scared, that crybaby. Evie had been excited, but not scared. So what if she got caught? What would they do to her other than tell her off and possibly send her to bed early? She could handle that. Her parents were unlike other parents. They were kind and understanding, and they never beat her or Robbie. Evie didn't have much interaction with children who lived in and around Jamestown, but she recognized the signs when she saw them in church.

The children looked askance at their parents, their eyes full of fear and apprehension, and they sat down carefully and seemed to suffer through the sermon more than anyone else did, shifting from side to side, probably because their behinds were still raw from the hiding they'd received. She was thankful that her papa never took a belt to her because she'd likely never sit again. She wasn't a very obedient daughter; she knew that. Evie briefly wondered if this was going to be the time that her parents finally broke down and punished her. Her papa was in no condition to beat anyone, but he could always ask Uncle Alec to take his place. Evie let out a giggle. The thought of Uncle Alec taking a belt to her was quite funny. He wouldn't beat a donkey, much less a girl.

Uncle Alec could be stern, but he wasn't cruel. And he never kept anything under lock and key, which meant that whatever the object was, it was something very special. The green light that magically appeared when she pressed the 'on' button was like nothing she'd ever seen before. What was that thing, and what was its purpose? And what was the other thing she'd seen? It looked like two oval bits of glass connected by something in the middle with two hornlike sticks extending outward.

What in the world was Uncle Alec up to in that study of his? Could those things be Popish objects of worship? The minister always went on and on about evil lurking everywhere and the devil seeking weak, easily led people to corrupt. Evie knew that Uncle Alec was Catholic, as was Aunt Valerie and her own mother. They were not weak or easily led, nor were they evil. Uncle Alec would never do anything to hurt anyone, she was sure of that.

Evie had walked for what felt like hours, but nothing looked familiar, and Jamestown seemed as far away as ever. She kept walking until painful blisters had appeared on the soles of her feet and her mouth had grown dry with thirst. It had to be late afternoon, and very soon the sun would begin to set, and she would be alone on this wooded road. She'd continued to put one foot in front of the other and kept her mind occupied with questions to pass the time, but she was suddenly overcome by such terrible fear that her knees buckled, and she had to sit down.

Where was she? How had she come to be here? And why had no one come for her? Evie had begun to cry, hot tears running down her cheeks and into her mouth. They tasted salty, and for some reason, that made her cry harder. She'd never been alone, not anywhere. There was always someone nearby, always someone looking out for her safety and welfare. She wanted her parents, or Uncle Alec and Aunt Valerie. She wanted Jenny. Or Minnie, or even Cook. She wanted an adult to come and save her.

Evie knew she should keep walking but couldn't bring herself to stand up. She was tired, hungry, and frightened. The first stars were already twinkling in the sky, and the last of the daylight would fade away soon. Did no one realize she was gone? Did no one care? Was this her punishment, to be left alone in the woods for the whole night? She cried harder, but self-pity only made her feel worse, so she had wiped her eyes with the back of her hand, wrapped her arms around her legs, and rested her chin on her knees, fixing her gaze on the road.

Evie had sat up straighter when she heard the sound of hooves and the creaking of wheels. Someone was coming. She was saved. She hastily tucked her hair into her cap and rubbed at her eyes to make sure she didn't look like she'd been crying. She didn't want to give them the satisfaction of thinking she'd been scared. She would look like she was simply sitting on the side of the road, having a bit of a rest. The first indication that something was wrong was when Evie saw the floating lights. They seemed to be moving toward her, the lights swaying from side to side. What were they? Evie wondered as the first twinges of panic began to take root in her heart.

The monstrosity that had finally come into view left Evie gaping with shock. It was a conveyance of some sort, with huge back wheels, a gleaming blue box decorated with gold leaf, and two lanterns attached to the front. Evie was accustomed to candles, but these lanterns had a sort of wick that burned on its own. There were glass windows covered by velvet curtains. A coachman wearing a strange triangular hat pulled on the reins, slowing the carriage to a stop next to Evie and making her recoil in fear. She'd scrambled back on her behind, but there was nowhere to go. The road was fringed by woods and running into the forest seemed even scarier.

Evie had breathed a sigh of relief when a woman's face peered from behind the curtain. She waited until the driver opened the door and lowered the steps, then accepted his hand and descended to the ground, making Evie gape in amazement. She wore a beautiful gown made of fine fabric, not homespun, and a strange hat that looked like a large flat circle held on the woman's head by ribbons tied beneath her chin. Her bosom was covered by a bit of lace that was tucked into the bodice of the gown and two long curls snaked over her shoulders and bounced as the woman approached. She wasn't young, but she was attractive, and clearly wealthy.

"Are you all right, child?" the woman had asked as she came toward Evie. "Are you ill?"

Evie shook her head, suddenly unable to speak. Perhaps she was just having a strange dream, and if she tried hard, she would wake up and find herself at home in her own bed. Evie squeezed her eyes shut and opened them again, but the woman was still there, watching her with concern. A gentleman got out of the carriage and stood behind the woman, staring at Evie. He was older than Uncle Alec, with strange white hair curled at the sides. His hat was also triangular but made of something finer than beat-up brown leather.

"What's your name?" the woman asked gently.

Evie was about to give her full name and title when something held her back. "Evie," she muttered.

"Are you lost, Evie?"

Evie nodded. "I don't know how I got here." She'd tried not to sound frightened, but her voice shook, and she sounded tearful.

"Well, where do you live?" the woman asked, all patience, unlike her companion who seemed eager to get going.

"I live at Rosewood Manor, ma'am."

"Is your mother one of the servants, or workers?" the woman asked.

"No, my uncle owns it, and my papa helps him run it," Evie replied. Everyone around Jamestown knew Uncle Alec and her father.

"Dear, our good friends, the Bartletts, reside at Rosewood

Manor. It has been in their family for several generations now. As a matter of fact, we were just coming from visiting them."

Evie stared at the woman. She'd heard that name. Uncle Charles had mentioned someone called Bartlett, but they certainly didn't live with them.

"What's your surname?" the man asked, not unkindly.

"Sheridan," Evie replied. She was really worried now. How could someone else live at Rosewood Manor? Where had everyone gone?

"Can't say that I know of any Sheridans in the area. Do you, Harold?" the woman said. "Well, we can't leave you here with night fast approaching. Come with us. We'll help you find your people come morning."

Evie was afraid to go with the unknown couple, but she was even more afraid to remain. The woman smiled playfully and rolled her eyes. "Oh, I'm sorry, dear; I should have introduced myself. How remiss of me. I am Mistress Robertson, and this is my husband, Harold. We have a house just outside Williamsburg. Our daughters are grown and married, with children of their own, but they would be glad to have you use their room tonight, wouldn't they, Harold?"

"Of course. Come now, Evie. Nothing to fear," he said as he held out his hand.

Evie had allowed herself to be handed into the carriage. She sat down gingerly, amazed by the pretty pink upholstery and soft, padded seat. She barely even felt the carriage jolt as it began to roll on its massive wheels. The Robertsons sat across from her, smiling benignly. They seemed like kind people and would help her get home. But where was Williamsburg? Evie had never heard of it before. What if they were taking her somewhere far away where her parents wouldn't be able to find her? Evie thought desperately.

Mrs. Robertson reached out and patted Evie's knee. "I know you're frightened, but I promise, we'll see you safe."

"Thank you, Mistress Robertson," Evie replied politely. "You're most kind."

"So nice to see such a polite child," Harold Robertson said. "Kids these days are so ill-mannered. You're quite the little lady."

"Yes," Evie replied, thinking that she was a lady—Lady Evangeline Sheridan.

SEVENTY-NINE

Mr. and Mrs. Robertson sat illuminated by a brace of candles, enjoying their glass of port, as they did every evening after supper. The fire blazed merrily in the grate, but Mrs. Robertson found herself unable to enjoy the wine.

"What's troubling you, Linda?" her husband asked as he watched her frown into her glass.

"Evie. She's so well-behaved, but there's something off about her, isn't there? Her clothes are old-fashioned, and she seems to be fixated on Jamestown."

"Perhaps that's where she is from," Harold suggested, bored with the topic. In his opinion, they should have left the child where they had found her. Doubtless, she wasn't too far away from home and would have found her way back or been rescued by her parents. Taking her to Williamsburg was a mistake. Her people would have no idea where to look for her, if indeed they were looking for her at all. Perhaps she'd been orphaned and was clever enough to try to find someone to take her in.

"She has a British accent," Mrs. Robertson continued, oblivious to her husband's lack of interest.

"So she does."

"Perhaps her people are Tories who fled the area," Mrs. Robertson suggested.

"And left their child behind?" Harold Robertson asked. "Doesn't seem likely, does it?"

"No, I suppose not. And why would she say that she lives at Rosewood Manor?"

"Search me."

"Harold, what if we don't find her family?" Linda Robertson asked, her voice trembling with hope.

"No, my dear. We can't simply take her in. She doesn't belong to us."

"But she is so lovely."

"Yes, she is, and she does resemble our Margaret, if that's what you're thinking, but that's no reason to make her a part of our family. That little girl belongs to someone. We'll take her to Jamestown tomorrow and see if we can find her kin."

"All right," Linda breathed, her hopes dashed.

Life had become so dull, so predictable since their girls had gone to Philadelphia with their families. Linda would follow them in a heartbeat, but Harold was loath to leave his printing business. It had belonged to his father, an indentured servant who'd come to Virginia with nothing but the clothes on his back. Harold was proud of his dad and wouldn't see his life's work sold to someone else, but they weren't getting any younger and with no sons to inherit, the shop would eventually go to someone else anyway.

Linda finished her drink in one gulp and stood, ready to retire. Tomorrow was another day. Perhaps they wouldn't find Evie's family, and then she'd have a stronger case. Harold was always like this, saying no and coming up with a slew of reasons not to do something, but she always managed to talk him around in the end, and this would be no different. Harold had been a doting father when the girls were little, and Linda was sure that he missed having a child around as much as she did. Evie wasn't some peasant. Her speech was cultured, and she had lovely manners, both so at odds with her strange clothes and shoes. Clothes could be changed, and homeless children could suddenly find themselves a part of a new family.

We'll just see what tomorrow brings, Mistress Robertson thought as she climbed the stairs to her bedroom.

EIGHTY

VIRGINIA OCTOBER 1628

The house was ominously quiet without Alec and Kit. The children were already asleep, having been uncharacteristically well-behaved and subdued all evening. They were worried about Evie and frightened that she was gone for good. Jenny, Valerie, and Louisa sat by the fire. Their eyelids were drooping with fatigue, but they couldn't bring themselves to go to bed, still hopeful that Alec and Kit would return with Evie. Cook had gone home to her cottage, and Minnie had retired. Both women believed that Evie was lost somewhere on the estate. Cook had suggested that all the indentures be utilized to form a search party and had been surprised when her idea was met with a lack of enthusiasm.

Louisa looked haunted, smudges of fatigue darkening the tender skin beneath her eyes and making them look bruised. She hadn't said anything in a long while, but her fingers constantly picked at her skirt, pleating and releasing the fabric absentmindedly. Valerie tried to give her some brandy, but Louisa had refused, preferring to remain alert. She started every time there was a noise outside, but it was nothing more than the sounds of evening on a farm. The lowing of cows, soft neighing of horses getting settled for the night, and the croaking of frogs at the pond didn't sound anything like two men and a child returning home.

"Lou, go to bed. I'll come and get you if anything at all happens," Valerie promised, but Louisa shook her head.

"How can I sleep when my baby is out there on her own, possibly sleeping in the woods? She might be cold and wet, but most of all, she's probably scared out of her wits."

"Yes, she probably is, but Alec and Kit will turn Williamsburg upside down to find her. You know that, Lou."

Louisa swallowed a sob. "Kit can barely stand, much less run around Williamsburg. He's probably in such pain. And what if Evie is not in Williamsburg? What if she's in Jamestown, or lost in the woods? You said yourself that she would have arrived somewhere between Williamsburg and the Mallory farm. How will they ever find her?"

Louisa was right, Valerie thought. Kit was probably in agony. Even if his bones had healed sufficiently, after months on bedrest, his muscles were weakened, and he'd tire quickly. He would have a hell of a time keeping up with Alec, who would likely be searching the area like a madman. It had taken them months to find Finn when he went missing, and Alec knew that the first twenty-four hours were crucial. If they didn't find Evie by end of day tomorrow, the trail would grow cold.

Louisa looked done in, so Valerie decided to take matters into her own hands. She went to the kitchen and heated up some milk, to which she added a few drops of laudanum. Louisa wouldn't drink the milk if she suspected, but she needed to rest before she had a breakdown, and maybe, just maybe, by the time she woke, Evie would be home, and life would go back to normal.

Louisa refused the milk at first, but then drank it bit by bit. She hadn't eaten anything at supper, nor had she eaten much during their picnic at noon. She was starving even if she didn't know it. Valerie watched as Louisa's eyelids began to droop and her hand stilled, her fingers no longer pleating the fabric. The laudanum was taking effect.

"Let me help you upstairs," Valerie cajoled. Louisa was too sedated to argue, so Jenny and Valerie walked her upstairs and helped her into bed.

"I don't know what I'd do if Ian went missing," Jenny whispered as they closed the door behind them. "I'd go mad. I'd die."

"Nae, ye wouldn't. Ye would turn the world upside down to find him, lass, as would I," Cameron said, having finally gotten Ian to settle. "I could do with a drink," he said. "Anything on offer?"

"There's brandy. I'd like one, too," Valerie said. She hoped Jenny wouldn't drink, being pregnant, but she could hardly say anything, given the customs of the day. But thankfully, Jenny refused.

"I'm for my bed," Jenny said. "This day has been one for the books."

"Goodnight, Jenny. Sleep well." Cameron gave his wife a tender kiss and sent her on her way. "Ian is sound asleep, so he should give ye some peace."

Valerie and Cameron went back downstairs and applied themselves to Alec's decanter of brandy.

"Ye know, this afternoon when Master Alec spoke of time travel, I thought he were mad," Cameron said.

"And now you don't?" Valerie asked.

"To be honest, I dinna rightly ken what I think. It's such a far-fetched notion. Who'd ever heard of such a thing? But then I watched them go. Just vanished, they did. There one moment, gone the next."

"It is true, Cameron. We've been to the future, and it's like nothing you can envision."

"Will ye tell me about it?" Cameron asked. "Dinna seem like either of us is getting any sleep tonight."

"What would you like to know?"

"Tell me about the time we're going to. I'd like to ken more about the twenty-first century, but that can wait. If we are to leave this place, I'd like to ken what to expect."

"You are very practical. I like that about you," Valerie said as she settled deeper into her chair.

"A poor man dinna have the luxury of being impractical. It can cost him dearly."

"Yes, I suppose it can. Well, I do know that there are many Scots in eighteenth-century Virginia. Some are on the side of the British, and some on the side of the Revolution."

"So, no one will immediately assume that I'm a criminal sent down to do penance for my crime?" Cameron asked, smiling sarcastically.

"No, they won't. They'll assume that you are an immigrant, like so many others. You will have a clean slate."

"A clean slate," Cameron repeated, savoring the phrase. "Most people never have a clean slate, not even if they've lived an exemplary life. I do look forward to that."

Valerie nodded, suddenly exhausted. She'd consumed a lot more brandy and the surge of adrenaline was finally wearing off.

"Ye look tired, Mistress Valerie. Shall I help ye up?"

"I can manage. Goodnight, Cameron."

"Goodnight. I'll just stay down here a wee bit longer, if that's all right."

"Of course."

Valerie trudged upstairs. She hoped she'd be able to sleep. Perhaps a miracle would occur, and Evie would be back by morning. If only.

EIGHTY-ONE
VIRGINIA OCTOBER 1781

Alec and Kit woke at dawn, ready to resume their search. The publican suggested that they have some breakfast, and Kit reluctantly agreed. He looked like death warmed over and needed all the sustenance he could get. They had porridge, bacon, and bread before setting off toward the livery at the far end of the street. They'd need to hire horses since Evie didn't appear to be in Williamsburg. Alec suggested that Kit remain at the inn and wait for word, but Kit was adamant about coming along. His shock at being in the eighteenth century had worn off, and he felt more confident about interacting with people.

"Where shall we begin?" Kit asked.

He gazed up and down the street that was just coming to life. Shops were opening, servants were heading to the market, and several wagons were making deliveries of fresh milk products and produce. Sunlight gleamed off large glass windows, making Kit wince.

"Are you all right, Kit?" Alec asked.

"I've a bit of a headache, but I'll be fine. Let's go."

It took a great deal of effort for Kit to mount his horse, but once he did, they proceeded to go up and down every street, searching for any sign of Evie. Although there were lots of girls fitting Evie's description, none of them turned out to be her. Kit's eyes followed a girl of about seven, who laughed at something her mother said as they passed by. Kit looked unbearably sad, making Alec feel even more helpless than he did already. They hadn't found any trace of Evie, which wasn't a hopeful sign.

By midday, Alec decided that they needed reinforcements. Evie wasn't in Williamsburg, and they needed to cover a broader area, extending their search from Williamsburg to Jamestown, and possibly even as far as Rosewood Manor. Evie might have figured out how to get to Jamestown and go in search of home. Alec had no idea who lived at the plantation now, but was sure they wouldn't be welcoming.

"Kit, we need to ask Finn and Sam for help. They know the area better than we do, and the four of us can cover more ground. We'll have a lot of explaining to do but finding Evie is the priority."

Kit nodded sadly. "I look forward to seeing Finn again, and meeting Sam," he said, trying to sound positive.

Alec thought it might be a good idea to leave Kit with Mrs. Mallory, who would look after him, but knew Kit would refuse. He looked gray, even in the sunlight, his mouth pressed into a thin line and his eyes glazed with pain, but he hadn't uttered a word of complaint, putting his own suffering aside to find his daughter. Alec turned his horse in the direction of the Mallory farm, hoping that he would find everyone safely at home. He felt a flutter of excitement at seeing Finn, Abbie, and his grandchildren, despite their grim mission. Besides, he was bursting to tell Finn their news.

EIGHTY-TWO
VIRGINIA OCTOBER 1628

Louisa's eyes fluttered open. The room was still dark, but objects began to melt out of the shadows, their outlines just barely visible in the gray light of pre-dawn. Louisa felt as if she had fought her way to the surface from some deep and frightening place that was full of darkness and danger. She was muddled, the sinister images from her dream still swirling in her mind even though she was awake. She shut her eyes and allowed herself to hover somewhere between wakefulness and sleep, hoping the oppressive somnolence would wear off. Sleep pulled at her, but she had to fight it. There was something important she had to do, but she couldn't quite remember what that was.

She must have fallen back asleep because when she woke again, bright sunshine was streaming through the window, reminding her that it was a new day and that her child was still missing. Louisa sat bolt upright, suddenly angry. Valerie must have drugged her last night, which explained the vivid, frightening dreams and the heavy slumber. She should have kept her vigil, but instead, she'd slept through the night, her sanity safeguarded against the heart-wrenching reality. They weren't back.

Louisa could tell just by listening to the sounds coming from downstairs. She could hear the clatter of pots, smell the aroma of baking, and just make out the whiney protests of the children as Jenny herded them outside for a walk after breakfast.

She couldn't hear Valerie, but instinctively knew that Valerie was in the house, waiting for her to wake up and ready to offer understanding and support. Louisa got up, dressed, splashed some water on her face, and made her way downstairs. She was angry with herself for being hungry, but the body demanded what it needed, and starving herself certainly wouldn't help Evie. She entered the kitchen and accepted a bowl of porridge from Cook, who went out of her way to avoid making eye contact for lack of anything positive to say. Louisa ate a few spoonfuls of porridge and pushed the bowl away, suddenly nauseated. She needed Valerie.

Louisa found Valerie outside, sitting on the porch, her eyes trained on the road from Jamestown. She looked up at Louisa and offered a guilty smile, which Louisa ignored. She was still furious about the laudanum, but she was grateful Valerie had given it to her. Had she not, Louisa would have been a madwoman by now. Louisa sat next to Valerie, who laid her hand over Louisa's in a gesture of silent support. There wasn't anything she could say. Alec and Kit were out there somewhere, searching for her little girl. Had Evie remained in one place, they would have found her by now, so it stood to reason that she had wandered off and where she'd gone was anyone's guess.

Louisa shuddered at the thought of never seeing Evie again. Perhaps this was divine retribution, the Universe's way of evening the odds. She'd been lucky enough never to lose a child, as Valerie had. Nor had she lost a husband. Valerie had been left by her first husband, who'd been her college boyfriend, and then lost Finlay shortly after they were married. Perhaps this was cosmic justice, a reminder that Louisa wasn't immune to loss and heartbreak.

"They'll find her, Lou," Valerie said, sensing Louisa's agitation. "They will. It took us months to find Finn when he disappeared, but we found him in the end. He was safe, and he was loved."

Louisa nodded, unable to respond. Finn had been sixteen. Evie was seven. She was intelligent and resourceful for her age, but still a child. She wouldn't be able to fend for herself, and if she found someone to take her in, God only knew what their motives might be. Pedophilia was not restricted to the modern age, nor was basic human cruelty.

"I can't just sit here," Louisa cried, jumping to her feet. "I'll go mad. I must do something."

"Why don't you go and see the children? Tell them a story. It always makes you happy when you do. I know you're not in the right frame of mind, but it will at least keep you busy for a few hours. Lou, you must remain calm. Nothing will be achieved by having a breakdown."

"Easy for you to say," Louisa retorted.

"No, it's not easy for me to say. It's actually extremely hard, but there's no other alternative. There is nothing we can do but wait."

"Fine," Louisa said. "But come and get me if there's any news."

"Of course, I will," Valerie promised. "Keep the faith."

"I'm trying," Louisa grumbled. "God, I'm trying."

EIGHTY-THREE
VIRGINIA OCTOBER 1781

Finn pulled on his clothes and descended the ladder, eager to get outside. There was much to do since Sam was effectively bedbound for a few more days at least. Finn was the only man around, except for Doctor Freeman, who knew less about farming than he did about the invention of the telephone. In either case, Doctor Freeman was joyfully spending time with Sue and his grandchildren and tending to Sam, so Finn was on his own. The girls pitched in as much as they could, as did Hannah, but a pall hung over the house, everyone lost in their own thoughts and memories of John. His specter loomed over everything, leaving his wife and children unable to accept his death and start the lengthy process of moving on.

Finn refused an offer of breakfast from Mrs. Mallory and strode from the house. He'd been unbearably angry these past few weeks, but his anger was directed mostly at himself. He'd left Abbie and his children alone, had put Sam in danger, and had come back to find his wife terrified, branded, and reeling from shock. And for what? His mother said that the Revolutionary War would end in victory for the colonists. What did it even matter if he'd helped the war effort? History had already been written, and his part in it was insignificant. He'd allowed himself to believe that he was making a difference, when all he was really doing was endangering the people he loved. What a fool he'd been.

Hannah Mallory had made Finn and Sam promise that neither one would go within a mile of the coming battle. It was bad enough that Jonah would be in the line of fire, but to have Finn and Sam face danger was more than she and the girls could bear. Finn would stand by his promise, but the thought of missing Cornwallis's surrender made him even angrier. Did he not deserve some satisfaction? He wouldn't fight, but he could observe. Well, for now, all he could do was milk the cows. And then have another argument with Abbie about Leo Sparks. Finn thirsted for retribution, but Abbie had put her foot down, forcing Finn to swear that he wouldn't exact revenge for what happened. Leonard Sparks was dead by Finn's hand, and Leo Sparks was barely holding on after being shot by Sam. That would have to be good enough.

Finn stopped walking, surprised to see a carriage rolling toward the farm. Such posh conveyances did not come this way often since the farm was not situated along any major road. Finn waited, curious to see who was coming and why. Perhaps Sparks had accused Finn of murder and the magistrate was on his way to arrest him.

Finn spread his feet, as if that would help him stand his ground. It would be rather ironic if the British executed him for a murder days before the end of their rule in Virginia. Finn relaxed marginally when he realized that the man driving the carriage was not in uniform. Couldn't be the magistrate then. Perhaps someone was lost. The carriage drew as close as it could to the farm, then rolled to a stop, a stout man in a wig and a tricorn getting out and stepping carefully onto the muddy path, mindful of his expensive shoes.

"Hello," he called, smiling at Finn as if they'd known each other all their lives.

"Hello," Finn replied. "Are you lost, sir?"

"No, no, my dear fellow. But I believe I have someone who might belong to you. My wife and I found this little girl on the side of the road yesterday evening. She says her family name is Sheridan, but upon further questioning this morning, she mentioned that she's also related to the Whitfields. I nearly forgot that John Mallory's son-in-law is called Whitfield, and then I recalled meeting you in Williamsburg. You came to my print shop."

"Oh, of course," Finn replied. Now he remembered the man. His name was Harold Robertson.

"How is John? I haven't seen him in eons, or so it would seem."

"Mr. Mallory died recently," Finn said, feeling a pang of loss at the mention of Mr. Mallory.

"Oh, I am sorry to hear that. A good man, John. The best."

"Yes, he was." Finn paused, suddenly realizing what the man had said. Who had he come across that was a Whitfield?

"The little girl," Finn prompted.

"Ah yes, of course. My wife is quite taken with her. Pretty little thing. Very composed. Name is Evie. Is she one of yours?"

Finn nearly gagged when he heard the name. There could only be one Evie, the daughter of his Aunt Louisa and Christopher Sheridan. What in the world was Evie doing in the eighteenth century on her own?

"Yes, she's one of ours," Finn replied carefully. He had no idea what Evie's reaction would be to him, but he had to keep her safe no matter what. Dear God, how was he going to explain this to Abbie and Mrs. Mallory? It was hard enough to explain his parents, much less try to weasel his way out of explaining a cousin he'd never met, who'd just appeared out of thin air, and whose parents were nowhere to be found.

Finn watched as the coachman helped a well-dressed woman out of the coach. A little dark-haired girl allowed herself to be lifted out and set on the ground, her eyes watchful in her small face. She didn't smile, nor did she cry. She just stood there, rooted to the ground.

"Are you Evangeline Sheridan?" Finn asked, hoping that knowing her name would put her somewhat at ease.

"Yes, sir." The child curtsied prettily, making Finn smile. His mother did say that Evie was quite the little lady.

"I know your mother, Louisa Sheridan, very well. Welcome, Evie. I'm so happy to meet you at last," Finn said. He prayed that the child would not dig in her heels and refuse to stay, but she turned to the Robertsons and thanked them for their help, ready to join Finn.

Mrs. Robertson looked as if she might cry, but she hugged Evie and kissed her on the forehead. "I wish you well, my dear. I'm so glad to see you reunited with your family."

Evie looked a bit dubious at the mention of family, but nodded and reluctantly moved toward Finn, her eyes wide with apprehension.

"You know my parents?" she asked.

"I haven't seen them in a long while, but yes, I know them. Lord and Lady Sheridan are my aunt and uncle."

The mention of her parents did the trick. Evie smiled at last, believing herself to be safe. "I want to go home, please."

"I know you do. Why don't you come back to the house, have some breakfast, and meet your cousins." *And I will wrack my brains as to how to explain your presence and get you back where you belong*, thought Finn.

Evie followed Finn into the house, hanging back once she saw all the people in the front room. Everyone stopped what they were doing and turned to Finn, who suddenly wished that the floor would open up and swallow him. "Eh, this is Evie," he said. "She's my cousin, daughter of my mother's sister, Louisa."

"Well, it's a pleasure to meet you, Evie," Mrs. Mallory said as she came around to smile at Evie. "Would you like to join us for breakfast?"

"I've already breakfasted, thank you," Evie replied, but she seemed a little less frightened.

"Perhaps just a morsel of something," Mrs. Mallory insisted with a smile.

"Come sit by me," Diana called out as she waved to Evie. "This is Eddie, my brother," she said, sticking her chin out in the direction of Edward.

Sarah scooted over to make room for Evie, who climbed onto the bench and accepted a slice of bread and a few rashers of bacon. She smiled at Annie as the older girl offered her a cup of milk to go with her second breakfast.

"Finn, outside please," Abbie whispered as she left Evie to the care of her mother and sisters.

"What in the world is she doing here on her own?" Abbie demanded as soon as they were out of earshot.

"I don't know. It seems that she was lost, and Mr. and Mrs. Robertson found her. They were kind enough to look after her and bring her to us."

"Where are her parents?"

"Beats me," Finn replied, feeling defensive and annoyed. He could hardly tell Abbie where Evie's parents presumably were, unless they had decided to take a holiday in the eighteenth century and were somewhere nearby.

"We have to look after her until someone comes for her," Finn said, hoping Abbie wouldn't object.

"Of course, we'll look after her, you dolt," she exploded. "Do you believe that my mother and I would put out a little girl who needs us? Seriously, Finn, you can be so strange at times."

Finn wanted to be angry, but suddenly a bubble of laughter welled up inside him. Yes, he was strange. Abbie had no idea just how strange. He imagined explaining to her where he came from and where exactly Evie belonged and burst out laughing, drawing a look of intense disapproval from Abbie.

"Why are you laughing?" she demanded.

"Because you are a bossy, cranky besom this morning. And I love you."

"I love you too," Abbie replied, and gave Finn a friendly shove before disappearing back inside.

Finn shrugged and turned his steps toward the barn. Evie or no Evie, the cows needed milking, the stable needed mucking out, the fence needed to be mended, and water needed to be brought from the well for the day's laundry.

I'll go and visit Sam as soon as I'm done and take Evie to meet the other half of the family, Finn thought as he sat down on the milking stool and pressed his head to the warm side of the cow, who breathed a sigh of contentment as Finn began to skillfully squeeze her udders. He was nearly finished when he heard hoofbeats. Who was it now? Had they found Tom wandering the streets of Williamsburg as well? Finn wondered as he moved the bucket of milk out harm's way and went to the door to check on the latest arrivals.

Finn's heart leaped with joy when he recognized his father. The man next to him could only be Kit. He barely remembered him, but was glad to see Kit again, especially since his daughter would no longer be his problem. Finn hurried toward the gate, eager to say hello. He instantly noted the lines of strain around his father's mouth and the sickly pallor of Lord Sheridan. The poor man looked as if he might faint. He was probably worried sick about his daughter. Finn smiled, anticipating telling them the news.

"Finn, we need your help," his father said as soon as the two men hugged. "Evie's gone missing. She found the device."

Finn tried to look serious as he shook Lord Sheridan's hand. "It's good to see you again, Uncle Kit."

"Likewise, Finn."

"Come inside. Mrs. Mallory has breakfast on the table, and I need a few minutes to get ready."

"We've no time to waste," Kit said. Finn noticed that he seemed unable to fully bend his leg and walked with the assistance of a wooden crutch.

"Just come in for a moment," Finn said as he led the way to the farmhouse. "You look like you could do with a drink."

Kit seemed a bit uncomfortable about the meeting that was about to take place, but he put on a brave face and followed Finn into the house with Alec bringing up the rear. Kit smiled pleasantly when he saw the group of women and children around the table.

"Good morning," he said, his eyes going to Mrs. Mallory.

Finn laughed out loud when Evie jumped off the bench and flew into her father's arms. "Papa! I knew you'd come for me. Oh, Papa, please don't be angry."

"Oh, my darling," Kit gushed as he held Evie to his heart. "My poor darling. Are you all right?"

Evie gave him a look of scorn. "Of course, I'm all right. I met Diana and Eddie, and Annie is going to show me how to make apple fritters, and Sarah said I can meet her friend Derek. And Abbie said that I can go over to her brother's house with her. He has three children: Ben, Nat, and Rachel. Their grandfather is staying with them at the present." Evie suddenly grew quiet, realizing that she would have to go home before she got to do any of those things.

"We must get going, Evie," Kit said gently. "Your mother is worried sick."

"Do stay a while. Where is her ladyship? I would so love to meet her," Mr. Mallory said, suddenly realizing that an honest-to-goodness lord was standing in her kitchen.

"She is at home with our son," Kit replied. He looked bemused, which entertained Finn to no end. What a day this was turning out to be.

"Where's John?" Alec asked, instantly dispelling Finn's good mood.

"He's gone, Alec," Mrs. Mallory said. "Much has happened since we saw you last."

She didn't mean to sound accusing, but Finn detected a sour note in her voice. She thought it was strange that the Whitfields couldn't be reached by messenger or post and hadn't come to John's funeral. And that there were so many other relations no one had ever met.

"You have my deepest sympathy, Hannah," Alec said. "Your husband was a wonderful man. I only wish I'd been able to pay my respects. Finn, perhaps we can go to the cemetery so that I may say goodbye."

"Of course, Dad. I just have some chores to finish. Sam's been unable to pitch in."

Alec gave Finn a curious glance but was deterred from asking any questions by Mrs. Mallory's closed expression and Abbie's pursed lips. He trusted Finn to explain later.

"Alec, we should get going. Louisa must be tearing her hair out by now," Kit interjected.

Evie's eyes filled with tears and she drew away from Kit. "But Papa, I don't want to go home yet. I still haven't met Ben, Nat, and Rachel, and I want to make fritters. I like it here," Evie wailed to the mortification of Kit, who looked shocked by her outburst.

"Darling, your mother is frantic. We must go back."

"You go back," Evie retorted. "Tell Mama that I am all right. I'd like to stay for a while. And bring Robbie when you come back for me. I'm sure he'd like to meet everyone," Evie added.

"Your lordship, we'd love to have her," Mrs. Mallory cut in, noticing Kit's embarrassment. "She is most welcome to stay for as long as she likes. The more the merrier, I always say."

"I couldn't possibly leave her here," Kit replied, but his answer was drowned out by the clamoring of children.

"Oh, please, let her stay," Diana begged.

"We'll look after her," Sarah promised.

Kit turned to look at Alec, who shrugged noncommittally. "Up to you," his eyes seemed to say.

"Papa, please," Evie begged. "I never knew I had so many cousins."

"All right," Kit replied, sorry the moment the words left his lips. Louisa would crucify him.

EIGHTY-FOUR
VIRGINIA OCTOBER 1628

Valerie sprang to her feet when she saw two figures in the distance, and instantly sat back down, her hand flying to her mouth. She could make out Alec and Kit, but there was no child with them, no Evie. How could they have given up so easily? Valerie forced herself to her feet, despite the weakness in her knees, and walked toward them. On closer inspection, they didn't seem too upset. Alec was smiling, and Kit responded to something he said with a grin of his own. What was going on?

Alec gave Valerie a cheery wave, and she waved back, more perplexed than ever. Why weren't they more upset? To top it all off, Valerie saw Louisa running toward them, having been on her way back from visiting the children at the barracks. Louisa looked wild, her mouth open in a silent wail of misery. Kit couldn't run, but Alec hurried toward her, eager to comfort her. Louisa flew into Alec's arms. Valerie couldn't hear what was said, but Louisa stared at Alec open-mouthed, her gaze sliding toward Kit. Valerie began to run, unable to stand the suspense any longer. Louisa had gone from looking stark raving mad to smiling smugly.

"What happened? Where's Evie?" Valerie cried once she

finally reached the trio. Alec and Kit shared a conspiratorial smile.

"She's at Finn's," Alec said. "She refused to leave. She was having too good a time."

"What?" Valerie asked, thinking she hadn't heard them correctly. "So you just left her there?"

"For the time being," Kit replied.

"What does that mean?" Valerie demanded. Louisa seemed surprisingly calm, looking at Kit with an expression of such love and longing that it took Valerie's breath away.

"We'll see her soon enough," Kit replied, grinning like the Cheshire cat.

"When?" Valerie asked. "What's going on?"

"We are coming with you," Kit said, his grin broadening. "We're going to the eighteenth century."

Valerie felt the prick of tears behind her eyelids. Was it really possible? Had Kit changed his mind? He must have because Louisa was jumping up and down, whooping and crying at the same time. They wouldn't be torn apart. They would stay together, all of them, except for Charles, but a separation from him wouldn't be as painful.

Valerie threw her arms around Louisa and they jumped up and down, laughing and crying, the way they had when they'd been reunited after years of separation. *Together*, was all Valerie could think, her mind and heart reeling with joyful disbelief. Together.

"Come, Val. There's so much to do," Louisa cried. There were tears streaming down her cheeks, but her eyes glowed with happiness and she was vibrating with a manic energy that was contagious. "We only have a few weeks to get everything sorted out."

She grabbed Valerie by the arm and pulled her toward the house, leaving Alec and Kit to make their own way home.

"Are you still sure?" Alec asked Kit, who looked a bit

bemused. "You can't change your mind now you've told Louisa."

"I've no wish to. I suddenly feel as if a great big weight has been lifted off my shoulders. I hadn't realized how bereft I was about parting from you and Valerie until I made up my mind to come with you."

"You'll be giving up everything," Alec replied, already knowing what Kit would say.

"Not the important things."

"Let's go have a drink to the future," Alec suggested.

"It's not even noon."

"Who cares?"

"Who indeed?"

EPILOGUE
VIRGINIA THANKSGIVING 1783

"Valerie, can you grab the cornbread on your way out?" Hannah called from her place by the hearth. She was still cooking, even though the trestle tables set up outside could hardly accommodate another dish. The day was chilly, but the men had built a bonfire in the yard and all the collective children were dancing around, whooping like Indians doing a war dance. Valerie set the dish of cornbread on the nearest table and stood back to watch.

They had been in the eighteenth century for two years, years that had flown by in a blink of an eye. Valerie cast her gaze over the assembled company. As at any large family gathering, the women were still bringing out food, admonishing the children, and making sure that there were enough plates and utensils to go around while the men were engaged in a heated debate about state politics, disagreeing as usual. Jonah, who'd had enough of politics, was by the fire with Gemma, the little girl breathless with excitement. Jonah seemed to be enjoying a moment of carefree abandon, but kept a wary eye on the little ones, especially Ian, who seemed to be getting too close to the flames. Valerie could see Tom's blond head as he danced around, thrilled to be spending time with his cousins. Edward and Diana were next to him, their faces already smeared with soot, something Abbie wouldn't be too pleased with once she got a look at them.

Valerie chuckled when she saw Evie coming out of the house, a dish carefully balanced in her hands. At nine, she no longer saw herself as a child and preferred to stay with the women, particularly with Annie, who had become her surrogate older sister. Sarah was on the other side of the bonfire, standing close to her intended, Derek. An engagement had been announced as soon as Sarah turned eighteen. John Mallory would have approved.

At long last, it was time to sit down, and there was a moment of chaos as everyone tried to pry their children away from the crackling, mesmerizing glory of the bonfire and get them to settle down. Cameron, who held Aurora, easily lifted Ian with his free arm and deposited him unceremoniously on Jenny's lap. Doctor Freeman cajoled Nat, Ben, and Tom to come to the table, while Sue rounded up the girls.

Everyone finally took their seats and grew quiet in anticipation of the annual recitation of what everyone was thankful for on this holiday. They started off with Hannah. Valerie looked around the table, taking each face in turn. The last two years had been good to them. Finn and Abbie finally realized their dream of opening a shop in Williamsburg and had invited Valerie and Alec to come in as their partners. They lived in a spacious set of rooms above the shop, a far cry from the loft they'd occupied at the farm. Finn and Alec ran the shop while Valerie produced and illustrated children's books, which were in constant demand. Abbie helped too, but she had her hands full with Diana, Eddie, and Johnny, named after the grandfather he would never meet.

After much deliberation, Louisa and Kit had opened a school, catering to all children, not just those who came from well-to-do families. There were two male teachers, since everyone still looked upon bookish women with suspicion, but Louisa taught several classes herself, enjoying the process of connecting with her students and watching them learn. Kit, meanwhile, had become quite involved in local politics and was considering standing for election in the near future. Valerie and Alec often remarked on the fact that he never seemed to regret his decision to forfeit his title and estate in favor of his nephew, Robin. He planned to leave a new kind of legacy for his son, completely different from the one Robbie had been born to.

Jenny and Cameron were happily running their farm. Jenny had truly blossomed in the past two years, finally content with her place in the world and within the family. Cameron missed Scotland from time to time, but he'd met several Scots who'd emigrated from the same area and found comfort in spending time with them and their families. Valerie suspected that another little one was on the way for those two, but Jenny hadn't said anything yet and Valerie didn't wish to pry.

Valerie's eyes traveled toward the Mallory clan. Jonah and Augusta sat next to Sam and Sue, who leaned affectionately against her father's shoulder. Doctor Freeman had chosen to remain in Virginia and had opened a practice of his own. His kindness and warm manner made him popular, despite his crisp British accent, and he was in high demand. Sue's sister Laura had written to say that she and her husband were planning to visit Virginia the following summer and Sue was glowing with anticipation, excited to have her family reunited at last.

Everyone except Hannah Mallory noticed the high regard in which Doctor Freeman held her, and the family secretly hoped that maybe, someday, the two would take their close friendship to the next level. Hannah was still grieving for John, but she wasn't yet fifty and had many years still ahead of her, and Valerie believed that although she didn't acknowledge it, even to herself, she wasn't indifferent to Joseph Freeman.

Valerie's smile faded somewhat when she caught sight of Sam. Sam was handsome as ever, but he was no longer the easy-going, happy-go-lucky young man Valerie had known. He looked older, and a few strands of gray now silvered his temples. His back had healed, but he had to avoid heavy labor to keep from putting undue strain on his spine, and he had never fully recovered his voice. He managed quite well despite his physical limitations, but still suffered from occasional anxiety attacks and periods of moodiness and depression. Valerie was no doctor, but she thought he might be suffering from post-traumatic stress disorder, given what he'd been through. He was considerably better though and improving daily under the watchful eye of his wife and Doctor Freeman.

Valerie looked around the table until she spotted Louisa, who sat next to Kit. He was laughing at something Alec had said, and the two men raised cups in a silent toast. Louisa's gaze met Valerie's and a slow smile spread across her face. She didn't have to say anything or speak publicly about what she was thankful for. Valerie already knew.

Louisa lifted her own cup and raised it in Valerie's direction. No words were needed. They were together, and this was home.

A LETTER FROM THE AUTHOR

Huge thanks for reading *The Ties that Bind*, I hope you were hooked on the conclusion of Valerie and Alec's epic journey. If you want to join other readers in hearing all about my new releases and bonus content, you can sign up for my newsletter.

www.stormpublishing.co/irina-shapiro

If you enjoyed this book and could spare a few moments to leave a review that would be hugely appreciated. Even a short review can make all the difference in encouraging a reader to discover my books for the first time. Thank you so much.

Although I write several different genres, time travel was my first love. As a student of history, I often wonder if I have what it takes to survive in the past in the dangerous, life-altering situations my characters have to deal with.

Thanks again for being part of this amazing journey with me and I hope you'll stay in touch – I have so many more stories and ideas to entertain you with!

Not ready to leave the world of the Whitfields, Sheridans and their extended family? Catch up with the whole clan in three bonus novellas in the Hands of Time series: *The Winter Solstice*, *The Summer Solstice* and *The Christmas Gift*.

Irina